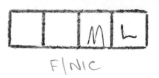

TO ALL ETERNITY

TO ALL ETERNITY

Christopher Nicole

This first world edition published in Great Britain 1999 by
SEVERN HOUSE PUBLISHERS LTD of
9–15 High Street, Sutton, Surrey SM1 1DF.
First published in the USA 2000 by
SEVERN HOUSE PUBLISHERS INC., of
595 Madison Avenue, New York, NY 10022.

British Library Cataloguing in Publication Data

Nicole, Christopher, 1930-
         To all eternity
         1.   Title
         823.9'14 [F]

         ISBN 0-7278-5498-4

Typeset by Palimpsest Ltd
Polmont, Stirlingshire, Scotland.
Printed and bound in Great Britain by
MPG Books Ltd, Bodmin, Cornwall.

Contents

Prologue   1

Part One   A Matter of Honour
  Chapter One   The Mission   19
  Chapter Two   The Bride   40
  Chapter Three   The Raid   57

Part Two   A Business of Intrigue
  Chapter Four   The Husband   83
  Chapter Five   The Voyage   95
  Chapter Six   The Flight   110
  Chapter Seven   The Offer   130

Part Three   A Question of Murder
  Chapter Eight   War   153
  Chapter Nine   The Lovers   171
  Chapter Ten   The Assignment   187
  Chapter Eleven   The Hand of Fate   207
  Chapter Twelve   To All Eternity   226

'Assassination is the extreme form of censorship.'
George Bernard Shaw

Prologue

The rain mist drifted down from the mountains, damp and clinging; it shrouded the peaks and the valleys, seemed to cling to the occasional tree, turned the track into a muddy bog; it deadened all sound save for the rustle of the rushing stream close by the path. And then, incongruously, the silence was split by the wail of a whistle, the thunderous roar of the Warsaw–Vienna express. The track was at least two valleys away, but the sound dominated the afternoon, briefly, before disappearing into echo.

Berkeley Townsend supposed it was a sign of the times, this burgeoning, still new twentieth century, that in this most desolate part of Europe there should be an express train, hurrying on its way.

He looked over his shoulder to make sure Lockwood was still there. Both were expert horsemen, both had the sense and the experience to allow their mounts to pick their own way through the sludge underhoof, but whereas Berkeley carried only his shotgun, Lockwood was laden with their equipment. The valet was also somewhat overweight, and his horse occasionally stumbled, bringing a snort from the red face, a hasty reaction from the heavy shoulders.

In contrast, Berkeley Townsend was perhaps underweight for his six feet of height. His face was somewhat long as well, but was not unhandsome, dominated by the clear blue eyes, the strong chin. He sat straight, and rode like the cavalryman he had been, until recently, and often wished he still was.

At Cambridge he had studied languages; that, he supposed, had been a mistake, if he intended to enter the army. Perhaps he should have been a schoolmaster.

"I'll be glad to be going home, sir," Lockwood commented.

"I'll say amen to that," Berkeley agreed.

A dog barked, and then another, and through the mist the roofs of houses came into view. The village of Seinheit had only one street, and this had been empty in the inclement weather. Now windows opened as well as doors; the tiny hamlet had few visitors. But the two horsemen were quickly recognised, even if they were not locals

1

and were, indeed, foreigners. People waved and called greetings as the two horses walked slowly down the street, accompanied by the dogs; the horses belonged.

The horsemen turned through the arched gateway into the inn, situated at the far end of the street. A groom hurried forward to take their bridles, and Berkeley slipped gratefully from the saddle.

Dittmann, large and round and red-faced, appeared in the doorway. "Welcome back, Herr Smith. Three weeks! I was beginning to think the good count had got you."

"He wasn't at home," Berkeley said, stamping mud from his boots as he limped up the steps. Although the wound caused by a Dervish spear, ten years ago at Omdurman, had long healed, it had been sufficiently serious to end his active service career, and was inclined to make itself felt when it was damp. "What I would like, Herr Dittmann, is a very large glass of beer and a hot bath. I assume you have kept our rooms?" His German was very nearly perfect.

"Oh, yes, sir. Your rooms are waiting. Anja! Beer for Herr Smith."

"And for Herr Brown," Berkeley said.

Anja, a plump fifteen-year-old replica of her father, giggled as she scurried behind the bar.

Berkeley went into the taproom, laid down the shotgun, and stood before the fire. It was July of this year 1908, but Seinheit was high up in the western Carpathians, and was already cool, while the damp made it positively cold. He slapped his hands together and steam rose from his clothes. Behind him, Lockwood brought the gear in, then joined his master.

As did Dittmann, who said, "You mean you saw nothing of the gentleman at all?"

"The gentleman does not exist," Berkeley said. "Except in certain imaginations."

"What a pity," Dittmann said. "You will be leaving now?"

"Well, when next the stage is in. The day after tomorrow, isn't it?"

"That is when it is expected. Now, I must tell you, Herr Smith, that we have other guests."

Berkeley raised his eyebrow.

Dittmann grinned. "I know. We are not always so popular. This is a couple on honeymoon. Very . . . how shall I put it?"

"Much in love," Berkeley suggested.

"Why, yes. That is it exactly."

"Well, we'll try not to get in their way."

Anja presented a tray, and Berkeley took a long drink of beer. "By God, that tastes good."

2

Lockwood obviously felt the same way.

"Now, a hot bath."

"Anja!"

She hurried off to fetch the tub.

Berkeley finished his beer and went up the narrow staircase, Lockwood following with the bags as well as the shotgun. He had been Berkeley's batman in the army, and rated him highly, although of course the officer took a lot of things for granted. He put it down to the gammy leg.

The corridor at the top of the stairs, leading between the bedrooms front and back, was as narrow as the staircase, and as Berkeley reached it one of the doors to the rear rooms opened and a woman came out. He checked, because with her bustle it would be a very tight squeeze if they tried to pass each other; equally, she was well worth looking at.

Of medium height, she wore a well-cut blue gown and black boots. Her hat was broad brimmed. She had a good figure, that was obvious, and a handsome rather than pretty face. Her real beauty lay in her auburn hair, at the moment gathered in a loose pompadour beneath the hat, but glowing with colour to set off her green eyes.

She smiled at him, and stepped back into the doorway. "You first," she said, speaking German with a pronounced accent. "You must be the Englander, Herr Smith."

"Why, yes," he said. "However did you know that?"

"Herr Dittmann told me. He is very full of you; the Englander who has come to find Count Dracula. But you did not succeed."

"And how do you know *that*?"

She smiled, and then did become beautiful. "If you had, Herr Smith, would you not have two little holes in your neck? And very big teeth."

"Good point. I didn't find him, because he doesn't exist, Frau . . ."

"Oh, forgive me. I am Hedda Harlinger."

"My pleasure, Frau Harlinger. Now I must get out of these wet clothes. Perhaps you and your husband would join me for a drink before dinner?"

"I am sure that will be a pleasure, Herr Smith. But . . . how did you know I have a husband?"

Berkeley smiled. "Dittmann told *me*."

"He's a great gossip," she agreed.

"What do you reckon, sir?" Lockwood asked, in English, while Anja filled the tub. The Englishmen shared two rooms, with an adjoining door, as they had shared most things during their years

3

in the army together, and since Berkeley had embarked upon his new career.

"Suspicious, Harry?"

"Well, sir, she didn't look like a honeymooner to me."

"How many honeymoons have you been on?"

"Well, sir . . ."

"Just pulling your leg. Thank you, Anja."

Anja gave one of her giggles and left the room. Lockwood hastily closed and locked the door.

"Everyone knows we've come to the Carpathians looking for Count Dracula," Berkeley said. "They may think we're mad, but there is no reason for anyone to be suspicious of us." Unless, he thought, they could have a look inside my bag. He opened it and spread the sketches carefully on the bed, making sure no water had got at them.

"She's too old," Lockwood complained.

"Eh?" Satisfied the sketches were undamaged, Berkeley stripped off and sank into the hot water with a sigh of relief. There was no room for his legs in the tin tub, but he would deal with them later. Instinctively, his fingers caressed the scar tissue that stretched up the front of his left thigh.

"Well, sir," Lockwood said, "I would put her down at about forty. Maybe more."

Carefully brought up as an officer and a gentleman, Berkeley did not make a habit of estimating women's ages. But now he thought about it, Lockwood was undoubtedly right; there had been a wealth of experience in those eyes, that face.

He soaped himself thoughtfully. "So just who do you think they are?"

He and Lockwood had fought shoulder to shoulder in the Sudan, and Lockwood had saved his life after he had received the wound that had ended his active service career. They trusted each other, and each other's judgement.

"I don't know, sir." He held the towel for his master as Berkeley stood up. "I agree with you that it's highly unlikely they could be after us. But . . . if they're honeymooning, I'll eat my hat."

"All without laying eyes on Mr Harlinger. They could be eloping."

"Now that would be interesting," Lockwood said. For all his somewhat stolid exterior, he was a romantic at heart.

"We'll investigate, this evening," Berkeley said.

"The *Morning Post*. That is a famous newspaper." Otto Harlinger returned Berkeley's card. He was an even less likely spouse for

4

Hedda than Lockwood had supposed might be the case. He was hardly taller than his wife, yellow-haired, with a fair moustache and slightly built.

"Thank you. We like to think so."

"And they sent you here to search for Count Dracula? As recounted by your Mr Stoker? I'm afraid I have not read the book."

"It was a runaway bestseller in England, oh, about ten years ago." Berkeley said, sipping his beer. "Then they made it into a play."

"And Mr Stoker is a friend of yours?" Hedda Harlinger asked.

"No, no. It's just that the book has been reissued, and my editor thought there might be something in the story. Something real."

"So you have had a . . . what do you say in English? A wild goose chase?"

"I'm afraid that's about it."

"Yet the story sounds very exciting," Hedda said. "Do you think it has been published in German?"

"I am sure of it."

"Then I must obtain a copy when we return to Vienna. Do you not think that would be a good idea, Otto?"

Otto was not listening, at least to her. "The dogs are barking," he said.

"Somebody must be coming," Berkeley suggested.

"At this hour?"

"Quite a few of them," Berkeley said, listening to the hoofbeats.

Harlinger stood up; his already pale face had turned quite white.

Dittmann hurried in, also looking agitated. "A squadron of hussars."

"Coming here?" Hedda asked.

"I am afraid so. What will you do?"

She looked at her husband, who was now trembling. "We must get away."

"There is no time," Dittmann said. "Listen, they may just be passing through. I will find out. Meanwhile, act naturally." He looked at Berkeley. "Dinner may be a little delayed, Herr Smith."

"I can wait," Berkeley said. "You'll excuse me a moment."

He went upstairs. Lockwood stood at the window which looked down into the courtyard.

"We've been scuppered," the valet said. "Like I said . . ."

Berkeley stood beside him, watched the white-clad horsemen dismounting in the yard. "I don't think they're after us."

"Those people?"

"Yes. Those people." Berkeley opened his bag, again took out the sketches he had made of Austrian military emplacements in the

5

mountains, folded them, and placed them in his wallet; their value would have to withstand a few creases. Also lying in the bag was the new Browning automatic pistol with which he had been issued before leaving London. He glanced from it to the shotgun. But there were some twenty Austrians in the yard. Long odds, and in any event they couldn't possibly be after him. His business was to keep a clean nose until he could get across the Swiss border, and that was a long way away.

There was a knock on the door. He straightened, looking at Lockwood, who had instinctively moved towards the gun. Berkeley shook his head, and nodded towards the door. The Austrians were still in the yard, being greeted by Dittmann.

Lockwood made a face, but opened the door instead. Hedda Harlinger almost fell into the room.

"Please," she gasped. "Will you help me?"

Berkeley nodded again, and Lockwood closed the door.

"Help you to do what?"

"Please. Those men are looking for a man and a woman. If you would say I am with you." Her tongue gave a quick sweep round her lips. "As your wife, or . . . or your mistress, as anything . . ."

"We would still be a man and a woman," he pointed out, more because he felt the need to say something to allay their mutual embarrassment than as an objection to her plea.

"They are looking for an Austrian man and woman. Well, for . . . not for an English man and woman. I speak English," she said, switching to that language with very little added accent.

Berkeley looked at Lockwood, who pulled his nose.

"What about your husband?" Berkeley said.

"Otto is not my husband. He will manage on his own."

They listened to booted feet stamping on the floor beneath them, and raised voices.

"Please," she begged. "It will only be for a short while. Dittmann will get rid of them."

Dittmann, Berkeley thought. A gentleman who would bear investigation.

"With respect, sir," Lockwood said.

He was a stickler for the matter in hand. From their point of view, the matter in hand was, having completed their mission, to get out of Hungary just as quickly and safely as possible.

Hedda Harlinger could see the indecision on his face. "If they take me," she said, "do you know what they will do to me?"

Berkeley made his decision; he well knew what they might do to her. "If you're to be my woman," he said, "your things should be in here. Harry, would you nip across and collect Mrs Harlinger's belongings."

Lockwood looked as if he would have protested again, then went to the door.

"There is only the one bag," Hedda said, "and two gowns in the wardrobe and some toiletries."

Lockwood gave a heavy sigh, and went into the corridor. Berkeley turned back towards the woman, and saw to his consternation that she was taking off her dress.

"Just in case they come in," she said, and sat on the bed to unlace her boots. Hastily he turned away from her, although she remained sufficiently well petticoated to be modest.

The heavy feet were now on the stairs. Lockwood could well be caught. He went to the door.

"Where are you going?" Hedda asked.

He looked back at her; she had rolled under the covers, which were drawn to her chin.

"Just checking," he said, and opened the door.

The Austrians were just reaching the corridor, four men following an officer. They stared at Berkeley, and he gave them what he hoped was a friendly smile.

"You are the Englander," the officer commented.

"John Smith, at your service," Berkeley said. "Anything I can do to help?"

"Just keep out of our way," the officer said. "Go to your room, and stay there."

"Ah," Berkeley said, "but you see . . ."

The officer was already opening the door of the rear bedroom, his revolver drawn. "You," he said. "Who are you?"

Lockwood had Hedda's bag under his arm.

"My man," Berkeley said.

The officer looked from one to the other.

"Just fetching something," Berkeley said.

Lockwood hastily dropped the bag on to the bed.

"I wish to know what is going on," the officer said. "I wish . . ." He was distracted by a shout from downstairs, and moved to the window, to watch Otto Harlinger sprinting across the field behind the inn, making for a copse about a quarter of a mile away. "Shoot him down," he snapped at his men.

"Here, I say," Berkeley protested, as he was thrust to one side by the soldiers moving to the window, carbines thrust forward. They were firing before he could say, or do, anything more. Harlinger threw up his arms and fell.

"You could have killed him," Berkeley shouted.

7

"Very probably," the officer agreed, and leaned out of the window. "Bring him in, Sergeant," he called.

Several soldiers emerged from the back door of the inn and ran towards the still figure.

"That was cold-blooded murder," Berkeley said.

"It was an execution, Herr Smith. Of a highly dangerous man. But it is the woman we really want. Have you seen her?"

"You mean Frau Harlinger?"

"I mean Anna Slovitza," the officer said. "Perhaps she was posing as his wife."

"We had a drink downstairs before dinner," Berkeley said. "They seemed a very pleasant couple. And now, to shoot Herr Harlinger down in cold blood!"

"Bah!" said the officer. "Now you, return to your room and stay there. With your man."

He seemed to have forgotten his enquiry as to what Lockwood had been doing in the room. Berkeley jerked his head and Lockwood followed him across the corridor and into their rooms.

Hedda Harlinger, or was she really Anna Slovitza? stared at them with enormous eyes, the sheet still held to her throat. "That shooting . . ."

"Was your husband being killed," Berkeley said. "But I gather he wasn't your husband."

"He was my partner," she said. "But . . . you mean he is dead?"

"I would say he is dead. He stopped several bullets."

"Poor Otto." She did not seem terribly upset.

"So . . ." Berkeley sat at the foot of the bed, while Lockwood stood by the locked door, "I think I am owed an explanation."

"I am sorry you have become involved," she said. "If I may just stay here until the hussars leave, then I will leave too, and you can forget all about me."

"I think that may be rather difficult," he said, realising that he meant it in more ways than one. "I'm afraid I'm a man who likes to know just what he's involved in. Your name is really Anna Slovitza, which I would say is neither Austrian nor Hungarian, but Serbian, perhaps."

She gazed at him with wide eyes.

"That was told to me by the Austrian captain," he explained. "He also said that you were far more dangerous than your so-called husband. Please, madame, I am assuming it really is madame, just what are you wanted for?"

She licked her lips. "Surely that is no concern of yours."

"Madame, you happen to be in my bed."

"Please . . ." she started as there came a knock on the door.

8

Berkeley and Lockwood looked at each other. But there was no way of concealing the woman, and at the moment Berkeley was not sure he wanted to take any more risks on her behalf, however attractive she might be.

He nodded, as the knock came again, and Lockwood unlocked the door. The officer came in. "I forgot to ask . . ." He gazed at the woman, who had sunk down until only her nose was visible; her hair however, remained exposed. "Well, well," he said. "You have been lying to me, Englander."

"You know how it is, Captain. Beauty in distress . . ."

"How romantic." He went to the bed, seized the covers and jerked them away. Anna Slovitza drew up her legs.

"We have an understanding," Berkeley said.

"Quite so. And your ladies always go to bed with their clothes on?"

"Am I under arrest?"

"You?" The captain gave a brief laugh. "No, no, Englander. You are not involved. The outrage was committed last week, and you were up in the mountains, looking for some legend. I have no doubt at all that this woman sought to become romantically involved with you. We will just remove her and save you a great deal of trouble. But let me give you a piece of advice: falling for a pretty face is not always a wise thing to do. You. Up."

Slowly Anna Slovitza swung her legs out of the bed and stood up. Once again Lockwood and Berkeley exchanged glances. But two of the hussars were standing just outside the door, their carbines in their hands.

"Did you say outrage?" Berkeley asked.

"Of course. Did you not realise that anarchy is this woman's trade? But it will soon end. Outside."

"My dress." Anna said.

The officer grinned. "You will not need that."

Anna looked at Berkeley. "You know what they are going to do to me?"

"I am sorry," Berkeley said.

She went through the door, followed by the officer. One of his men closed it behind them.

"Whew!" Lockwood said. "I thought we were for it."

"She is certainly for it."

"Well, sir, I think we have done all we can for her. And if she really is wanted for some criminal act . . ."

He checked as a scream echoed through the inn. It came from very close at hand.

"Damn," Berkeley said.

9

"Sir . . ."

There came another scream.

Berkeley opened his bag, took out the Browning, checked the magazine. He had only ever fired it on the range and would have far preferred his service revolver. But the magazine did hold nine cartridges.

"Sir," Lockwood protested. "We were sent here to do a job of work. We have to get those sketches back to England."

There was a third scream.

"You take the shotgun," Berkeley said.

Lockwood swallowed, but he knew nothing was going to stop his master now. He picked up the shotgun, inserted two cartridges.

"Bring spares," Berkeley said, and opened the door.

A hussar stood immediately outside, leaning against the wall, but straightened as he saw the Englishman. "You are to stay inside."

"I need the air," Berkeley told him, and swung his hand, holding the pistol, into the soldier's midriff. He doubled up, and before he could straighten Lockwood hit him on the head with the shotgun. He went down with a thump.

"That's torn it," Lockwood commented.

"Good man," Berkeley said.

The door of the bedroom opposite opened. "Hans?" asked the hussar who emerged. He took in the situation at a glance, and leapt backwards. But Berkeley had followed him and now he kicked the door in while the hussar was trying to shut it. The man tumbled into one of his comrades, and Berkeley charged into the room. Anna Slovitza occupied the very centre of the space, suspended by her wrists from the rafter above her head. She had been stripped to her stockings and boots, and was being whipped by the officer, who was using his riding crop; there were red weals on her back and buttocks.

The captain dropped the crop to reach for his revolver holster, and Berkeley shot him in the chest. His white tunic flared red and he went down without a sound. The three other men in the room, who had been watching the woman being tortured, all reached for their carbines and met the full blast of Lockwood's shotgun, as he fired twice.

Berkeley drew one of their swords to slash the rope holding Anna Slovitza, and she collapsed into his arms, sobbing.

From below there came shouts.

"Cover the stairs," Berkeley snapped. "Madame, I know you're in pain, but put something on."

He released her, somewhat reluctantly, and she sat on the bed, then hastily stood up again.

10

Berkeley leant over the shattered men. Two and the officer were dead; the other two were badly wounded.

"Company," Lockwood called.

"Stop them."

"Halt there," Lockwood shouted.

For reply, there were several shots, followed by the heavier explosion of the shotgun. Then there were shouts and clattering noises.

Anna Slovitza was dragging on her underclothes. "What can we do?"

"For the moment, keep your head down."

This was madness, he knew, and a complete dereliction of duty, but how his brain sang with an exultation he had not known since the Sudan; he had still been hobbling on crutches when the Boer War had started. Too long.

The two wounded men were groaning and writhing. They were terribly cut up by the shotgun blast at close range, and there was nothing he could do for them. He went into the corridor, at the end of which Lockwood crouched. There was no way anyone could get at him, save one at a time round the last bend in the stairs, and Berkeley guessed that, lacking an officer, they would be less keen on risking their lives. Besides, Lockwood had been trained as a machine gunner before becoming his batman, and knew all about controlling fields of fire.

Behind him the hussar who had been guarding his room was sitting up, rubbing his head and groaning. Berkeley nudged him with his toe. "Get up."

The man staggered to his feet, looked for his carbine.

"Leave it," Berkeley said. "Tell your comrades that you are coming down, with two wounded men. Tell them to send Dittmann up to help you. Only Dittmann, mind."

The hussar licked his lips, staggered to the end of the corridor and shouted as instructed down the stairs.

Anna Slovitza came out of the bedroom, fully dressed

"How much do you trust Dittmann?" Berkeley whispered.

"He will help us if he can."

Berkeley nodded, listened to feet on the stairs. "If it is Dittmann, let him through," he told Lockwood. He gave Anna his pistol. "I assume you know how to use this, madame?"

"Certainly I do."

"Then keep our friend covered, and if he tries anything, shoot him."

He went into his own bedroom, looked down on the front yard. There were several hussars down there, looking up, and when they saw him they began firing at the window. He stepped back hastily

11

as the bullets splattered into the ceiling. Behind the soldiers, quite a crowd had gathered at the inn gate and on the street beyond, but he felt they were more hostile to the Austrians than to the foreigners. More important, the evening was drawing in; it would be dark in half an hour.

Then, as he watched, a horseman came out of the stables and the gate was opened for him. The crowded parted, and he cantered down the street and on to the road leading south. Berkeley wondered how close the possible reinforcements were.

He returned to the corridor, to see Dittmann emerging up the stairs. The innkeeper looked into the back bedroom, his jaw dropping as he saw the bodies.

"Come in here, Herr Dittmann," Berkeley said.

Dittmann came into the front bedroom.

"What is happening down there?"

"There is much confusion, much argument. Some are for rushing the stairs, regardless of the casualties. Others are for waiting. One even wishes to set fire to the building. My inn, Herr Smith."

"But they are not going to do that?"

"The sergeant is against it. He has sent for help and instructions."

"How soon can help reach here?"

"I do not think before tomorrow morning."

"We must be away by then. I wish you to prepare a knapsack of food, food that will keep for a few days."

"But they will see me and arrest me."

"Not if you do it as part of preparing their dinner. They must be hungry by now. Talk them out of any further action until they have eaten. Do not fail me in this, Dittmann. If we are taken, Frau Slovitza will implicate you."

Dittmann licked his lips. "I had nothing to do with what happened in Budapest. I was here."

"But you gave shelter to the anarchists," Berkeley reminded him, "knowing who they were. Now hurry. Put the sack of food outside the back door."

Dittmann returned to the back bedroom, where Berkeley removed the dead and wounded men's cartridge belts, and stacked their carbines. Then the innkeeper and the remaining hussar heaved up the two wounded men and carried them to the stairs. Covered by Lockwood, they got them round the bend and down to the taproom.

"What happens now, sir?" Lockwood asked. "I reckon they still number about fifteen."

"With more on the way." Berkeley went into the back bedroom, looked out at the fields and the woods, and the mountains. He had come to know those mountains very well over the past three weeks.

"Once we are in the open, they will hunt us down," Anna said at his shoulder. "They will use dogs."

"They'll need a lot of them." Berkeley checked the weaponry. They had four carbines and nearly a hundred rounds of ammunition, together with his pistol, the shotgun, and the captain's revolver. Cartridges for these were limited – he had only the two spare magazines, and Lockwood perhaps half a dozen shells left, but the captain's pouch contained a dozen bullets, apart from those still in the chamber. Resolutely used, there was sufficient firepower to discourage any close pursuit not equipped with a machine gun.

"And anyway," Anna said, "the mountains . . . there is only Russia on the other side."

"Wouldn't you rather face a Russian than an Austrian right now?"

She sat on the bed, glanced at the dead man sprawled across it, shuddered, and stood up again.

"Don't tell me you've never seen a dead man before?" Berkeley said. "He described you as an anarchist."

"I planted a bomb," Anna said sulkily.

"Which I assume went off. How many people were killed?"

"I do not know. It had a timing device."

"So you were well away when it exploded. Do you not think that is a cowardly way of doing things?"

"They are many, we are few. They are tyrants, we are—"

"Assassins."

"Yet you are helping me."

"Yes," he said thoughtfully.

She caught his hand. "I wish you to know that, should we escape, I shall be forever in your debt." Her eyes were enormous. "My life will be yours. You may ask anything of me, and you shall have it."

"We will escape," he said.

"Well, then . . ." her tongue circled her lips.

"Let's do it first."

He returned to the front bedroom to look down. There were still a dozen men in the yard, but as he watched several went inside, called in by Dittmann to be fed. The street remained crowded with people awaiting the denouement of this strange intrusion of violence into their lives; and they probably did not yet know that at least three men were already dead.

With how many to follow? And what then? The woman? He was being a complete fool. Were he sitting in the smoking room

13

of his club in London, reading *The Times*, and he came across an item regarding a Serbian woman arrested and probably hanged after planting a bomb in Budapest, he would undoubtedly say to himself, serves the creature right. She would have no actuality to him; how she looked and smelt and talked would have no meaning. Now, because this woman had meaning and reality, he was acting like . . . an officer and a gentleman? But he was no longer an officer and a gentleman, in real terms. He was a spy; really the lowest form of human existence.

Lower than a professional assassin?

But as he *was* a spy, he folded his drawings into a small satchel, in which he also placed the spare magazines for his pistol, as well as his travel documents. During the week he had spent in the village before his expedition into the mountains he had become fairly well known, so there was no hope of concealing his identity, even if it was a false one, but he would need some form of identification to get into Russia.

He also packed his belt of gold sovereigns, which would probably be even more important.

It was now nearly dark. He put on his coat and hat, fetched Lockwood's from the adjoining room, as well as his passport, and went into the gloomy corridor.

"Any movement?"

"Just a lot of chat, sir. They're eating. And drinking," he said sadly.

"Put these on and be ready to move."

"Our gear?"

"We'll have to abandon it." He tapped the satchel. "I have what matters." He went into the rear bedroom. "Hat and coat. Nothing else, I'm afraid. You have travel documents?"

She nodded.

"Give them to me."

She hesitated, then obeyed. He stood at the window to look at them. "Are these real, or forged?"

"They are real enough," she said.

"Well, the Russians are your friends, are they not?" He added them to the contents of the satchel.

"Dittmann has put out the food," she said.

Berkeley looked out of the window, saw the sack lying beside the back door. There was no way of knowing what was in it; the innkeeper had to be trusted.

It was now dark enough to make the wood an indistinct blur. "Time to leave, I think. While they are eating."

"Do you not think they will be keeping a watch?"

14

"I doubt it. They'll reckon we'll feel safer up here." He went into the corridor, touched Lockwood on the shoulder. "You first," he said in a low voice. "It's about twenty feet to the cobbles. Use the sheets from the bed. Then wait for the lady."

"And you, sir?"

"I'm the rearguard. Now, Harry, should anything happen to me, you take the lady across the mountains and into Russian Poland." He gave the valet his satchel. "Everything you need is in there."

"Begging your pardon, sir, but shouldn't you go with the lady?"

"I intend to do that, Harry, as soon as we're out of here. Now be a good fellow and do as I say."

Lockwood went into the bedroom, and Berkeley took his place, one carbine on his lap the other at his side; both were repeaters. He listened to some good cheer from downstairs; the Austrians might have lost three of their people and had two more wounded, but they were enjoying their food and wine. He guessed, knowing what he did about the Austrian army, that they hadn't been all that fond of their officer, anyway.

Anna knelt beside him. "You are sending me away with your servant?"

"Briefly. Do get on with it."

She hesitated, then kissed him on the cheek and returned to the bedroom.

He waited, listening, heard the scrabbling sound as she climbed out of the window on to the rope of sheets. The noise below him was increasing as the hussars tackled the wine. Then someone wagered he could get upstairs. Berkeley levelled his carbine, listened to the steps, and as a face peered round the corner fired three times. He did not aim at the face, as he felt he had done enough killing for one evening, but the man disappeared, and could be heard tumbling back down the stairs to the accompaniment of roars of laughter from his comrades.

Now was the best time. Berkeley slung both carbines and retreated into the bedroom. There had been no noise from the back of the inn. Now he swung himself out of the window, down the sheet-rope, landed on the cobbles. Lockwood and Anna had already disappeared into the gloom.

He ran behind them and had covered about half the distance when he heard shouts from behind him, followed by shots. But he knew the Austrians couldn't see him; they were shooting blind.

"Here, sir," Lockwood called.

He panted up to where they were waiting, at the first of the trees.

"Keep going," he told them.

15

They could hear the sound of hooves as the hussars mounted up and rode out of the yard. The three fugitives pressed on into the trees, whipped by low-hanging branches, tripping over fallen tree trunks, but always climbing.

"Shouldn't we stop those fellows, sir?" Lockwood gasped. He was carrying the heavy knapsack of food.

"Let them come into the trees," Berkeley said. "You all right?" he asked Anna, who was hampered by her heavy skirt.

"I am all right," she panted.

They climbed, listening to the horsemen shouting as they rode into the trees, becoming separated as they did so. They and their horses were making so much noise they could not possibly hear the fugitives, and after some minutes there came a bugle call, summoning them back.

"They'll mount a proper pursuit in the morning," Anna said.

"By which time we'll be far away," he said. "But we can take ten minutes' rest, now."

She collapsed to the ground, as did Lockwood, taking off the knapsack.

"What's in there?" Berkeley asked.

Lockwood opened the bag. "Going by feel . . . a ham, a cheese, some loaves of bread, even a couple of bottles of wine. He's done us proud."

"Dittmann is loyal," Anna said. "Will they hang him?"

"Only if they can prove he helped us. He would have to be betrayed for that."

"We were betrayed," she said bitterly. "Poor Otto."

"Were you lovers?"

She glanced at him, but he couldn't make out her expression in the dark. "We had known each other a long time," she said. Which wasn't really an answer, he supposed.

"What will you do?" he asked. "After we reach Russia?"

"I must get back to Belgrade. Will you come with me?"

"No," he said. "I must get back to London."

It was tempting to ask, will you come with *me*, but he decided against it.

Part One

A Matter of Honour

'What is honour? A word.'
William Shakespeare

The Mission

"Hm," remarked General Gorman, using a magnifying glass to study the drawings on his desk. "Hm. These are awfully good, Townsend."

"Thank you, sir." Berkeley stood in front of the desk.

"However . . . the cost." The general laid down his magnifying glass and raised his head; he looked rather like a large bulldog. "You were sent to the Carpathians to report on the Austrian military capabilities *vis-à-vis* the Russians on the other side. There was no intention that you should virtually start a war."

"I was overtaken by events, sir."

"The events, as I understand it, being a considerable rustle of skirts. You should be ashamed of yourself."

"The lady was being tortured by the Austrians, sir. I considered it my duty as an officer and a gentleman to go to her assistance."

"The lady," Gorman mused, opening a file and picking up a sheet of paper. "Anna Slovitza. In 1894, she shot at the Emperor. She missed. In 1896, she planted a bomb intended to blow up the Archduke Franz Ferdinand. It went off prematurely. In 1896, she and her associates held up a train at gunpoint and escaped with a considerable amount of money and valuables taken mainly from the mail compartment. In 1898, she was traced to a house she was using in Vienna, and there was a gun battle in which three policemen were killed and two wounded. She escaped. In 1902, she and her husband, Milan Slovitza, were arrested after a shoot out in Banja Luka. Slovitza was captured, taken across the border into Hungary, and executed. Again, she escaped. It was thought by the Austrians that the death of her husband might have ended her career. And now this, blowing up a railway station in Budapest simply because the Minister of the Interior was arriving there. Twelve people were killed, and thirty-odd injured. On this occasion several of her accomplices were taken, but needless to say she and one other escaped. To the village of Seinheit, where they were traced by the Austrian army. But once again she escaped, with the assistance of a British subject, a newspaper reporter, after another gun battle,

19

which left another four men dead. The woman is the original human equivalent of a hungry lioness."

"I was unaware that we kept a file on her, sir."

"We don't. This has been supplied to me by the Austrian Embassy. Well, not to me personally; to the Home Secretary, who is very unhappy about it. The Austrians don't yet know who you really are, you see. They have identified John Smith as a newspaper correspondent; but as the editor of the *Morning Post* has never heard of you, even the Austrians understand that John Smith is almost certainly a pseudonym. But they are still applying for his extradition to face charges of murder. If that extradition procedure were to reach the courts, and you then be identified as a serving British army officer engaged upon undercover work within the Austrian Empire, well, it could be a very nasty business indeed."

"Yes, sir. With respect, sir, when I went to Madame Slovitza's assistance, I was not in possession of the information you have just divulged."

"You were unaware that she was a wanted anarchist?"

"I realised that she had just committed an anarchist crime; that she had planted a bomb in the Budapest railway station."

"Aha! But you still went to her help, shooting down anyone who got in your way."

"As I have explained, sir—"

"Yes, yes, *noblesse oblige* and all that." Gorman leaned back and stroked his chin. "What happened to the woman when you reached Russia?"

"We agreed to part company, sir. It was my duty to return to England with those drawings just as rapidly as I could, and she conceived it to be her duty to return to Serbia just as rapidly as *she* could."

"Do you suppose she got there?"

"I would imagine so, sir."

"A single woman, alone in a strange country, many miles from her home – how was she going to manage?"

"I gave her some money, sir."

"You mean you gave her some of His Majesty's Government's money."

"That is correct, sir. It can be stopped from my pay."

Gorman's expression indicated that there had to be some doubt as to whether Berkeley was still going to receive any pay. "And you still think she will manage. Is she good-looking?"

"Very, sir."

"Then she is probably lying raped and robbed and perhaps murdered in some ditch."

"I doubt that, sir. Madame Slovitza is a very formidable woman. And she was armed."

"Good God! You didn't give her a British service weapon?"

"No, sir. I gave her a revolver I took from the Austrian captain."

"Well, that's something. At least the Austrians won't be able to trace that back to you. Now tell me, you were alone with this woman for several days . . ."

"Not alone, sir. I had Lockwood with me."

"Lockwood?"

"My valet, sir. An invaluable man."

"I suppose he was also engaged in killing Austrians. I don't want to hear about it. At least they haven't named him. Just another person who was involved in the criminal activities of this fellow Smith. But you haven't answered my question."

"With respect, sir, you haven't asked it."

"You know what I mean, Townsend."

"Well, sir, I am bound to say that Madame Slovitza was very grateful to me for saving her life."

Gorman pointed. "You, Townsend, are a cad."

"Yes, sir."

"Aren't you engaged to that lovely Gracey girl?"

"Ah, no, sir. We are not actually engaged. There is an understanding."

"And are you going to tell her about your Serbian bit?"

"I hadn't thought of doing so," Berkeley said, "as it would involve telling her what I was really doing in Hungary, and that is top secret, is it not?"

Gorman cleared his throat, noisily.

"Sir," Berkeley said, "I will admit I acted hastily and perhaps irresponsibly. In my defence I would claim, however, that *any* English officer would have acted as I did when he saw a lovely and appealing woman being tortured."

"Hm, I hope most British officers would have a greater sense of responsibility. However, the question remains: what are we to do with you? I hope you understand that were we to let the Austrians extradite you, they would certainly hang you for murder, quite apart from the international scandal that would result from it being discovered that you are a serving British officer. The Kaiser is already making all manner of anti-British pronunciamentos. He is furious over the way we backed France at the Algeciras Conference. He would love to stick another needle into us. And Germany is allied to Austria. He would have a field day. I suppose you have been relying all along on the fact that we cannot allow this to happen."

21

"I hadn't really considered it that deeply, sir. I did what I considered to be my duty, and will stand by that decision."

"Even if your so-called duty were to bring down the government, eh? It seems to me that we have only a couple of possible alternatives. One is to bury you alive in some outpost of the Empire, so remote that not even the Austrians will wish to follow you there." He paused to gaze at his subordinate. "This would have to be for a period of several years, and would, I'm afraid, put the kybosh on any plans you might have for either marriage or promotion for that time."

"Yes, sir."

"Does that idea appeal to you?"

"Not in the least, sir."

"But there is another alternative, which could clean the whole thing up in a matter of weeks, and put you, and the government, entirely in the clear."

Berkeley waited.

"One gets the impression," Gorman said, "that the Austrians are less concerned that you killed some of their people than that you assisted this most dangerous anarchist to escape when they actually had her under arrest. You will have noted, no doubt, from that brief biography I read to you just now, that she appears to be getting both better and bolder at her job. They really feel she should be stopped before she does manage to kill a member of the royal family, or blows up any more railway stations. So it does occur to me that if we were to offer to exchange Madame Slovitza for the dropping of all charges against you, they may agree."

"Unfortunately, sir, it is a matter of first catch your hare."

"Yes," Gorman said.

Berkeley swallowed. "I hope you're not serious, sir."

"The Austrians," Gorman said, "have an almost insuperable problem, unless, of course, they can catch her on the job, as they so nearly did in Seinheit. For the rest, having committed her crime, she disappears across the border back into Serbia. I understand from the report that she is actually a Bosnian by birth, and it is of course the Austrian designs on Bosnia-Herzegovina that are causing all the trouble. However, Madame Slovitza is using Serbia, where anti-Austrian feelings are running high, and where she is safe. Even if they could find out exactly where she was at any given moment, for Austrian agents to attempt to arrest the lady would result in their lynching on the spot. What is required is an agent who can travel freely in the Balkans, a national of a nation which is known to be sympathetic towards Serb aspirations. If, in addition, this agent is someone known to Madame Slovitza, and trusted by her, as would necessarily be the case if he had once saved her life, well, I would say his task would be made extraordinarily simple."

"I am sorry, sir, but I must decline," Berkeley said. "It would be the most underhand act in history."

"I think it is something you need to consider very carefully," Gorman said. "You speak of it as underhand. Let us analyse what this woman did to you. She appealed to you for help, a woman on the run from what she represented as a minor anarchist action. You, being a gallant British gentleman, responded most effectively. Now, Townsend, if this woman had come up to you and said, I need your help, but I must tell you that I have just killed twelve innocent people, having already, over the past few years, killed several more and attempted to kill another several more, that I am a cold-blooded international assassin with a list of crimes to my name that is a yard long, and that if, with your help, I am enabled to continue my career I will undoubtedly kill quite a few more people, many of whom may well again be innocent bystanders . . . would you have been quite so anxious to rush to her help, no matter how attractive she might be?"

Berkeley bit his lip.

"Exactly," Gorman said. "You acted as you did because you were not in possession of all the facts. Now that you are, you must realise that you made a mistake, a mistake which could have the most serious consequences unless it is set right, and very quickly. You, and you alone, have the ability to correct your own mistake."

Berkeley sighed. Everything the general was saying was true. But it would still be a despicable act. "May I ask, sir, is this idea yours, or did it originate with the Austrians?"

"I will take the credit, Townsend. But as I have said, I have no doubt that the Austrians will go for it. They will also be prepared to keep it a secret, as will we. No one will know of your exploit, outside a few army officers, of senior rank, and a very few government ministers."

"And Madame Slovitza."

"I don't think anything she may have to say will be of much importance. While you, on your return from this mission, will receive your majority. As I am sure you are aware, any army officer needs to be a major by the time he is thirty-five, or he may find further advancement difficult."

"Yes, sir. I will need to take Lockwood with me."

"Very good. Having arrested Madame Slovitza, you will convey her to the Austrian border and hand her over. There is no need to do more than that. Once your mission is accomplished, I suggest you and, ah, Lockwood, return home just as quickly as possible, travelling through Hungary and Austria, as I do not imagine you will any longer be very popular in either Serbia or Bosnia. I will attend to the details, passages, false passports, safe conducts, etc., but of course I must not be involved in any way."

"And should Madame Slovitza, or her associates, discern what I am doing and shoot me, sir? And Lockwood?"

"Then you will have died doing your duty to King and country. But do you really think that is likely?"

"No, sir," Berkeley said.

Berkeley took the train up to Northampton and hired a trap to ride out to the village where his parents lived. He was an only son, and the more highly prized for that; they had in fact been very relieved when his wound had meant the end of his active service career – as far as they were aware. Equally, they were pleased that he had not been discharged, but had been continued in the army, both as a superb horseman and for his abilities as a draughtsman. "So how was Hungary?" John Townsend asked, shaking hands with his son. A retired civil servant, he relished the quiet of the countryside after a lifetime spent in London.

"Wet. Lockwood arrived yet?"

"He came yesterday. No use asking him anything."

Berkeley grinned. "That's why he's such a good servant."

He went into the garden to hug and kiss his mother.

"Did you find any good horses?" she asked.

"A few. They're being shipped over."

How easy was it to lie, even to his own parents.

"I know Julia wants to see you. She and her parents were over here last week. They . . . well, now you're past thirty, they're wondering when you'll tie the knot."

But lying to one's wife on a daily basis would be an entirely different matter. And he really hardly knew the girl, for all that they had been thrown together as often as possible by their respective families, as being the ideal match.

"I'll go over and see them," he said. "Tomorrow."

"I understand she's been seeing quite a lot of Harvey Braddock," Alicia Townsend remarked. Berkeley wondered if that might not be a good thing.

Lockwood had already unpacked their gear. "How was the War Office, sir?"

"All hell has broken loose," Berkeley said, and outlined the first part of his conversation with General Gorman.

"Well, sir . . ."

"You are quite entitled to say, I told you so, Harry."

"What I was going to say, sir, was that if they hand you over to the Austrians, they have to hand me over as well."

"Good fellow. However, we have been given a way out." He repeated the second half of his conversation with the general

Lockwood listened with a frown. "We go into Serbia, find the lady, arrest her, convey her to the border, and hand her over to the Austrians? Just like that?"

"Simple, isn't it?"

Lockwood scratched his head. "And then we just leave again."

"Even more simple, wouldn't you say?"

Lockwood made a whistling sound through his teeth.

"Yes," Berkeley said. "If we get through this one our nine lives will have been reduced to one, I should think. But . . . King and country and all that."

"And the lady, sir? I had the impression—"

"Oh, fuck it, Harry! Of course I found her attractive. And compelling. Another week and I'd have fallen in love with her. Even if I'd known she was a murderess."

"The Austrians will hang her, sir. After . . ."

"Yes, Harry. After tossing her about a bit. Believe me, I am trying desperately to think of some way to get us, and her, off the hook."

"But we are going to Serbia, sir?"

"Yes, Harry. We are going to Serbia. Because we have no alternative. We'll just have to see what turns up."

Rationalise, he told himself, as he walked his horse over the rolling countryside to Gracey Farm, some ten miles away. He *had* acted irresponsibly, in terms of his mission, in getting involved with the anarchists. It had, as he had told Gorman, been a knee-jerk reaction to an appeal for help from a beautiful woman. Had he known she was a multiple killer he *might* have rejected her. Now it was simple: that as she was a multiple killer, and as he had wrongly killed several men in her defence, it was his duty to atone for that crime by arresting her and handing her over to the Austrian judiciary, even knowing that it would involve hours, perhaps weeks, of torment with a rope in a public square at the end of it. But that knowledge could not be allowed to interfere with his duty, any more than the memory of that naked, voluptuous body dangling from the beam to be whipped, or even more the memory of that same voluptuous body writhing naked beside his own beneath their blanket in the Carpathian Mountains.

She had been repaying him for saving her life; she had not pretended otherwise. And had he attempted to come between her and what she considered *her* duty, she no doubt would have shot him without a moment's hesitation. Whatever his memory of her, he had been an object to be used. When they had parted, after crossing the Russian border, she had not looked back. That was better. That was a recognition of the facts. They were two people who had drifted together, and who, for a brief few days, had been forced to fight and exist, shoulder to shoulder. But basically they were enemies, whose duty it was to destroy each other if necessary. As now. If only he could feel certain that it wasn't the Austrians, in their brutal suppression of their Slav minorities, who weren't the real enemies. Just as he wished he was not accepting this mission simply to save himself from disgrace.

"Berkeley!" Paul Gracey, bluff and red faced, worked his own land and was in the field by the road supervising the harvesting. "Welcome home." He stamped across the mud to reach up and shake Berkeley's hand. "Successful trip?"

"On the whole. Julia at home?"

"Indeed. And she'll be the happier for seeing you. Go on in. I'll be down as soon as we've got this field finished."

Berkeley continued to walk his horse, down the drive now, between more recently harvested fields towards the farm house, large and four-square. Dogs barked, and a maidservant appeared, to duck back inside, no doubt calling her younger mistress. A groom emerged from the stables to take Berkeley's bridle as he dismounted, and he patted the shaggy mastiffs on the head.

"Berkeley!"

When away from this young woman, he often forgot how attractive she was. Or perhaps today he needed her to be more attractive than usual. Julia Gracey was tall and slim. As she was twenty-four years old, he had to presume that she would remain tall and slim until she perhaps began to put on weight in middle age. Her face was piquant, with small, attractive features. He would never have called her pretty, a word which he disliked anyway, but equally she could not be described as beautiful. The most appropriate word was attractive. And she had splendid pale brown hair and eyes; the hair was worn long unless she was dressed for an occasion, and the eyes were huge.

"It's good to see you," she said. "Did you have a successful trip?"

"Yes," he said, and kissed her. It was a chaste kiss, but then, their entire relationship was chaste. That was the way of the English gentry, certainly those who lived in the country. It would be quite impossible to imagine Julia, no matter what the circumstances, entering the bedroom of a man she had just met, much less asking permission to get into his bed! But then, living in rural England in this year of 1908, she could be a million miles from oppressive regimes, from bombs and whips and revolvers and simmering hatreds.

Long might it remain so. And yet, he thought, as she withdrew her closed lips and gave his hand a gentle squeeze, might that not be an important factor in his behaviour towards Anna Slovitza, this apparent lack of passion, of intensity among his own womenfolk?

Suddenly he knew he needed to find out if passion was *there*, urgently, before he could contemplate marriage to even this charming creature. And if it was there, and would be there to come back to, would that not make his mission the easier to accomplish?

"Mother!" Julia called, as, still holding his hand, she led him into the house. "Berkeley's back."

"Berkeley!" Joan Gracey bustled out of the kitchen drying her hands on her apron. Like her husband, she believed in playing an active role in the running of her household. "So good to see you. Did you have a successful trip?"

Hopefully, this would be the last time he would be asked the question. "Oh, indeed, Mrs Gracey. Excellent."

"Well, there's roast lamb for lunch. In an hour, so you've time for a wash and brush-up."

"I'm sure Berkeley and I have a lot to talk about," Julia said. She was every bit as positive as her mother.

"Of course. One hour, mind." She bustled back into the kitchen.

"Do you want a wash and brush-up?" Julia asked.

"I'd rather talk to you, first."

She pulled a bonnet from the stand by the door, put it on, and led him through the low-ceilinged drawing room, and out the back door into the orchard. It was a warm August day.

"So," he said, "what have you been doing with yourself?"

"The usual things. I don't live a very exciting life."

"I understand you've been entertaining."

She glanced at him. "People come to call."

"Harvey Braddock?"

"Why, yes."

"I gather he's been making a habit of it."

She nodded, pink spots gathering in her cheeks. "He doesn't seem to have much else to do, not being a soldier."

"I thought Foreign Office people worked harder than soldiers."

She had walked as far as a rustic bench, some hundred yards from the house. Now she sat down. "They do. But not at weekends. And they're always in the country. Don't tell me you're jealous?"

He sat beside her. "Of course I'm jealous. Has he proposed?"

"As a matter of fact, yes."

"And?" He wasn't sure he wanted to hear.

"I told him he'd have to wait."

"That must have cheered him up. Wait on what?"

She turned her head to look at him.

"So I'm still number one?"

"Perhaps."

They gazed at each other, then he took her in his arms and kissed her. This time he did not allow her lips to remain closed, but forced them open to get at her tongue. She made a startled sound, which changed into another sound as he rested his hand on her breast, caressing the soft mound he could feel beneath her bodice. For a moment she didn't resist, perhaps because she was too surprised. Then she got her own hands up to push him away.

"Gosh," she said.

"I'm sorry. I needed to do that."

Her cheeks were flushed. She glanced at him, then looked away again. "What are you trying to say?"

"That I love you and would like to marry you. But . . . I am a passionate man."

"So I gather," she said.

"Was that so repulsive?"

"It was . . . unexpected."

"Too much so?"

"I don't know."

"But will you marry me?"

"I don't know," she said again. "It's all rather sudden."

"Sudden?" he cried. "We've known each other all our lives."

"Have we?" she asked.

"Ah," he said. "But love is about passion."

"Tell me what happened in Hungary," she said.

"Hungary? I went there to buy remounts for the cavalry, and—"

"The truth."

"I beg your pardon."

"You've come back . . . different; as if you've had some kind of experience. I think I'm entitled to know what it was."

"Before you can make up your mind to marry me." And he had supposed the decision was all his.

"Well . . . I don't think a husband and wife should have any secrets from each other."

"Then . . ." he changed his mind about what he would have said, that she knew very little about marriage. "I'm sorry, Julia. I went to Hungary to buy remounts for the cavalry. That is all I am prepared to say, all I can say."

He gazed at her, willing her to understand.

Her face was composed, but the pink spots were back. "Then you are asking me to marry a man part of whose life must be a secret from me."

"That's how it is, with the army."

"There was some talk of you giving that up."

"I'm afraid that's not possible, right this minute. It's my career, and, incidentally, my livelihood. Dad's income doesn't rise to giving me an allowance substantial enough to live on, much less support a wife."

"And you will continue to go on secret missions, the purposes of which you will not be able to divulge to your wife?"

"I will continue to go where I am sent," he said carefully. "I have no choice."

"You would not say that is an intolerable burden to place on a wife?"

"I'm sure it is. But there are quite a few thousand wives bearing such a burden. Not all of them are unhappy."

At last she turned her head. "You are rebuking me."

"I am endeavouring to point out that you would not be unique. For God's sake . . ." he seized her hands, and she did not pull them away. "I love you. I suppose I have loved you, in a vague sort of way, all of our lives. Now I do so as a man. I want you to be my wife. So I am an actively serving officer; that will soon be over. I will have promotion, and a settled place, and I will be home even more often that your Harvey Braddock. You will no doubt become bored with the sight of me."

"And when there is another war?"

"There is hardly likely to be one, involving us, for a very long time. We have proved, to the Boers, to the world, what we can do when we are roused. Anyway," he made a face, "I am hardly likely to receive a field command with a gammy leg."

"Then may I ask what are your plans, or the army's plans for you, in the immediate future? Where you will be stationed?"

"I'm afraid I have to go away again."

"More remounts?"

"We cannot have enough horses."

"And where do you hope to obtain these horses now?"

"The Middle East. In the first instance, Greece."

Now she did pull her hands free. "I could never marry a man who lied to me."

His mouth opened, and then shut again. "I am going to Greece. Athens. I can show you the ticket."

"But not to buy horses."

"Well . . ."

29

She stood up. "I hear the lunch gong."

"Then your answer is no."

"No. My answer is, please ask me again when you come back. And perhaps are more settled."

"The Devil," John Townsend commented at dinner. "Turned you down flat? I never expected that. You should've worn uniform. Gals always go for a handsome man in red."

"Oh, really, Father. Hasn't she seen me in uniform often enough? Anyway, she didn't turn me down flat. She said to ask her again when I come back from my next overseas trip."

"You can't really blame her," Alicia Townsend said. "A woman likes a settled life, children, a husband she's going to see at least once a day. Next trip? You never said anything about another trip, Berkeley. Aren't you due some leave?"

"Actually, I am. But the War Office have discovered there are some good horses to be had in Thrace, and they want me to go out there and look them over, negotiate a price for them if they are worthwhile."

"Thrace," John Townsend said. "That's actually Greece, isn't it?"

"There's a difference of opinion as to whether it belongs to Greece, Bulgaria, or Turkey," Berkeley said. "I don't suppose the horses know, either. However, Lockwood and I have passages booked for Piraeus, next Monday."

"So soon?"

"You know what the War Office is like, Mother. It shouldn't be a long trip. Not more than a month."

"But you'll be careful," his mother admonished. "Those people are so *wild*."

"I'm sure they won't trouble me, Mother. Or even Harry."

"But you're not going for a week," his father said. "Are you going to, ah . . ."

"Certainly not," Berkeley said. "She said to ask her again when I come back. I shall do that."

"A month," Alicia said darkly. "She may have been suited by then."

"That is entirely up to her," Berkeley said.

He almost hoped she would be. Because, if she had not entirely rejected his physical advance, she had certainly not responded to it. They lived in different worlds, and it had been foolish of him ever to suppose the gap could be bridged. But didn't he then also live in a different world to his own parents?

As for the world in which he would be living when he returned from this jaunt; he did not care to consider that.

He gazed at the mountains of the Peloponnessus, glowing to the west in the sunset as the steamer turned Cape Malea and headed through a calm sea, north for Piraeus, the port for Athens. The people here were so *wild*, his mother had said. It's an unlucky mother who does not know her own son, he reflected.

"Well, sir, at least it'll be different," Lockwood commented, leaning on the rail beside him. "I've never arrested anyone before. And as for that Madame Slovitza . . . do you think she'll come quietly?"

"No," Berkeley said.

"Ah." Lockwood considered this for some seconds, no doubt wondering how his master would reconcile those undoubtedly passionate moments he and the lady had shared during their escape from Hungary, with having to treat her as a criminal. Even if she was; Lockwood had read the file. "Could be tricky."

"It will be tricky. We shall need to employ subterfuge until we get her within striking distance of the Austro-Hungarian border."

"Sounds nasty. Will you . . ."

"Harry," Berkeley said. "We have been given a job to do. As you say, it looks very nasty. But we will employ all the means in our power to carry it out."

"Yes, sir." As he had made obvious from the beginning, Lockwood did not approve. It was worth remembering that the only time in their entire relationship, which now went back ten years, Lockwood had questioned a decision of his master's had been in the bedroom in Seinheit, when he had realised Berkeley intended to help the woman. But he would continue to obey whatever orders he was given.

But what orders would he be given? Berkeley had wrestled with this problem through the last three weeks. He had sought a quick, easy answer, that Julia should fall into his arms so passionately and without reservation as to allow him to regard Anna as what she really was: a cold-blooded murderess deserving only of hanging. That hadn't happened. Which did not in any way make Anna less of a cold-blooded murderess, but also did not allay his desire for her as a woman. That had to be exorcised. By being harsh and ruthless and treating her as . . . a cold-blooded murderess.

He didn't know he could do it.

Early next morning they nosed up to their anchorage off the little seaport that had been the scene of so much history. Instantly the steamer was surrounded by bumboats and launches from the shore, some containing customs and immigration officials, but one delivering an attaché from the British Consulate.

"Mr Jones?" The attaché seemed uncertain.

"I am he." Berkeley shook hands.

"I have train tickets for you and your man as far as Belgrade. I was informed that you would not be staying any time in Athens." He seemed relieved about that.

"That's right," Berkeley agreed. "There was also to be a dragoman; I don't speak Serbian."

The attaché nodded. "I have one waiting. You will find, though, that many Serbs speak at least a variation of German."

"Thank you. That will help."

The attaché hesitated. "The train ticket is one way . . ."

"That's right," Berkeley said again. "We won't be coming back."

The interpreter was a small, round man, who wore a Greek hat and smelled of garlic; this was, fortunately, a vegetable of which Berkeley was fond.

"I show you everything," Pathenikos said. "There is much to see in Belgrade." He rolled his eyes.

"I just wish to find someone," Berkeley said.

Pathenikos rolled his eyes some more.

"I am a solicitor. You understand this?"

"Sol-i-ci-tor?"

Berkeley hoped his Serbian was better than his English. "It means lawyer. There is a woman in Serbia for whom I have some money. I need to find her."

"Ah, money. Yes, I understand. But in Serbia? This is a big country, sir."

"I think, if we ask in the right places in Belgrade, we will be able to find her."

The distance from Athens to Belgrade, following the valleys through the mountains, was a good 800 miles, involving crossing the border into Macedonia, thence north to the province of Kosovo, all Turkish territory this, then up the valley of the Morava to Belgrade itself. As the train seldom made more than twenty miles an hour, because of the age of the engine, the overcrowded carriages, and the various gradients, and as it only worked for twelve hours a day, the journey would in any event have taken more than three days. But as it also stopped regularly, sometimes for more than an hour while passengers embarked or disembarked in a most leisurely fashion, and the drivers and conductors engaged in long conversations with the various stationmasters, punctuated by much arm waving and gesticulating; and as all the border guards were highly suspicious and insisted upon examining, slowly, the papers of every passenger, it was actually five days before they stepped down at Belgrade Central.

Berkeley found it a very interesting and informative, if disturbing, trip. He had known before he left England that the Turkish Empire was in turmoil, with the Sultan virtually a prisoner and his government being carried on, spasmodically, by the so-called Young Turk Party. These internal problems had meant that the Turkish grip on its European provinces had been weakened, as a result of which those little countries, such as Bulgaria and Serbia, which within the last generation had gained full independence, were flexing their muscles and seeing what might be picked up if, as was generally supposed would soon happen, the Turkish Empire was to disintegrate entirely.

What was more serious, both Russia and Austria were dipping their fingers into the Balkan pie. The Russians claimed to be behaving honourably, as traditional defenders of the Slav race, but the British at least suspected that they had their eyes on the possible acquisition of Constantinople, a Russian dream for many years, and one which Whitehall was determined to frustrate.

The Austrians were being much more blatant in their desire to get hold of the province of Bosnia-Herzegovina, still officially Turkish but overrun with Austrian traders and merchants. It was pretty generally accepted that the only reason the Austrians had not simply marched in and occupied the province was fear of Russian reaction. This could well provoke a war, which might spread; if Austria was officially allied to Germany and Italy, these were essentially defensive arrangements growing out of fear of Russia and France, who were also allied. Hence the Austrian desire to remain friendly with Britain, which was legally allied to no one save Japan, despite all the press agitation about the Entente Cordial.

It did seem to Berkeley, however, that with so much suspicion and ambition on every side, the Balkans were a possible source of big trouble, and even if he was on a specific mission it was still his duty, as a serving British officer, to observe and report anything that he supposed might be of use or value to his government. This he fully intended to do, when he got home. But as the train entered Serbia, he became aware of an even more disturbing feeling.

Serbia was the first of the old Turkish provinces to have gained independence. This had been achieved with both Austrian and Russian assistance, and Serbia had settled down to become a usefully powerful little state, despite being rent within from the rivalry, which in the past had involved even murder, between the two families of Karageorgevich and Obrenovich. The current King, Peter Karageorgevich, had come to power only five years previously, following the murder of Alexander Obrenovich, and the country remained in a very disturbed state.

He asked Pathenikos about it.

"Ah, it is very bad," the Greek said, as usual rolling his eyes. "Since the assassination of King Alexander . . . you know about this?"

"Remind me."

"They say it was his marriage."

"I remember reading about it. Not everyone approved. Of the lady."

"The lady, Mr Jones? She was hardly that. Her name was Draga Mashin and she was lady-in-waiting to the King's mother, but was dismissed because of her immoral misconduct. She was ten years older than the King, and she was said to rule him like a mother. So she was very unpopular. But the King was already unpopular, because he ruled like a dictator. His father was forced to abdicate, you must remember. The Serbs have always regarded the Russians as their friends and protectors, but the King excluded the pro-Russian faction from his cabinets and leaned towards Austria."

"But didn't I read that Tsar Nicholas II of Russia attended the marriage?"

"Yes, he did, sir."

"Didn't that give it the seal of approval?"

Pathenikos shrugged. "No doubt he was advised to do so by the pro-Russian faction. The point is that the people were very unhappy about the King's pro-Austrian stance. And when in addition he brought his father back from exile and made him commander-in-chief of the army, well . . ."

"So a group of army officers invaded the royal palace and shot the King and Queen Draga. But that was five years ago."

"Yes, sir. And as a result of that, the Karageorgevichs regained control. King Milan is virulently anti-Austrian, so the entire government policy has been reversed. Yet the country remains unsettled. There are those who side with King Milan, but there are also those who fear the might of Austria, and wonder if the support of Russia is really of any value, certainly since that débâcle in the Far East, and all the social trouble in Russia itself."

Berkeley wondered how all this political turmoil was helping Anna Slovitza . . . or otherwise.

Being badly in need of a bath and a shave he checked them in at a hotel, and sampled some Serbian wine with his dinner. Next morning he paid a visit on the chief of police, who he discovered spoke good English. So Pathenikos was left outside.

"Mr Jones," Colonel Savos said thoughtfully. "That is a common name in England, is it not?"

"Actually, it's Welsh," Berkeley said. "Although my family has been English for generations."

"Quite so. And you were a soldier before you became a lawyer, and have been wounded."

Berkeley raised his eyebrows. He hadn't really expected to meet a Sherlock Holmes clone in Belgrade.

Colonel Savos smiled. "It is very simple, really, Mr Jones. Your movements have the precision of a man trained in drill. But you also walk with a limp."

"Very good," Berkeley said. "I was in the Sudan as a soldier, yes. But after I was wounded, I had to try something else, don't you know."

"I understand. And now . . ." He lifted the letter Berkeley had given him and frowned at it. "Anna Slovitza. Inheriting money in England. Very odd."

"Do you know the lady?"

"We have never met. Do *you* know the lady?"

"I'm afraid I don't. Only her name."

"Yes. Well, I am bound to tell you, Mr Jones, that I do not believe this letter."

"I'm sorry, I do not understand."

"I do not believe that Madame Slovitza has inherited any money in England."

"My dear fellow . . ."

"Oh, I am not impugning you, sir. But I think you are being duped."

"Duped?" Berkeley demanded, suitably outraged.

"I think this is a means of conveying money from England to Madame Slovitza, certainly, but the money itself, I suspect, is a donation to her cause."

"Her cause?"

"Madame Slovitza is a well-known anarchist, Mr Jones. She is a member of a secret organisation known as the Black Hand. This organisation is directed against Austria. Specifically, the organisation is opposed to an Austrian takeover of Bosnia-Herzegovina. Well, I suppose, so are a lot of people. But not all of them spend their time blowing up trains or railways stations, or assassinating Austrian officials."

"Madame Slovitza does this?" Now Berkeley was suitably horrified.

"There is an application before our courts for her extradition to Austria on a charge of murder, at this moment."

"Good lord! Will the application succeed?"

Which would let him neatly off the hook.

"I doubt it," Savos said. "We live in a divided society, Mr Jones. Austria is our near neighbour, and is a most powerful neighbour. She is our biggest trading partner. But all this talk about the possible annexation of Bosnia-Herzegovina . . . Were that to happen we would be half surrounded by the Austrian Empire. The army would favour closer relations with Russia. I do not think the judiciary would dare risk the wrath of the army by handing over Madame Slovitza to the Austrians for trial and public execution."

So, Berkeley thought, I could well be taking on the entire Serb army. He wondered if Gorman knew that.

"And where do you stand in this, Colonel?" he asked.

Savos gave a cold little smile. "I endeavour to keep the peace, Mr Jones."

"But you have not actually arrested Madame Slovitza."

Savos spread his hands. "She has committed no crime in Serbia. I have no reason to arrest her. Unless the Austrian deposition is successful in the courts."

"And you don't think that is likely to happen. But I have an idea you know where she can be found."

"Certainly. As far as I know, she is at her home in Sabac. That is a town to the south-west of here, quite close to the Bosnian border. It is convenient for her, as if things were to go against her here, she could slip across the border before we could arrest her."

"Ah. As a matter of fact, that is something else that puzzles me. The lady is apparently Bosnian, yet she seems to be able to come and go through Serbia as she chooses. And you describe this place Sabac as her home."

"It is not as complicated as you suppose, Mr Jones. Anna Slovitza *is* Bosnian, as you say. But she was married to a Serb, named Slovitza, and thus has Serbian nationality."

"You said, was married."

"Yes. Her husband was captured by the Austrians a few years ago, and executed. Which is one reason why she continues the fight, almost recklessly."

"I see. I assume you have her address, in this place Sabac?"

"I do. You mean to go there?"

"I was sent here to contact Madame Slovitza, and inform her of her inheritance. I'm afraid it's not my province at this stage to enquire whether it is an inheritance or a means of conveying money for her support. I can only act as instructed by my client in England."

"You would not care to divulge this client's name?"

"No, I would not," Berkeley said. "It would be highly unprofessional."

"Of course. My secretary will give you the address. But if I may offer a word of caution, Mr Jones: Madame Slovitza is by the nature of her life and occupation a somewhat suspicious person. I think you need to proceed with caution."

"But, Colonel, you said she has never committed a crime here in Serbia."

Once again Savos' smile was cold. "She has never committed anything I would consider a crime, Mr Jones."

"Which probably means that if she or her friends lynch us they won't be arrested," Berkeley suggested to Lockwood.

"But we are hoping she won't do that, aren't we, sir? We saved her life."

"Yes," Berkeley said, feeling more of a despicable cad than ever.

The line from Belgrade to Zvornik passed through Sabac, and as the distance was only some twenty-five miles they were there quite early the next morning. Now they had come down from the mountains, following the River Sava, and found themselves in a fertile plain. Sabac itself was a bustling river port.

"It's just along to the left," Berkeley said, having committed to memory both the address given him by the Belgrade police and the town plan he had procured.

Lockwood and Pathenikos hefted the bags and Berkeley strode out in front as well as his limp would let him, swinging his cane. He had formulated an initial plan of action, but that was to account for his return. As for getting her out . . . this had to be in the nature of a reconnaissance. Sabac was, as Savos had said, only a few miles from the Bosnian border. But he doubted that would be the right way to go. There were Austrian agents in Sarajevo, but he did not think they would dare arrest, or even take delivery of, Anna Slovitza. They would need to go north, to Hungary. That meant she would either have to be duped into accompanying them, or physically kidnapped. He rather suspected it would have to be the latter.

What an occupation for an officer and a gentleman.

But however he went about it, it would have to be very carefully planned; and if he had some ideas on how it could be done, nothing could be considered until Anna was first of all located, and it was discovered just how well protected she was.

He deduced very rapidly that English gentlemen were not usual visitors to Sabac. He and his two servants aroused a great deal of interest, and soon there was an honour guard of small boys, and mongrel dogs yelped at him.

"They want money, your excellency," Pathenikos explained.

"Tell them I have nothing to give them," Berkeley said.

Pathenikos shouted at the crowd, but did not have any effect, except that the boys shouted back. A few minutes later they were at the address, one of a row of tall, somewhat narrow houses, a few blocks from the river. Berkeley went up the steps and rapped on the door with the handle of his cane. He had to do this several times before a small window was opened.

Pathenikos had already taken up a position in front of this, and now he spoke in Serbian. Berkeley understood the words English and Madame Slovitza.

The face – Berkeley decided it belonged to a woman – peered left and right. Then it asked a question.

"Madame Slovitza," Pathenikos repeated.

The woman made a terse remark and closed the window.

"She says no one by that name lives here," Pathenikos explained.

"Then she is lying."

"Perhaps the police gave you the wrong address, your excellency."

"I do not think they did." Berkeley rapped again, and when the window opened he thrust his cane into the aperture so that it could not be closed. "Tell her that I have some very important news for Madame Slovitza. From England. From John Smith."

Pathenikos translated and the woman replied. "She says we must wait."

"Very well. But I am not going to remove my stick."

The woman muttered, and disappeared.

"What did she say?" Berkeley asked.

"It is not repeatable, your excellency."

Berkeley grinned, and while he waited, surveyed the crowd which had now grown to include several men and women. These were all talking loudly.

"What are they saying?" he asked.

"They are hostile, your excellency. They ask why you are making this trouble."

"I am not making trouble," Berkeley pointed out. "Yet."

There was movement beyond the door, and he heard the scraping of bolts. A moment later the door swung in. The hall was gloomy, but Berkeley stepped inside, to be seized by the shoulder and half thrown forward. He stumbled against a chair, and turned to see the door being slammed and bolted before either Lockwood or Pathenikos could enter.

"I say," he said. "My people."

His eyes had still not become accustomed to the gloom. But now a man stepped against him, and said something in a low voice. At the same time a long knife was presented to his throat.

The Bride

The man was speaking to him in a language he did not understand, and the knife was very close to his throat. Berkeley did not doubt he could deal with him, if necessary, but now that his eyes were accustomed to the gloom he realised there were several other men in the room, and he had not come here to get himself beaten up.

"Listen," he said. "I do not understand you. Do you speak German? *Nein verstehen?*"

The man apparently did not speak German. He was in any event distracted by a banging on the door. Faithful Lockwood. Lockwood had the baggage, and in the baggage were their guns. But he would hardly start shooting on the street.

"Listen," he said again, and had an inspiration: he had a few words of Yiddish. "*Ikh heys* John Smith. *Ikh bin an guter fraynd* Madame Slovitza."

At last, communication. "You are lying," said the man, also speaking Yiddish.

"Why don't you ask her?"

There was more banging on the door. The man with the knife gave instructions in Serbian, and two of the other men came forward, each taking one of Berkeley's arms, to push him through an inner doorway. Here there was another hall, and a flight of steps leading up. He realised he had lost his hat, but was not given the opportunity to look for it.

"We go up," one of them said.

"My people?"

"They will be sent away."

"Listen, old boy," Berkeley said, "you are not attempting to imprison me, are you? I am a personal friend of Colonel Savos."

Which was drawing the bow a bit, but these people couldn't know that.

They reached the first floor, and a corridor. A door on the right was opened, and he was pushed into a surprisingly well-furnished reception room, although here again, as there were shutters over the windows, it was extremely gloomy.

"Colonel Savos sent you here?" asked one of the men.

"No, he did not send me. But he knew I was coming; he gave me the address. He is expecting me back in Belgrade tomorrow morning."

"You are a police spy."

"Don't be ridiculous. I am a close friend of Madame Slovitza's. I saved her life, quite recently. Perhaps you know of this. Now I need her help in return."

The two men considered him, and spoke to each other in Serbian. Then the spokesman said, "You will wait here."

It was Berkeley's turn to consider. But he could not break his way out without engaging in a great deal of violence and possibly endangering his life; and to attempt it would not help him get close enough to Anna to arrest her. Lockwood was quite capable of operating on his own for a few hours.

"You mean, I must wait for Madame Slovitza?"

"Perhaps. Do not make trouble."

They closed the door behind themselves, and he heard a key being turned in the lock. They had definitely taken him prisoner.

He opened the shutters but predictably there were bars beyond, and he was looking down at an inner courtyard in any event. But at least he had allowed some daylight into the room, and his first impression of comfortable elegance was confirmed. The home of an anarchist chieftainess, he thought. But there was money here.

He took a turn around the room, looking at the various photographs in the gilt and silver frames on the dark-polished table and mantelpiece: a strikingly handsome man, in an absurd Napoleonic pose, one hand thrust into his jacket, chin tilted; the same man and a young very handsome Anna, wearing a wedding dress; Anna, seated on a settee, cradling a baby. That gave him a surprise; he had not supposed she was a mother. But why shouldn't even anarchists be mothers?

Then a photo of mother and daughter, wearing black, their faces sombre. But what faces! Anna was a most handsome woman; but her daughter, who had had an even more handsome father . . . she would be about twelve, he supposed, when the photograph had been taken, a child of quite unworldly loveliness, perfectly chiselled features framed in straight hair. In the photograph the hair appeared dark, but he suspected it might be the same colour as her mother's.

He wondered what had happened to her, heard the key turning in the lock, and gazed at her.

She was now about eighteen, he supposed. She was taller than her mother, but had, as far as he could see under the loose dress, an even fuller figure. And her hair was indeed auburn, worn loose beyond her shoulders, while her face, if it were possible, had even grown in beauty.

At the moment her expression was a mixture of caution and curiosity. "You are Mr Smith," she said in German. "My mother has told me of you. She says she owes you her life."

"I was actually taking care of both of us," he said. "She never told me she had a daughter."

"I do not think she ever expected to see you again." She closed the door behind her. "I am Caterina Slovitza."

He took her hand, softly warm. Pray to God, he thought, that she is not an anarchist and a murderess like her mother. "Now it is I asking for *her* help," he explained.

"And I know she will give it to you," Caterina Slovitza said. "But she is not here at the moment."

"Then, if you will tell me where she is, I will go and find her."

Caterina smiled, and like her mother, redoubled her looks. "That will not be necessary. She will return tomorrow. You may spend the night here and wait for her."

"That is very kind of you, Miss Slovitza. I have a man . . ."

"Here?"

"Your people locked him out in the street."

"Then I will have him admitted."

"There is also an interpreter."

"Very well."

"Him I will send back to Athens," Berkeley said. "He was just to see me as far as here."

"You are very well organised," she remarked, and went to the door. There she hesitated. "I wish to apologise for the way you were treated by our people. But as you know my mother, and what she does, you will understand that we need to be suspicious of strangers."

"I do understand that," he said. "Are you coming back?"

There was so much he needed to find out about this girl.

"I will see you at lunch, Mr Smith."

Lockwood and Pathenikos had remained on the street, watching the house. Now they were brought inside, together with the bags.

"Bit of a turn up, sir," Lockwood remarked.

Pathenikos rolled his eyes.

"It's all turning out all right, actually," Berkeley said. "I think you can go back to Athens, now, Pathenikos." He peeled off several notes from his roll and gave them to the dragoman. "Many thanks for all your help."

"You wish me go to Colonel Savos, in Belgrade?"

42

"No, I don't think that will be necessary. Just get back to Greece and avoid talking with strangers."

Pathenikos touched his hat, and departed.

"You don't reckon it might be a good idea to let the police know where we are, sir?" Lockwood asked.

"I have no doubt at all the police know just where we are, Harry. And we certainly don't want them muscling in."

A white-gowned maid led them upstairs to a very comfortable apartment on the next floor. Here the windows looked out over the town and the river, and the countryside beyond.

"Is there any change in our plan, sir?" Lockwood asked.

"At the moment, none," Berkeley told him.

But only at the moment, he thought.

He and Caterina lunched alone, in a dining room every bit as elegant as the reception room; he gathered that Lockwood was being entertained by the servants in the pantry. They ate with old silver and drank from crystal goblets, and she had changed her dress to a becoming morning gown, although she had left her hair loose.

The surroundings at least gave him an opening for a probe. "As you know, your mother and I were thrown together, briefly, by circumstances," he remarked. "I really know very little about her. But, if you'll forgive me, I find it remarkable that with so much to live for and enjoy . . ." he gestured at the room ". . . she finds it necessary continually to risk her life, for, well I am not sure just what the cause is. To keep the Austrians out of Bosnia-Herzegovina?"

"To fight the Austrians, for as long as she has a breath left in her body," Caterina said.

"Ah . . . I know that I'm English, and less involved in these things than I might be, but is that not a dreadful waste of a life?"

"It is an act of honour, to avenge her murdered husband."

"Your father."

"Yes, Mr Smith. My father."

"May I ask how old you were when he died?"

"I was thirteen when my father was hanged, Mr Smith."

"I am truly sorry. It must have been, well, an awful experience."

"Yes, Mr Smith."

"Were you here when you heard the news?"

"I was standing on the gallows beside my father," she said, "when they sprang the trap."

Berkeley stared at her in total consternation.

"We were taken together, you see," she said. "We were told my grandmother was very ill. She lived in a place called Banja Luka, in Northern Bosnia. We felt we had to go and see her, perhaps for the

43

last time. But it was a trap; the house was filled with Austrian agents. Mother shot her way out, Papa was taken, together with me. We were smuggled across the border into Hungary and tried as terrorists."

"You, a thirteen-year-old girl, was tried as a terrorist?"

"No. But they wished me to give evidence against my father. I refused to do this, so when he was condemned anyway, I was made to watch him die."

Berkeley licked his lips. "Forgive me," he said, "but when they were trying to make you give evidence against your father, did they . . ."

She gazed at him, her eyes enormous. "Yes, Mr Smith," she said. "They did things to me. Things that made me ashamed." She gave a little shrug. "Then they beat me, and let me go. I suppose they felt that I was too young, and too frightened, ever to be a threat to them again. They did not know my mother very well, then, you see."

Berkeley couldn't think of anything to say; even less could he think of anything to do, now. Anna Slovitza, and perhaps her daughter as well, were cold-blooded killers. But didn't they have a reason?

"May I ask, have you helped your mother in any of her ventures?"

"She will not let me. She says I am too young."

"Thank God for that."

She raised her eyebrows.

"I would hate to think of you falling into the hands of the Austrian police, again."

She nodded. "I would kill myself first." Then she smiled. "But perhaps I would kill some of them, first."

"But you haven't yet killed anybody?" He couldn't keep the anxiety out of his voice.

"No, Mr Smith. I have never killed anybody. Would it bother you if I had?"

"Very much. Killing is no occupation for beautiful young women."

She regarded him for several seconds. "That was a very nice thing to say," she said at last. "But I am tarnished goods, Mr Smith."

"I do not think you could ever be tarnished, Caterina. You do not mind if I call you Caterina?"

"I should like you to." She drank the last of her wine. "Now, I must go out this afternoon. You are welcome to stay here. I will be back this evening."

"Are you going to meet your boyfriend?"

"I do not have a boyfriend, Mr Smith."

"Ah. Then may I come with you? Wherever it is you are going?"

Another slow consideration. Then she shook her head. "It would be best for you to remain here, Mr Smith."

Berkeley lay on the bed with his hands beneath his head and stared at the ceiling; presumably, Lockwood was disporting himself downstairs with the serving maids. Had Lockwood yet seen Caterina? He wasn't sure, but he didn't suppose it would make too much difference to him. As a general rule, Lockwood left the making of plans and decisions to his master. This also, conveniently, left matters of ethics or conscience to his master as well.

So, what am I doing? Berkeley asked himself. And more important, what am I going to do?

On what might be called level one, he was embarked on a mission, the failure of which would undoubtedly mean the end of his career; if it did not involve his being extradited by the Austrians as a kind of sacrificial lamb.

To carry out the mission successfully, he would not only have to dupe and betray a woman who regarded him as a friend, but virtually condemn her to death. Before which, like her daughter, she would have "things done to her". That was a quite unacceptable thought.

What made it even more unacceptable was that to carry out his mission might involve Caterina. It would certainly involve her lifelong hatred, and he suspected that she could, and did, hate just as deeply as her mother.

But there was a level two that was even more disturbing. He had never supposed he was worse than any other man in his susceptibility to sex, the excitement of the pursuit of a beautiful woman. Nor, he knew, did he have the morally correct attitude towards faithfulness that might be approved by the Church. He accepted that he might, one day, if he survived this jaunt, marry Julia Gracey, become a father, and hopefully, when that happened, a faithful husband as well. That had been his attitude before he had gone to Seinheit. But it had not stopped him falling for the flamboyant beauty of Anna Slovitza. Not that, had she been a genuine honeymooner, he would have dreamed of having an affair with her. But the circumstances had been exceptional.

Knowing just what she was, he had been prepared to betray her to get himself off the hook on which she had hung him. A bad choice of word. But now he was absolutely smitten by her daughter. That was unethical and immoral, as he had had sex with the mother. It was also highly dangerous, in that Caterina had left him in no doubt that she supported her mother in everything and could hardly wait to get hold of a gun or a bomb and start on a career of anarchism herself.

The only good that could possibly come out of this whole sorry affair would be if she could be saved from that. But she certainly would not be saved by having her mother carted off for execution. She would merely have an added incentive to kill and maim and destroy, until she was herself sucked into the vortex of political and racial hatred which could only end in death.

What a mess!

Lockwood appeared to help him dress for dinner.

"Tête-à-tête with the young lady, sir?"

"As far as I know, Harry. Who are you dining with?"

"Ah, well, sir, there are some lively spirits in the pantry. Goes against the grain to have to turn them in. But I don't suppose the serving girls will be involved. Will they, sir?"

"I see no reason why they should be, Harry."

Lucky for some, he thought, and then changed his mind when he went down to the reception room, where Caterina waited. Now she wore an evening gown, off the shoulder, which appeared to be supported only by her magnificent breasts. Her shoulders were very white, and glowed. Her hair was swept up in a pompadour to expose them and her neck, again glowing white.

"Why, Mr Smith," she said, "a dinner suit does become you."

"Hardly as much as that gown becomes you, Caterina."

"And you are a master of the compliment," she remarked, and poured wine. It was white and bubbly, not champagne, but very pleasant if a trifle sweet. "Let us drink to our friendship."

"Oh, indeed." They sipped, and she gave him one of those every intent stares which seemed to strip his mind of the ability to think. Except of one thing. "Ah . . . when do you expect your mother back; tomorrow?"

"The train gets in from Belgrade just after ten. You were on it, this morning."

"So I was. Good Lord! You mean your mother has been in Belgrade all of this time?"

"But you did not know that," she pointed out. "Now you will regard your journey as entirely wasted."

"No journey could be wasted that involved meeting you, Caterina."

Another long stare. Then she asked, "Are you my mother's lover?"

As usual, he was left speechless.

"I think you must have been," she said. "Briefly. But she speaks very kindly of you, and not just because you helped her escape from the Austrians. Is that why you have come back? To be with her?"

"Not exactly."

She raised her eyebrows, and he decided he might as well begin his campaign now; he could do so without finally committing himself either way. "I came back because I am out of a job."

"Explain, please."

"Well, you see, as I am sure your mother gathered, I am, was actually, a British soldier, engaged in discovering what fortifications the Austrians had in the Carpathians, opposite Russian Poland."

Now her eyes were enormous. "You, the English, are going to war with Austria?"

"Sadly, I think that is extremely unlikely. No, it was just part of our desire to know just what the other fellow, all the other fellows, have up their sleeves. All governments, all armies, do it all the time. Being engaged in that duty, of course, it was not intended that I became known to the Austrian government, but because I decided to help your mother, I killed several of their people."

"Mother has told me this."

"So, this upset the Austrians, who applied for my extradition. So I was dismissed the service, and told to make myself scarce."

"How terrible!" She looked genuinely concerned. "All because you helped my mother."

"All because I disobeyed orders. So, having no family and very little money, I thought I'd look your mother up and see if she had any employment for me."

"With your faithful servant. I find that very romantic. I am sure my mother will employ you, Mr Smith. She may even . . ." She refilled their glasses. ". . . wish to renew her liaison with you." She held his out. "Would you like that?"

Their fingers touched as he took the goblet, and he drew a deep breath. If he was going to be the absolute cad, then he was going to be the absolute cad. "If you'd asked me that this time yesterday, I would probably have said yes."

Another long stare, then she said, "Supper is ready."

They ate the first part of the meal in silence. He was in her hands now, even more than when he had first entered the house. It was not until they were into the dessert that she said, quite suddenly, "I have never known a man. With love or tenderness."

"Then I am seeking a great responsibility. Can you forgive me, for having known your mother?"

"Oh . . ." She made a dismissive gesture with her hand. "Mother does not know men. She uses them. She can do this, because of her beauty, her femininity and her ruthlessness. As she used you, regardless of what it might do to you, your career, your life. And she will use you again, if you stay here. You must understand this. If all she has told me of you is true, you could be of great value to her."

"And you?"

Now the adrenalin was flowing.

"If what she has told me is true, I think you could be of great value to me as well," Caterina said. "I have dreamed. I have felt, experienced, what men can do. It was brutal, and frightening, and painful. My mother has told me it is not always so, need not be so, with a man who would be gentle, and kind, and loving. She described you as such a man. So perhaps I dreamed of you, without even knowing what you looked like."

My God, he thought, what have you got yourself into here, Berkeley Townsend? But he could still try to do some good.

"And if I turned out to be such a man, would that enable you to stop hating the Austrians? Wishing to kill them?"

"I don't think anything could do that, Mr Smith," she said.

"Ah."

"But it would make my life more acceptable."

She stood up and held out her hand. Berkeley realised that whatever other plans he might have, and was now developing, they would have to wait on the here and now. And perhaps, afterwards, his situation would be more acceptable.

In any event, she was irresistible. She had been, from the moment he had laid eyes on her.

She led him up the stairs and into her bedroom, a place of soft scents and a huge four-poster bed.

"You are the first man ever to enter here," she said.

She was making sure he understood what she was giving, a responsibility almost beyond belief.

Now she faced him. "What do you wish me to do, first?"

"I would like you to undress." How calm was his voice, at total odds with the raging desires in his brain.

She removed her dress and her underclothes with no hint of coquetry, each layer uncovering more beauty: long, well-muscled but slender legs, flat belly, rounded buttocks, thickly coated pubes, well-formed feet and toes. She was the epitome of what a man might wish in a woman.

And he was here to destroy her? That could never be. Then what of King and country? And his oath as a soldier?

Naked, she faced him.

"Do you know," he said, "now I wish to kill Austrians as well. At least, the men who raped you."

"And who murdered my father," she said.

"Yes," he agreed. "Them too."

He had been sitting to watch her, now he undressed himself.

48

She remained standing, watching him. Once again, she showed no embarrassment or even uncertainty, until he uncovered the scar. Then she gave a little gasp and dropped to her knees before him.

"Can I touch it?"

"Of course."

Her finger stroked down his thigh, only inches away from his manhood, but ignoring that.

"Does it hurt?"

"Sometimes, when it rains."

"Is it a bayonet wound?"

"No. It was done by an African spear, when I was there with the British army, ten years ago."

She kissed it, then seemed to realise what was beside it, and kissed that too. "Be gentle with me," she said.

A man would have to be a monster to be anything else than gentle with such beauty. It was not that she gave the impression, like some women, of being fragile, easy to hurt, even if accidentally. It was the flawlessness of her beauty that was at once irresistible and made him almost afraid to touch her. He laid her on the bed and stroked her, taking possession of her with his fingertips, carefully exploring every hill and every valley. When he rolled her on her face to do the same for her back, she moved without demur, spread her legs for him, would, he knew, have accepted everything and anything he might have desired, as long as he did it with love.

But he wanted only the orthodox, to feel her against him, to kiss her mouth while he entered her body. She moved beneath him and murmured, but he knew enough about women to doubt she had an orgasm, although she was well aware when he climaxed, and then lay beside him, nestling.

"I would not like you ever to leave me," she said.

"I hadn't thought of ever doing that," he told her.

Until tomorrow?

But when he awoke, tomorrow, it was to gaze at Anna, standing at the foot of the bed.

Caterina was apparently still in a deep sleep. Berkeley sat up, uncertain whether he might be about to die.

"John Smith," Anna said. "I could not believe my ears when my servants told me someone by that name was here. Did you come to see me, or my daughter?"

Caterina had apparently not been asleep after all. Now she also sat up, pushing hair from her eyes. "He came to see you, Mama."

"And encountered you."

"He needs your help, Mama. He has lost everything, because of you."

Anna regarded them both for several seconds. She was in every way exactly as Berkeley remembered her, even to the large droopy hat – but this had to be a new one, as she had lost the other in the escape from Seinheit.

"If you would care to get dressed, Mr Smith," she said. "We can breakfast together, downstairs."

She closed the door behind herself, and Berkeley looked at Caterina.

"Just tell her you love me," she said. "And she will not be angry."

Berkeley kissed her and got dressed, trying to remember if at any time in their Carpathian adventure he had told Anna that he loved *her*. He did not think he had; which would not, in the eyes of most mothers, provide the slightest excuse. But this was an unusual mother. And daughter.

He went downstairs to the dining room, where Anna was seated at the table pouring coffee.

"We thought you were coming in on the Belgrade train," he said, lamely. But he was also curious.

"I decided to come early. On horseback."

"Was that a sudden decision?"

"My life is composed of sudden decisions, Mr Smith."

"Were you in danger?"

She smiled. "I was informed that there was a man in Belgrade, looking for me. I preferred to meet this man on my own ground, shall we say."

"You mean Colonel Savos told you about me."

"Colonel Savos, no. But I have friends in the police department, or I would not still be here. So tell me why you are really here."

"What Caterina said was the truth."

"And you came to me? I find that hard to accept."

"I hate to admit it, but I came here because I felt you owed me something."

"I do. My life. And you suppose the way for me to repay you would be to employ you? Are you not aware that most of those I employ wind up dead?"

"Including your own husband."

"Including my own husband," she agreed. "I would hardly call that adequate repayment."

"You told me once, in justification of your actions, that you are fighting a war. I am a soldier. I know nothing but wars. Yours would appear to be the most justifiable war going, at the moment. There is

50

also the fact that we know each other, that you know my capabilities. As for being killed, that is an occupational hazard, for a soldier."

She gave him one of the long, appraising stares indulged in by her daughter. Then she asked, "Did you enjoy sex with Caterina?"

"Very much. I should explain—"

"Explanations for things past, things done, are usually a waste of time. It is the future that matters. I assume she told you about herself."

"Yes."

"And so, were you acting out of sympathy, or because the thought of that beautiful creature being repeatedly raped and beaten aroused you?"

"I was acting because I think she is the most beautiful woman I have ever seen, and because I felt that she wanted it as badly as I. With respect, Anna."

Another long stare. "Very well," she said. "You will be married. Today."

His head jerked. "Married?"

"Is it not the custom, even in England, that a man should marry a girl with whom he has had sex?"

"Ah . . ." Think, goddamit. But that was impossible at the moment. "Yes, it is."

"So, then, would you not like to be married to my daughter? Then you could have sex with her every night, when you are here."

"Yes," he said. Shit, shit, shit, he thought. But had he ever been going to hand her over to the Austrians? "I think that would be wonderful."

"Good. And do not worry about her mind. It is very strong. It has not suffered because of what happened."

"Even if it has left her dedicated to killing Austrians."

"It has left her dedicated to avenging her father, Mr Smith. As your life will now be similarly dedicated, as she will be your wife."

"Is it permissible to ask, sir, exactly what is going on?" Lockwood said. "The talk below stairs is of a wedding. Your wedding. Today."

"Yes," Berkeley said.

"Sir?"

"I'm afraid I have got us into a right royal mess, Harry. I am to marry Miss Slovitza."

"*Miss* Slovitza, sir."

"That's the one. We were caught *in flagrante delicto* by her mother, and I must pay the price. Not that I wouldn't want to marry her, all things being equal."

"But they aren't, sir."

"Oh, quite."

"Can you . . . ah . . . complete our mission in these circumstances, sir?"

"No, Harry, I don't believe I can."

"Did you ever mean to, sir?" Revealing that Lockwood was far more perceptive than he appeared.

"I don't believe I did, Harry. I've been playing it by ear, and hoping that something would turn up."

"And so it has, by jingo. If you'll pardon me, sir."

"Oh, indeed."

"So, are we going to make a run for it?"

Berkeley raised his eyebrows.

"Well, sir . . ."

"If we make a run for it, Harry, or if I make a run for it, I will in any event have failed in my mission, and may well find myself extradited to Austria on charges of murder. If I stay here, well . . . things may turn out."

"How, sir? Apart from the girl, of course."

"I really don't know. I have been dealt a hand; I suppose you could say I dealt it to myself, and I must play it to the best of my ability. But there is no need for you to be involved. You have my permission to return to England. I have sufficient funds for that purpose. Once there, you had better report to the War Office that I have deserted, and then I would also like you to report to my parents."

Lockwood considered. "And Miss Gracey, sir?"

Berkeley sighed. "Her too, I suppose."

Lockwood considered some more. "I would rather remain here with you, sir."

"Harry, that is damned decent of you, but I am about to become an anarchist. If you stay, you will become one too. I am not sure we will ever be able to return to England, but in any event, it will not be for a very long time."

"There's a shame, sir. But as you say, if it's the hand we've been dealt . . ."

"Your family?"

"I have no family, sir."

Berkeley considered. He most certainly did have a family. He would have to write to them. Would they understand? He doubted that they would. As for Julia . . . not to mention England, Home and Beauty.

He had never expected it to turn out this way. But at least he would have Harry. "Well, then, Harry," he said. "Shoulder to shoulder, eh?"

"As always, sir." Lockwood winked. "Who knows, I might

get married myself, one of these days. They're a handsome lot, below stairs."

However unexpected had been the decision of Anna Slovitza to have her daughter married, the preparations were made with both speed and gusto. Great quantities of food and wine were brought in accompanied by numbers of people and a regiment of black-garbed and high-hatted priests: it was to be an Orthodox ceremony.

Berkeley understood that he was required to do nothing but remain in his room until six that evening when the ceremony would begin, but he was surprised to be visited by his bride in the middle of the afternoon.

He was a man who had always prided himself on his pragmatic approach to life, tinged of course with that romantic streak which was a definite weakness. Thus he had spent his time trying to rationalise his situation. He could remind himself that had he refused this mission, Gorman would probably have carried out his threat and despatched him to some remote and dangerous – if only from disease – corner of the Empire, where he would not have seen his family or been able to marry Julia in any event.

Was his present situation any different, save that he had accumulated a beautiful bride?

He could also remind himself that he had come here to commit a really dreadful crime, all in the name of keeping the peace between Great Britain and Austria. While all his instincts had pushed the other way. He had nothing against either the Austrian or the Hungarian people; most of those he had met had been charming and friendly. But the Hapsburg tyranny they had accepted and allowed to permeate their lives was about the most hideous regime in the world, after that of Tzarist Russia. Because it did permeate every aspect of their lives. The regime was based on an unholy marriage between a mind-deadening bureacracy and a soul-destroying secret police. The people of Serbia could hardly be blamed for fearing their immense, greedy neighbour; the people of Bosnia-Herzegovina could equally hardly be blamed for taking the law into their own hands in their efforts to prevent themselves being swallowed alive.

Obviously it was not cricket to go around planting or throwing bombs amidst innocent people; the idea was abhorrent. But neither, he had felt more than once in the past, was the entirely British habit of sitting behind a machine gun flanked by repeating rifles and mowing down thousands of savages armed with spears who were only trying to defend *their* homeland.

Hardly acceptable thoughts for a British officer. Well, that was behind him now; and so was his oath of allegiance to King and

Country. That was the damnable thing. But at least he could never be required to fight against them. He had not changed sides, only sidestepped the issue.

That was better. And now . . . he gazed at Caterina.

"Is it not bad luck, for us to see each other before our wedding?"

"On our wedding day," she pointed out. "But we have already seen each other today, before we even knew we were going to be wed."

He took her in his arms. While she was there, he had no doubts.

She turned back her head to look up at him. "I wish you to know that I am sorry."

"Eh?"

"I wanted to have sex with you. I did not mean you to be dragged into a marriage you cannot want."

"I do want it."

"You wish to devote the rest of your life to this clandestine existence?"

"I am going to devote the rest of my life to you. If that means fighting the Austrians, then I am content. I only want you to say that *you* wish this marriage."

"Of course I do."

"A man you have only just met?"

She shook her head. "I met you long ago, because of what my mother told me. When you came, I realised that you were everything she had said of you."

"And you can forgive me for having, well . . ."

Caterina smiled. "Had her first? Does that not create a bond?"

"Between you and her, or you and me?"

"Between the three of us. John. Is your name really John?"

The last, and perhaps final decision. But he had lived a lie long enough. "No," he said. "Nor is it Smith."

Anna was amused, when she in turn came to see him, shortly before the ceremony was due to begin. "Is your name really Berkeley Townsend?"

"I'm afraid it is."

"And do you wish this widely known?"

"I'd prefer not. But I did not wish to marry your daughter under an assumed name."

"I do not know what to make of you, Berkeley. You are such an honourable man, and yet . . ."

"I am throwing in my lot with a bunch of murdering brigands."

She raised her eyebrows. "Is that how you see us?"

"No. That is how my family and superiors in England will view the situation, when it becomes known to them."

"But that will not be for a while yet, and in that time we may be able to accomplish a great deal. What name are you actually travelling under at the moment? Your own?"

"It was thought better to use a pseudonym."

"Not John Smith again?"

"No. That is the name of the man the Austrians are looking for. My name is Walter Jones."

"That is the name Savos knows you as?"

"Yes."

"And you have travel documents for this Mr Jones?"

"Yes, I do."

"That is excellent. Excellent. Walter Jones. Your bride awaits you."

As the entire service was conducted in Serbo-Croat, Berkeley understood very little of it. He contented himself with responding to Caterina's nods as their wrists were bound together and the priest placed his hands over them. Anna produced a ring, very old and somewhat ornate for a wedding band, but he placed it on Caterina's finger and kissed her on the lips. She affected him as powerfully as ever, and she also seemed impatient.

But then she was away to dance, to be seized and whirled in the air by every man present while the guitars strummed and the guests clapped. Berkeley was also required to dance, with all the women in turn. They hugged him and kissed him and chattered at him and he did not understand a word they were saying. But at last it was over, and he was escorted to bed with his bride. For the second time that day, he thought. But this time she was even more responsive.

What have I done? he wondered, as he lay awake in the darkness, Caterina's head on his shoulders, her scent clouding his nostrils. He was reminded of the Dracula story, as told by Bram Stoker, of the law clerk Jonathan Harker, sucked into a nest of vampires, beautiful and deadly. Harker, as he recalled the story, had resisted to the best of his ability, unavailingly. *He* had jumped in with both feet, enthusiastically. He wondered how soon he would have to pay the price.

Or was he actually the destroyer, come to root out a band of murderers, no matter how beautiful?

It was not a matter he could determine for at least a fortnight: a fortnight he wished would never end. It was, Berkeley thought, perhaps the happiest period of his life. He had torn up his past.

He did not know if he had a future. But he had a very beautiful present.

Whatever the Austrians, or indeed the Serbians, might think of Anna Slovitza, she was popular, and therefore safe, in Sabac and the immediately neighbouring countryside. Autumn was now setting in and it was surprisingly cold; the fields were fallow. He and Caterina could gallop their horses across the open country, Caterina's hair flowing in the wind. They could walk, too, the narrow streets of the old town, greeted everywhere by the locals, most of whom seemed to have known Caterina since birth. They could sit together in the library while Caterina painstakingly taught him the Serbo-Croat dialect, and he responded by teaching her English. They ate sumptuous meals, smiling at each other along the length of the oak table.

And they made love endlessly, with their bodies in bed, and their eyes and lips and fingers at other times.

Anna was often absent; and with her, the dark-visaged man, Karlovy, who had taken Berkeley prisoner when he had first entered the house. Only once did Berkeley raise the question. "Does your mother carry out her schemes, even in winter?" he asked Caterina.

"More often in winter than at other times," Caterina said. "There is more darkness."

"And is she planning something now?"

"I do not know. She does not confide in me." She gave a little giggle. "Perhaps you should ask her."

Berkeley decided to let her come to him. And on the fifteenth day of his marriage he was awakened before dawn by Anna.

"We leave in an hour," she said.

The Raid

Berkeley sat up, as did his bride.

"So soon?" Caterina asked.

"It has been planned," her mother told her. "Berkeley's presence is a bonus. Will your man accompany you?"

"He will wish to."

"Then he will be welcome. Summon him and tell him to prepare."

"I will come too," Caterina said, getting out of bed.

"You will stay here," her mother commanded.

"I must go with my husband."

"You will stay here and wait for him to return to you."

Caterina looked at Berkeley.

"That is the most sensible thing, my darling," Berkeley said.

Quite apart from the unbearable thought of her being hit or captured, he still hoped to prevent her from ever actually becoming a killer.

"Say goodbye," Anna said. "You have five minutes."

She closed the door behind herself.

Berkeley sat beside his naked wife, embraced her.

"You will come back to me?" she asked.

"I hope to."

"She frightens me," Caterina said, resting her head on his shoulder while he caressed her velvet flesh. "Sometimes I hate her."

"Your business is to love – me. And your mother, to be sure." He kissed her. "I must go."

Berkeley rang the bell for Harry, but was already half dressed by the time he arrived. The valet studiously avoided looking at the bed, where Catarina had retired beneath the sheets.

"Where are we going, sir?"

"I have no idea. But I imagine it is north."

Harry rolled his eyes. North was where they had intended to go, taking Anna Slovitza with them.

He kissed Caterina again, and went downstairs for a hasty breakfast. Anna was alone.

"Just us?" he asked.

"And Lockwood, to be sure." She smiled. "No, no. We have a support group, but they left two days ago. We rendezvous as Kiskunhalas. Szigeti expects us."

"It would help if I knew what was going on," Berkeley said.

"You will know, in time enough. You have your weapon? That automatic pistol?"

"I do."

"And Lockwood will bring his shotgun."

"Will they let us cross the frontier with guns?"

"Of course. All Englishmen travel with sidearms. They would be suspicious did you *not* have a weapon. In any event, our story is that we are going to shoot in the Balaton area. It is a famous hunting ground."

"Balaton," Berkeley said thoughtfully.

"We are taking a train ride, into Hungary," Anna said.

Lockwood nearly choked on his coffee.

Anna glanced at him. "There is no need to be alarmed, Harry. Only a few of our enemies actually know what I look like. Nor are you likely to encounter anyone able to recognise you, or your master. Nor is there any chance of anyone recognising your name. We are an English couple, Mr and Mr Walter Jones, travelling for our health, with our faithful servant." She smiled. "As we did in the Carpathians."

"Mr and Mrs . . . Anna, that is over."

"Because you are married to my daughter? In our business, Berkeley – or perhaps I should practise calling you Walter – we need to use all the weapons we possess. And you, as an itinerant Englishman with the documents to prove it, are a gift from heaven. Caterina will not mind, believe me. In any event, she will never know . . . unless you tell her. Now hurry, the train leaves in half an hour."

"We are returning to Belgrade?"

"This is the northbound train, for Subotica, and the frontier."

"And then?"

"I will tell you at the frontier."

From Sabac to the frontier was just about a hundred miles, and they were there for lunch. They had only two carpet-bags with a couple of changes of clothing, and shared a first-class compartment with two men, who it was quickly established did not speak English. But as Anna did have some knowledge of the language, Berkeley and Lockwood could not discuss what was on Lockwood's mind until Anna left the compartment to go to the toilet.

Then Lockwood said, "It's a rum do, sir."

"That's life."

"When you think, well, we spent so much time brooding on how we were going to get the lady up to the Hungarian border, and here she is taking us there herself. I mean, you couldn't have planned the whole thing better if you *had* planned it."

"Only I didn't."

"Yes, sir. But . . . well, talk about fate."

"If fate is running this show, Harry, then all we can do is play the cards as they are dealt. We have taken our decision, and we're not going to change our minds now. It would be an absolute betrayal of trust."

"Yes, sir," Lockwood said, and sighed.

Berkeley couldn't blame him for being tempted; he was even tempted himself. As Harry had said, they couldn't have planned it better. Once across the border, all he had to do was hand Anna over to the police, present his other documents of which she knew nothing, and be whisked across Hungary and Austria to Switzerland; and thence home, promotion, his family and Julia Gracey. The fact that he would be marrying her bigamously was hardly relevant as no one in England knew of the existence of Caterina Slovitza.

Who would wait, and linger, and mourn, and hate. He shook his head to rid his mind of such unthinkable behaviour.

Anna returned. "You will have to do the talking at the border," she said. "My English is not good enough."

"I doubt theirs will be either," he said. "I'll stick to German as much as possible."

She nodded. "Good. Then I will understand what is going on. Now, from the border, we go to a place called Kiskunhalas. It is only another twenty-odd miles further on; we will get there this afternoon. There we will leave the train. I have an agent there, Paul Szigeti. He will be waiting for us, and we will spend the rest of the day in his house, although you may take me for a walk, if you wish. Kiskunhalas is a famous lacemaking centre. I am sure a travelling Englishman would wish to buy a piece of lace for his wife."

It occurred to Berkeley that she was having the time of her life, travelling with him, even if this time it was into danger instead of out of it. But he needed to remember that she had, at least for a few minutes, been very frightened in Seinheit.

She smiled at him. "You can even buy a piece of lace for your other wife," she suggested.

Berkeley gazed out of the window at the almost flat countryside rushing by the track. While he was rushing at his destiny. He could still change his mind, still betray both Anna and Caterina. Once they had crossed the border and linked up with this man Szigeti, he would be an anarchist, against whom every law enforcement officer in Europe would be ranged.

"And what do we do after Kiskunhalas?" he asked.

"I will tell you, in Kiskunhalas," she promised.

Subotica was actually a few miles south of the border, and the train stopped there to allow the passengers to stretch their legs and have some lunch.

"Now the adrenalin begins to flow," Anna said, drinking wine.

"Are you afraid? Do you ever get afraid?"

"Apprehensive. Is that not what soldiers feel before they go into battle?"

"And we are going into battle?"

"In our own fashion, yes."

The train slowed to a halt at the frontier post. Armed border guards marched along the corridors, demanding to see passports. The guard who entered their compartment spoke neither English nor German, and had to summon one of his comrades, who spoke German, of a sort.

"Where do you go, in Hungary?" he asked Berkeley.

"Lake Balaton."

"This is your first visit?"

"Yes, indeed."

The guard looked at Anna, then at Harry. "Enjoy your stay," he said.

"That was easy enough," Berkeley remarked, as the train moved on.

"Perhaps too easy," Anna muttered. "He did not even wish to look in our bags."

For all her dismissal of his suggestion that she might be afraid, she was becoming tense again. But as she had said, only an hour later they were in Kiskunhalas and disembarking, Harry carrying the bags.

Waiting for them was a short, thin man with a hatchet-face and a small moustache. He kissed Anna's hands then regarded Berkeley with some suspicion.

"My husband, Mr Walter Jones." Anna introduced him in German. "And our servant, Lockwood. Walter, this is Paul Szigeti."

Berkeley shook hands. Szigeti had a trap waiting and they were loaded in, Lockwood sitting beside the driver, who was Szigeti himself. They drove through the town to a house in a quiet suburb. On a cool September day there were few people about.

"Is all well?" Anna asked.

"As far as I am aware, madame."

"You have not seen Karlovy?"

"He will be here tonight, with the horses. We will meet him at a rendezvous outside town."

"And the manoeuvres?"

"They started last week Much banging of cannon. The money will be on time."

Berkeley could only continue to be patient. They arrived at the house and were greeted by Madame Szigeti, a stout lady who perspired, and her two teenage daughters who were clearly in awe of their visitors even if surely, Berkeley thought, they could not know the truth of it. But they, like their parents, accepted the fact without comment that Anna, who they clearly knew quite well, had suddenly accumulated a husband.

But at last they were alone in the bedroom they had been given.

"Whew." Anna unlaced her boots, kicked them off, threw her hat in a corner, scattered her hair, and stretched on the bed. She made an entrancing picture, and Berkeley had to remind himself that she was his mother-in-law. "I am exhausted. We had better get some sleep, as there will be none tonight."

"I think I need to know what we are doing, Anna."

She sat up. "Of course you do." She got off the bed, opened her bag and took out a map which she spread on the table. "We are here."

Berkeley took in the position of Kiskunhalas relative to the rest of the country: the border twenty miles to the south, Budapest perhaps a hundred to the north. To the east, the Hungarian plain continued, to the west . . . He frowned. "Aren't those marshes?"

"Yes. They are caused by the River Duna bursting its banks over many centuries. To the south is the town of Mohacs. Have you heard of this place?"

"Mohacs," Berkeley said thoughtfully. "Yes. It was at Mohacs that the Hungarian army was utterly destroyed by the Ottoman Turks of Suleiman the Magnificent. 1526."

"You are a student of history," Anna observed. "Well, at Mohacs and in the surrounding country, the Austrian army is currently carrying out manoeuvres."

"In September?"

"They think this is necessary, to train their people to fight and move in these conditions. The Austrian army is trained to look in only one direction: east. They do not doubt that they will one day, perhaps one day soon, have to fight Russia. Thus they prepare for warfare in Russian conditions."

"They have a point. And what have Austrian manoeuvres got to do with us?"

"Very simply, armies need to be paid. The money left Budapest the day before yesterday, if my information is correct. The convoy – it is only two wagons – will travel non-stop, and will reach the village of Tolna just after dawn tomorrow morning. We shall be there to meet it. Tolna is only about twenty-five miles from here, due west."

Berkeley stared at her in consternation. "You intend to steal an army payroll?"

"It will be the easiest thing in the world," Anna said. "I have told you, there are only two wagons. Each has a driver and a guard, and they are accompanied by an escort of twenty horsemen."

"Only that?"

"Well, no one has ever dared attempt to interfere with an army payroll before."

"Because it would be committing suicide."

"Not if it is properly planned and carried out. As this will be. In Tolna, at dawn, the drivers and the escort will be stopping for breakfast. They will be tired from the night and they will be relaxing because they will be within a few hours of their destination, Mohacs. They will also be within a few miles of the border. This is very convenient for us. Now come and lie down."

She took off her dress, but to his relief did not undress any further, He took off his boots and coat and lay beside her.

"You have additional people?" he asked.

"We have Karlovy and his three men. They are coming on horseback. They will be here tonight."

"And you, me, and Lockwood . . . six men and one woman, taking on twenty-four professional soldiers?"

"We have some secrets up our sleeves," she said.

By which he presumed she meant that she, and they, would be throwing bombs, wounding and maiming indiscriminately where they did not kill.

"And this is really necessary?" he asked.

"Yes," she said. "It is really necessary. For two reasons. One is that we are running low on funds, and need the money."

"You reckon you can spend Austrian pfennigs in Serbia and not have them traced back to you?"

"Not at all. But I find it useful to keep a store of various currencies, for when I am travelling. It is in the strongbox in my room. I will show you when I return. As for the rest, the bulk of the money, there are people who will exchange it for us and the movement. They can launder the money through Bosnia."

She certainly seemed well organised.

"And the other reason?"

"It will cause a great deal of trouble between the Austrian government and the Serbian. This is good."

"I think you are trying to provoke a war."

"I would like to see that happen, certainly," Anna confessed.

"Have you any idea what war is like? Real war? What it would be like, fought with modern weapons? Serbia would be wiped off the map."

"I do not think that will happen," Anna said. "Russia would not permit it. If Austria were to attack Serbia, Russia would come to our aid. They have promised this."

"That assumes the Russian army is worth a damn after the mauling they got from the Japanese, and that the Tsar is in any condition to go to war with anyone else, right now. He has troubles at home."

"He has given his sacred word," Anna insisted.

She appeared to go to sleep, breathing slowly and evenly. She had no conscience, no apprehension of what tragedies her deeds might perpetuate. And he was her sworn partner. Yet eventually he slept himself; he had had very little sleep the night before. When he awoke, Anna was washing herself in the basin. She was, as always, a delight to watch. But he had awakened to some very odd thoughts.

"Is this your first visit to Hungary since Seinheit?"

"Yes. It took me a month to get home, through Russia."

"And then I would say you immediately sat down and started planning this raid."

Anna used a towel to pat her face dry. "Of course. As I said, we need the money."

"But you did not know I was going to come back."

"No, I did not." She began brushing her hair. "I told you, that was a bonus."

"On which you acted very quickly."

She smiled. "I am good at making quick decisions."

"Did you know Caterina would seduce me? She did, you know."

"As I did not know you were coming, Berkeley, I could hardly have known she would seduce you, although I will not argue that she did. However, I think it has all worked out very well. Having an Englishman along will make our escape very much easier."

"The Austrians will trace me."

"By the time they do, we will be safely back in Serbia, and you can always change your name again. Or even use your real one." She secured her hair with a ribbon on her neck, rather than putting it up. "Now come, it is time to get dressed. We will need a meal before we leave."

Berkeley got up, still brooding. "There is something else on my mind. Does Szigeti know what we are planning, where we are going?"

"No. He only knows that I needed to use his house for a rendezvous with Karlovy."

"You've used his house before."

"Several times. He is a sympathiser to our cause."

"And you trust him."

"He has never failed me in the past."

"You told me you had been betrayed in Buda."

Anna glanced at him. "Not by Szigeti."

"Are you sure? Did you not use this house on that occasion?"

Anna frowned. "Otto and I spent the night here, on our way north. But Szigeti knew nothing more than that we were going to Buda. He had no idea what we were planning to do."

"Yet, in Buda, you were betrayed. How?"

"Our getaway vehicle was not where it should have been, and the police were." She shrugged. "It could have been bad luck. When I said we had been betrayed I was angry. But Szigeti knew nothing of our plans. He is a sympathiser and a go-between who risks much for our cause. He is not an anarchist himself."

"And does he know where we are going this time, when we leave here?"

"No," Anna said. "He does not know."

Berkeley had to accept her confidence. They finished dressing and went downstairs where Lockwood and a meal were waiting for them. Then Szigeti got out his trap and drove them out of the town and along a lonely road to a copse a mile away. There was no moon and it was very dark. As they approached the copse they heard the stamping and rustling of horses, and a moment later saw four horsemen waiting in the darkness; with them were eight other horses, and two pack animals, heavily laden.

Szigeti brought the trap to a halt, and they got down; Lockwood unloaded the bags.

"Did you have any difficulty?" Anna asked Karlovy.

"None. We told the border guards we were taking the horses for sale in Buda."

"And the gun?"

"They prodded the bags, but the weapons were too well broken up."

"Excellent. Well, Szigeti, thank you for everything, as usual. You will receive your money in the usual way."

Szigeti kissed her glove. "I look forward to our next meeting."

"Of course."

They watched the trap disappear into the darkness.

"Gun?" Berkeley asked.

Anna chuckled. "I told you that we had hidden resources. Let's move."

There was apparently no longer any reason for concealment of their true purpose. Repeating rifles, divided as Karlovy had said into several pieces, were taken from the packs and fitted together, cartridges were handed out. Berkeley strapped on his Browning and put two spare magazines in his pocket. Lockwood had the shotgun. Anna equipped herself with a revolver. Then they rode into the night, which if anything grew even darker, but Karlovy's men were sure of the way, even when they came to the marshes and were splashing through vast areas of bogs.

"Just let the horses find their way," Anna advised. "They will do it."

They came to the river and swam the horses across. By now it was past midnight.

"This is some show, sir," Lockwood remarked, riding beside Berkeley.

"Nothing like the Sudan, eh?"

Another two hours, the horses walking now on firmer ground, and they saw lights.

"Tolna," Anna said.

"Do you have an agent here as well?" Berkeley asked.

"No. It would be too dangerous. We must act very decisively, but very quietly. Karlovy checked the town out earlier this year. He knows where to go."

The horses' hooves clipped the cobbles as they entered the little town.

"Halt there."

It was the night watch, two men armed with staves.

"We are on our way to Lake Balaton, to hunt," Karlovy explained.

"In the middle of the night? It is forty miles to Lake Balaton."

"We wish to get there tomorrow," Karlovy said. "In fact, today."

The watchman raised his lantern the better to see him, and then the others, pausing when he uncovered Anna; and then found himself looking down the barrel of her revolver.

"Make a sound and I will shoot you," she said.

The other man was speechless as Karlovy's men dismounted to secure their arms.

"You will come with us," Anna said.

They proceeded into the town, arriving at the main street.

"This is the Budapest road," Karlovy said. "That is where they will come."

"And where do they stop?"

"At the inn on the corner." He pointed.

The inn was in darkness, save for a light hanging outside the door.

"That will be our position," Anna decided. "You said there was a garrison."

"The post is at the other end of town, but it is only a sergeant and six troopers. With the army only a few miles away, there is no reason for more."

Berkeley listened. There was no sound from the south. The army might be on manoeuvres, but it believed in a good night's sleep.

A cock crowed.

"Let's do it," Anna said.

They walked across the street, leading their horses, still stamping river water from their boots, and into the yard. A dog barked, and an upstairs window opened. "Who is there?"

"Weary travellers," Karlovy said.

"We are closed."

"I beg you to open. We will not trouble you until it is time for breakfast. We just wish to stable our horses and rest our bones."

The innkeeper closed the window, and a moment later they saw the flare of a light. Karlovy and one of his men stood at the door. The two watchmen were immediately behind them, held by Berkeley and Lockwood and menaced by Anna's revolver. Karlovy's other two men held the horses.

The dog continued to bark, and was beside his master when the door was opened. He was a big dog and bared his teeth, instinctively recognising the intruders as enemies.

"What the . . ." the innkeeper gazed at the rifle presented to his chest.

"Obey us, and live," Karlovy said. "And keep that dog under control."

The innkeeper gasped and seized the dog's collar just as it seemed the animal was about to launch an attack.

"Back up," Karlovy commanded.

The innkeeper retreated into the taproom and the anarchists followed, save for the two men with the horses which were now led round the side of the building to keep them out of sight from the street.

The innkeeper was carrying only a candle. Karlovy went behind the bar to find a lantern, which he lit. The innkeeper stared at the two watchmen, eyes huge. The dog growled. Then the innkeeper's eyes grew even larger as he gazed at Anna.

"What are you doing?" he asked. "There is nothing here to rob."

"Let us be the judge of that," Anna said. "How many people are in the building?"

"My wife and son, and two travellers."

"Karlovy, you and Pietr go with him, find them and lock them up. Put the dog in the side room and shut the door."

Karlovy nodded, and pushed the innkeeper in front of him.

"Berkeley, will you and Lockwood fetch the gear," Anna said.

"What about these two?"

Anna smiled. "They are not going to misbehave themselves. Sit down, gentlemen."

The watchkeepers obeyed, faces working behind the gags.

Berkeley and Lockwood got the bags down from the horses and brought them inside.

"I assume you know how to assemble a Hotchkiss gun?" Anna asked.

"I do. Are you saying there is a Hotchkiss in here?"

"Did you not tell me that Harry was a machine gunner in your army?"

Berkeley and Lockwood looked at each other. Then they put the gun together, arranging the belt of bullets. "This is one hell of a weapon."

"It cost me a great deal. And unfortunately, it will have to be abandoned. Still, we should make enough this morning to pay for it."

"Where do you want it?"

"Just inside the door. They must come into the yard before we open fire." She wore a watch on her lapel, and this she now checked. "It will be light in an hour, and they are due immediately after that."

From upstairs there came the sound of a strangled scream. The dog was still barking.

"I should shoot that animal," Anna said. "He will wake up the town."

"Not so fast as the sound of a shot," Berkeley said.

Karlovy and his man came down the stairs.

"All correct?" Anna asked.

"All correct. They will be able to get free in time."

"Not in sufficient time. Let's eat."

They ate bread and sausage, and Anna made some coffee. It began to grow light outside.

"Take your positions," she said.

Karlovy went outside to join his two men in the yard; they had now tethered the horses all of which had been saddled. Armed with rifles, they took up their positions just inside the gate to the yard, so that they would be behind anyone entering. In the building, Lockwood sat behind the Hotchkiss gun, hand on the crank. Anna, Berkeley and the fourth man were armed with rifles.

"You understand," Anna said. "We shoot to kill."

Berkeley swallowed, but he was in too deep to have any other ideas.

Slowly the town began to come to life. The innkeeper's dog had now grown tired of barking and appeared to have gone to sleep. But other dogs in the town barked and there were sounds of movement. A slow clatter of hooves and wheels marked the approach of the milk float.

Berkeley glanced at Anna, who again looked at her watch. "They are late."

The milk float turned into the inn gates. The milkman walked beside his horse, patting it on the rump. The bottles clinked. Noticing nothing wrong, he came right inside, only pausing when he heard movement behind him. Karlovy stepped up to him. Inside the inn they could not hear what he said, but the milkman visibly blanched, then led his float towards the side of the building, escorted by one of Karlovy's men.

"We are running out of time," Berkeley said.

"They will be here. They . . . Listen."

They heard the clatter of hooves, the rumble of wheels. A moment later, two dragoons rode into the yard and drew rein, looking left and right; they wore pale blue capes over red breeches, and crested black helmets. Their carbines were slung on their backs. With Karlovy and his men concealed, there was nothing out of the ordinary. The second dragoon had remained at the gate, and now he waved his arm. The rumbling grew louder and the two wagons rolled through the gate into the yard, their escort to either side and behind. "Now," Anna said.

Lockwood glanced at Berkeley, and received a quick nod. He began cranking the handle and the Hotchkiss emitted a hail of bullets. The two lead dragoons, one already dismounting, were the first to fall. Then the gun was moving to fire into the escort.

"The drivers," Anna shouted.

Berkeley levelled his rifle and fired, and one of the men on the driving seat of the first wagon uttered a shriek and fell. The other also went down, by whose shot he didn't know. Those on the second wagon attempted to turn their vehicle but were cut down by Karlovy's people. The dragoons at the rear swung their horses to escape the hail of bullets, but they too were scattered left and right by the rifles. Only one appeared to be unhurt as he galloped the length of the street towards the military post.

"He will alarm them," Berkeley said.

"Six men and a sergeant?" Anna said, contemptuously. The sound of the firing and the cries of the wounded and dying men had awakened the town. Shouting people joined the barking dogs, but as Karlovy sent two shots down the street no one came to investigate. "Hurry. Lockwood, stay with the gun." Anna ran out of the building. There were bodies scattered everywhere; the cobbles were red with blood. The dragoon captain rolled on his side, groaning as he reached for the revolver he had dropped when he fell. Anna levelled her own pistol and shot him through the head. "Hurry," she shouted again, her voice unemotional.

Two of Karlovy's men ran to the horses to fetch the saddlebags. Karlovy himself kept the gate watching the street, and occasionally firing at anyone who showed himself. Berkeley joined Anna and the third man to tear open the canvas hoods of the wagons, exposing the boxes inside. These were locked, but were opened by shots from the rifles. Inside were both paper and coin,

"Take the paper," Anna commanded, and the saddlebags were packed.

"Action," Karlovy called.

"Get the gun down there," Anna said.

Two of the men ran to the inn and helped Lockwood manhandle the Hotchkiss down to the gate.

"Keep your head down, Harry," Berkeley called.

As each saddlebag was loaded it was taken to one of the horses; these had now been brought out into the yard.

The first wagon was empty, save for a few scattered notes, and the silver.

"Now the other," Anna said.

"Don't you think we have enough?" Berkeley asked.

"No," she said, clambering into the second wagon in a flutter of skirts.

At the gate Lockwood was cranking a stream of bullets down the street. Karlovy was still firing his rifle. The town had become a huge hubbub of sound: people shouting, women and children screaming, dogs barking, horses neighing. Anna kept on calmly filling saddlebag after saddlebag,

Now there were shots from along the street, as the garrison post finally began to return fire. They also heard the clatter of hooves.

"They've sent for help," Karlovy said. "We'd better be off."

Anna nodded. "That's enough." She watched the last of the horses being loaded. "We need a rearguard."

"Lockwood and I will see to it," Berkeley said.

"One man will do, with the Hotchkiss."

"If Lockwood stays, I stay," Berkeley said.

She considered him for several seconds. "And what am I to tell Caterina?" she asked at last.

"I will tell her myself," he said.

Another brief hesitation. Then she reached up and kissed his cheek. "I believe you will. When you leave here, ride to the west. You will catch us up."

She signalled her men and they all mounted.

"God go with you, Englishman," Karlovy said.

Berkeley knelt beside the perspiring Lockwood. "Any sign of them?"

"Not at the moment, sir."

The street was empty, save for two or three bodies sprawled in the agony of death.

"Civilians?" Berkeley asked.

"They got in the line of fire, sir. It's a right fuck-up."

"It was always likely to happen," Berkeley said. "Open up again."

"No target, sir. And there's not all that much ammo left."

"Then let's get rid of it." Berkeley ran back to where the two horses waited restlessly. The milkman was looking round the corner of the building; when he saw Berkeley he hastily ducked back again. From the upstairs of the inn there was now a considerable noise as the innkeeper and his family and friends got free. The dog started to bark again.

"Let's go, Harry," Berkeley shouted.

Lockwood sent a last rattle of bullets down the street, then left the gun and ran to his horse, vaulting into the saddle. They rode round the back of the building, past the terrified milkman, and jumped their horses over the low fence at the rear. Beyond was open country, and they galloped their horses as close due west as they could calculate, away from the rising sun. Behind them some shots were fired, but none came even close.

"Well sir," Lockwood panted, "I reckon Jesse James would have been proud of that."

"Let's get across the border before we start congratulating ourselves," Berkeley suggested. "Where the hell are the others?"

But a few minutes later they saw Anna, sitting on her horse on a slight rise, waving her hat.

*   *   *

"A great coup," Anna cried as they rode along. "A great victory. When the news of this reaches Vienna, that ghastly old man will have a seizure. Now we turn south, for the border."

"How far?"

"Forty miles."

"Then we had best slow down. The horses won't last."

"That is why we have the remounts."

"And the Austrian army?"

"We must outrun them."

She was totally confident. But so were her men, chortling to each other as they rode along; one had even brought a bottle of wine, and this was passed to and fro.

They topped a rise, and Anna drew rein to give the horses a much needed breather. Steam surrounded them from the sweating, panting beasts. Anna had a pair of binoculars, and with these she swept the country both before and behind them. "No pursuit," she said. "They think we are too strong. Our only problem is that galloper they got away." She studied the south-east. "No movement there, either."

"They will make for the border," Karlovy said.

"No doubt. How far have we come?"

"Twenty miles, maybe. Do we change horses now?"

"No. We will keep these for a while, and change when we know we will have to gallop."

They resumed their journey, at a slower pace now.

"This is the border with Serbia, we are seeking?" Berkeley asked.

"It is the border with Slovenia. The Austrians regard it as a province."

"Then will not the army follow us there?"

"They will not find it easy, except in strength. The Slovenes prefer to think of themselves as independent. Anyway, where we are going it is not far – only about five miles – from Serbia. We will make it, Berkeley."

He could only hope she was right. Now they either walked or cantered their horses. They came to a village and even stopped at the inn for a meal, as it was midday. Anna continued with her story that they were a hunting party, only now returning from Lake Balaton. No one appeared to find anything suspicious about them. But much, Berkeley thought, might depend on how far the Austrian army had developed the use of the new wireless telegraphy.

In the middle of the afternoon the ground fell away to the plain, and with Anna's glasses they could make out the wide, deep River Drava. "That is the border," Anna said.

71

"And there is the bridge, with a squadron of dragoons guarding it," Berkeley pointed out.

"But we are not going to use the bridge."

"You reckon on swimming our horses across? That river must be five hundred yards wide."

"But you see, it bends. There." She pointed. "At that point it ceases to be the border, which continues to the east until just south of Mohacs. That is then the border with Serbia."

Berkeley used the glasses. "There is water down there as well."

"It is just a stream. We will cross it without difficulty."

"And those Austrian soldiers?" He pointed.

She took the glasses back, refocussed them, then gave them to Karlovy. "What do you reckon?"

Karlovy studied the situation for several minutes. "A company of foot," he said. "And a squadron of horse. Marching west." He swung the glasses. "There is another body further to the east. But it is about two miles distant."

"And the border is two miles further on," Anna said. "That gap is where we shall make our break. We will change horses, now."

They unsaddled their weary mounts and saddled the remounts.

"We need a diversion," Karlovy said, "to draw off the cavalry." He looked at his men.

"I will do it," one of them said.

"You understand they will hunt you down?"

"If they can," the man said.

"Very well. We will go down to that little wood. Lead your horses."

They made their way down the slope, keeping to gullies and the protection of the trees until they reached the plain, still sheltered by a small wood. Now the first contingent of Austrians was to the right, the cavalry walking their horses behind the infantry. They looked smart but Berkeley thought there was a certain lack of discipline. That had to be to the fugitives' advantage.

"Walk your horses to the far edge of the wood," Karlovy said to the decoy, "and then ride like hell. Once your free animals are at the gallop, detach yourself and double back. By then, those of the enemy who have not followed you will be following us. If you remain here until dark, you should be able to get across."

The man nodded, gathered up the reins of the rejects and walked them through the trees.

"Will he make it?" Berkeley asked.

"If he is lucky. Now, be ready."

They waited until the decoy reached the end of the wood. Then he burst out with the horses behind him, neighing and galloping.

Instantly there was a bugle call from in front of them, and half of the cavalry detached themselves to give chase.

"Only half," Anna said in disgust.

"That is the best we could expect. Go!"

"Stay beside me, Berkeley," she said, and kicked her fresh mount forward. Berkeley obeyed, knowing that Lockwood would be at his shoulder. They galloped out from the trees and made straight for the water. Now there were bugle calls from their left as well, as the second Austrian body saw them. But in front of them was the shallow water of the stream. They splashed across this and out the far side. Now shots were fired, but at this distance and from the back of a galloping horse it was impossible to hit anything.

"We are there!" Anna shouted, rising in her saddle to wave her hat.

"Keep going," Karlovy bellowed. "Keep going."

But surely they were at the border, Berkeley thought. Surely . . .

From out of a shallow dip in front of them came a patrol of Austrian infantry.

There was no means of avoiding the unexpected enemy; the cavalry were close enough behind to take advantage of the slightest delay.

"Charge them!" Anna shouted, drawing her revolver.

Berkeley drew his pistol and Lockwood unslung his shotgun. Karlovy and his men also levelled their guns.

They all fired together, as did the Austrians. But the soldiers had been as surprised as themselves, and most of the bullets were wide. Two of the Austrians went down, then the horsemen were through them. Now more men appeared in front of them, but these were not soldiers, and at the appearance of the Slovenians the Austrian cavalry drew rein.

"Safe!" Anna shouted. "Safe!" And she fell from her saddle.

The men dismounted, while several of the militiamen hurried towards them. "You must keep going," one said. "They will come across as soon as they receive orders."

Berkeley looked up at the Austrian cavalry, lined up a hundred yards away. Then he looked down at Anna. Her eyes were open, but her face was twisted from the pain.

"Go," she muttered. "Take the money and go."

"Not without you," He rolled her over. The bullet had struck her in the shoulder, and he reckoned the bone was utterly splintered. She was also losing blood.

"I have bandages," Karlovy said, unrolling a first-aid kit. "But we must hurry."

When they bound up the wound Anna cried out in pain.

"I don't suppose we have any laudanum?" Berkeley asked.

73

"I have brandy."

"Give her some."

He didn't suppose it would help very much. Even after she had drunk, Anna continued to moan and groan in pain.

"There is a doctor in Oscijek," the Slovenian sergeant said. "But if the Austrians are ordered across, they will look for you there."

"Better Apratin," Karlovy said. "It is across the Serb border, and there is a doctor there too."

"How far?" Berkeley asked.

"Five miles."

Berkeley drew a deep breath, but there was no alternative.

"Leave me." Anna moaned again. "Take the money and go."

"No," he said. "You are my mother-in-law."

He scooped her up and mounted her on his horse in front of him; his clothes were stained with her blood.

"The pain," Anna whispered. "I do not think I can stand the pain."

"You have to." Berkeley gave her some more brandy to drink, and the little cavalcade set off again, covered for the moment by the Slovenian militia.

"Will they fight the Austrians?" Berkeley asked Karlovy.

"Not if they come across in force. But they have bought us some time."

It took them half an hour to reach the border. By then Anna had thankfully fainted from the pain, but that she was seriously hurt could not be doubted.

They rode directly for Apratin, relying on the fact that they would get there before any news of what had happened in the north reached it, but it was necessary to pass through a customs post.

"This woman is badly hurt," said the captain. "How did this happen?"

Karlovy stuck to the original story. "I was guiding this Englishman and his wife and servant to go shooting at Lake Balaton, and the Austrians fired on us."

"So what did you do?"

Karlovy grinned. "We rode like the Devil. But the madame was hit."

"And badly," Berkeley said. "We need a doctor."

The captain gave instructions, and Anna was taken to a doctor's surgery. The doctor pulled his beard as his nurse slowly stripped away the blood-soaked jacket and blouse, and he removed the improvised bandage. Anna woke up and began to scream, and he gave her some laudanum. "This is very bad," he told Berkeley.

"I can see that. Will she live?"

"Very bad," he said again. "The bullet is still in there. But we will do what we can."

He and his nurse began removing the rest of Anna's clothing, and Berkeley ushered the men out of the room.

"What will you do?" Karlovy asked.

"I must stay with Madame Slovitza. But you had better get on with it."

"And the money?"

"The money is Madame Slovitza's responsibility."

"And if she dies?"

"Then it is mine."

The two men gazed at each other.

"You would not think of robbing us, Englishman?"

"Either I, or Madame Slovitza herself, will bring the money to Sabac," Berkeley said. "I would like you to go there now, and inform my wife of what has happened. Tell her I am bringing her mother home."

Karlovy considered for a few seconds, then nodded. "I must trust you. And pray for Madame Slovitza." He held out his hand. "I will do as you ask, and look for you, in Sabac, at the house of Madame Slovitza."

Berkeley and Townsend watched the three men ride off; there was no sign or word of the fourth – the decoy.

"I thought he was going to turn nasty," Lockwood said.

"They have too much respect for Anna," Berkeley said. "Or maybe they fear her too much." He heard a dreadful scream from the next room and opened the door.

There were two nurses now, both holding Anna down. The doctor straightened at Berkeley's entry and turned towards him. His apron was smothered in blood.

"What are you doing to her?" Berkeley asked, his voice harsh.

The doctor held out the distorted piece of lead. "The bone is quite shattered."

"Had you nothing to give her?"

"Not enough."

Anna's gasps and writhings were slowly diminishing.

"I will give her some more laudanum," the doctor said. "And perhaps she will sleep. But the pain must be considerable."

"Will she live?"

The doctor sighed. "She has lost a great deal of blood."

"Give me a straight answer."

"She might live, if we could get her to a hospital where they have proper facilities including transfusion equipment."

"Where is the nearest hospital?"

"In Novi-Sad."

"Which is . . ."

"About fifty miles to the south-east. On the road to Belgrade."

If it was fifty miles towards Belgrade, Berkeley thought, then it was also some way towards Sabac.

"But to move her," the doctor went on, "would be very dangerous. I will stop the bleeding, if I can, and bind her up. If the wound were to open again, on the road . . ."

Berkeley gazed at the tortured, still beautiful features. Her mouth was working, but uttering no sound.

"But if she stays here, she will die."

"I am afraid so."

"Then she must be moved. At least she'll have a chance. Can you purchase me a cart and two horses?"

"A cart. And maybe one horse."

"One horse," Berkeley agreed. "It must be done now."

The surgery was visited by the captain from the bridge.

"It is very dangerous for you to stay here, Mr Jones. The Austrians are demanding that you be handed over."

"They are in Apratin?"

"No, no, they cannot cross the bridge without permission. But they are saying that you are not what you say you are, that you are an anarchist, that you robbed the military payroll in Tolna. They are seeking an order from the magistrate for you to be arrested and handed over to them. With your wife, and . . ." He glanced at Lockwood. "Servant."

"I thought you said they couldn't cross the bridge?"

"Their soldiers cannot cross the bridge, without permission. But I could not stop a civilian agent from doing so."

"Well, as I am sure you know by now, my wife is badly hurt. I am arranging to get her out, in a couple of hours. Can you give us that much time?"

The captain considered. "I will see what I can do," he said. "But you understand, if we resist the Austrians' legitimate demands, this could well become a major incident, which would be bad for us. Bad for me. I need to know the truth. Did you rob the payroll?"

"Do I look like a robber to you?" Berkeley asked. "Would I attempt to rob the Austrian army, with my wife? We are English travellers, proceeding peacefully on our way, when we were attacked by the Austrians. I intend to make representations to my government."

Another consideration. Then the captain said, "You understand I cannot delay proceedings for very long."

"I understand," Berkeley said. "Two hours."

The captain nodded. "Two hours."

"And then?"

"I can truthfully tell the magistrate that you have left Apratin. I do not know where you are going. A report will then be forwarded to Belgrade, and it may be that there will be more trouble for you when you arrive. If that is where you are going. But this will take several days to be sent and processed and decided upon."

"Thank God for Balkan bureaucracy," Berkeley said.

"Is it possible to look at your wife?"

Berkeley frowned. "Why do you wish to do that?"

"I am doing you a great favour, Mr Jones. Can you not do me a small one?"

Berkeley's turn to hesitate. But what the captain had said was perfectly true. He opened the door. The doctor was attending to other patients, having sent one of his servants to arrange the wagon. Anna was the only patient in the operating theatre, still lying on the hard bed and watched by a nurse, who looked up as the two men entered.

"She is asleep," she said.

"We won't wake her. Well, Captain?"

The captain gazed at Anna, nodded, and stepped outside again. Berkeley joined him.

"That is not your wife," the captain said. "That is Anna Slovitza. I have seen her photograph."

"Why should Anna Slovitza not be my wife?"

The captain glanced at him. "She may be, Mr Jones, but she is not an Englishwoman, and she does not spend her time travelling peacefully about Europe. You have lied to me. You did rob that payroll. Where is the money?"

"I sent it off with Karlovy," Berkeley said, looking him in the eye.

"I have the power to arrest you," the captain said.

"And hand me and Madame Slovitza over to the Austrians? I would not be hanged, Captain; my government would see to that. But Madame Slovitza would be. And your name would be forever damned. *I* would see to that."

The captain wiped his brow. "I give you two hours, Mr Jones, to be out of Apratin." He left the room.

"Seems to me we're skating on very thin ice, sir," Lockwood remarked.

"So we have to move very fast. See if that transport has arrived yet."

* * *

The transport was, literally, a horse and cart. The doctor and his nurses carried Anna out to it, laid her on a blanket over the bare boards and spread another blanket over her.

"There is also this tarpaulin to spread over her should it come on to rain. Or . . ." He looked at the sky. "To snow. You have food?"

"No."

The doctor gave instructions to his staff, and they bustled off to return a few minutes later with a sack of food.

"If you have no trouble, it will take you about twelve hours to reach Novi-Sad," the doctor said. "That is, if you travel all night."

"We intend to," Berkeley said.

Lockwood was tethering their horses to the cart; the precious saddlebags he loaded in beside Anna and covered with the tarpaulin.

"Take this as well," the doctor said, and gave Berkeley a quarter-full bottle of laudanum.

"Is this all you have?"

"Yes. Use it sparingly. There is some brandy in the box. Use that too if you have to."

"We are deeply in your debt, doctor."

"I am honoured to have been of some assistance. God go with you."

"Amen," Berkeley said, and snapped the whip.

The sun was setting behind heavy banks of cloud, and it had become very cold. They attracted some attention as they walked the cart through the little town, but as Townsend and Lockwood were both heavily-armed no one attempted to interfere with their progress; and once they were away from the houses the road was empty in the gathering gloom.

Anna began to wake up, moaning and groaning. Berkeley was not surprised, as the road surface was poor and the cart was unsprung. He gave the reins to Lockwood, sat beside her in the cart and fed her some of the laudanum so that she lapsed into semi-consciousness. But she was again losing blood, seeping through the bandage and even the blouse and blanket.

"Is she going to make it, sir?" Lockwood asked.

"It's up to us to see that she does," Berkeley told him.

Around midnight there was a flurry of snow. Berkeley covered Anna with the tarpaulin and they rumbled on their way into the night, the two men huddled in their greatcoats on the driving seat. The snow did not last long, but the sun came up to a countryside scattered with white; even in September it was not that much above freezing, Berkeley reckoned, as he could hear frost crunching beneath their wheels. But in the distance they could see the church spires of Novi-Sad.

Two hours later they had crossed the bridge over the Danube and were in the streets of the town, regarded curiously by people on their way to work. Berkeley had enough Serbian, as taught him by Caterina, to ask the way to the hospital, and half an hour later they were in the yard.

"We have a very sick woman in the cart," Berkeley said. "Will you fetch someone with a stretcher?"

The porter lifted the tarpaulin to look at Anna, then went inside. When he returned, it was with a doctor as well as two male nurses and a stretcher. The doctor nodded briefly to Berkeley, then himself raised the tarpaulin and peered at Anna, lifting her eyelids and taking her pulse. Then he raised his head. "This woman is dead," he said.

Part Two

A Business of Intrigue

'. . . my bloody thoughts, with violent pace,
Shall ne'er look back, ne'er ebb to humble love,
Till that a capable and wide revenge
Swallow them up.'

William Shakespeare

The Husband

B erkeley touched the cold cheek, held the cold hand. He doubted his were any warmer, unprotected by gloves.

The doctor was peering at the bloodstained clothes. "Take her inside," he told the porters.

"No," Berkeley said.

The doctor raised his head in surprise.

"If she is dead," Berkeley told him, "I will take her home to be buried."

"But . . . where is her home?"

"Sabac. That is only about twenty miles from here, is it not?"

"That is correct. But there should be a post-mortem."

"To what purpose? She suffered a gunshot wound, and has died from loss of blood and exposure."

"There will have at least to be an inquest. How did she get this wound?"

"Contact the captain of the frontier guard at Apratin, and he will explain it to you."

The doctor looked thoroughly uncertain; he was used to having people do what he told them to when it came to matters of sickness and death. "This is highly irregular," he said. "I shall have to report it to the police."

"Do so," Berkeley agreed. "I will wish you good day."

"At least tell me her name," the doctor begged.

"Her name is Anna Slovitza."

"Anna . . ." The doctor gulped, and he stepped up to the cart again, to peer at the still features, relaxed in death.

"I am taking her to her people," Berkeley said. "I would strongly recommend that no one attempts to interfere with me. Not even the police."

He drove out of the hospital yard.

"Here's a pretty kettle of fish," Lockwood opined.

"It was always liable to happen," Berkeley said.

Which he knew was perfectly true. Yet he had not expected it

83

to happen. Not to Anna. And certainly not while she had been in his care.

"Do you think they'll come after us, sir? The police?"

"I'm hoping they'll think long enough about it for them to be unable to catch us."

They rode in silence for some time. Then Lockwood said, "Strange how things turn out."

Berkeley had been thinking the same thing, but he did not reply.

"What I mean is, sir," Lockwood went on, "we were sent here to kidnap the lady and hand her over to the Austrians, who would have hanged her. Well, now they've shot her."

"So, from the point of view of both the Austrian and British Governments, we have accomplished our mission. That thought had crossed my mind."

"Well, sir, here we are with a dead woman and a very large sum of money . . ."

"You are a scoundrel, Harry."

"Just considering all the options, sir. I mean, the Austrians have no idea that we were involved in that robbery and shoot-out. They'll find out it was a Mr Jones, an Englishman, but they won't be able to take it further than that if we get out now. While if we stay . . ."

"They'll trace our true identities, given time. But we are going to do the honourable thing, Harry . . . and maybe get back to England as well."

Supposing Caterina could be persuaded.

But first her grief had to be endured. They encountered people they knew when within a mile of Sabac. One of the men had been with Karlovy and had obviously been sent to look out for them. Now he gazed at Anna's body for several minutes, then wheeled his horse and galloped into the town.

By the time they got there the streets were crowded, people crossing themselves as the cart rumbled over the cobbles. When they reached the house, Karlovy and several men were waiting for them. Silently they lifted Anna's body and took it inside and up the narrow staircase, into the reception room. Here Caterina waited. She had already donned black, and wore a black veil which entirely concealed both her hair and her face. She watched her mother's body laid on the table, never moving. Then she said, "Leave us."

Karlovy nodded to his people, and they filed from the room. Lockwood hesitated, but Berkeley nodded and he followed the Serbs.

"Do you wish to be alone?" Berkeley asked.

"With you."

Berkeley closed the door and went to stand beside her.

"Karlovy told me what happened," she said. "He told me you were very brave, and very gallant. I am grateful for this."

There was nothing he could say.

"And you brought the money?" she asked.

"It is downstairs."

"Gregory will be pleased," she said.

"Gregory?"

"He is our master. He will mourn Mother, but he will be pleased to have got the money."

Berkeley found it difficult to envisage Anna having had a master.

"And you? Us?"

Her face twisted. "Now we have two parents to avenge."

They buried Anna the following day, almost the entire town turning out to watch the coffin being conveyed to the little cemetery and lowered into the earth. Caterina stood at Berkeley's side, Lockwood and the other servants behind. Karlovy and his people, now a dozen strong, stood on the other side, while the black-robed priest stood at the head of the grave and intoned his prayers. The townspeople were gathered around the inner group. Berkeley tried to study them, but there was no way of telling if any of them were officials of the Black Hand.

"Was Gregory there?" he asked Caterina, when they returned to the house.

"There was no time. He will come tomorrow."

"There are things we need to discuss."

"We will discuss them with Gregory," she said.

That was not what he had in mind at all, but he knew he had to be patient. Caterina had taken her mother's death with a massive calm; too much so, he felt. He suspected there might be an explosion lurking in there and he was in no hurry to provoke it.

Besides, Gregory might be a sensible man, and accept that Caterina could not possibly be expected to take on her mother's mantle at the age of eighteen.

Gregory arrived in time for lunch the following day; he had apparently taken the train from Belgrade. He was escorted to the house by Karlovy and his men who were clearly in awe of him, but to Berkeley's surprise he did not in any way suggest an anarchist. Short and stout with a little beard, he was well dressed, carried a silver-hilted cane and wore spats and a Homburg hat.

He exuded confident well-being.

"My child!" He held Caterina's hands and kissed them. "Every time I see you, you grow more beautiful. Even in grief."

Caterina bowed her head.

"And you are the famous Englishman," Gregory said, taking Berkeley's hands in turn, "who brought us the money."

"The money is there," Berkeley agreed.

"But at what a cost, eh? What a terrible cost." He waited, but as Berkeley made no comment, continued. "Anna was motivated. And now you will be motivated."

Berkeley frowned. "I'm not sure what you mean. I rode with Anna because she was my mother-in-law, and she wished it. When she was wounded, it was my duty to bring her back here. Now . . ."

"Now you must take her place," Gregory said. "And lead us in the field."

Berkeley gulped. "I know nothing of anarchism, of Balkan politics, of your cause."

"Of politics and our cause, you will learn," Gregory assured him. "In the field, you have every prerequisite: courage, boldness, decisiveness, an understanding of what needs to be done and the determination to do it. Karlovy has told me of you. He will willingly follow you."

"Why can Karlovy not replace Anna?"

"He does not have . . . what is the word? The charisma."

Berkeley looked at Caterina. Her eyes were gleaming.

As Gregory could see. "I am sure this is what your wife would have you do."

"It is something I need to consider," Berkeley said. "Something my wife and I need to discuss."

"Of course," Gregory said smoothly. "I shall return tomorrow."

"Will you not stay here?" Caterina asked.

"No, no. I have lodgings arranged in the town. I would not interfere in your discussion." He kissed her hands again, shook Berkeley's hands again, and left.

"So he is the great panjandrum," Berkeley said, pouring them each a glass of wine.

"I do not know this word, panjandrum," Caterina said.

"What the Americans would call the boss; who never goes into the field himself."

She sipped. "He organises."

"Quite. In absolute safety. He does not even provide his own funding."

"You did not like him."

"I would regard him, at least indirectly, as the cause of your mother's death. Perhaps your father's, as well."

86

"The Austrians killed Father and Mother," she said. "We are fighting a war. People get killed in a war."

"Like your mother, you really have no idea what a war is like," he said. "She discovered when it was too late." He took the glass from her hand, placed it on the table beside his own, led her to the settee and sat beside her.

He had to choose his words with great care, remembering his cover story for why he had come here in the first place. "Caterina, my dearest girl, do you not see that this is a war we cannot win? Austria-Hungary is one of the five great nations of Europe. Serbia cannot ever fight her. You think the Russians will support you in a war? I do not think they will be able to do that. Nor do I think their support will be of any value. Your parents devoted their entire lives to fighting Austria, and they both died in that cause. Are you going to do the same?"

"Yes," she said fiercely. "Yes."

"You are my wife," he said. "I cannot permit it."

"You are my husband," she retorted. "You swore an oath."

"I took marriage vows," he said. "I swore to honour and respect you. Neither of those can be reconciled with having you become an outlaw. Listen. I would like to take you to England."

"You said you had had to flee England."

"I did not. I said I had been dismissed from the army. I would like to take you there and introduce you to my parents. I will obtain a job, and you will live a normal, happy life. We will have children, and in time you will forget all the horrors with which you have been surrounded all of your life."

"And the Austrians who killed Mother and Father? Who raped me?"

"You do not even know who they are any more. And you cannot kill the entire Austrian nation."

She pulled her hands free. "I thought you were a man of courage."

"I believe I am. I have the courage to know when something is possible, and when it is not."

"Then leave me. If you wish no part in my future, then I wish none in yours."

"If you stay here, you will not *have* a future," he almost wailed.

"I will kill Austrians," she said. "Before I die."

She locked herself in her bedroom after dinner, and Berkeley retired to the rooms he had originally occupied where he was joined by Lockwood.

"Here's a pretty . . ."

"Just don't say it," Berkeley recommended.

"It's just that I really thought we were going to get away with it."

"We are," Berkeley said.

He took out the marriage papers; he had been given a copy of the certificate. He couldn't read all the printed words, but his own as groom and Caterina's as bride, with her mother as a witness and Karlovy as the other, were clearly written, as were the signatures. And the whole was signed and attested by Father Michael. It might have been a Greek Orthodox ceremony, but he did not doubt it would be legally binding anywhere in the world. He was Caterina Slovitza's husband.

More importantly, for his purposes, Caterina Slovitza was his wife.

So, at the end of the day, he would after all be betraying her, as she would see it; but he would be saving her life.

"How do you reckon we are going to do that, sir?" Lockwood asked.

"Listen very carefully."

The house was sleeping, as apparently was Caterina. Silently, Berkeley entered Anna's bedroom, which was as she had left it for the last time. Candle in hand he hunted around. She had spoken of her strongbox, and there it was, in the bottom of her wardrobe. He lifted it out, placed it on the bed. It was secured with a padlock but he did not suppose that was going to prove difficult.

He took the box to his own room, where Lockwood waited, and between them they sawed through the hasp easily enough. Inside there was, as Anna had claimed, a considerable sum of money: dinars, zlotys, pfennigs, marks, even some English sovereigns. Most important of all, there was a large wad of drachma.

"We'll take it all," Berkeley said. "After all, it belongs to my wife, and by Serb law what's hers is mine."

For the furtherance of his plan even more important were the several certificates, which included Anna's own marriage certificate and Caterina's birth certificate. These he stowed in his wallet as well.

They replaced the padlock, and restored the now almost empty box to the wardrobe.

"What's a strongbox?" Lockwood asked. "After an army payroll."

"My friend," Gregory said, embracing Berkeley. "My own true friend. I knew you would wish to work with us. Are you not proud of him, Caterina?"

"I am proud of him," Caterina said, uncertainly. His volte-face had taken her by surprise.

"I did not wish to, in the first instance," Berkeley confessed. "I felt it my duty to protect my wife and save her from the dangers of this life. But when I realised how determined she was to avenge her mother, I knew I could do nothing else."

"Admirably put, and it is a brave man who can tell the truth about such matters. Now, be happy while you can. I must return to Belgrade. I will be in touch as soon as our next venture is arrnged."

"Will it be soon?" Berkeley asked.

"It will not be for a few weeks. We must lie low for a while. All southern Hungary is in a ferment. Budapest is in a ferment. Vienna is in a ferment. There are representations being made. There is even talk of the Serbian government being forced to act against us. They will not, of course. But we cannot afford to embarrass them too much until this furore dies down."

"Do they know that Madame Slovitza is dead?"

"There are only rumours at the moment. But they will find out soon enough." He squeezed Caterina's hand. "When they are sure of it they may relax their pressure somewhat."

"Do they know about me?" Berkeley asked.

"They know that Anna was assisted by an Englishman as well as her own people. He is identified as a Mr Jones. But Mr Jones does not exist, does he?"

He does in Whitehall, Berkeley thought grimly. But he didn't doubt he could talk himself out of that situation as well.

"I need a week," he said. "To visit Athens."

Gregory raised his eyebrows. "Athens?"

"As I did not know how things here were going to work out," Berkeley explained, "before leaving England I arranged for some funds owed to me to be sent to a bank in Athens. The money should be there by now, and I would like to pick it up. A week will do it."

"Very well. But make the journey as rapidly as possible. Will Mrs Townsend be going with you?"

"Of course," Berkeley said.

"Why must I go to Athens?" Caterina asked. "I would rather stay here."

"That is one reason why you must come with me. You have spent too much of your life here. When last did you leave?"

"I have not left Sabac since I returned here after Father was executed. Mother would not let me."

"Exactly. My dearest girl, that was six years ago. You must get out and see something of the world, meet other people. Besides, you will love Athens. It is one of the great historical cities."

"A week," she said. "And then we will return here."

"Of course."

Once he had told himself he could never contemplate marriage, if it involved lying to his wife!

But she was content, and allowed him into her bed that night. They left next morning; Berkeley intended to be out of the country, and indeed out of the Balkans while Anna's death was still only a rumour. However, it was necessary to spend the night in Belgrade while awaiting the train south. Not entirely to Berkeley's surprise there was a knock on the door within an hour of their moving in to a hotel; he had never doubted that the Serbian police kept the Slovitza family under constant surveillance.

Two men stood in the corridor.

"My God," Caterina muttered as Lockwood opened the door. "The police!"

"I expected them," Berkeley said.

"Mr Jones?" One of the men asked Lockwood.

"I am Jones," Berkeley said.

"Would you come with us, please?" He spoke German.

"No," Caterina said. "You must not go."

"I don't think I am in a position to refuse, my dear. I won't be long." He put on his coat and went to the door. "I assume you are from Colonel Savos?"

"That is correct," the man said, and glanced at him. "You know Colonel Savos?"

"We're old friends," Berkeley assured him.

"Sit down, Mr Jones. Have a cigar." Savos pushed the box across the table. "From Havana. The best."

Berkeley took one, and Savos waited while he lit it. Then he remarked, "It is not quite three weeks since last you sat in that chair, Mr Jones. A great deal has happened in that time."

"I'm afraid it has."

"Is it true that Anna Slovitza is dead?"

"I'm afraid so."

"You can prove this?"

"There is a death certificate."

"Presumably signed by her doctor in Sabac. One of her close associates."

"There is also a body. I assume you would have no difficulty in obtaining an exhumation order."

90

"I think I may well do that. The Austrians would like to be assured that there is no risk of a mistake. And now you have taken up with the daughter, I understand."

"The daughter, as you put it, Colonel, happens to be my wife."

Savos raised his eyebrows. "And of course you have a certificate to prove it."

"I do. Plus a few hundred witnesses to the event."

"All in three weeks." Savos shook his head. "You come, you see, you marry, you watch your mother-in-law die . . . and of course, you took time out of your honeymoon to rob an Austrian payroll wagon and kill several people. Tell me, Mr Jones, did you also find the time to inform Madame Slovitza of her 'inheritance'?"

"Am I under arrest?" Berkeley countered.

"At this moment, no. But the Austrians I believe are applying for your extradition. As the charge is murder and you are not a Serbian citizen, Mr Jones, I believe their request may well be granted. They are very angry about what happened."

"I'm sure they are. But you can only arrest me if I am in the country, right?"

Again Savos raised his eyebrows. "You are leaving Serbia? With your child-bride?"

"I would hardly describe her as a child, Colonel. Yes, we are leaving Serbia."

"I think that is a very sensible decision. May I ask where you are going?"

"In the first instance, Athens."

"You understand that the Austrians will also be able to extradite you from Greece."

"Supposing I am still in Greece."

Savos nodded. "I have an idea they will hunt you down, Mr Jones. Even as far as England itself." He smiled. "But then, I do not suppose your name is really Jones. I will wish you good fortune, Mr Jones. With your beautiful bride. But let me give you a word of advice. I do not recommend that you ever return to Serbia again. Or indeed, anywhere in the Balkans."

"Was it very bad?" Caterina asked at dinner.

"Not in the least. As I told his people, the Colonel and I are old friends."

"But what did he want?"

"To tell me that the Austrians are after me. But they're looking for Walter Jones, not Berkeley Townsend."

"Will they not trace you to Sabac?"

"Perhaps they will. But surely in Sabac, I, like your mother, will be safe."

"Oh, yes," she said. "We would never let anything happen to you."

"Well, then." He raised his wine-glass to her. "Here's to Athens."

As he had hoped and anticipated, Caterina was quickly bound up in the excitement of the journey. She had never been on a long train trip before, and she had never seen the mountains of southern Serbia and northern Greece. When, three days later, they rolled into Athens, tired and dirty, she was on a high of expectation as to what might come next. Berkeley checked them into a hotel, and they bathed and changed while Lockwood, as instructed, set off immediately for Piraeus.

"What does he do there?" Caterina asked.

"We have some unfinished business," Berkeley told her, and carried her off to look at the Acropolis. This occupied the rest of the morning as she was quite awestruck, and by the time they returned to the hotel for lunch, Lockwood had also returned.

"All done?" Berkeley asked.

"All done, sir."

"Well, this afternoon I must go to the bank and see what they have for me. How would you like to go shopping, my dear? Lockwood will escort you."

"Oh, may I? But do we have any money?"

"Enough." He gave her some of her mother's drachma.

"Hm," remarked the Embassy secretary. "Hm." He studied the various papers Berkeley had placed before him. "These all *seem* to be in order, Captain Townsend. I should think we will be able to issue your wife with a British passport. It will take about a week."

"Today," Berkeley said. "Or at least, tomorrow. No later."

"My dear sir, that is quite impossible. A week."

"I would like to send a telegram to General Gorman at the War Office," Berkeley said. "My commanding officer," he explained.

A form was produced, and he wrote out the message: Mission accomplished. Forced by unforeseen circumstances to return Greece. Require all possible assistance from Embassy. Please confirm. Townsend.

"Well, I say," the secretary commented. "Friends in high places, eh?"

"You should get a reply to that by tomorrow morning," Berkeley said.

"I'm sure we shall. Very good, Captain Townsend, if it is a matter of national importance, your wife's passport will be waiting for you tomorrow morning."

"I have been a naughty girl," Caterina confessed. "I have spent so much money."

Berkeley surveyed the several dresses laid out on the bed, the underwear, the boots and shoes, the hats. "I am sure they will all suit you very well."

"I have never seen such lovely shops," she said.

Hopefully, he thought, she would find those in London even lovelier, even if it might be expensive for a while. "I don't suppose you thought to buy an extra bag to put this stuff in?"

"Ah . . ." she looked at Lockwood, eyebrows arched.

"I'll attend to it in the morning, sir," Lockwood promised.

"And tomorrow afternoon I thought we'd go down to Piraeus," Berkeley said brightly.

"What is there at Piraeus?" Caterina asked.

"The sea. Ships. Have you ever seen the sea?"

"No, I have not," Caterina said. "Is it so wonderful?"

"Let's say, there's more of it than anything else."

He had worked out his schedule with great care. He collected Caterina's passport in the morning, as arranged, while she and Lockwood were buying the extra suitcase. They lunched at the hotel, and afterwards took the train down to the seaport; naturally they left all their luggage behind – as far as the hotel, and more important, Caterina was concerned, they would be returning that night.

Caterina was, predictably, fascinated by the ships and the sea. They strolled along the various piers, looking at the big vessels moored out in the roads.

"Why, Captain, sir," Lockwood suddenly said. "There is our old friend Pathenikos."

The dragoman was effusive in his greeting, but then he had been well paid. "Mr Jones! And your so beautiful bride. I saw you, madame, when I was in Sabac with Mr Jones. But I do not suppose you remember me."

"I remember you very well," Caterina said.

"And what are you doing here?" Berkeley asked. "Waiting for a client?"

"Oh, indeed, sir. Actually, I am on my way out to speak with him now, make arrangements for his trip into the interior. Would you like to accompany me?"

"Eh?" Berkeley simulated astonishment.

"Well, sir, it would be a feather in my cap if I were able to introduce you as a previous client, one who was entirely satisfied with my services."

"Well . . ." Berkeley looked doubtful. "Would you like actually to go on board a ship, Caterina?"

"Could we? I have never been on a ship."

"I have a boat waiting," Pathenikos said. He was very nervous, but Caterina did not seem to notice; she was very nervous herself at the thought of getting into the waiting rowing boat.

"You wait here, Harry," Berkeley said.

"Of course, sir." Lockwood agreed. It was his business, as soon as they were far enough away, to return to Athens with all haste, pay the hotel bill and bring their luggage to the dock.

Berkeley assisted his wife down the steps and into the boat; she gave a little shriek as it moved beneath her feet, but then she was seated on the transom with him alongside her, and the oarsmen were pushing off.

"Oh," she said. "The feeling . . . it is so strange. This water . . . how deep is it?"

"Here? About twenty feet, I would say. It gets much deeper out at sea."

She shuddered.

Ten minutes later they were pulling into the side of the rather battered-looking tramp steamer; her sides were streaked with rust. Fortunately, as she knew nothing about ships it did not occur to Caterina that this was a strange sort of vessel on which to find an important visitor. A torn and stained Red Ensign drooped from her stern, and the accommodation ladder was down. Caterina gave another little shriek as she was assisted on to the platform with the sea now surging gently only inches beneath her.

"Just hang on to the lines," Berkeley told her. "And go straight up."

She obeyed, pausing every now and then as the ladder swayed; the breeze fluttered her skirt and petticoat and revealed her boots.

"I will leave you now, sir," Pathenikos said.

"No. Stay here until the matter is completed," Berkeley said. "We do not want her to become suspicious."

"I hope you know what you do, sir," the Greek remarked.

Berkeley looked up to the gangway, where Caterina was having her hand kissed by the waiting captain. "There is nothing for you to concern yourself about, Pathenikos," he said. "It is not possible for a man to kidnap his own wife."

The Voyage

Pathenikos looked doubtful, as well he might, Berkeley supposed; he himself had no idea of the actual legality of what he was doing. He was relying on the journey for a reconciliation.

He went up the ladder to join Caterina.

"Captain Lukeman?"

"That's me. You'll be Mr Jones. And Mrs Jones, to be sure. You'll come up to the cabin deck." He spoke English.

"Berkeley," Caterina asked in German, "what is happening?"

"There's this man wishes to see us," Berkeley explained. "Just up here."

The captain led the way, while his mate touched his cap. The crew watched with interest, but Berkeley did not think any of them were English, or, for that matter, German; he reckoned they were mostly Egyptian.

Caterina was slightly out of breath by the time they reached the accommodation deck. Here they were shown into a somewhat grubby saloon, presided over by an even more grubby steward, whose white jacket had definitely not seen a laundry for several weeks.

"The cabin's along here," Captain Lukeman said. "We don't carry passengers as a rule, but your man said there'd be another hundred when we dock at Marseilles."

"That's right," Berkeley agreed.

"You've the money with you?"

Which confirmed Berkeley's suspicion that this character might not be above a bit of kidnapping himself, or at least piracy.

"My man will bring the money when he joins us this evening."

He had no intention of having Captain Lukeman leave earlier than arranged, thus losing Lockwood, his back-up.

"Aye, well," Lukeman said. "I hope he's on time. I've a tide to catch."

Berkeley grinned at him. "Come now, Captain, there are no tides in the Mediterranean."

The captain glared at him, then went down the corridor and opened a cabin. "In here."

"And my man?"

"He'll be opposite. This is all there is."

"Let's have a look."

He held Caterina's arm and escorted her down the corridor.

"Berkeley," she said, "I do not understand what is happening. And I do not like this man."

"Join the club," he said. "But he'll have to do."

They reached the cabin, which was actually cleaner than he had hoped. Although the bunks were an upper and lower, and neither was very wide, there was a hanging locker and it even had its own washbasin, dating perhaps to the days when the ship had had a more salubrious existence – and a more salubrious crew.

"Berkeley," Caterina said. "Please tell me what is going on?"

"You can leave us, and close the door, Captain," Berkeley said. "My man will be here in a couple of hours."

Lukeman grunted and closed the door.

"I feel as if I am being kidnapped," Caterina complained.

"Come and sit beside me," Berkeley said, sitting on the lower bunk.

Caterina hesitated, then obeyed, frowning.

"Now listen carefully," Berkeley said. "This ship is going to take us to Marseilles. From Marseilles we will take a train across France to Calais, and at Calais we will catch the cross-Channel ferry to Dover, and be in England in time for Christmas. Won't that be fun?"

Her eyes were enormous. "Marseilles? France? Calais? Dover? England?"

"You are going to see a bit of the world."

"But . . . aren't we going back to Sabac?"

"No."

"But . . . you were going to take field command of the Hand?"

"I'm afraid I lied about that," he admitted. "I'm simply not cut out to be an anarchist."

"You promised! You told Gregory . . ." Her voice had risen an octave.

"I know I did. But that was all a lie, too." He held her hands. "Listen to me. I do not want ever to have you involved in anarchy. I do not want ever to have to watch you bleed to death in agony as did your mother. I want you to live a normal and happy life, with me, as my wife."

Now her eyes were blazing. "You have no right to do this! You swore an oath!"

"To honour you, and cherish you. I am endeavouring to do that."

She pulled her hands free, leapt up, and ran for the door. He caught her shoulder, spun her round, and she fell across the bunk, on her face. When she tried to rise, he put his hand on her back to force her down again. She threw back her head and screamed, but the porthole was closed and he did not suppose Lukeman or any of his crew would interfere.

"You are going to make me angry," he warned her.

She panted. "You have no right . . ."

"I have every right. You are my wife."

"I will kill you," she gasped.

"No you will not. You will sit up and behave yourself." He moved his hand.

"Never," she spat. "Never. I will . . ." But she did push herself up.

"One day you will thank me for what I have done," he told her.

"Thank you? You are a crawling thing, a creature from the gutter, a—"

Berkeley slapped her face. She had got to her feet, now she sat down again with a bump.

"You are being hysterical," he told her. "Now, behave yourself, or I shall have to tie you up."

She licked blood from her cut lip. "I shall kill you," she said again. "No matter how long it takes. I will watch you die."

While she was in this mood he didn't think he could leave her alone, and free.

"Lie down," he told her.

"I will not have sex with you," she said. "Not now, not ever again."

"Right now, nothing could be further from my mind," he assured her. "Lie down; and if you attempt to fight me, I will hit you again."

She lay on the bunk. He unlaced her boots and took them off, then threw up her dress and petticoat and pulled down her stockings. These he also took off, using one to bind her ankles together, and the other for her wrists. This last he left with a tail, which he secured to the stanchion by the bedhead; her arms were extended, but he reckoned she would be quite comfortable, at least for a while. She stared at him with hate-filled eyes, but made no effort to resist him.

He placed a pillow under her head. "Now," he said. "If you have any sense you will lie there and think about what I have said. If you throw yourself off the bed you will be most uncomfortable, so I advise against it. If you wish to scream, go ahead; but if you make too much noise I will have to gag you. Please be sensible, Caterina. Please try to understand that I have only your safety in mind. Your life itself."

Caterina spat at him.

Berkeley went on deck, locking the cabin door behind him. He climbed the ladder to the bridge where Lukeman was walking up and down.

"Your wife is not happy, eh?"

"I'm afraid not, at the moment," Berkeley said. "She'll get over it."

"But she *is* your wife?" Lukeman asked.

"Would you like to see the marriage certificate?"

"No, no, sir. Who am I to doubt the word of a fine gentleman like yourself? A *rich* gentleman. But you understand, Mr Jones, that if this is an abduction, it could turn out very badly for me."

"A man cannot abduct his own wife, Captain."

"Of course, sir. Of course. The young lady is not Greek."

"No, she is not."

"And definitely not English," Lukeman mused. He was plotting his course.

"No, she is not English, Captain," Berkeley said. "And what she is, and who she is, is absolutely no business of yours."

"Of course, sir. Of course."

Lockwood was back on time with the luggage, and was ferried out by the same boat as they had used earlier.

"Am I glad to see you," Berkeley said. "Where the devil did Pathenikos find this one?"

"Well, sir, you'll agree the situation is a bit difficult. He had to find a captain who is more interested in money than ethics."

"And he has certainly done that," Berkeley agreed. "I think we are going to have to keep a fairly close eye on things until we reach Marseilles."

"And how is Mrs Townsend?"

"Mrs Townsend is currently below."

"Went off all right, then, did it, sir?"

"No, Harry," Berkeley said. "It did not go off all right. Mrs Townsend is presently tied to her bunk."

Lockwood gulped. "Well then, sir . . ."

"We just have to see what the next few days will bring."

"If it's all right with you, Mr Jones, I'd like to raise anchor now," Lukeman said. "I have clearance from the port authority."

"Whenever you're ready, Captain," Berkeley assented, and went below.

Caterina had not moved very much in his absence. Nor had her eyes in any way softened.

"We shall be at sea in an hour," he told her. "Is there any chance of your agreeing to come up to watch? And perhaps have some supper afterwards?"

"I will come up," she said.

That was too easy.

"Thank you," he said.

He released her, and she sat up to rub her wrists and ankles.

"Am I allowed to put on my stockings?"

"Of course."

He waited while she dressed herself, then summoned Lockwood from across the corridor. "She's in your charge."

"You'll excuse me, madame," Lockwood said. He threaded his own belt through that of her skirt, retaining the end in his hand.

"Is this necessary?" she asked.

"I'm afraid it is," Berkeley said.

She snorted. "I am not going to commit suicide, husband."

"I am very glad to hear it."

"I am going to stay alive to kill you," she said.

Lockwood swallowed.

They stood together on the bridge, behind Lukeman and his mate whose name was Arnold, while the anchor was raised and the engine began to rumble. Then the *Wanderer* slowly made her way through the outer shipping and into the Aegean Sea.

"How many days to Marseilles?" Berkeley asked.

"Much depends on the weather, sir," Lukeman said. "At this time of the year it is not good. But if all goes well, about a week."

Berkeley looked at the sky. "Doesn't seem too bad at the moment."

"Ah, sir, who can tell? It can come on to blow with hardly a cloud in sight." He glanced at Berkeley. "You have people meeting you in Marseilles."

Still laying plans, Berkeley thought.

"Of course," he said.

Lukeman smiled.

Caterina joined them for dinner in the saloon. She was behaving in a most civilised manner, although there was no indication that she had at all softened her resolve; indeed, her icy politeness was as disturbing as her earlier anger.

After the meal, with the night already dark and cold – the breeze was not strong but it was from the north – they walked the deck together, Lockwood as always in attendance although he remained out of earshot.

"I should like to ask for your cooperation," Berkeley said. "Look at things rationally. You feel you are duty-bound to avenge your parents, by remaining in Serbia and working with the Black Hand.

I feel I am duty-bound to preserve your life, as the alternative is to die like your mother. That is a matter which can, and must, be resolved between us. I do not think I am being irrational in asking you to return to England with me, as my wife, to meet my parents to whom I am as strongly attached as you are to yours. When we have done that and you have sampled the life I can offer you, if you are still determined to return to the Balkans and resume the fight against the Austrians, then I give you my word that I shall not stand in your way."

She glanced at him. "But you will not come with me."

"I may well do that. But I think you should give my way a trial first."

She stared back at the dwindling lights of the Piraeus.

"However," he said sensing victory, at least in the short term, "our first business is to reach Marseilles. I'm afraid, as I knew you would not willingly leave Sabac, I had to trick you, and that meant taking whatever ship Pathenikos could provide. He didn't do us very well. This captain is a thug, and I am quite sure his crew are too. They reckon I'm a wealthy man, and I have an idea their idea is that some accident should befall us, and that we should never reach Marseilles at all. I have no doubt that Lockwood and I can deal with them. We are professionals and they are amateurs, when it comes to killing. But obviously it would be a handicap to have you in the opposite camp, or even a camp of your own, as it were. And you do need to remember that if anything were to happen to us and you be left to the mercy of this lot, well . . . it would be the Austrian police all over again."

"I understand. I will support you against these people. Give me a gun. I can shoot as well as Mother."

"I have her own gun with me." He smiled. "I hope you will not use it to shoot me."

"I will use it to shoot these people," she said, seriously.

"Right. But please don't shoot anybody until I say so."

Berkeley was well pleased with the way things were turning out. Although Caterina remained cold to him physically – they slept in separate bunks, she in the upper – she gave every appearance of being a faithful and loving wife when they were in the presence of Lukeman or his crew. Nor, remarkably, did she suffer from seasickness; although by morning the wind had freshened quite a lot and the seas had become lumpy. Berkeley stuck with his plan that the three of them should remain together at all times, and he gave Caterina her mother's revolver, loaded, which she placed in her handbag.

The *Wanderer* continued to waddle to the south; she only made about seven knots, but with the wind behind her she was quite comfortable. It was not until that evening when they rounded Cape Malea to take a westerly course with the wind on the beam, that she began to roll heavily. The breeze had freshened as Lukeman had suggested it might.

Dinner was amusing, with plates and glasses and bottles and cutlery sliding to and fro; and the steward, whose name was Perryman, staggering around the saloon as he tried to serve the meal.

"Is it going to be like this all the way to Marseilles?" Caterina asked.

"I shouldn't think so,' Berkeley said. "But I've a notion it'll get worse before it gets better."

He had spent the day finding out what he could about the ship, without appearing too inquisitive. He deduced that there were twelve deckhands, and about six crew in the engine room; plus the two officers, of course, together with the steward and the cook. But with the seas quite heavy and the ship in a fairly busy lane, he reckoned they were safe for the time being.

"Tell me about England," Caterina said, as they lay in their cabin in the dark that night, while the ship thumped and rolled and the wind howled. "Are there great mountains?"

"None at all, I'm afraid. Nothing you would call a mountain. In Wales and Scotland, maybe. But we will live in Northamptonshire."

"Is it a big town?"

"Well, what I am talking about isn't a town at all. It's a county: what you would call an administrative district. There is a town called Northampton, but we're some distance away from it."

"I have only ever lived in a town," she commented.

Berkeley wondered how she would find the peace and quiet of Northampton and the surrounding farmland compared to the narrow streets of Sabac, crowded with desperadoes.

She was thinking along the same lines. "Is there much anarchy in England?" she asked.

"There is no anarchy at all. Unless you consider the Sufragettes to be anarchists."

"What are the Sufragettes?"

"Women who want the vote."

"The vote for what?"

"The vote for who is elected to parliament."

"Why do they wish this?"

"Well, you see, parliament makes the laws, and there are a lot of women who feel that the laws in Britain unfairly discriminate against women. Thus they feel that if they could have a say in who

101

is elected, they could perhaps have some of the laws changed, or at least modified."

"Laws are made by men," Caterina said, with some finality.

"Quite," he agreed. "But these women feel so strongly about it that they throw stones and smash things up, whenever they can. They don't shoot people, though."

"Then it is not a matter of life or death to them. Are they executed when they are caught?"

"Good Lord, no. There would be no possible reason for it. They do not threaten the state."

"You English are fortunate," she remarked. "You have no Austrians sitting on your border, waiting to take your land."

He found himself wondering what might happen if she did settle in England and joined the Sufragettes.

Next morning they were well clear of Greece, and crossing the southern end of the Ionian Sea towards the channel between Sicily and the Maltese Islands. The wind had dropped, but there remained heavy clouds and a high swell: from crest to trough was some thirty feet, Berkeley reckoned.

"There is more bad weather ahead," Lukeman said at breakfast. "A mistral, out of the Gulf of Lyons."

"That's a good way away, isn't it?" Berkeley asked.

"Ah, sir, a big mistral can stretch all the way down to below Sardinia. September is a bad time to be at sea in the Mediterranean."

"What's a mistral?" Caterina asked. She had picked up enough English to understand the gist of what was being said.

"A north-westerly wind which comes out of France. It can be quite strong, and sometimes lasts for days."

"Will it be bad for us?"

"Not dangerous. But uncomfortable, as we'll be going into it."

Lukeman grinned. "You know a lot about the sea, Mr Jones."

"I've travelled a bit," Berkeley conceded.

Lukeman made his play that afternoon. It was actually quite a pleasant day, with patches of blue sky and the sun from time to time visible as it sank to the west. The wind remained fresh and cold, however, and the sea lumpy, and it was more comfortable to stay in the saloon, where Berkeley continued to teach Caterina English. She was an alert and quick-witted pupil, and appeared keen to master her new language.

Lockwood had retired to his cabin, but the door was hooked open.

It was four o'clock when the captain appeared, followed by Arnold and two of the crew. "It is my decision, Mr Jones," Lukeman said without preamble, "that you should pay the remainder of the passage money now."

Berkeley leaned back in his chair and let his hands droop; they were within inches of his holstered pistol which was invisible to the captain. "And it is my principle, Captain, never to alter an agreed procedure."

"But I must insist," Lukeman said. "You wouldn't like us to harm the little lady, now, would you?"

"I think you'd be very unwise to try," Berkeley said, and whistled.

Lukeman's head jerked, but before he could react, Lockwood stood in the doorway, shotgun in his hands. The captain stepped back, as did his men.

"I think," Berkeley said, "in the circumstances, that we will have to change our plans after all. We'll put in to Valletta, tomorrow morning, Captain. There I will pay you a further fifty pounds."

Lukeman licked his lips.

"The agreement was for a hundred."

"For delivery to Marseilles. But you are only taking us halfway, you see. So you only get half."

Lukeman glared at him. "You are trying to take over my ship. I will hand you over to the authorities."

"You have it backwards, old man. If you deliver us to Valletta without any more trouble, I may just refrain from handing *you* over to the authorities. You are flying the Red Ensign. That means you are subject to English law. And I happen to be an officer in His Majesty's army, travelling on official business. I am fully entitled to requisition this ship. Now . . ." He drew his Browning, and Lukeman gaped. "We will come with you, Captain, and you will show me what arms you have on board. And please, no funny business."

"I have no arms," Lukeman growled.

"Show me, anyway."

"Well, there is a rifle in my cabin."

"Show me." He signalled Lockwood and Caterina to stay close to him.

The rifle turned out to be an old Mauser, rusty and badly in need of a cleaning.

"I reckon anyone firing this would be in more danger than his target," Lockwood commented.

"So get rid of it," Berkeley said.

Lockwood threw it over the side.

"Hey," Lukeman complained. "That's my property."

"It was," Berkeley agreed. "Now, Captain, alter course for Malta. And remember that I know enough about navigation to check you out. We shall stay on the bridge, with you, for the night. You can have our dinner sent up."

Lukeman muttered to himself, but set the new course. The motion eased as the *Wanderer* turned slightly away from the wind and waddled up and down the troughs.

"That was well done," Caterina said. "I can see why my mother valued you so highly."

"Unfortunately, we're not in Malta yet," Berkeley reminded her.

"Do you think they will try something?"

"I'd be very surprised if they didn't."

"But we have the captain."

"Yes," he said thoughtfully. That they *would* try something was as certain as anything in this life; they would rely on the fact that an English army officer would never shoot someone in cold blood. They did not know that he was also a professional anarchist as well as a spy.

The helmsman was changed every four hours, as if everything was normal. Their dinner was brought up, as requested. It included a bottle of wine, but just to be sure, Berkeley made Lukeman drink some of it first.

The captain grinned. "You think I would drug your wine, Mr Jones? How am I to do that?"

"I was thinking more of poison, old man," Berkeley said. "But as you're still breathing . . ."

It was now getting dark, the sun having disappeared behind a bank of cloud on the horizon. The sea seemed absolutely empty. So did the ship; from the bridge none of the crew, not even the mate Arnold, were to be seen, but Berkeley posted Lockwood and his shotgun at the top of the ladder to discourage anyone coming up, save for the relief coxswain.

Just aft of the bridge was the captain's cabin, and Berkeley sent Caterina to sleep in there. She didn't want to go, but he insisted. "You can be up at the first sign of trouble," he told her.

There was also a toilet and washbasin, which was useful.

Then it was just a matter of waiting, as the ship muttered on its way. Lukeman sat on the deck and appeared to go to sleep. Berkeley, well used to sleepless nights, patrolled the bridge and watched the compass. He remained certain that the crew were going to try something rather than steam tamely into what was virtually a British seaport, but he didn't see *what* they were going to try and by dawn they should be well within sight of the islands.

The answer should have been predictable. At midnight the engine stopped.

"Eh, eh?" Lukeman jerked awake and scrambled to his feet.

The helmsman released the wheel and the roll increased.

"Your play," Berkeley commented. Lockwood looked in from the ladder. "Stay alert, Harry."

"I knew nothing of this," Lukeman protested.

"Well, call down and find out what the trouble is, and how long it'll take to fix."

Lukeman blew down the voice tube.

Caterina appeared from the cabin, carrying her revolver. Lukeman blinked at it; he had not realised that she too was armed.

"Joseph," he said. "Are you there Joseph?"

An unintelligible sound came up the pipe. Lukeman listened, then raised his head. "He says it is a serious matter. He wishes me to go down and see for myself."

"No chance," Berkeley told him.

Lukeman blew down the pipe again. "You know the ship has been taken over by these people," the captain shouted down. "They will not let me come down. You will have to come up."

More unintelligible gargle, then Lukeman replaced the cap. "He says it is very serious. He says we are making water. He is coming up."

"Just him," Berkeley warned. "You mean he has opened a seacock?"

"You think I would scuttle my own ship?"

"I'd bet on it, to keep out of gaol."

"There's this fellow on the ladder, sir," Lockwood called.

"Let him through," Berkeley said.

The heavy-shouldered engineer appeared on the bridge, looking curiously from Lockwood's shotgun to Berkeley's pistol to Caterina's revolver, then more appreciatively at Caterina herself.

"So what's the problem, Chief?" Berkeley asked.

The engineer looked at the captain.

Lukeman shrugged. "He's taken command. Tell him."

Joseph, who also appeared to be Egyptian, wiped his brow. "We have thrown a propeller blade and it has cut into the hull. We are making water."

"You are a lying bastard," Berkeley told him. "Had we thrown a propellor blade, the engine would have half shaken itself to pieces, not just stopped."

"I tell you we are making water. If you do not believe me, come down and see for yourself."

"You can forget that idea as well," Berkeley told him. "I recommend you get the pumps working, shut that seacock, and restart your engine."

"We are sinking," Joseph declared. "The pumps are broken. We must abandon ship."

Presuming they *were* prepared to sacrifice the ship, it was such a simple plan. And so effective. If the passengers were to enter the lifeboat with the crew, at such close quarters they could very easily be overpowered and murdered. At the same time, none of them could risk running the gauntlet of the entire crew by going down to the engine room to close the cocks themselves.

"I will give the command to break out the boat," Lukeman volunteered.

"No one is launching the boat," Berkeley told him. "If the ship goes down, then we all go down. You'd better tell this fellow to go turn off that seacock."

Lukeman and Joseph exchanged glances, then they and the helmsman acted together. Joseph charged Lockwood, Lukeman went for Berkeley, and the helmsman dived at Caterina. As they did so, the rest of the crew, led by Arnold, who had been crouching in the darkness at the foot of the ladder, came swarming up.

But they had no idea with whom they were dealing. Lockwood fired his shotgun, and Joseph screamed as he arched backwards, his chest blasted into flying red. Caterina also fired without hesitation, and the helmsman tumbled back, shot through the head. Berkeley had also fired, and the captain went down, but from his curses he was only wounded.

The other crewmen came to the head of the ladder, but they could only do so one at a time, and Lockwood fired the second barrel of his shotgun to send Arnold screaming back down, taking several men with him. Lockwood felt in his jacket pocket and reloaded, moving back to the top of the ladder.

"Cease firing," Berkeley commanded. "Are you all right, Caterina?"

She was panting, and he realised that for all his plans, she had still killed a man.

"You are murderers," Lukeman shrieked. "Murderers."

"You had better hope we are not," Berkeley said.

"There's a bit of a list, sir," Lockwood shouted. "Think those people have any fight left in them?"

"I would say so. Lukeman, if you want to live, tell your people to shut down that seacock."

"I am bleeding to death," Lukeman complained. "You have broken my bones."

"Give the order, and we'll look after you."

"They will not obey me now."

"Have a go," Berkeley recommended. "Caterina, have a hunt in the cabin and see if you can find some first-aid kit."

Lukeman dragged himself to the rail and began shouting, presumably in Arabic. Someone shouted back out of the darkness.

"They're launching the boat, sir," Lockwood said. "Shall I fire into them?"

Berkeley sighed. The sailors were unarmed, they were terrified, and they were not posing a threat. "Let them go," he said.

"They are leaving me here," Lukeman complained.

"You're safer with us," Berkeley told him. "Besides, you're going to gaol. With them, when they're picked up."

The boat splashed into the water and the men swarmed down the sides of the steamer, each carrying a bundle of belongings.

Caterina returned from the cabin. "I can find nothing."

"We'll have to use the sheets from the bunk. He's bleeding pretty heavily."

Lukeman had again subsided down the rail and was lying against it, groaning.

"Are they away, Harry?" Berkeley asked.

"Well away, sir."

"Right. Come here, tear up the those sheets and bind up the captain. But keep an eye out, and if those fellows try to come back, then you fire into them."

"Yes, sir."

The ship was now definitely taking on a list. Berkeley slid down the ladder, ran along the deck to the engine room hatch. This was open, and from below there came an ominous swish of rising water. It was utterly dark down here, and although he found the light switches and threw them, all that happened was a faint fizzling sound as the fuses went.

As he had absolutely no idea where the seacocks were situated, even if he could get to them beneath the already considerable amount of water in the hull, it was clear that the ship was going to founder. And fairly soon.

He went on deck and had to hold on against the increasing slope. There had only been one boat, but on the upper deck there was a wooden slatted life-raft. It would have to do.

He climbed the ladder to the bridge. Caterina and Lockwood had between them bound up the captain, and he seemed to have fainted.

"There's a couple of ribs broken, I'd say, sir," Lockwood remarked.

"Well, he'll have to suffer. We have to get off this ship before she goes down."

Between them, he and Lockwood lifted the captain down the ladder and to the lower deck. Caterina followed, hanging on to the rail as the ship went ever further over. Berkeley climbed back up to the life-raft, and secured a retaining line which he passed back down to Lockwood. Then he cut the raft free.

It slid over the side and went into the water with a splash, but Lockwood had made the line fast and it was a simple matter to pull it back to the side of the ship, although it rose and fell on the still considerable swell. The rail was now close to the water, and there were considerable groanings and creakings from the ancient hull.

Berkeley ran up to their cabins, secured the carpet-bags and suitcases and handed them down to be placed on the raft; it was about twelve feet long and six wide, so there was sufficient room. Then came the difficult bit, getting Lukeman over the side. He came to, screaming in agony, but Berkeley and Lockwood got him down and stretched on the wooden slats. Then they handed Caterina down, before following themselves.

They pushed the raft off as hard as they could; but it only travelled a few feet and now the *Wanderer* was settling fast.

"Hold on," Berkeley said, and lay across Caterina, toes and fingers dug into the slats. But actually there was less turbulence than he had anticipated. Two waves rushed at them as the steamer went under, and the raft rocked vigorously while water splashed over them. Then the sea subsided again, utterly silent.

"What do we do now?" Caterina asked.

"We wait," Berkeley told her.

The sun rose out of a cloudless sky, and it was clearly going to be a very hot day. Without water! But as Berkeley had anticipated, when he rose to his knees to look west, he could see land on the horizon. That had to be Malta's sister island, Gozo. And where there was land there would surely be fishing boats, hopefully sooner than later.

Unfortunately, when he looked to the east he could make out the lifeboat, slowly approaching them, water glistening as it flicked from the oars.

"I am dying," Lukeman groaned. "Dying. Water! I must have water."

"You'll have to wait a while," Berkeley told him.

"They will have water on the lifeboat," Lukeman said.

"I'm not having them alongside," Berkeley said. He cupped his hands and shouted, "Keep away."

The lifeboat kept on approaching, so he drew his pistol and fired into the air. That checked them. There was a conference on board, but the oars had stopped pulling. They remained perhaps fifty yards away, rising and falling on the swell.

"I will die without water," Lukeman begged.

"Ah, shut up," Lockwood said. "Or I'll bat you one."

Caterina moved, slowly and painfully, to sit up. "I am thirsty, too."

"We all are."

"All this water . . . can we not drink it?"

"It's not recommended. This water is salt, you see. It will only make you thirstier."

She regarded the sea for some minutes. He had been impressed with her serenity at their first meeting, and again with the way she had accepted her mother's death. He was again now. She was in an utterly strange environment, in grave danger of her life, yet she seemed more curious than apprehensive.

"Are we going to die?" she asked.

"It is not my intention that we should."

She looked up at him. She was so beautiful, even with her hair scattered and undressed, her clothes torn and disordered.

"I love you," he said. "I ask your forgiveness for everything that I have done. I did it out of love for you."

"I know," she said. "I think you are an honourable man, Berkeley Townsend. Mother thought so too. If we do not die, I shall be pleased to be your wife."

"But you still intend to fight the Austrians, and avenge your parents."

"Of course," she said. "We will do it together." She smiled. "After I have seen your home."

She had an agenda all mapped out. It would be up to him to change it. But he knew he would have to go very carefully. Survival was the first requisite.

And there it was.

"I see a ship," Lockwood said, waving his arms.

The Flight

"I suspect you are really quite the most amazing scoundrel in the whole history of the British army," General Gorman remarked.

"I was given a mission, sir, and that mission has been carried out."

"*You* did not carry it out."

"No, sir. I did as I was instructed and infiltrated my way into Madame Slovitza's home. But before I could implement my plans for conveying her to the Hungarian border she went off by herself, with some companions, and got herself shot."

"You are aware that she was robbing an Austrian army payroll when this happened?"

"I have heard rumours, sir."

"I see. There is no chance you went along on this raid? The Austrians seem to have the idea that there might have been a foreign national involved."

"I was honeymooning at the time, sir."

"I see. That is another matter that disturbs me: you were sent to arrest Madame Slovitza, yet according to your report, you managed to marry her daughter."

"Well, sir, I had very little choice in the matter. It was Madame Slovitza's wish."

"I am sure she had a reason."

"Yes, sir, she did."

"You have got to be the most ruthless, amoral rascal who ever walked the face of this earth."

"Yes, sir."

"And now, this business in Malta . . ."

"It was actually off Malta, sir. The crew of the ship in which we were travelling attempted to rob us. We had to defend ourselves."

"In your well-known fashion, by shooting several of them."

"It was their lives or ours, sir."

"You understand that the Maltese authorities will require you to return there to give evidence at the trial of this Captain Lukeman, and his people?"

"Yes, sir."

"Now, this young woman . . ."

"Happens to be my wife, sir."

"I appreciate that. And I can believe that your marriage took place at the end of a shotgun. However, it took place without any permission from your commanding officer."

"I am applying for that permission now, sir. There really wasn't time to do so before."

Gorman stroked his chin. "You do not think, in all the circumstances, that it would have been better just to leave her in Serbia?"

"I'm afraid I could not consider that, sir."

"You're not pretending that you have fallen in love with her? Or is she pregnant?"

"I do not know if she is pregnant or not, sir. But I have fallen in love with her, yes. That is not the point, however. I went to Serbia to destroy her mother. Whether I actually caused it to happen or not, Madame Slovitza is now dead. Had I abandoned Caterina, she would merely have taken over where her mother left off, and no doubt come to the same end. I could not allow that."

"An honourable rascal," Gorman remarked, sceptically. "And where is the young lady now?"

"At the Hotel Cecil, sir, where I have taken a room."

"At your own expense, I hope. Well, I suppose I should congratulate you, not only on succeeding in your mission, however deviously, but, as usual, having fallen on your feet. Very good, Captain Townsend. I will put it to the Austrians that you completed your mission, if in a back-handed manner, and hope that we will hear nothing more of the matter. I will also give permission for your marriage. You are entitled to some leave. Take it and honeymoon. Spend it at your home. I will contact you when next we have an assignment for you. Failing that, return to London at the beginning of November and resume your duties at the War Office. Understood?"

"Yes, sir."

Berkeley remained standing before the desk.

Gorman looked up. "Was there something else?"

"The matter of my promotion, sir."

"Hm. Yes. I will have to take that under consideration. Much will depend upon if we can bury this business. Good day to you."

"As you said, it is all flat," Caterina commented, as the train made its way north. She had shown no interest in Berkeley's visit to the War Office, or the outcome of his meeting with General Gorman. She appeared to think that he operated entirely on his own.

"What did you think of London?" he asked.

"So big, so noisy, so many people . . . and those machines!"

"They call them automobiles, and they're all the rage."

"Do you have one?"

"Ah, no. A bit beyond my pocket. Anyway, I prefer a horse."

"Are we rich, or poor?"

"We're a bit of neither." He hadn't told her he still had a large part of her mother's money in his satchel.

"Mother was always rich."

"She always seemed rich, certainly. But actually, when she needed money, she simply went out and stole it."

"Only from the Austrians."

"Absolutely. A real female Robin Hood."

"Who was Robin Hood?"

"An English folk hero who only robbed the villains. So they say. You know, you could become a wealthy woman in your own right, if you were to sell the house in Sabac. It is yours, isn't it?"

"Of course it is mine. But how can I sell it? We will need it to live in when we go back."

Not a subject to pursue at this moment. Besides, there were more important matters rushing at him, at least from his point of view.

Caterina had equally shown no great interest in the society into which she was going, the family into which she was moving; clearly she still regarded this as a transient as well as temporary part of her life. Berkeley, on the other hand had considered at some length the right approach to follow as regards his parents. But he really had had very little choice. He and Caterina had spent two weeks in Malta waiting for a passage to England. He had still, technically, been under War Office orders, which meant letting no one know where he was or what he was doing. The voyage home had taken another week, but he had still been under orders to contact no one until he had been to the War Office. Then they had spent the last two days in London while he had been waiting to see Gorman. He could have written to his mother and father from the Hotel Cecil, but he supposed he would have got home about the same time as the letter.

And how could he possibly explain what had happened in a letter, again without betraying trade secrets, as it were?

He looked across the compartment at his wife. She was wearing some of the clothes she had bought in Athens: a white dress with a matching broad-brimmed hat. She looked an utter delight. But . . .

"You understand," he said, "that my parents must not know the truth of it."

She frowned at him.

"I mean that your mother was engaged in anarchism, that she killed people."

"There was nothing dishonourable in anything Mother did," Caterina riposted. "She was fighting for her people, and to avenge her husband. Anyway, you helped her."

"Yes. The point is that people in England regard anarchists, regardless of their reasons or their cause, as criminals."

"They regard you as a criminal?"

"No, because they do not know of it. Nor can they."

She considered this. "What will you tell them?"

"As much of the truth as is practical. They think I was sent to Greece to buy remounts for the British cavalry. I will tell them that while I was doing this, I met your mother and yourself, and that when your mother died, I married you."

"Out of pity."

"Of course not out of pity. I married you because you are the most beautiful, the most delightful, the most enchanting woman I have ever known."

He was surprised to realise he had been actually telling the truth. Certainly Caterina was pleased.

"You say the sweetest things. Will they think that of me, too?"

"Yes. Providing they do not find out about your mother. Or your father," he added.

"You are asking me to live a lie."

"I am asking you to give my parents the opportunity to love you as I do. Then it may be possible to tell them the truth at a later date."

"Very well," she said, "if that is what you wish."

He could read her mind; from her perspective it could only be a temporary measure, in any event.

"Will they be at the station to meet us?" she asked.

"No."

She raised her eyebrows.

"They do not know we are coming."

She gazed at him.

"There simply hasn't been time to let them know," he said. "And these things are difficult to explain, by letter."

"It will be more difficult for them, when I just appear."

"I hope it won't be. But there is something else."

Her eyes were watchful; she was being given rather a lot to think about at short notice.

"My parents do not speak German. You will have to do the best you can with English."

He had continued to teach her on the voyage home from Malta, and she could string one or two sentences together.

"It will be amusing," she said.

Berkeley hoped she was right.

There was a trap for hire at the station, and Lockwood loaded the bags while Berkeley and Caterina seated themselves. Lockwood sat beside the driver, and they trotted out of the town. It was a crisp, early October day. It had rained recently and there was a fresh northerly wind.

"It is so cold," Caterina remarked.

"Doesn't it get cold in Serbia?" Berkeley asked.

"Of course it does. But it is a different kind of cold. This gets into the bones."

He put his arm round her shoulders. The village was only a few miles from the town and the drive took them less than an hour. Then they were turning into the short front drive of the Townsend house. Dogs barked and people emerged.

"Mr Berkeley," said Trant the butler. "Welcome home."

He looked at Caterina uncertainly.

"This is Mrs Townsend," Berkeley explained.

"Good heavens. Welcome, madam."

Caterina looked just as uncertain, unsure whether to curtsey or give him her hand to kiss.

Trant held the front door open for them. "Shall I announce you, sir? I'm afraid Mr Townsend is out, but madam is in the conservatory."

"We'll announce ourselves," Berkeley said. "Perhaps you'd give Harry a hand with the bags." He held Caterina's arm to escort her into the house.

"I am nervous," she confessed.

"Don't be. No one is going to harm you."

They walked through the drawing room, Caterina looking left and right with interest, and emerged into the glass-fronted conservatory. Alicia Townsend was seated with her back to them, doing some needlework. "Who was it at the door, Trant?" she asked without looking up.

"Me," Berkeley said.

"Berkeley!" She put down her sewing and stood up, turning in the same moment. "Oh, you're back for Christmas. I am so glad." Then she stared at Caterina with her mouth open.

"This is Caterina," Berkeley explained.

"Caterina," Alicia said, slowly.

"I am so 'appy . . . to . . ." Caterina glanced at Berkeley.

"Meet you," Berkeley prompted.

"Meet you," Caterina said.

"I'm afraid her English isn't all that good," Berkeley explained. "But she's learning."

"Ah . . ." Alicia looked from one to the other.

"She's my wife," Berkeley said.

"Your . . . Good Lord!"

"You do not like me?" Caterina asked, watching her mother-in-law's expression.

"Ah . . ." Alicia looked at her son again.

"She's just a little surprised," Berkeley said in German, and then reverted to English. "Ah, Trant. Is there any champagne on ice?"

"There is champagne, sir," Trant said. "It will be cool."

"Then let's have a bottle. Now, come and sit down, Caterina. You too, Mother." He seated them on the settee, with himself in the middle. Alicia continued to look utterly scandalised, Caterina apprehensive. "We met in the Balkans, you see, and fell in love; and married."

Alicia opened her mouth and then shut it again. "You've only been gone two months."

"Yes, I know. It all happened rather quickly."

"But couldn't you have let us know?"

"There were no telegraph offices in the vicinity. And well . . . her mother died, you see, and there was a lot to do."

Alicia digested this. "Her mother died . . . before or after the wedding? I mean, you *are* married?"

"Of course we're married, Mother. I'll show you the certificate. It was an Orthodox ceremony."

"But you're Church of England."

"I know, but it was the only way to do it. I thought we could have a Protestant ceremony here. Caterina would like that." He squeezed her hand, as she was looking more and more uncertain as she tried to follow the conversation.

"What people will say . . ." Alicia muttered.

"People can say what they like," Berkeley said. "Caterina is my wife, and there is an end to it. Ah, Trant! Good man."

The butler presented a tray with three full glasses.

Berkeley raised his. "Here's to Caterina."

Caterina drank, and after a moment, Alicia did also.

"I hear Mr Townsend," Trant said.

Alicia gave a sigh of relief.

All the explanations had to be gone through again. John Townsend, having an eye for beauty like his son, was less flabbergasted than his wife. At least by Caterina; the event remained startling.

He took Caterina in his arms for a hug and a kiss, looking at his wife over her shoulder while Caterina looked at Berkeley.

"There'll have to be an announcement," John said. "We'll have to throw a party."

"Do you think that's necessary?" Berkeley asked.

"It would be nice to 'ave a party," Caterina said.

"I think it should wait until after you have been, well, properly married," Alicia suggested.

Caterina looked at Berkeley, having caught only the gist of what had been said.

"We are not married?" she asked in German.

"Of course we are, my darling. But not under English law. We should do it again. Would you not like to do it again?"

"Oh, yes," she said.

The parents were waiting, anxiously.

"How soon can we have the ceremony?" Berkeley asked.

"Well, there'll have to be banns . . ."

"Can't we get a special licence?"

"Well, we could. But it'll be expensive. And it'll take at least three weeks to organise the reception."

"I only have a month's leave," Berkeley pointed out. "So we had better start now."

"Yes, of course," Alicia said. "Now, lunch . . ."

"Wash 'ands," Caterina said. "And face."

"Oh, good heavens," Alicia said. "You poor dear. And I haven't even showed you to your room. Do come along." She went to the door, and there checked, to look at Berkeley. "You . . . ah . . ."

"Of course we are going to share a room, Mother. We're married."

"It will have to be the spare bedroom. Yours only has a single bed."

"Then the spare bedroom it will be. Shall I come up with you?"

"I think we should have a chat," his father said.

Caterina was looking from face to face, anxiously.

"You go up with my mother," Berkeley said. "I'll be with you in a little while, and we'll sort things out."

The two men waited until the women had disappeared, then John Townsend refilled their glasses.

"Quite a beauty."

"I think so."

"But not, hopefully, only skin deep."

"No."

"Two months," John Townsend said, sitting down. "A truly whirlwind romance. Love at first sight, and that sort of thing."

Berkeley also sat. "Something like that."

"I don't suppose you'd care to tell me the truth of it?"

Berkeley considered. His father was a shrewd man. "You know most of it."

"Tell me what I don't know."

"It's not very flattering to me. Well, I had to stop for the night in this village, at a house owned by Caterina's mother. She wasn't there at the time. One thing led to another, and Caterina and I were caught *in flagrante delicto* when the mother returned the following morning. I told you it wasn't a very pretty tale."

"It's also not a very truthful one," John suggested.

Berkeley shot his father a look.

"Oh, I don't want to pry into your military affairs, Berkeley," John said. "But when you produce a wife like a conjuror with a top hat, I think I am entitled to probe just a little. Frankly, Caterina doesn't look the sort of girl who would climb into bed with a complete stranger on the occasion of their first meeting. And if she were, then she would hardly be a suitable wife for my son."

Berkeley had no desire to quarrel with his father; the two were friends. "Well," he said, "that is actually what happened. Save that I wasn't a complete stranger. I met Madame Slovitza some time ago."

"Madame Slovitza being Caterina's mother."

Berkeley nodded.

"Now deceased."

"I'm afraid so."

"And you met her some time ago. Presumably in Hungary, or somewhere central."

"Yes," Berkeley said. "I was able to do her a favour, and she said if I was ever in her part of the world to look her up. This I did, and met Caterina. So we were not actually strangers, although we had never met. Her mother had told her a great deal about me."

"It must all have been very good," John remarked, drily. "But just let me get this straight. You met the mother in Hungary; you visited her in . . . Thrace?"

"Yes."

"And going by her name, she is Serbian."

"Yes. Well, the populations in the Balkans are apt to be a little mixed up."

"I can imagine. So, Madame Slovitza found you in bed with her beautiful daughter, and reached for her shotgun."

"It wasn't quite like that."

"Of course it wasn't. You felt obliged to do the decent thing because Madame Slovitza was dying? She must have been dying, and quite obviously, as she did so a few days later."

"Ah . . . yes," Berkeley said. "She had been ill for some time." Which he felt was not all that much of a lie, when referring to a woman who had risked her life almost on a daily basis for several years. "And, well, you see, Caterina had no one left. Her father died

117

some years ago. Don't get me wrong; it really was love at first sight, Dad. I think I would have married her anyway, all things being equal, but of course after a decent courtship. As it happened . . ."

"All things weren't equal. Well, I would say you came out of it with considerable credit. Does she love you? Or does she just regard you as her saviour? She's quite a lot younger than you, isn't she?"

"Twelve years or so. I don't think that has anything to do with it. I believe she loves me. She gives every indication of it."

"If that is so, it would make me very happy," John said. "Believe me, your mother and I shall welcome your wife as if she were our own daughter, if she will accept that."

"I shall encourage her to do so," Berkeley said.

"Excellent. Now, there is just one other matter." He gazed at his son.

"Yes," Berkeley said.

"Was there an understanding between you and Julia?"

"There was no formal engagement," Berkeley said. "I asked her to marry me, certainly, and she put me off."

"But as I remember you told me before leaving for Greece, she didn't actually refuse you."

"She suggested I ask her again when I returned."

"Exactly. I'm afraid she seems to have regarded that as an understanding. She has been visiting here regularly. Her demeanour is that of someone soon to become part of the family. My impression is that she has made up her mind that, when you returned and asked her again, she would say yes."

Berkeley stroked his chin.

"Bit awkward," John said.

"She cannot have it both ways," Berkeley protested. "She told me to ask her again. There was no agreement that I should not ask someone else in the interim."

"I suspect she took that as read. It's a damned tricky business, particularly in your profession. Remember the Duke of Wellington? He proposed marriage to Kitty Pakenham when he was a very junior officer, and she turned him down because he did not appear to have any prospects. When he returned from India a famous soldier and a general, she reminded him that he had once proposed, and he felt obliged to marry her."

"The Duke of Wellington," Berkeley said, "has a great deal to answer for. And that was over a hundred years ago. Times change."

"Not for an officer and a gentleman. He set a precedent."

"Well, Dad, there is damn all I can do about it now."

"I still think you need to do the decent thing."

"Which would be?"

"You must go and see Julia, and explain the situation to her before we publicise it."

"I think I'd prefer to write her a letter."

John shook his head. "It needs to be done personally. If you are an officer and a gentleman." The two men gazed at each other. "As you have proved in the case of Caterina," John added, gently.

"Where are you going?" Caterina said after lunch, as Berkeley pulled on his riding boots.

"There is someone I must see."

"Can I not come with you?"

"Not this time, darling."

She hugged herself. "You are leaving me all alone, in a strange house, with strange people . . ."

"Your mother and father-in-law, who are prepared to take you into the family and love you like their own, if you will give them the chance."

She pouted. "I wish to be with you."

"And you will be, always, just as soon as I have paid this visit."

"I would like my gun back."

"Now don't be ridiculous, Caterina. Young ladies don't carry guns."

"Suppose I need it?"

"You won't. This is England, not the Balkans. We don't have anarchists in England. Nor do we have secret police or armies rushing about killing people. This is the safest place in the whole world. Please believe that."

She sat on the bed, her hands on her knees. "It is so strange."

He sat beside her, put his arm round her. "You'll get used to it. Then you'll enjoy it."

As usual, he could only hope he was right. But now . . . He braced himself as he walked his horse down the road towards the Gracey Farm. He had absolutely no idea what to expect, but he knew he'd rather be facing an Austrian cavalry patrol than the coming ordeal. So, shoulders back, chin out, and take what was coming like a man. He supposed it was all really a matter of interpretations. He did not think he was under any obligation to Julia. He could only hope she would accept that point of view.

But he drew rein within sight of the farm, to compose himself. He really was very anxious. He looked left and right, but at the beginning of October the harvest seemed to have been completed; the fields were empty of men as much as wheat. Then he looked up the slight slope at the main road, and frowned. A horseman stood there, man and beast motionless, gazing at him. The man was too far away to be identified, but there could be no doubt that *he* knew who he was watching.

Berkeley frowned. It was quite absurd to suppose there could be anything sinister about a lone horseman in central Northamptonshire in utterly peaceful England. Yet it made him uneasy.

However, there was nothing to be done about it at the moment; he had more important matters to deal with. He approached the house. As usual, the dogs gave the first warning of his approach; they brought out the groom to hold his bridle as he dismounted.

"It's Mr Berkeley," a housemaid called, and a moment later Julia emerged from the front door, cheeks pink, hair loose.

"Berkeley!"

She came towards him, both arms outstretched. He caught her hands and kissed them; she subsided, slowly, a faint frown between her eyes.

"We were wondering what had happened to you."

"It's a long story." He looked past her at her mother and father, all smiles.

"Welcome home, Berkeley," Paul Gracey said. "Good to see you."

"Did you have a successful trip?" Joan Gracey asked.

"On the whole, yes," Berkeley said.

They escorted him inside, and he was offered some tea.

"I think Julia and I need to have a talk," he suggested.

"Of course you do," Joan agreed.

Berkeley looked at Julia, who moved to the garden door.

"I've a bottle of champagne," Paul Gracey whispered to Berkeley. "Just give me a signal, and you'll hear the cork pop."

"Ah . . . yes," Berkeley said, and followed Julia into the garden.

She had not bothered to put on a hat, and was walking slowly towards the bench by the orchard. "Did you find lots of fine horses?" she asked over her shoulder.

"Not really."

She stopped and turned, then went on to the bench and sat down, her hands in her lap.

Berkeley sat beside her.

Julia waited for several seconds, then she said, "You've something on your mind."

"I'm nervous as hell," he said.

She turned her head. "You, Berkeley? You weren't nervous last August."

"That was different."

"I'm afraid I don't understand."

120

Berkeley drew a deep breath. "Something has happened, since last August."

She raised her eyebrows, but didn't speak.

"I . . . I have got married," he said.

The frown was back, far deeper than before, as was the pink in her cheeks.

"I felt I had to come and tell you," he said. "The moment I got home. That was this morning."

"Did you think I would be interested?" Her voice was cold.

"Ah . . . probably not. But you see, the announcement of the wedding will be in the newspapers in a couple of days' time, and I didn't want you to read about it there. I mean . . ." He was flushing. "I felt I had to tell you in person."

"That was very good of you. Very gentlemanly." She used the word as if indicating it was probably the only gentlemanly thing he had ever done. "Is your wife from around Northampton? Perhaps I know her."

"You do not know her. My wife is Serbian. Well, half-Serbian and half-Bosnian."

Her mouth opened a little, then closed again. "One of your purchases, perhaps."

He felt that really deserved a slap on the cheek, but he had done enough damage. He stood up. "I had hoped we might remain friends."

"Friends, Captain Townsend? Were we ever friends?"

There were tears in her eyes. Oh, Lord, he thought. "I really must be going."

"Back to your wife." Each word was like a drop of vitriol.

But now he was angry; he had done his best to be civilised. "Yes," he said. "Back to my wife. I'll bid you good afternoon, Miss Gracey."

He went up to the house, leaving her sitting on the bench.

Paul Gracey was waiting by the door. "Overcome, is she? Women are like that. I'll pop that cork, and you can take a glass down to her."

"I'm afraid Julia and I are not going to be married, sir," Berkeley said.

"Good God! Not get married? But it was settled long ago. Wasn't it?"

"No," Berkeley said.

"But . . . you're not going to tell us she turned you down?" Joan Gracey asked from the back of the room.

"No, she did not, Mrs Gracey. I came here this afternoon to inform Julia that I am now married."

There was a moment of utter silence. Then Paul Gracey said, "Good God!"

"You'll leave, sir. Now," Joan Gracey said, and hurried out of the door to be with her daughter.

"I'm sorry about this, Mr Gracey," Berkeley said.

"Good God!" Gracey said again. "I suppose you'd better go."

"Yes, sir." He started to hold out his hand, then changed his mind. "Good afternoon."

He had to wait for several minutes while his horse was brought from the stable; the groom had not expected him to be departing so suddenly. He mounted and walked the animal out of the yard and up the road. At least the mysterious figure had disappeared.

He had not yet reached the high road when he felt an enormous impact.

Berkeley did not immediately lose consciousness. He was aware of hitting the ground with a very heavy thud, which left him breathless. There was no other pain at the moment, but he knew he had been shot.

Vaguely he heard shouts and the sound of running feet. Then he did slide into oblivion, unsure whether or not he was dying. But when his eyes opened again he was in a bed, and now the pain was severe.

Faces peered at him. Joan Gracey. Paul. A maid. And Julia, hovering, features contorted with fear and horror.

"His eyes are open! He's alive!" Paul exclaimed. He bent over the bed. "We've sent for the doctor. And your parents."

"And your wife," Joan said.

Berkeley opened his mouth, and it closed again of its own accord before he could speak. The whole lower half of his body seemed gripped in a vice of pain.

"Laudanum," Julia said. "He must be given laudanum."

The morphine mixture was brought and he was fed a little. Then he fainted again.

More familiar faces: his mother and father, and Caterina, weeping as she held his hand. And of course Harry Lockwood, looking more concerned than Berkeley could ever remember. The Graceys had faded to the back of the room. And Dr Cheam, who he had known all of his life. The doctor's face was severe but composed, and Berkeley felt a little more in control of himself. He gathered he had been tightly bandaged.

"Two ribs," Cheam said. "You're a lucky fellow, Berkeley. That bullet was meant for your heart."

"Always aim for the head, if you can," Berkeley muttered, attempting a smile.

"Oh, Berkeley, my darling," Caterina said in German. "Who could have done this?"

"I think we need to find that out."

"You said things like this did not happen in England."

"It seems I was wrong."

"How soon can he be moved?" John Townsend asked.

"I have sent for an ambulance."

"We take him home?" Caterina asked.

"He must go to hospital first," Cheam insisted. "He needs more care than I have been able to give him here, and he needs a transfusion. He has lost a lot of blood."

They heard the sound of hooves on the drive.

"It's here," Cheam said, with some satisfaction. "Now, please, my people will move him."

"He not die, doctor?" Caterina begged. "Like my mother."

The slip for the moment went unnoticed.

"He's not going to die, Mrs Townsend," Cheam said.

Berkeley turned his head to look from Caterina to Julia. One stood on either side of the bed, and they were looking at each other. For the first time he realised that he had been undressed. He wondered who had done that.

"I'm sure he's not going to die, Mrs Townsend," Julia said.

Berkeley was exhausted: that was partly loss of blood and partly the various sedatives with which he was being fed.

"Aspirin," he muttered. "Why don't you try aspirin?" The latest wonder drug.

The pain continued to be intense.

"I don't think aspirin is going to be too much use in this case," Cheam said.

"Now, how do you feel?"

It was the next day.

"Bloody," Berkeley said.

"Are you up to answering some questions? Inspector Watt is here."

"I suppose I'll have to," Berkeley said, trying desperately to think. The would-be assassin had to be from the Balkans, but from which side of the fence? He did not think it could be the Austrians. Even if they had managed to work out that Mr Jones and Mr Smith were one and the same man, and that both were really Berkeley Townsend, surely they would go through the proper channels to have him arrested, as they had in the summer, rather than just attempt to have him murdered? No, it had to have been a member of the Black Hand. As far as Gregory Masanovich was concerned, Berkeley had not only deserted the organisation, but had also kidnapped Anna Slovitza's daughter; which made him both a traitor and a criminal.

And he was absolutely right on both counts.

"Well, now, Captain Townsend, here's a rum do." Inspector Watt was rotund and red-faced, and breathed heavily.

"I'm afraid it is," Berkeley agreed.

"I mean to say, shooting at people on the high road. We don't have that kind of thing up here."

"Do you have any idea who it was?"

"I was going to ask you that, sir."

"Isn't there any evidence at the scene?"

"Well, sir, we hunted around. There was a horse there, for sure. And we found a spent cartridge."

"Well, that's something, isn't it?"

"A rifle cartridge, sir. Three-o-three. It was a powerful weapon."

"I'm aware of that, Inspector."

"Indeed, sir. Well, that is a military weapon."

"Yes."

Watt waited. Then he asked, "Does that give you any idea who it might have been, sir?"

"English soldiers do not usually go around shooting at their officers, Inspector. You say you found horse's tracks. Couldn't they be followed?"

"Not on the road, sir. It's been pretty dry. What we found was sufficient manure to make it seem likely a horse had stood in those trees for some time. But we have found the horse, sir."

"Oh, good man. Why didn't you tell me that before?"

"Well, sir, it ain't going to do us all that much good. The horse was found at the railway station at Weedon Beck, just this side of the canal. That's just about four miles away from the Gracey Farm. It had just been tethered and abandoned. The assassin caught the train there."

"How do you know? How do you know it was his horse?"

"Well, it seems likely, sir. It had been hired at a livery stable in Northampton that very morning by a foreign-looking gentleman. And it was a foreign-looking gentleman boarded the train at Weedon Beck, for London."

"Did you have the train met?"

"I sent a telegram, sir. But by the time I did that the train had reached London. The horse wasn't reported to us until yesterday evening, you see, sir, when the stationmaster realised the animal was still there, untended. Then he felt he should get in touch with the stable first, seeing as how it was one of theirs, and, well . . . it took time."

"So our foreign-looking gentleman had already disappeared," Berkeley said.

"I'm afraid so, sir. I've been in touch with Scotland Yard, and they say they will keep an eye out for him. The Channel ports are being watched. But, well . . . foreign gentlemen come and go."

"Indeed they do," Berkeley agreed.

"And we've no proper description to go on. Unless you can help." He paused hopefully.

"Well, I can't," Berkeley said.

"I suppose there is no chance it wasn't the foreign-looking gentlemen, sir?"

Berkeley knew what the policeman was after; an outraged husband, perhaps? Berkeley was a handsome young man.

"The theory is yours, Inspector."

"Oh, yes. Quite. Well, we'll keep looking. Good day to you, sir."

The family came to see him.

"I wonder if I could have a moment alone with Caterina," Berkeley requested.

His parents dutifully filed out, followed by Lockwood.

"Your friend Gregory appears to bear grudges," Berkeley said.

Caterina sat beside him. "I have thought this too. We should go back."

"If and when I go back to Serbia, the first thing I am going to do is put as much lead into him as he has had put into me."

Her face seemed to close.

"However, as that is unlikely to happen for some time," Berkeley went on, "we have to decide what to do next. When he discovers I am not dead, do you think he will try again?"

"I will write him a letter, and tell him not to," Caterina volunteered.

"Do you honestly suppose a letter from you will have any effect?"

"Well, he obviously supposes you kidnapped me. You did kidnap me. If I write him and tell him that we are reconciled, and that I am perfectly happy . . ."

"Darling," Berkeley said, "you have got hold of entirely the wrong end of the stick. I do not think Gregory has the slightest interest in your marital affairs, whether you are happy or not, I suspect even whether you are alive or not. What is on his mind is that I know too much about the Black Hand, about how it works, about who many of its members are. I know who *he* is, for God's sake."

"Then what are we to do? Now you *must* give me back my gun."

"It's not you he's after. But I might just do that."

"England," she said. "Ha! Where there are no anarchists."

"I was thinking of the home-grown variety. Still, maybe they'll catch this one."

"Oh," she said. "I hope—" She bit her lip.

"You hope they don't, because he's likely to be a friend of yours. Maybe one of Karlovy's people. Maybe Karlovy himself."

"He did not kill you," she said sulkily.

"He certainly tried," Berkeley said, and squeezed her hand. "Just stay happy, my dearest girl."

She kissed him, but there was no warmth in it.

Berkeley could understand that it was a moment of supreme crisis for her. The people she had left behind in Serbia were her friends and even relations; she had grown up among them, shared their heritage, their ideals and their determination never to be ruled by Austria. Additionally, she had the deaths of her parents to avenge.

He had taken her away from all that, and although he had a hopeful suspicion that she was actually relieved to be out of the Balkan maelstrom, she undoubtedly felt guilty at having abandoned her roots and had not yet become reconciled to the possible permanency of that. And now those roots had risen up to remind her, most forcibly, where she belonged.

At the cost of her husband? There was a battle going on in her mind, a battle he was sure he could win, given the opportunity. But he was stuck here in this bed. He began to fret, so much so that Cheam became a little anxious.

"You're running a temperature," he said. "There's no reason for it. I'm sure the police will catch the blighter. Now, I feel you shouldn't have any visitors apart from family at this moment, but there's an officer from the War Office demanding to see you. Shall I send him away?"

"One doesn't send away officers from the War Office, doctor. If one is a soldier."

"Major Toby Smailes." The man was short and slim, but wore a large moustache.

"Sir."

"What exactly happened here?"

"I was shot."

"Here?"

"Not in this hospital, no, sir. On the road."

"I meant here in Northamptonshire. People don't get shot in Northamptonshire."

"It's rare," Berkeley agreed.

"Have you been fooling around?"

"Obviously you haven't met my wife, sir."

"Then it's to do with this Serbian business, eh?"

Berkeley gazed at him.

"Oh, I'm in General Gorman's confidence," Smailes said.

"Then I would say it's to do with this Serbian business."

"An Austrian agent, eh?"

"I wouldn't know, sir. He is described as a foreign-looking gentleman. Around here that could mean a Scotsman."

"Very amusing," Smailes observed. "But it is not amusing at all. We cannot have our officers being shot at. And hit!"

"Yes, sir."

"How long do you have to remain in hospital?"

"I'm afraid a couple of weeks, sir. So the doctor says."

"Damnation. The general will not be pleased about that."

Berkeley gained the impression that the general not being pleased would have less to do with his being shot than with his being out of action.

"Has something come up?"

Smailes got up to walk about the room. "Yesterday the Austrians moved into Bosnia-Herzegovina."

Berkeley frowned at him. "That's not possible."

"I'm afraid it's happened. We received a telegram from our man in Sarajevo. He had just watched a regiment of Hungarian cavalry ride past his apartment."

"But . . . the Russians?"

"There seems to have been some sort of agreement between them. Presumably, in return for giving the Austrians a free hand in Bosnia, the Austrians are giving the Russians a free hand somewhere else. It's a damned disturbing business. Could lead to a whole lot of trouble."

Berkeley's brain was whirring. "You say you received the news . . ."

"At dawn today. It'll be in the evening editions in London, and in all the papers tomorrow."

"Shit!" Berkeley muttered.

"The general thought you should know, in view of your connections."

"He's not assuming that Madame Slovitza's death had anything to do with it?"

"Not her death, her raid. That was probably the straw that broke the camel's back. If it gets out that an Englishman was involved, there may well be questions asked. The general feels it would be a

127

good idea for you to take an extended leave of absence from duty, and spend it out of the country."

"I can hear him gnashing his teeth," Berkeley said. "There is also the matter of my wife."

"Your wife?"

"She happens to be Madame Slovitza's daughter. It took me a great deal of time and effort to persuade her to leave Serbia in any event. When she learns that there is to be a shooting war back home . . ."

"Hopefully there won't be."

"The Serbs are going to accept a *fait accompli?*"

"There are a few sabres being rattled, both in the Serbian army and the Serbian parliament, but the Russians, supported by the French and I may say ourselves, are making every effort to persuade them not to declare war. I think we will be successful. Serbia cannot possibly fight Austria-Hungary on her own and hope to win, or even to escape defeat. We have the idea that if they can be persuaded to accept the situation, and Russia guarantees them against any further encroachment of territory by the Austrians, well . . ."

"You'd be sewing the seeds of a future war."

"Possibly. But the situation should hold for a while. I'm sorry about your wife. But you'd do best to keep her out of it as well." He picked up his cap. "I'll report on the situation to the general. Two weeks, you say. We'll try to keep things quiet, as regards you at least, for that time. Then we'll have to see about transferring you to the West Indies, or West Africa, or some place. Good luck, old man."

Good luck, Berkeley thought. But of course it had nothing to do with luck. It was a natural progression of events, given the continued activities of the Black Hand and the refusal of the Serbian government to harness it.

But where did that leave Caterina, and thus himself?

She would have to be told, before she could read it in the papers. He frowned at the ceiling. Of course, she did not read English very well, and she had never shown any interest in the newspapers. But he couldn't chance anyone inadvertently mentioning it to her. No, she would have to be told, by him, today.

She had already paid her daily visit to him. He called the nurse. "I need to see my wife," he said. "Urgently. Can you have a message sent to my parents' house?"

"Well," she said, "I'm not sure. Aren't they on the telephone?"

"No."

"I'll have a word with the doctor, and see what we can do."

She disappeared, and Berkeley was left to continue staring at the ceiling and chafing.

Dr Cheam came in. "Fretting again? That soldier upset you. I should never have let him in."

"He did have to see me," Berkeley said. "Are you sure I have to stay here another two weeks?"

"Absolutely. You have to give time for those bones to knit. And then it's going to be another fortnight at least, convalescing."

"That is absurd," Berkeley said.

"That is, if you ever intend to sit a horse again," Cheam said severely.

Berkeley made a face.

"Now you just have to relax a little," Cheam said, "or I am going to have to give you a sedative. And you are putting back your release from hospital."

By which time, Berkeley thought, Serbia and Austria could be at war. He had no great faith in diplomacy when the issue was an annexation of territory which would leave the Serbs virtually surrounded. He wondered if Anna had really intended to provoke the Austrians into such a reaction. But whether she had or not, all the time she had been carrying out her little pinpricks the Austrian and Russian Governments had been negotiating a diplomatic arrangement of which she had known nothing.

He wondered if Savos had known what was going on.

And where the devil was Caterina?

"Did you send that message?" he asked the nurse.

"Yes I did, Captain Townsend," she said, irked.

"Then why hasn't my wife come to see me?"

"You will have to ask her that, Captain Townsend. When she comes to see you."

He was left to fret. Lunch came and went – he could hardly eat a thing – and it was after six when Lockwood appeared.

"Thank God," Berkeley said. "Harry, I need to have a word with my wife. Urgently."

Lockwood looked thoroughly unhappy.

"Don't tell me; she's heard the news about Bosnia-Herzegovina."

"That is possible, sir."

"And how has she reacted?"

"Well, sir . . ." Lockwood looked even more beset. "She's gone."

Berkeley stared at him, uncomprehending. "Gone? What do you mean?"

"Just that, sir. She's disappeared."

The Offer

"Gone?" Berkeley asked, incredulously. "Disappeared? What the devil are you talking about, Harry? How can she have disappeared?"

"Well, sir, after Mrs Townsend came to visit you this morning, she returned to the house and said that she wished to go into Northampton. I drove her in myself. I was to return to collect her at four o'clock, sir, under the clock tower. Well, I did that, sir, but she wasn't there."

"Let me get this straight," Berkeley said. "You took my wife into Northampton, and left her there? Why didn't you stay with her?"

"Well, sir, she didn't want me to. That was the third time."

"The third time?"

"Yes, sir. Mrs Townsend has been into town twice before, since you were hit. I suggested I stay with her, knowing her English isn't that good, but she sent me home. The arrangement was always the same: the clock-tower at four o'clock. And both the previous times she'd been there. Today she wasn't. And no one had seen her. So I returned home, in case she had caught a lift with someone else, but she hadn't been home either. Mrs Townsend – I mean your mother, sir – went up to your room, and could find nothing. I mean, all Mrs Townsend junior's clothes were there, but she wasn't. Quite agitated your ma and pa were, sir. So they told me to come over here and ask you if you wished them to inform the police."

Berkeley tried to think. "She must be found."

"Well, sir, if she planned to leave, it could have been when I first dropped her in Northampton, at eleven this morning. That's seven hours ago. She could have reached the south coast by now."

Planned to leave, Berkeley thought grimly. Obviously she had been meeting someone almost every day. Someone – his would-be assassin? "She must be traced. It can't be that difficult. She is exceptionally good-looking, and she speaks broken English. Get hold of Inspector Watt and ask him to come and see me."

"Yes, sir," Lockwood said doubtfully.

He went off, leaving Berkeley to some very disturbing reflections.

His father came to see him that night. "This is a terribly upsetting business," John Townsend said.

"That's one way of putting it," Berkeley said.

"Do you suppose Caterina is all right?"

"I would say she is."

"But she's left you. Just like that. Without a word to a soul. I wonder if there are certain things you haven't told me, Berkeley."

Berkeley sighed. "Yes, Dad. There are some things I haven't told you. And I can't tell you now."

"Because they are military secrets?"

"Partly. And partly because it would be safer for you not to know."

"Then you will have to allow me to draw my own conclusions. I don't believe in coincidences. You have just returned from the Balkans, with a most attractive but you'll have to admit somewhat unusual young lady as your wife. On the day you got home you were shot by an unknown man of foreign extraction. A couple of days ago the Austrians occupied Bosnia-Herzegovina. And on the day that news is made public your wife disappears. I'm afraid there can be no doubt in my mind that those four events are linked." He paused, waiting, but when Berkeley did not reply, sighed himself. "What do you intend to do?"

"Get her back."

"In your condition? And she has probably left the country by now."

"I know where she's gone," Berkeley said.

Inspector Watt came to see him the next morning. "Not good news, Captain Townsend," he said. "The young lady boarded the train to London at Northampton Station at noon yesterday; the ticket clerk distinctly remembers her. Well, she's not the sort of young lady one forgets, is she? She would have been in town by about two o'clock. Where she went after that is difficult to say. The Metropolitan Police are cooperating, and we should get a sighting soon."

"Tell them to concentrate on the boat train for Calais or Boulogne," Berkeley said.

But she was gone, gone, gone.

Watt cleared his throat. "There is something else, sir."

"Cheer me up, Inspector."

Watt looked doubtful about that. "Well, sir, when Mrs Townsend bought her ticket, she had a gentleman with her. As a matter of fact it was the gentleman bought the ticket. And one for himself. They boarded the train together."

"Gentleman?"

131

"Well, sir, a man. Foreign-looking. But he spoke good English." The inspector began to look embarrassed. "You don't reckon it was same gentleman, man, who shot you, do you, sir?" He was hopeful.

"I have no idea," Berkeley said.

Because if it was then Caterina had been part of a conspiracy to have her husband murdered, so that she could return to Serbia. But he just couldn't believe that she could have acted her part so convincingly, appearing to be reconciled to him, and her display of grief when he had been hit had surely been genuine. If it had not, he did not suppose he could ever trust a woman again.

"You see, sir," Watt was saying, "it's a little difficult. What the ticket clerk had to say does not give the impression that Mrs Townsend was being coerced in any way. In other words, she was travelling with this gen— ah, man, of her own free will. So, really, unless we have some crime to follow up, we do not have any reason for apprehending them, even supposing we can find them. Especially as they are not even British citizens."

"In my opinion, Inspector, you have every reason for apprehending them," Berkeley said. "The young lady is travelling on a British passport. She is not yet twenty-one. In fact she is not yet twenty. And she happens to be my wife. I am entitled to have her back."

Inspector Watt departed, unhappily, and Berkeley returned to his hopeless reflections. He even attempted to get out of bed and get dressed, but was apprehended by several nurses, and put back. Dr Cheam came in, very angry. "Are you trying to commit suicide?" he demanded.

"Listen," Berkeley said. "My wife has run off."

"That's damned bad luck. But there is nothing you personally can do about it until this wound is healed. And you're doing your damnedest to put this back by several weeks. Now, are you going to behave yourself, or am I going to have to sedate you and put you in a straitjacket?"

Berkeley knew he had to submit. It was the first time in his life that he had been in such a position. When he had been wounded at Omdurman, he had had the comforting knowledge that the battle was won, that Khartoum would fall, that Gordon's murder would be avenged. Heady stuff. And if the wound had taken far longer to heal than he had expected, and he had early been warned that his career as a field officer was finished, he had also been assured that he would remain on the staff. No one had told him then that it would be as a travelling spy, because of his abilities as an observer and a draughtsman; he had just been happy that he could remain a soldier.

Since then, and up until that fateful act of gallantry in Seinheit that summer, life had followed a fairly even course. He did not enjoy being a spy – military observer the War Office called it – but it had been an easy enough occupation. Wealthy English gentlemen were fairly common on the continent; that his habits were somewhat more absurd than the norm had only amused, not concerned the various Austrian, German, Russian, Turkish and even French officials with whom he had come into contact. But all the while the frustration had been growing, without him even being aware of it, to explode in the defence of Anna Slovitza and throw him into a vortex from which there was no certainty he would ever emerge.

Then emerge now, he thought, his brain only half active under the drugs Cheam pumped into him. He had met, wooed, and married the most beautiful girl he had ever seen. Now she was gone. She might even have been responsible for the attempt on his life. Was this not the moment to say, good riddance? She had been called back to the catastrophe that was Balkan politics. He had no part in that. She had cost him dear, for the few precious moments he had held her in his arms, and loved her.

But he *had* loved her. He did love her, there was a problem. And she was his wife. He was still enough of an English officer and a gentleman to feel that was vitally important, that his rights as her husband were vitally important, to his manhood, to his very personality.

And he could do nothing about it, save lie in this bed and feel pain, in his mind as much as his body.

"We've a visitor for you," the ward sister said brightly.

As at least one of his parents, not to mention Lockwood, came to see him every day without such an announcement, he feared the worst. But it was no one from the War Office. Julia Gracey hovered anxiously in the doorway.

"May I come in?" she asked.

"Please do."

He was sufficiently healed now to be propped up in bed.

She advanced, stood beside the bed. "You look awful."

"I don't feel all that good," he agreed. "But it's mainly weakness. They're letting me out next week. Then it'll be a matter of regaining my strength."

She sat in the straight chair beside the bed. She wore a little hat with flowers on the brim, tilted forward over her eyes. "I'm very sorry," she said.

"About what, exactly?"

"Well, your wife leaving you . . ."

"Wives do these things, from time to time."

133

There was a brief silence.

"Are you going to divorce her?"

"I haven't thought of it. It wouldn't be very easy to do, anyway, as I believe she's left the country."

Another brief silence.

"I'm to marry," Julia said. "Harvey Braddock."

"I'm sure you'll be very happy."

"He keeps asking me," she said as if he hadn't spoken. "And . . . well there was no longer any reason to put him off."

"Absolutely."

"It's not official yet. I just thought you should know."

"That was good of you."

She was fishing, desperately. She wanted to marry him, not Harvey Braddock. The slightest hint that he might be planning to secure his freedom would have her in his arms, he was sure. Another temptation to turn his back on the Balkans.

But he couldn't, not on the woman he loved, and not to a fate like her mother's, which would surely happen if she rejoined the Black Hand.

"Well," Julia said at the end of another brief silence, "I must be getting along. I do hope you'll be well enough to come to our wedding."

"I'll look forward to it," Berkeley said.

"Mrs Townsend and her companion took the ferry to Calais, as you suspected, Captain Townsend," Inspector Watt said. "In Calais, they boarded the train for Paris, but they had secured through tickets to Marseilles. After that, the trail is cold. The French police are being cooperative, but I'm afraid, well, there are quite a few of what we might describe as foreign-looking gentlemen in Marseilles, as well as good-looking young women. The odds on them being found, at least soon enough for any action to be taken, before they leave Marseilles, are remote. And as you know, sir . . ."

"You have nothing legally to have them arrested for," Berkeley said. "Thank you very much, Inspector. I think you can call off the hunt, now. I know where my wife can be found."

"Yes, sir," Watt said unhappily.

"I don't suppose you've had any success with the fellow who took a pot-shot at me?"

"Sadly, no, sir. I would say he also has escaped to the continent."

Berkeley nodded.

"You can, of course, make representations to the British Consul in Belgrade," John Townsend suggested.

"Do you really think that would have any effect?"

"Well, she is your wife, Berkeley."

"Far more important than that, Caterina is a member of an organisation which is virtually a law unto itself, in Serbia."

"Organisation?" John Townsend said uneasily.

"I shouldn't have said that. You'd best forget it."

"So you mean to go after her yourself."

"As soon as I can. Cheam says I can leave hospital next week."

"Yes, he did. But he also says you need at least another month's recuperation. Surely you can spend Christmas at home."

Berkeley nodded. He owed them that, at any rate.

The day before Berkeley was due to leave hospital, the ward sister was in a state of high excitement.

"A general," she squealed. "A real live general. I never knew you were so important, Captain Townsend."

"You learn something every day," Berkeley said. "You'd better show him in."

General Gorman was in civilian clothes and wore a bowler hat, a rather futile exercise in discretion Berkeley supposed, if he had announced himself as a general; he looked even more like a bloodhound on the scent than usual as he peered around the room. He was accompanied by Major Smailes, also in mufti.

"Shut the door," he growled.

Smailes obeyed, and remained standing by it, as if on guard.

Gorman stood by the bed while Berkeley endeavoured to lie to attention.

"They tell me you're almost fit again," the general remarked.

"I'll be out of this bed soon, thank God," Berkeley said. "But there's talk of a month's recuperation before I'll be fit for active service."

"Time, unfortunately, waits for no man," Gorman pointed out, and sat in the straight chair by the bed. "What are your plans regarding your wife?"

Berkeley could not stop himself from raising his eyebrows; he could not imagine the general being remotely interested in his domestic affairs.

"I would hope to get her back, sir."

"Commendably loyal," the general remarked, disparagingly. "I understand she has returned to Serbia."

"I believe she has, sir."

"For what purpose? Has she relatives there?"

"I don't think so. But her home is there, and all her friends."

"She came away with you happily enough. Didn't she?"

"Ah . . . yes, indeed, sir."

135

"So, she has gone back because of the crisis. And I can tell you, Townsend, that the crisis is deepening every day."

"I understood the Kaiser has retracted the remarks he made to the *Daily Telegraph*."

"Yes, he has, and it is not that I am talking about. Everyone knows Kaiser Willy is as mad as a March hare, which does not mean he isn't dangerous. We're pretty sure he's encouraging Austria; and it is that crisis that concerns us. The Austrians have mobilised an army on the Serb frontier. The Serbs have also mobilised. That no shots have actually been fired yet is because no one knows what Russia's attitude will be. If she backs the Serbs, as the Serbs are begging her to do, we could have a full-scale Balkan war. If she doesn't back them, well . . . it will still leave the area in a very unsettled state. The French and ourselves have put forward a peace package, which consists of persuading the Serbs to accept the *fait accompli* in Bosnia-Herzegovina in return for guarantees of their frontiers, and a comprehensive trading agreement with the Austro-Hungarian Empire which will greatly enhance their financial position. Unfortunately, the acceptance of these proposals also waits on the Russians, and they are in a mess. It appears that their foreign secretary agreed to the Austrian takeover of Bosnia-Herzegovina in exchange for Russian rights to build a railway through the Balkans, without reference to either the Tsar or the rest of the Russian government. So there is some argument going on in Moscow, against which has to be set the fact that the Austrians are in possession, and it is going to take a very large army to get them back out, especially if they are supported by Germany."

"As you say, sir," Berkeley commented. "A right royal mess. May I ask what the Turks think of it all? The provinces were technically theirs."

"Still are, legally," Gorman said. "But the Turks are in no condition to fight anyone at the moment. The point I am making is that the whole business, peace or war in the Balkans, is hovering on a knife-edge of diplomacy and hopefully goodwill. The slightest incident could spark off shooting. I am talking of the behaviour of your wife's friends, the Black Hand. They have been keeping a low profile since Anna Slovitza's death. Presumably they are again looking for a new leader in the field, having thought they had found him, but managed to lose him. Am I right?"

"Yes, sir." Berkeley said.

"They may also be waiting on the result of these various negotiations. However, in view of their past record, we must assume not only that they will find a new field commander soon enough, but that they will also grow tired of waiting. So," Gorman said, "we have decided it would be a good idea for you to go after your wife and find her . . . I assume you know where to look?"

"She will have gone back to Sabac."

"Excellent. So you will go there, make it up with her and settle down to a life of domestic bliss until further notice."

"Sir?"

"Officially, we are retiring you, Townsend. This will be entirely honourable, and will be on account of your wounds which render you unfit for active service, or indeed any service. Officially. Being retired, you will, as I have indicated, join your wife and settle down. You will be funded, unofficially, through our people in Belgrade, and you will of course, remain a British officer. You are being assigned to a very special duty, and that is to keep the Black Hand out of trouble, or from causing trouble."

"I'm afraid that will be difficult, sir. If not impossible."

"I think not. You told me that you were offered command of the field part of this society."

"Which I declined, sir."

"Now you must accept it. You are fired by the Austrian action."

"Supposing, just supposing, they do accept me back, sir, and it is doubtful, it will be because I convince them I am, as you put it, fired by the Austrian action. In which case, they will expect me to do something about it."

"You will have to procrastinate."

Berkeley gazed at the general. "I don't think you quite understand the situation in the Balkans, General. Those people hold life very cheaply. If they suspected for a moment I was not doing my best for them they would cut my throat."

"You're a soldier, Berkeley. Soldiers take risks."

Berkeley gulped; the general had never addressed him as Berkeley before.

"It shouldn't be for very long," Gorman went on, as winningly as a battered bloodhound could. "Once we get the Serbs to sign up to a treaty with Austria, we can then bring pressure to bear upon them to get rid of the Black Hand people."

"Of whom I shall be one," Berkeley observed. "Their commander in the field, if all goes according to plan."

"You will have sufficient warning to get out," Gorman promised him. "With your wife."

Berkeley sighed. He reckoned he was once again being sent on a suicide mission. But oddly enough, it was what he wanted to do; just to be with Caterina again, to see that marvellous smile, to hold all of that beauty in his arms. Even if it brought him a knife in the ribs.

"You will, of course," Gorman went on, "also use your advantageous position to keep an eye on the entire Serbian situation. You will be our man on the ground. Or perhaps I should say, *in* the ground." He gave one of his wintry smiles. "In this regard, we would like you to report any events or developments which may be of importance to His Majesty's Government. You will have to use your discretion in making a judgement on these matters. However, whatever you have to report must be top secret." He snapped his fingers and Smailes came to the bedside, carrying a small book he had taken from his briefcase. "This is a personal code book. There are only half a dozen of them in existence. I have one, of course. Now you do too. Guard it with your life. You will use this for any message you wish to communicate with me personally. You will not communicate with anyone else, and no one else must know what you are sending. In normal circumstances you will use the mails. However, if the matter is urgent and you need to telegraph, you will use our Embassy in Athens."

Berkeley opened his mouth, and then closed it again. Gorman seemed to assume that Athens was a mere day's journey away from Serbia, much less Sabac.

"So, your passage to Greece is booked for next Friday," Gorman said.

"I am supposed to convalesce for a month."

"There is no better way to convalesce than a sea voyage," Gorman assured him.

"My people were hoping I'd spend Christmas with them."

"I am sure they'll understand," Gorman said, and stood up. "Oh, by the way, as of today you hold the rank of major. This will be gazetted, as it is normal procedure when an officer is retired. Any questions?"

"Am I allowed to take Lockwood?"

"Of course."

"I will have to tell him what we're about."

Gorman frowned.

"He is absolutely trustworthy," Berkeley said. "He has proved this time and again. And I cannot ask him to undertake what may be a very dangerous mission in the dark, as it were."

Gorman cleared his throat. "I take your point, Major. Very well On your head be it." He held out his hand. "This is a business of great importance. It could mean the difference between war and peace."

Berkeley clasped hands. "I shall do my best, sir."

"You don't have to come, Harry," he told Lockwood. "My wife's people may take one look at me and shoot. And anyone standing alongside me."

"But you don't expect them to do that, sir."

"I'm an optimist. And I can't believe that Caterina really means me ill."

Lockwood looked doubtful. "She did threaten to kill you on board that ship."

"We sorted that one out."

"Yes sir. Well, I shall of course accompany you."

His tone suggested that he felt Berkeley needed a keeper.

"But . . ." John Townsend was horrified. "You said you'd be home for Christmas."

"I'm sorry, Dad. I have to go."

"Because you've been sacked? We'll find you a job here."

"It's not quite as simple as that. I must go to Caterina."

"After she walked out on you?"

"We don't know she wasn't coerced, or certainly tricked. She is my wife. I have a duty towards her."

"I hope you'll remind her that she has a duty towards you," John Townsend said.

"But are you really well enough to travel?" Alicia asked.

"The voyage to Greece will take several days. Cheam says it will be good for me."

"But then you have to go into the mountains, don't you?"

"By train," Berkeley reminded her. "I shall travel in complete comfort."

Déjà vu, he thought, as the train rumbled into Belgrade Central. However, the atmosphere was more tense than when he had first come here the previous year; now it had even spread into Greece which was openly mobilising. He and Lockwood had visited Pathenikos, who at the very sight of them had begun to tremble; no doubt the story of the incident of the *Wanderer* had reached Athens. He had declined to accompany them into Serbia. "There will be a war up there at any moment," he said.

And on this occasion, of course, he could expect no assistance from the Embassy, at least regarding his personal affairs.

The Turks in Macedonia had also been in a highly agitated state, and spent even more time inspecting papers than they had on his last visit. Serbia was a ferment of troop movements and new defences, only now they had to take account of the Austrians in Bosnia-Herzegovina as well, which gave them a very long frontier to defend.

There were, however, some things that never changed.

"Mr Jones," Colonel Savos said. "Is it Mr Jones today?"

"Jones will do, Colonel."

"Welcome to Belgrade. I had not really expected you to return."

"My wife is in Sabac."

Savos nodded. "This I know. You intend to go there?"

"That is my intention. Unless you propose to stop me."

Savos shrugged. "If you mean, do I have an Austrian warrant for your arrest, I believe there are several lying about the place. But at this moment we are not serving Austrian warrants of arrest."

"I had hoped that might be the case."

"On the other hand, I doubt that the Austrians are any longer your chief enemy. I would have supposed that going to Sabac would be, for you, a highly dangerous business."

"Which is why I am reporting to you, first, Colonel."

Savos raised his eyebrows.

"I just wish you to know where I am, and I wish the people of Sabac to know that you know."

Savos stroked his moustache. "I'm afraid that will offer you very little protection, should you, ah . . . disappear."

"It is still a measure of protection." They shook hands. "I will see you when next I am in Belgrade."

"I shall look forward to that. Tell me, Mr Jones, when the shooting starts, will you be on our side?"

"I should think so. You tell me, Colonel, when will the shooting start?"

"Some time quite soon, I would say. We are in the mood to fight."

"Austria? With or without Russian help?"

Savos gave a quick smile. "Somebody. As I said, we are in the mood to fight."

The colonel, Berkeley reflected, knows something that I don't. And he didn't think the War Office knew, either.

They took the train to Sabac. Again, *déjà vu*. The little town had hardly changed in the few months he had been away; the river port was as busy as ever, the fruit sellers lined the wharfs. And there was the usual crowd of little boys, some of whom remembered him and shouted his name; but they called him Mr Slovitza.

He was also very aware of being watched, as he and Lockwood made their way towards the big house. He could not help but feel certain that one of the people watching him was very probably the man who had tried to kill him.

He rapped on the barred door, and it opened immediately; they had seen him from an upstairs window.

"You are . . . Marie," he said, remembering.

She gave a little curtsey, her face crimson as she looked past him at Lockwood.

"Aren't you going to let us in?" Berkeley asked.

She moved backwards so quickly she almost fell over.

"Is your mistress at home?" he asked.

"I am here," Caterina said from the top of the stairs.

"Am I welcome?"

"As long as you have not come to take me away."

He climbed the stairs towards her. She was even more beautiful than his memory of her.

"I will not take you away. But there was no reason for you to sneak off like a thief in the night. Had you waited, I would have come with you."

"I do not believe you," she said.

He reached her and stood against her, put his arms round her, held her close, kissed her forehead and her hair and her mouth. She did not resist him, but her body remained stiff.

"I adore you."

"You adore my body," she said.

"May I tell Lockwood to settle in?"

"Of course." She looked past him. "Welcome back, Harry."

"Good to be here, madame."

"Give Mr Lockwood food and wine, Marie," Caterina commanded, and led Berkeley up the next flight of stairs and into the drawing room. She went to the sideboard, poured two glasses of wine and gave him one. "So, if you did not come here to take me away, why did you come here?"

"To be your husband."

She gave him one of those appraising stares he remembered so well. "How is your wound?"

"It twinges every so often. I still need a few weeks' recuperation."

"And your career?"

"It is over."

Another long stare. "That is what you told Mama last year. And it was a lie."

"This time it is the truth. I will show you my discharge papers. They do not think I will ever recover sufficiently from my wounds to be a soldier again."

"Is that true?"

He shrugged. "According to the requirements of the British army, I suppose it is."

"I am sorry you got shot."

141

"I'm very glad to hear you say that. I assume you know the man who did it?"

"It is better for you not to know who it is."

"Which means that you do."

"I have said, it is not a matter we should discuss."

Nineteen years old, and she was treating him like a child. And he had to accept it.

"I would like you to know," he said, "that everything I did was for your mother and yourself."

"I do not believe you," she said, and looked at the door.

Which opened to admit several men, led by Karlovy. All were armed, and Lockwood and their guns were far away.

"I could not believe my ears," Karlovy said.

Berkeley looked at Caterina, who did not seem the least surprised by the intrusion.

"You sent for them?"

"There are matters to be discussed," Caterina said.

"Matters?" Karlovy enquired. He jerked his head and his men filed into the room, spreading out along the walls. The last closed the door.

"There is really no need to be quite so cautious," Berkeley said. "I am unarmed."

Karlovy pointed. "You are a traitor to the cause. You deserted us. You abducted Caterina. You have brought calamity upon us. You have been condemned to death by the supreme council."

Berkeley refused to be alarmed by the rhetoric. "And I assume the sentence was carried out, in England. Ineptly."

"You had a lucky escape."

"I agree with you. But I did escape and it is an axiom of the law that a man cannot be executed twice for the same crime."

Karlovy looked at Caterina in bewilderment.

She actually smiled, for the first time since his return. "My husband is very skilful with words and ideas, and has much knowledge," she said.

"No matter," Karlovy said. "We will try him again, on another charge, and condemn him again, and this time the execution will not be botched."

"Nothing will be done to him," Caterina said. "You will send for Gregory."

"Why wait for him?" Karlovy sneered. "It was Gregory who signed the death sentence."

"Exactly," Caterina said. "Therefore it is Gregory who must now rescind it."

"Rescind it?" Karlovy demanded.

"My husband will not be executed," Caterina said.

"He is a traitor to our cause," Karlovy shouted.

"He is the father of my child," Caterina said quietly.

Karlovy and his men left, faced with a situation they did not know how to handle.

Berkeley wasn't sure he knew how to handle it either.

"My dearest girl," he said. "When did you know?"

"I knew in England," she said. "But it is possible to miss one period and not be pregnant. Then when I missed a second, on my way back here, it could have been all the things that had happened. But now I have missed a third, and I have been examined by a doctor in Belgrade. He says there is no doubt of it."

"I am so pleased for you. For us." He frowned at her. "Are you not pleased?"

"I hope to be," she said. "If you will live here with me and be my husband."

"Believe me, that is all I wish to do."

"We have no money. I have no money. We may have to sell this house."

"I have money," he assured her.

"But you say you have been dismissed from the army?"

He nodded. "My parents have agreed to pay me an allowance. The money will be sent to Belgrade every month."

When would he be able to stop lying?

But at least he could make her happy. "So, you see, we can keep the house."

"I am glad," she said. "I was born in this house. I would like my child also to be born here."

He needed time to think, to evaluate the position. Suddenly the immediate future had taken on an altogether different aspect. He could actually look forward to it.

On a very basic level there was the delight any man would feel at becoming a father, and by a woman like Caterina. He hastily wrote to his parents to let them know they would soon be having a grandchild; he gave them the impression that he would be returning soon to England with his little family.

But on what might be called the political level things had turned out even more satisfactorily. Caterina was very definitely out of action for at least a year, as he did not doubt she intended to feed the babe herself. As a desperately loving husband, he could not be expected, and he certainly was entitled to refuse, to leave her side for any madcap adventures which might end with his being killed and she left a widowed mother. And by the end of the year he would have her pregnant again.

This last would obviously take some careful preparation, as for the time being she refused to allow him into her bed. She explained this very simply by saying her mother had always told her not to have sex while pregnant. Trying to convince her that it could not possibly harm the baby had no effect; when she had made up her mind that was that.

But he also had a nagging suspicion she was still not convinced that she could trust him. Restoring that mutual trust was essential.

But he had time, he reckoned. Gregory Masanovich needed to be dealt with first.

Gregory arrived a week after Berkeley's return. He looked as professorial as ever, and not in the least agitated.

"What do you say in English?" he asked. "The bad penny?"

"Very appropriate," Berkeley agreed, offering him wine. They were alone in the drawing room.

"I am amazed at your temerity."

"I came looking for my wife. I am amazed at your gall, Gregory, sending someone to kill me."

Gregory spread his hands. "It was a committee decision. You had broken our laws and abducted my godchild."

"Is Caterina your godchild? She never told me that. But you know it is not possible for a man to abduct his own wife."

"What is possible and what is not, is for me to decide."

"Not your committee?" Berkeley asked, innocently.

Gregory glared at him, then lit a cigar. He did not offer Berkeley one. "Why have you come back?"

"To be with my wife."

"To kidnap her again, perhaps."

"I shall not do that, Gregory. For one thing I have given her my word, and for another she is carrying my child."

"Do you believe that?"

"Of course I do."

"Well, I congratulate you. What are your plans?"

"To be a good husband and father."

"You have money?"

"I have a private income. Now tell me, Gregory, what are your plans?"

Gregory snorted. "We can make no plans, while this crisis continues."

"I am glad to hear that," Berkeley said, with genuine relief. "Do you have any idea what is going to happen?"

"Yes," Gregory said disconsolately. "Serbia is going to accept the terms imposed by the powers."

"You know this?"

Gregory nodded. "I have friends in high places. It is a bitter pill and nobody is happy with it, but we cannot fight Austria by ourselves."

"And Russia will not help?"

"Russia is close to revolution, and there is a famine. In the Ukraine, the breadbasket of Europe! People are dying like flies. They say they can undertake no foreign adventures."

"Well, as I understand the terms of the proposed treaty, they should bring considerable financial advantages to Serbia."

"You are speaking of a layer of icing on the top of a poisoned cake," Gregory said. "We have the Hungarian border lying to our north. Now we have the borders of Bosnia and Herzegovina lying to our west. All Austrian. To our south and east is Turkey. So the Austrians will increase their trade with us, and perhaps even invest in Serbia. They will not be risking anything, even their money. When the time is ripe, they will simply take us over as they took over Bosnia-Herzegovina. They mean to own all the Balkans."

"And you don't think that will stir up the Russians? Or even the Turks?"

"The Turks did nothing about Bosnia-Herzegovina, my friend. They are in no condition to do anything about anything. And Russia, I have told you, Russia is in a state of collapse. It is my opinion that the ripe time I have spoken of, as evaluated by the Austrians, will be when Russia dissolves into revolution."

"You envisage a disintegrating world," Berkeley suggested.

"From our point of view, certainly."

"So . . ." He drew a deep breath. "You are disbanding the movement?"

Gregory sighed. "The movement is disbanding itself, Berkeley. Anna's death was a heavy blow. I had hoped, Karlovy had hoped, that you would step in and lead us with her enthusiasm, her talent, her skill . . ." He raised his head to look at Berkeley.

"I told you once: anarchy is not my profession," Berkeley said.

Another sigh. "People are leaving the movement in droves. Financial support is drying up. Even Savos has got into the act and warned us against any overt activities. Perhaps, if you were to come back to lead us after all . . ."

"Forget it. I told you, I came back to be a good husband and father to Caterina. And to keep her out of trouble."

"I am sorry," Gregory said. "Truly sorry. I saw in you a man of looming greatness."

"I am sorry too," Berkeley said. "What will you do?"

"About the organisation? There is nothing I can do. Save wait, and hope."

"I meant, what will you do for a living? Do you have a profession?"

"Of course I have a profession. I am a schoolmaster."

"Good heavens! I would never have thought it."

"So, I will go back to schoolmastering." He stubbed out his cigar, finished his wine and stood up. "Give my regards to your wife."

"I can't pretend I'm sorry," Berkeley told Caterina. "My only regret is that this did not happen before your mother got killed."

"It could not happen were Mama still alive," she said fiercely.

"You could be right."

"And now I suppose you expect me to forget all about her, and about Papa, and about all those others who died, about my own mistreatment and the rape of my country."

"No, Caterina, I do not expect you to forget any of those things. They are not things one forgets. But there comes a time when one must accept facts. The Austrians hold all the high cards. If they are too powerful for Serbia to fight, they are certainly too powerful for any single man or woman to do so."

"I shall always hate them," she said. "And one day . . ."

"One day," he agreed. "Until then, for God's sake try to smile, and be happy."

He wrote to Gorman, acquainting him with developments, and feeling able to assure him that there would be no further activity from the Black Hand for the foreseeable future. Then he settled down to enjoy the life of a Serbian country gentleman. Living was very cheap and he still had a fair amount of Anna's capital left, while his salary arrived regularly from England. There were horses belonging to Anna's stable, and game such as wild boar to be hunted in the hills and forests. There was little social life, but as her stomach became swollen, Caterina did not wish to go out and see people in any event. Karlovy and his henchmen had entirely disappeared.

"I have to say, sir, that this is the life," Lockwood confided, as they cantered over the open country south of the town. Here they were quite close to the border of Herzegovina, but there was little sign of any activity there.

"I won't argue with that," Berkeley said.

It could be his life for the rest of his life. Would that be such a bad thing? He corresponded regularly with his parents, and they seemed to have accepted that there was no way he could return until after Caterina's delivery. They were contemplating visiting Serbia, but he advised against it until the political situation settled down. As Gregory had prophesied, the Serbs had finally accepted the proposals made by the powers, but resentment was still running high.

"I was wondering, sir, if you would have any objection if I tied the knot?" Lockwood asked. "Seeing as how we seem to be settling here."

"Why, Harry, I would be delighted," Berkeley said. "Who's the lucky girl?"

"The maid, Marie. She and I, well, we get on together."

"Brilliant. I know Mrs Townsend will be pleased."

Caterina was pleased.

She had settled into a regular routine. Despite her now-heavy pregnancy, she continued to oversee the running of her household, from the cleaning to the menus, but in the evenings she would sit with Berkeley while he read to her, or continued with her English lessons. She reciprocated by teaching him Serbo-Croat, as she had begun to do during their brief honeymoon period. She was friendly and good-humoured but clearly had not yet made up her mind whether they would ever resume conjugal relations. In any other circumstances he would have found this galling, but he reminded himself that it would not have been possible anyway while she was pregnant. He needed to be very patient while he restored himself in her esteem, even if he considered that the faults were all on her side, as she was the one who had attempted to end their marriage.

She never spoke about that, or about how the Black Hand had contacted her, but it seemed obvious that the organisation had been tracking their movements ever since they left Sabac the first time; and the lengthy stay in Malta had given Gregory ample time to get his people across the continent and into England.

And he still didn't know who had fired that near-fatal shot. But his stay in hospital had clearly given Gregory's people the opportunity to get at Caterina. He wondered what her reaction had been when, having got back home filled with determination to strike at the Austrians, she had discovered she was pregnant?

"However," she said, "the marriage must not take place until my figure has returned."

"I'm sure they'll be happy to wait," Berkeley said. He did not doubt the event had already been consummated.

Anna Townsend was born in June 1909. Caterina was disappointed, as she had hoped for a boy, but Berkeley was pleased, and not only at becoming a father.

"We shall have to try again," he told her.

This was a delight, as she welcomed him to her bed, even if he felt she had not yet forgiven him for their estrangement. And when he broached the subject of perhaps returning to England, for a visit, she was adamant.

"I shall never leave Sabac again," she said.

He did not feel he could press the matter, wrote to his parents to explain, and suggested that they might, after all, like to visit Serbia. But affairs in the Balkans remained too unsettled for them to wish to risk the journey.

He felt his best course was to wait and see the direction things took. He received no communication from Gorman, but his retainer arrived every month without fail so he had to presume he was still on the payroll. He supposed no one could have been given a simpler assignment, as the Black Hand appeared to have disbanded itself. On one of his visits to Belgrade he asked Colonel Savos if he knew anything of them.

"I had been hoping you might be able to tell me," Savos admitted.

"It is strange, the way they have just melted away."

"I do not believe they have," Savos said. "Organisations like the Black Hand never disappear. They submerge, and then they resurface when they are ready. However, if you are ever again approached by them, I would be grateful if you would inform me."

"I might just do that. Would you be prepared to act against them?"

"I would be prepared to prevent them from causing any trouble with Austria, at this time."

"So everything that has happened is to be history."

Savos gave one of his cold smiles. "For the moment, certainly. Tell me, Mr Townsend, how are your beautiful wife and daughter?"

"They are well. My wife is expecting again."

"Then I most heartily congratulate you, sir. Now tell me something else, do you never get bored, sitting in that little provincial town, watching the barges drifting up and down the river?"

"I do not get bored," Berkeley said, not entirely truthfully. "Have you something in mind for me to do?"

Another cold smile. "I might. Perhaps I may come to see you, one of these days."

Berkeley wondered what he could possibly have in mind. But for the time being he was more concerned with domesticity, as Caterina gave birth to a son in October 1910. He they named John, after Berkeley's father. Lockwood and Maria were also parents by now, while Sabac remained sunk in the somnolence of the country town it was. Even the border was quiet, and there was no sign of any activity by the Black Hand. Caterina always declined to discuss politics, nor was it a subject Berkeley chose to press. He knew she adored her little family, and he felt that the longer he could keep her involved in home affairs the more chance he had of weaning her from thoughts of vengeance. She was still only just twenty-one, and when, in the spring of 1911, she became pregnant again, he felt he was winning his private campaign.

Thus he was totally surprised, one June morning when he returned from his usual gallop, to find Colonel Savos waiting for him together with two other men; not even the colonel was in uniform, which was in itself strange, but there could be no doubt that all three were soldiers, from the way they stood.

"Mr Townsend," the policeman said, "I hope you do not object to this intrusion?"

"Well," Berkeley said, signalling an anxiously hovering Lockwood to pour some wine, "that must depend upon what you are intruding."

"May I introduce Brigadier-General Petrovich, and Colonel Markos," Savos said.

Berkeley shook hands and Lockwood served the drinks.

"Your wife is well, I trust," General Petrovich asked.

"Very well. I'm afraid she will not be coming down. She is several months pregnant."

"Our congratulations." They waited.

"Well," Berkeley said, "sit down, and tell me what this is all about."

"We have come," Petrovich said, "to offer you a commission in the Serbian army."

Part Three

A Question of Murder

'The angel of death has been abroad throughout the land; you may almost hear the beating of his wings.'

John Bright

War

For a moment Berkeley was too surprised to respond. Then he said, "My dear General, I am not a soldier."

"Of course you are a soldier, Major Townsend. We know all about you. You held a commission in the British army, and you commanded a field force of the Black Hand."

"I'm afraid those are only half-truths, sir," Berkeley said. "If you know so much about me, then you will know that I was retired from the British army on account of my wounds. I walk with a limp."

"You can still ride a horse," Savos pointed out. "You do so every day."

"Besides," Markos put in, "we have automobiles."

Berkeley decided to ignore that line. "Additionally, you must know that I have never commanded a Black Hand field force. I was under the orders of Anna Slovitza. My mother-in-law," he reminded them.

"For whom you fought nobly and well," Petrovich said. "And were offered command of the organisation's field force."

Berkeley looked at Savos. "That is history."

The colonel smiled. "There is no such thing as dead history, Mr Townsend. It keeps coming back."

"We are in the process of expanding our army," Petrovich explained, "and we have a position for a man such as yourself, a proven field commander and someone who knows the Balkans, the ground over which we shall require you to serve."

Berkeley signalled Lockwood to pour some more wine. Despite his predisposition to reject the proposal, he was intrigued. Besides, it promised information.

"If you are expanding your army," he said, "it must be with the idea of going to war with someone. Or you are expecting someone to go to war with you."

"That is true enough," Petrovich agreed.

"Am I allowed to know who this potential enemy is?"

"We are surrounded by enemies," Petrovich pointed out.

"But perhaps one more than the others," Berkeley said. "Gentlemen, in my opinion, for Serbia to go to war with Austria, unsupported, would be suicide."

"I am sure you are right," the general agreed, blandly.

"Ah," Berkeley said.

"I am sure you understand that I am not in a position to give you the thoughts of my government or any other government with whom we may be in consultation," the general said. "However, I would remind you, Major Townsend, as I mentioned earlier, Austria is certainly not our only enemy. Well, sir, I have said enough. I am in a position to offer you a colonelcy in a regiment of horse. Will you accept?"

Berkeley's mind raced. It seemed fairly obvious that the Serbs did *not* intend war with Austria – at least at this moment. That left only one possible antagonist . . . and a far more historical one than even Austria.

And that meant he would at last have to earn his living again.

"You will have to give me a few days to consider," he said.

"And discuss it with your wife, perhaps," Savos suggested.

"Of course."

"I need to go to Athens for a few days," Berkeley told Caterina.

As she began to swell, she was uncomfortable in the summer heat and thus irritable. "It is necessary, now? What business do you have in Athens? I hope you are not expecting me to accompany you?"

"Of course not." He kissed her. "We agreed that I would not kidnap you again, remember? It is to do with my allowance; there may be a hitch."

"Those men yesterday . . . one of them was Colonel Savos."

"Correct."

"Is there trouble?"

"Not for us. They offered me a commission in the army."

"You? But . . ."

"Absolutely. There are a whole lot of questions."

Her eyes lit up. "You mean we are going to war with Austria?"

"No, sweetheart, I don't think we are going to do that."

"Oh." Her face fell. "But you will accept? I should like to see you in uniform, as a Serbian officer."

"I shall be in the cavalry. If I accept."

She clapped her hands. "It is so romantic."

Berkeley considered. Like the Austrian dragoons, the Serbian cavalry wore light blue tunics and hats over brilliant red breeches, although kepis rather than helmets. "I'm not sure it's really me. Anyway, I have been given a few days to come to a decision."

"But you will accept?" she asked again.

"That depends on the situation with my allowance."

Lockwood naturally accompanied him, and on the train Berkeley outlined the situation.

"Well, sir, it wouldn't be a bad thing to get back into uniform," Harry said. "But if it won't be to fight the Austrians . . ." He glanced left and right as the Turkish ticket collector entered the compartment.

"Yes," Berkeley said.

He was aware of tension, and even more in Greece where there were large numbers of soldiers to be seen on the street. He made sure they were not being followed, and went to the Embassy.

"Well, really, Mr . . ." The clerk peered at his card. ". . . Townsend, his excellency is really very busy."

"This is a matter of national importance," Berkeley said. "If his excellency is in any doubt, ask him to wire London and ask for confirmation from General Gorman."

It took some time, but eventually Berkeley found himself in the ambassador's office.

"You've been here before," the ambassador said. "Something about a passport . . ."

"That is correct, sir."

"I was informed that you are a British agent," the ambassador said.

"I assume you have verified this with London, sir?"

"I have. They tell me you are to be allowed the use of our coding machine. Will not ordinary diplomatic channels do?"

"In this instance, sir, no. The matter is very urgent, and I must use the wire."

"Hm. Very good. London says I am to cooperate in every possible way. I shall, of course, require to see the telegram before it is coded. And the reply."

"I'm afraid you will have to request London's permission for that, sir."

The ambassador glared at him for several seconds, then rang the bell on his desk. "Take this, ah . . . gentleman to the coding room, Andrews," he told his secretary. "Give him whatever assistance he requires."

"I'd say you've rubbed the old man up the wrong way," Andrews suggested.

"I'm sure it happens all the time." Berkeley looked around the small office which contained three male clerks. "Would you get rid of these people."

"You mean you wish to be left alone? In the coding room?"

"If that is where I am, correct."

Andrews hesitated, then recalled his chief's instructions, and ushered the men from the room. "How long will you require?"

"I will let you know when I'm finished."

He sat at the desk, drafted his message.

Am in possession of information that Serbia intends war with Turkey in near future. This is not practical alone, so suggest possibilities of an alliance, possibly with Bulgaria but probably Greece as well, are investigated. Have been offered colonelcy in Serbian army. Please advise as to acceptance. Immediate reply requested.

This he encoded, using his own book which he returned to his satchel when he was finished. Then he opened the door, to find Andrews waiting in the corridor together with the three clerks.

"I'd like this sent immediately," he said.

Andrews studied the sheet of paper. "This is not our code," he remarked.

"No, it's mine," Berkeley said.

"This is very irregular."

"Like you, Mr Andrews, I'm sure, I only obey orders," Berkeley said. "Immediately, please, it is most urgent."

"Ah, yes. Right away." He snapped his fingers and one of the clerks hurried forward. "To be despatched right away."

"That means now," Berkeley reminded him.

The clerks went into the office with the sheet of paper.

"There won't be a reply for some hours," Andrews said. "Let's see, it's eleven in the morning here . . . Why, they'll still be at breakfast in London."

"Ideal. They should have a reply ready by lunch, in London, and we'll have it in time for tea, here," Berkeley said, pleasantly.

Andrews frowned, as if he was unsure whether or not he was having his leg pulled. Then he brightened. "Lunch. Sir Patrick has invited you to lunch with him."

Berkeley raised his eyebrows.

"Well," Andrews said, "you are obviously a man of some importance."

"And that's what matters," Berkeley agreed. "When and where?"

"Where are you staying?"

"The Excelsior."

"Ah, just round the corner. You'll be lunching at the residence. That is just outside of town. Very pleasant."

"You'll have to give me some advice on how to get there."

"Mr dear Major Townsend, our car will call for you. At a quarter to one."

Surprisingly, Berkeley had never driven in a motor car before. There were quite a few on the streets of Athens, blaring their horns and frightening the horses, and presumably there were even more on the streets of London; there had been some on the occasion of his last visit, nearly three years ago. But he had never felt tempted to use one; he was a horseman, and did not see these heavy, noisy, smelly, and essentially slow-moving vehicles, handicapped by being limited to road surfaces, ever replacing a good mount, certainly for military purposes.

But the ambassador's car was very grand, an open tourer called a Rolls-Royce, with comfortable seats and a uniformed driver, and capable of going quite fast, on the road, although nothing could negate the constant grind of the engine.

Equally imposing was the ambassador's residence, set in the midst of olive groves rather than houses, a glitter of white marble, outside which were several more automobiles and a clutch of uniformed servants.

As well as his host and hostess.

"Major Townsend, is it?" inquired Lady Goodall, a statuesque woman whose rather long neck was enclosed in a pearl choker, beneath which the bodice of her gown was festooned with pearl necklaces. "How good of you to come. But is your beautiful wife not with you?"

Now how the devil did this woman know he had a beautiful wife? Berkeley wondered. "I'm afraid not, milady. My wife is several months pregnant."

Lady Goodall did a double take; in her circles the word pregnant was not considered proper, certainly not between the sexes. "How happy for you," she remarked. "Now, come inside and meet our guests."

There were another dozen couples, a few Greek but in the main from the Embassy, as well as two officers off a British warship in Piraeus. And then, almost the last to be introduced, because they had deliberately hung back . . . "I think you have met Mr and Mrs Braddock," Lady Goodall said.

So that's where she got her information, Berkeley thought. But he was again totally surprised.

"Berkeley, you old devil," Harvey Braddock said jovially. Berkeley supposed he could best be described as a jovial man, short, stocky and red-faced. "Fancy meeting you here."

Berkeley allowed his hand to be squeezed while he gazed at Julia who was flushing. "You're looking well," she murmured.

157

"Well, no one has actually got around to shooting me for the past year or so," he said. "But you are looking splendid, Julia."

This was a lie. Julia Braddock was dressed in the height of fashion, in a grey-green costume with green braid and button trimmings, worn over a white lace blouse; her collar and cuffs were white. Her felt hat was fawn, with matching gloves and handbag, and was decorated with dark brown ostrich plumes. She should have been the most attractive woman in the room, but she had lost weight and could now be described as thin; this was especially noticeable in her face, which was gaunt, while there were shadows under her eyes.

"I'm sure you have lots to talk about," Lady Goodall suggested, and bustled off.

"I'm in a fog," Berkeley confessed. "Are you on a visit?"

"Good Lord, no," Harvey said, jovially. "I was posted here two years ago. Third Secretary, what."

"Two years," Berkeley said thoughtfully.

"It was the wife's idea that I should apply for this posting, what," Harvey said. "Always wanted to see Greece, she said."

"It is a most beautiful country," Julia murmured. "But perhaps not as beautiful as Serbia."

"I'm prejudiced," Berkeley said.

"And is Caterina well?"

"As well as can be expected. She's pregnant."

"Oh. Will this be your first?"

"Our third," Berkeley told her.

"Oh. Good Lord. I suppose I've been out of touch. I mean, with your parents."

"Have you children?"

"No," she said.

Julia was placed next to Berkeley at lunch, probably because, he supposed, Lady Goodall felt that having known him before she was the least likely to be shocked by anything he might say.

"Have you now made your home in Serbia?" she asked.

"You could say that. It is my wife's home, and Caterina is very attached to it. Anyway, there is nothing for me in England, now."

"I think the army treated you very shabbily."

"They pay me a pension. I can't complain."

"And are you happy?"

"I think so." But she had given him an opening. "Are *you* happy?"

She glanced at him, cheeks pink, and fiddled with her fork. "I think very few people actually know what happiness is."

"That's an interesting suggestion. But it can only be based on certain essentials."

"Tell me of them."

"Well, good health is a priority." His turn to glance at her, but she did not respond. "Then . . . security, financial and physical. A loving companion. And, as I am discovering, successful parenthood."

"And you have all of those things," she mused. "You are to be envied, sir."

"And you do not. Would you care to tell me why?"

"It is not a subject for lunch parties," she said. "Will you tell me where you are staying in Athens?"

"The Hotel Excelsior."

"May I ask for how long?"

"I imagine I will be leaving again tomorrow."

"Such a short visit," she remarked, and engaged the man on her left in conversation.

Well now, he thought; here was an interesting situation.

He was returned to the hotel about three and had a siesta, being awakened by Lockwood at four with a cup of tea, and, "There is a gentleman here to see you, sir."

"A gentleman?" Berkeley asked in surprise, allowing himself to be wrapped in an undressing robe.

"From the Embassy, I believe, sir."

"Oh, of course." He had almost forgotten the telegram.

It was Andrews. "This arrived half an hour ago, Major Townsend. His excellency suggested I bring it right round."

Berkeley took the envelope. "Thank you, Mr Andrews. You may tell the ambassador that I am most grateful for his assistance."

Andrews waited. "Aren't you going to open it?"

"Certainly. As soon as I am alone."

"His excellency should be informed of the contents."

"Have you received instructions from London to that effect?"

"Well, no. But it is our policy that the ambassador should see all correspondence, especially that in cypher."

"Yes. Well, the moment London authorises or instructs me to give the ambassador the transcript of this message, I shall do so."

Andrews glared at him. "I assume you are aware that there has been a revolt against Turkish rule in Albania. It is generally supposed this has been fomented by the Italians."

"I was not aware of that, Mr Andrews."

"You are saying that neither you, nor this clandestine exchange of messages with London, have anything to do with it?"

"As I have said, until you told me, I was unaware of the Albanian situation," Berkeley said. "As for my exchange of messages with

London, I cannot form an opinion until I have read this telegram. Thank you, Mr Andrews."

Andrews hesitated a last time, glanced at Lockwood uncertainly, and left the room.

"Lock the door, Harry," Berkeley said, and took out his code book before sitting at the table.

It was from Gorman.

Information appreciated and understood. Our estimation is Italy will strike first. Serbia and friends will hope to pick up pieces. Consider it very useful for you to be involved. Seek highest possible level. Priority remains avoidance of conflict with Austria. G.

"Intriguing," Berkeley said, handing the transcript to Lockwood.

"I didn't know Italy was involved in the Balkan situation, sir."

"She isn't, and I shouldn't think she wants to be. But the Balkans represent only the tiniest part of the Turkish Empire. In any event, it looks as if we are going to be soldiers again, Harry. We'll take the early train back to Belgrade."

"Yes, sir. That leaves tonight free." He paused, hopefully.

"Indeed it does," Berkeley agreed. "I'm feeling a bit tired, Harry. Heavy lunch and all that. Why don't you go out and have a good time. It may be your last opportunity for a while."

It's a sad thing when one descends to lying to one's oldest friend, he thought. But this was a white lie, and Lockwood was delighted.

"If you're sure, sir."

"Absolutely," Berkeley said.

He waited for Lockwood to leave, then went down to reception and placed some notes on the counter. "I am expecting a visitor," he said. "I don't know when, precisely. But when the lady arrives, please direct her to my rooms."

The Greek clerk revealed no curiosity or even disapproval, merely bowed and pocketed the money. Berkeley, having secured a bottle of champagne and an ice bucket, retired to his room to wait.

He wondered what he was planning. Adultery? He wasn't sure. As Caterina was following her usual agenda when pregnant, he could certainly do with some sex. It was an interesting thought that had he not encountered Julia at the lunch party, he might well have accompanied Harry to a brothel this evening. That certainly would not be considered adultery, even by Caterina.

So, was he intending to treat Julia as a whore? That was not possible. He was intending to treat Julia exactly as Julia wanted to be treated . . . it would be intriguing to find out. Just as it would

160

be intriguing to discover just what had reduced her to such a wreck of the strong, healthy girl he remembered.

And who he had known nearly all his life.

She came at nine o'clock, a gentle tap on the door.

He let her in, closed and locked the door. She was breathless.

"I did not know if they'd let me up," she said. "But the clerk . . ."

"I told him what to do."

He poured champagne.

Julia's chin tilted as she took off her hat. "You were sure I'd come."

"I've always been an optimist."

He gave her a glass, and they stared at each other. Then she sipped, and he took the glass from her hand and kissed her. For a moment it was chaste, and then they were tightly in each other's arms.

"Oh, God," she said. "I didn't come here—"

"How much time have we got?" he asked.

"As much as we wish. On Saturday nights Harvey plays cards with his friends. Then they go on to a brothel for a couple of hours. He's seldom home before dawn."

How amusing it would be, Berkeley thought, if Harvey chose the same house as Harry. But to the best of his knowledge, the two men had never met.

"Well, then," he said. "We have the time to talk, at least. That's why you came here, isn't it?"

He sat down, sipped champagne; Julia roamed about the room, nervously. "I've never done anything like this before," she said.

"I am sure you haven't."

"But . . . seeing you . . . I asked Harvey to apply for this posting. I was sure that as you had used Athens before you would do so again, regularly, and that we might meet. I suppose I'm not very good with maps and things. I had no idea how far way Serbia is. Two years . . . and suddenly, there you were."

"You're not going to say that you regret not having married me?"

She had been standing by the window. Now she turned. "Do you mean to humiliate me?"

"I hope not. I just want things to be straight up between us."

She sighed and sat on the bed, shoulders hunched. "Yes, I wish we could have got married. I know I made all of those objections, I kept putting you off. I know the fault was mine. I wanted too much. I didn't realise that in this life one has to settle for the best one can get."

"And Harvey?"

She shuddered.

"He always struck me as being a very congenial type," Berkeley said. "Of course, I don't know him all that well."

"He stops smiling when he enters his own front door," Julia said.

"Ah. You mean he just becomes unsociable, or . . ."

"He is physically violent," she said. "Especially when he has been drinking."

Berkeley moved to sit beside her. "I am very sorry."

She turned her head to look at him. "Why should you be? It is not your concern."

"You are my oldest living female friend. Apart from my mother."

"And you would like to help me?"

"Yes, I would."

"What, would you challenge him, and shoot him down? In this country I do not suppose you would be arrested for murder."

"Probably not. And then?"

"I don't know. You are married . . ." She hesitated.

"And a father."

"And you and your wife are still very much in love."

"As you and I are being so straight with each other, I will say that I am still very much in love with her."

She frowned. "And?"

Berkeley sighed. "Caterina hates more than she loves. She has every reason to. Hers has been a fairly violent life."

"But she does not hate you."

"I think she does, sometimes. When she feels I am not hating her enemies enough."

She smiled. "Then you do not, after all, have the best of all possible worlds."

"I never said I did. I merely outlined what, in my opinion, were the roots of true happiness."

"And I naturally supposed you were speaking of yourself. But you have most of those roots, and perhaps in time you will have them all. You cannot help me, Berkeley. At least, not in the long run. But just for a moment . . ."

What does one do with a woman in such desperation? Well, Berkeley thought, what one does *with* her is straightforward enough: it is whatever she wants to be done. But what does one do *about* her? When she is married to another man, and when one is oneself married, to another woman? Julia had condemned herself to a life of misery. But what had been the alternative, when Berkeley had

162

dropped out of the running? A lifetime of spinsterdom? And Harvey must have appeared an attractive prospect.

But now . . . He supposed he had always loved her, without ever being able to penetrate her cocoon of good breeding and natural reserve to uncover the passion that could lie beneath, if it was there. He was sure he would have married her, had Gorman not set in train that sinister sequence of events that had brought him to Caterina. That was being unfair to the general. Caterina was one of the great experiences of his life. He had only slowly come to accept that he ranked second in *her* life, to what she conceived as her essential mission.

Again he had to accept that the fault was his. His impatience to save her from the consequences of her birth and background and upbringing, but more importantly, he knew, to make her entirely his, had led him to that disastrous kidnapping. For all his promises since and her apparent acceptance of them, she had not forgiven him and never would, thus she would never fully trust him again. Even her delight at the idea that he should join the Serbian army had been because she anticipated that army, one day, going to war with Austria. As that was not going to happen in the immediate future, her pleasure would soon dissipate in disappointment.

Yet she was his wife, and the mother of his children. He did not know if the Orthodox Church permitted divorce – he doubted it – but he knew that if he proposed it she would declare war on him, and his children would be lost to him, even supposing he himself survived.

The other side of the coin was Julia. Their failure to marry had been a result of her refusal to accept anything but her own terms, her own concept of how a marriage should be. Now, after two years of marriage to Harvey Braddock, she in was the mood to surrender. She had indeed just surrendered, everything. She knew very little about the art of love, and Harvey had clearly not wasted any time in teaching her. A woman's business in bed was to lie on her back with her legs apart, or on her front, again with her legs apart, and let the man get on with it; she did not expect to be pleased or in any way aroused, much less satiated.

This last hour had been a new world to her. She had looked at him in consternation when he had used his hands before entry. She had given little whimpers of uncertain ecstacy as he had brought her to orgasm, the first in her life, he estimated. She had moaned with pleasure when his entry had created another. She had clung to him fiercely when he had in turn climaxed, as if this was a moment she did not ever wish to end.

She was his, all his, for all eternity. And he could not take her.

She lay on her side, facing him, small breasts crushed together between her arms. "Tell me what you wish me to do," she said.

He sighed. "I wish I knew."

"You mean you would like me to leave."

He rolled towards her. "I mean I would like you to lie there for the rest of our lives."

"But I can't. So . . ." She rolled away from him and sat up.

He caught her round the waist and brought her back to him. Her head lay on his chest, her still-rich hair scattered.

"Say the word," she said, "and I will leave Harvey. I know you cannot marry me. I will be your mistress."

"My dear girl, you'd be ostracised."

"Do you think I give a damn for any of these people?"

"And at home?"

"Them too. If I could be with you, only occasionally."

"Unfortunately, that isn't on."

She sat up again, and this time kept on going, out of the bed before he could catch hold of her again.

"It's not that I don't want to do it," he said. "I would set you up as my mistress tomorrow . . ."

She turned to face him, long and slender and white. "But?"

"I am to join the Serb army within the week. And we are going to fight a war. I cannot tell you more than that. But I do not know for how long I shall be involved, just as I do not know if I will survive. I cannot ask you to ruin your life for a dream which may never happen."

She began to dress, slowly. "Harvey's tour of duty here has still three years to run," she said. "Will your war be over in three years?"

"I should think so."

"Well, then, I will wait," she said.

He got out of bed, held her in his arms. "And consider what you do."

"I have done that," she told him.

Berkeley and Lockwood caught the eight o'clock train north. Berkeley did not ask Lockwood about his night, and Lockwood made no comment regarding Berkeley's night; but as he was a valet he knew Berkeley had not slept alone, even if the lady was long gone by the time he came home.

In any event, they were distracted when they reached the border, where the guards had been doubled and their travel documents were examined for several minutes, while armed soldiers patrolled the platform. As Berkeley spoke no Turkish it was difficult to discover what was going on, but he did manage to get some information from a Greek businessman who was travelling on the same train.

"The Italians have served an ultimatum at Constantinople," the Greek explained.

"To what end?"

"They wish the surrender of Tripoli, and indeed, all Libya."

"Just like that?"

The Greek shrugged. "It is the beginning of the end for Turkey."

"So that's what Gorman meant, that the Italians will do it first," Berkeley remarked, as the train finally moved off.

"Tricky business," Lockwood agreed. "And you think the Serbs will come in on the Italian side?"

"Let's hope they don't until we are across the border," Berkeley said.

But although the evidence of Turkish agitation and suspicion grew throughout the next two days, they reached Belgrade without mishap. Berkeley went immediately to see Colonel Savos.

"Exciting times," the colonel remarked. "I am glad you got back safely, Colonel Townsend."

"Would you tell me what is going on?"

"Why, the Italians have invaded North Africa."

"Invaded?"

"They were bombarding Tripoli and landing troops even as the ultimatum was being delivered in Constantinople," Savos said. "Our information is that they are now ashore in large numbers, and that the Turkish governor has fled."

"And what are the powers doing about it?"

"Nothing. We are informed, through diplomatic channels, that Italy cleared its action with Britain and France before undertaking it."

The bastards, Berkeley thought. "And Albania?" he asked.

Savos shrugged. "The Albanians are always revolting. In my opinion, they are a revolting people." He smirked. "No doubt the Italians will make what use of it they can."

"Are we going to join in?"

Savos raised his eyebrows. "What, fight the Turks, with the Italians? Or worse, the Albanians? Why should we do that, Colonel?"

The two men gazed at each other.

"But you would still like me to accept your offer," Berkeley said.

"Of course. When a war begins, shall we say, on your doorstep, it pays to be ready yourself, does it not?"

"What you mean is, should the Italians get a bloody nose,

the Turks might feel in the mood to do some muscle-flexing up here."

"Who can tell what a Turk will do," Savos agreed.

"While should the Italians win . . ."

"Informed military opinion is that the Italians must win," Savos said. "It is expected their fleet will sail up ·the Bosphorus and bombard Constantinople."

"And then?"

"Who knows, my friend. The Turkish Empire may well fall apart. We must be ready to pick up the pieces. Will you help us?"

"Yes," Berkeley said.

"Excellent. I will inform you of where and when you are to report. In the meantime, go home to your wife."

To my wife, Berkeley thought.

But Caterina was in an excellent mood, the more so when she learned that he was definitely accepting a Serbian commission.

"We anticipate fighting the Turks," he reminded her.

"One war often leads to another," she said happily.

Unfortunately, he knew she was right.

However, this war hurried slowly. By the end of October the Italians had taken Tripoli, and on November 1 they carried out the first aerial bombardment in history, on Tanguira Oasis in Tripolitania. Four days later the Italian government announced the annexation of Libya, Tripolitania and Cyrenaica. The total collapse of Turkish authority west of Egypt – which was actually controlled by the British – sent shock waves through the Balkans, and indeed the world. The French hastily annexed Morocco, at the other end of the North African coast. There were mobilisations everywhere. Berkeley, just joining his cavalry depot at Novi-Sad, expected war momentarily. But instead, King Peter went off to Paris to meet with the French president. The Serbs were taking no risks.

In fact, after the initial Italian claims, the war went into a complete stalemate. Libya was actually far from conquered, and various Turkish outposts continued to hold out. The Italians declared they would land troops in Albania to invade the Turkish Balkans, and were brought up short by the Austrians, who refused to accept such a step and said they would go to war with Italy if necessary. As Austria and Italy were officially allies, with Germany, against France and Russia, this caused a further diplomatic furore.

But the various machinations in the eastern Mediterranean were completely overshadowed the following April by the disaster of the RMS *Titanic*. While that news was winging round and round the world, the declaration of the Greek government that it had signed a pact of mutual assistance with Bulgaria against any common foe went almost unnoticed. But those two countries could only have one possible common foe.

"It is all coming together," Brigadier-General Petrovich said when he came to inspect Berkeley's regiment that spring.

Berkeley had worked hard over a bitter winter. He had found he commanded a regiment of lancers, also armed with sword and carbine; good men, mountain people who had served for some time already, excellent horsemen who only needed proper training and discipline to form a formidable force. The training and discipline were his province, with the assistance of Lockwood who he made a sergeant-major. He was also supported by an enthusiastic group of officers, among whom he was delighted to find Captain Horovich, who had commanded the frontier crossing at Apratin, when he had been bringing Anna home to die.

"Now we are on the same side, eh?" Horovich said.

"We always were, you know," Berkeley told him.

Sadly, with war likely at any moment, he had not been allowed to give any of his men leave, or take any himself. Thus he could not be with Caterina for the delivery of her third child, but she sent word that it had been simple enough; it was another girl, who she announced she would christen Alicia, after Berkeley's mother. He wished he could be with her.

While he wondered about affairs in Athens.

"It is crumbling," Petrovich told him. "The Turkish edifice. Of course the Austrians are being awkward; they suspect that if the Italians ever get into Albania they will never leave again. But we can work with the Italians. It is the Turkish beast we must destroy."

Having seen some evidence of the Turkish mistreatment of their subject peoples, and read of the Armenian catastrophe, Berkeley was inclined to agree with him.

"Am I allowed to give my people leave, General?" he asked. "They have been cooped up here all winter."

"Yes, give them leave, but staggered, of course. And subject to instant recall should the situation deteriorate."

"And my officers?"

"Them too." Petrovich chuckled. "And yourself. One week. You have a new child to see, have you not?"

Sabac was as quiet as Berkeley had ever remembered it, an oasis of peace in a world which seemed close to falling apart. It was now summer, and the people seemed prosperous and content.

Even Caterina was in the best of humours, and the children were delighted to see their father. Berkeley looked forward to a week of complete rest, and was unpleasantly surprised, on his third day, to see Karlovy on the street.

Karlovy also obviously saw him, because he immediately disappeared. Berkeley returned to the Slovitza house.

"Did you know Karlovy is back?" he asked.

"I did not know he had ever been away," Caterina said. "This is his home, you know."

"He has been away," Berkeley pointed out, "as for three years we have not seen him. Has he been here?"

"Why should he come here?" she asked.

She was lying, he knew. But as he had to return to his regiment in less than a week Berkeley decided against making a scene. Instead he paid a visit to Belgrade. He went first of all to Gregory's school where he was shown into the headmaster's office.

"Berkeley, my old friend," Gregory said, embracing him. "How splendid you look in that uniform."

"Thank you. I have come to find out if you are up to your old tricks."

"Me? Old tricks?" Gregory gave a twisted smile. "I am a schoolmaster. I deal in schoolboys. Look. It is a break."

He went to the window and Berkeley joined him. The yard beneath was filled with young men, soberly dressed, walking to and fro, talking; some of the younger ones were kicking a ball about.

"These are my followers now," Gregory said.

"And do you indoctrinate them with hatred of all things Austrian?"

"Every good Serb must hate all things Austrian, Berkeley."

"You don't think there are more important antagonists?"

Gregory spread his hands. "Not if you come from Bosnia-Herzegovina."

"And some of your pupils are from there?"

"Oh, indeed. They are the children of parents who fled when the Austrians took over. I do not have to teach *them* how to hate, my friend."

"I'm sure," Berkeley said, and went to the door. There he checked. "Oh, by the way, have you seen anything of Karlovy recently?"

"Karlovy? Why no. Should I have?"

Another liar, Berkeley thought, as he went to police headquarters. But as he spent so much time lying himself, he supposed he should not complain.

"Why, Colonel Townsend," Savos said. "How splendid you look in uniform."

"Thank you," Berkeley said. "Tell me about the Black Hand."

Savos raised his eyebrows. "It no longer exists."

"Colonel Savos," Berkeley said, "I do not wish to be rude to you, but you are lying to me. Everyone is lying to me. The Black Hand exists, and it is busily reconstituting itself. Gregory Masanovich is again in control, and I believe he is recruiting from among the schoolboys at his academy. I think it would be good for you, for all of us, were you to keep an eye on him, and it."

"Then I shall do so," Savos agreed. "But I can assure you that there will be no problem with the Black Hand until after the war with Turkey."

Berkeley wondered how he could be so sure.

But the war with Turkey was now very close. At the end of the week Berkeley received an order cancelling all leave and instructing him to rejoin his regiment; the cavalry brigade was to leave Novi-Sad and move south to Nish, close to the Macedonian border.

"I am so proud of you," Caterina said, checking his belts and sidearms, adjusting his cap to sit squarely on his head. "You will come back covered in glory. I know it."

It did not seem a possibility to her that he might not come back at all; or if it had occurred to her, she was not revealing it.

He held her in his arms. His beautiful, beautiful bride, who knew only hatred. Once he had felt so sure he could wean her away from that. Now he was realising it would never happen.

Unless Austria were to be crushed, somehow, and there did not seem the least possibility of that happening.

He kissed and hugged the children; Anna was just old enough to put some words together, and in English.

"You go beat the Turks, Papa," she said.

It was not a question.

"Oh, indeed," he said, and mounted his horse.

How sad it was, he thought, that he should feel relief at leaving his wife and family, his home and his people. No, never *his* people.

He found his thoughts drifting to Athens. But there was no hope of returning to Athens until the business in Macedonia had been completed.

The brigade moved south, and found itself part of a steadily growing army concentrating on the southern border. They marched through villages and were escorted by cheering crowds; girls and women threw garlands of flowers, small boys and dogs marched beside them. It was impossible not to feel a sense of euphoria Berkeley had never experienced before. In Egypt and the Sudan the British had been an occupying force, and although a large proportion of the population – those who were opposed to the Mahdi's fundamentalism – had appeared to welcome them, there had been no real enthusiasm.

But how odd it was, he thought, that having for a dozen years been regarded as unfit for active service by the British, he should now be riding at the head of a column of brightly clad and enthusiastic horsemen. But then, no British officer would ever consider leading, for example, the Household Cavalry into battle in full dress.

Even odder were his personal feelings. Like most Englishmen, brought up on Gladstonian revelations of Turkish horrors committed against the people of the Balkans and the Armenians, he certainly had no feelings of sympathy for the enemy. But although he was proud of his men and knew it was an honour to lead them, he felt no affinity for them, or for their country's aspirations. He could not help but feel that the Serbs, and their allies the Bulgarians and the Greeks, were like hyenas, seeking to prey on a decaying colossus. From what he had seen he did not believe that they could replace it with anything vastly better, or that they would not fall out amongst themselves when the spoils came to be divided.

He was here, risking his life, simply because General Gorman had willed it. And because it pleased Caterina, to be sure. But he was increasingly coming to wonder if that was any longer relevant.

The Lovers

The concentration on the Macedonian border was the largest Berkeley had ever seen; the Serbian army totalled some 80,000 men, a mass of gaily flying flags and splendid uniforms and rows of neat tents and supply wagons. The cavalry were met by Brigadier-General Petrovich, and instructed as to where to set up their encampment. They were to mount pickets along the border.

"But under no circumstances are they to cross the border," he told the regimental commanders.

"Are we not here to fight?" someone asked.

Petrovich smiled. "Indeed we are, Colonel. When the moment is right."

That evening Berkeley sat his horse beside Lockwood's, on a bluff overlooking the Morava and the twinkling lights on the far side of the river.

"They're well back," Lockwood remarked. "They must know we're here."

"I'm sure they do," Berkeley agreed. "But they're desperate not to provoke an incident."

"Is that what we are here to do, sir?"

"We," Berkeley said, "are waiting on the Italians."

He hoped they wouldn't take too much longer to complete their victory and move on Turkey itself; it was already into October and growing very cold. He didn't relish the prospect of the army, and himself, sitting in these hills for a very bitter winter.

He wished there was some means of communicating with Gorman, if only to find out exactly what was going on, but he dared not take the risk that anyone in the Serbian army might discover he was actually an English spy.

A week later the commanding general of the Serb forces, Putnik, arrived, and summoned all field officers to a conference.

Radomir Putnik was a short, heavy-set man with a clipped white beard. For the last nine years he had been either Chief of Staff to King Peter or Minister of War in the Serb government, and the soldiers worshipped him. He had seen service as a junior officer in the wars of the eighties, but not since then, and was now

171

sixty-five years old. But there was no apparent diminution in energy.

"Gentlemen," he said, "I have grave news. As a result of their defeats in Africa, the Turkish government has sued for peace. The Italians have agreed."

He paused to let this sink in.

"A conference is taking place in London at this moment to agree terms. This means that our plan to take part in an assault upon the Turkish territories in the Balkans, in conjunction with our Italian allies, has collapsed. The Italians will presumably get Libya, which is all they really wanted. While we . . . well, they do not appear to have much interest in what we might want."

Another pause.

"So," the general said, 'we are going to operate on our own."

A rustle of relief ran through the room.

"Even without the Italians," Putnik went on, "with our other allies we have an ample superiority over the Turkish forces here in the Balkans, and this superiority will be accentuated by the low morale we may expect on the other side following their defeats by the Italians. We anticipate being able to complete our campaign, successfully, before the Turks can bring any additional forces from the rest of the empire. Now . . ." He turned to the huge map of the region pinned to the wall. "We are here." He touched the area around Nish with his wand. "Eighty thousand of the best fighting men in the world. The Bulgarians are here . . ." he indicated the country just east of the Macedonian frontier, ". . . with one hundred and eighty thousand men. And the Greeks are here . . ." he touched the southern Macedonian border, ". . . with fifty thousand men under the command of Crown Prince Constantine. There are also the Montenegrins here." He pointed to the Adriatic seaboard. "They have about thirty thousand men under arms, but frankly, these cannot be considered front-line troops, no matter how useful they may be as guerillas.

"The Bulgarian task is to guard our eastern front, and undertake their own invasion of Thrace. The Greeks and ourselves will clear Macedonia of the Turks. To this end we are going to advance south into the valley of the Vardar, here . . ." He traced the river, in the lower half of Macedonia. "The Greeks will come up from the south, and between us we will squeeze the Turks into total collapse. So, gentlemen, you will receive your battle instructions within the week, and then . . . we seek the liberation of the Balkans from Turkish rule. I know you will all carry out your duties. May God go with you."

Hostilities commenced on October 20, 1912. The previous afternoon

General Putnik came to the cavalry encampment, and inspected the troops in the company of Brigadier-General Petrovich. He then assembled the senior officers for another conference.

"As you will have observed," he said, "the Turks are not manning the border in any strength. Our first business must be to seek out their army and destroy it. You are our eyes. Discover the enemy dispositions, and report. You will not undertake any aggressive actions against superior forces until the infantry have come up. Thank you, gentlemen."

Petrovich summoned Berkeley, and Putnik shook hands.

"You are the Englishman who fights for us," he said. "I congratulate you, Colonel Townsend. Will your countrymen support us?"

"If you mean here in the field, sir, I'm afraid not," Berkeley said. "The Balkans are a long way from Great Britain."

"Of course. I met an English journalist, quite recently, who thought Belgrade was the capital of Bulgaria. But will we at least have their sympathy?"

"I believe you will, sir."

"Then that is a step in the right direction."

"But only if the war is conducted in a civilised manner, sir."

Putnik looked at him. "Is it possible to conduct a war in a civilised manner, Colonel? Godspeed."

At dawn the next morning the cavalry crossed the river.

Still maintaining the pretence that nothing was happening, the Turks had not blown the bridges and the crossings were entirely unopposed.

"Eerie, sir," Lockwood commented, riding at Berkeley's right hand; the trumpeter was on his left, and the three squadrons, a total of 450 men, were in column behind him. The other two regiments of the brigade were about a mile away, to either side, and immediately in front of Berkeley's command there rode Brigadier-General Petrovich, with his staff. In front of him, a further half-mile distant, was a screen of some fifty men, widely spread out. "You wouldn't think there was a Turk for a hundred miles."

"I imagine they're closer than that," Berkeley said, surveying the hills through his binoculars.

The country was indeed so crumpled any one of the tree-shrouded valleys could have concealed a sizeable enemy force, but throughout the first day, during which the cavalry advanced some thirty miles, not a shot was fired. Petrovich sent a galloper back to report to headquarters, and he returned a day later to inform the brigadier that just about the entire Serb army was across the frontier.

The following day the scouts reported enemy forces, and Petrovich himself went up to the next ridge to survey the country ahead.

Berkeley and the other two colonels went with him, and they looked down on yet another valley, and here there were certainly troops; Berkeley estimated a regiment of blue-coated cavalry, with some infantry behind.

In the distance there could just be made out the roofs and minarets of a town. "Where is that?" Petrovich asked his guide.

"Kumanovo, your excellency."

"Colonel Townsend, how many men would you estimate are down there?"

"A few hundred, sir."

"Well, then, I would not say we were outnumbered. Gentlemen, let us see what those fellows are made of." He turned to his adjutant. "Captain, send a galloper to General Putnik to inform him that we are engaging a small enemy force covering the town of Kumanovo."

The captain saluted and hurried off and Berkeley returned to his command, where his officers were anxiously waiting.

"Take your positions, gentlemen," he said. "We are about to advance."

Various bugle calls rang out and the three regiments came into line, lances removed from rests. Brigadier-General Petrovich came back to them, and drew his sword. The other officers did likewise.

"Sound the march, bugler," Petrovich commanded.

The notes rang out and the line of horsemen advanced, topping the ridge to look down on the valley. Their manoeuvre had been observed, and the Turkish horse began to withdraw. A trap, Berkeley wondered. But there was no time for further consideration as the bugler now sounded the charge, and the blue and red lines went careering down the slope.

Now the Turkish horsemen were in full retreat, while their infantry support fired one volley before themselves hurrying back towards the safety of the town and the several cannon emplaced on its outskirts. These opened fire and the bugler sounded the halt. The lancers dragged their steaming horses to a stop as the shells began to burst. Berkeley looked over his shoulder. Several men had fallen and were being tended by the medical staff. He could not see any Turkish casualties.

Now it was their turn to withdraw out of range of the guns. "Well, gentlemen," Petrovich said, "at least we now know where they are. And that they prefer to fight behind fortifications. We'll soon have them out of there."

The Battle of Kumanovo was fought the next day, October 24. If it could be called a battle, Berkeley thought. The main Serbian army came up overnight, and the cavalry were kept back for the anticipated pursuit. By then Berkeley had inspected his men, spoken with the wounded, and overseen the burial of the three of his command who had been killed. Everyone was still full of fight and confident in the morrow.

As they had every right to be. The Serb artillery pounded the town – they did not seem concerned with causing civilian casualties – and then the infantry attacked. Resistance was minimal, and by afternoon the cavalry were ranging over the countryside south of the town, sweeping up survivors. As he had feared would be the case, Berkeley had a difficult job keeping his men in hand. They had seen some of their comrades killed, they had a long history of warfare against the Turks, and they were out for blood. But with the help of Lockwood and men like Captain Horovich he managed to prevent their captives from being massacred, and even the few women they found with the Turks from being raped. What would happen to them in the rear he could not say.

General Putnik reviewed them the next day. "You have done well," he said. "Now we must pursue. It is our business to destroy the main body."

It was obvious, both from the casualties and from interrogating the prisoners, that this had been no more than a covering force to allow the concentration of the full Turkish army.

In private, the general was less sanguine.

"It appears that we will have to do this job ourselves," he told his officers. "The Greeks have been defeated."

So that's why we have been meeting with limited resistance, Berkeley thought; the Turks have been concentrating in the south.

"There is also trouble with the Bulgarians," Putnik went on. "As I told you, their business was the invasion and conquest of Thrace. But Bulgarian units are also moving south-east, towards Salonika. The Greeks wish to have Salonika, but so do the Bulgars. This possibility is naturally distracting the Greek command. But we will continue our advance."

Two days later they were at the Vardar.

Here the bridges had been broken, but there was still only sporadic Turkish resistance. By now the Macedonians were taking an active part in the war, on the Serbian side – there was still no sign of the Greeks – and the cavalry were shown fords which enabled them to get across and clear the south bank while the sappers reconstructed the bridges sufficiently for the infantry and artillery to follow.

"Where is the Turkish army?" Berkeley asked one of the peasants.

"They say they will hold the Babuna Pass," the man said. "It is a few miles to the south."

"With how many men?"

"It is the main Turkish army, your excellency. Perhaps forty thousand men."

Berkeley duly reported this intelligence to headquarters before resuming his advance. They reached the head of the pass the next morning, and came under heavy artillery fire. So he withdrew to await orders.

The general surveyed the situation through his binoculars, surrounded by his staff. The pass was guarded by serrated peaks, impassable to a large army. "That is a strong position," he remarked. "I begin to understand their strategy, now. They have allowed us virtually a free run through Macedonia. Now they will hope to hold us here for an indefinite period, both to allow the onset of winter, and to enable them to deal with the Greeks in the south. We must not permit this to happen. The Turks must be kept on the run."

"You will force the pass?" Petrovich was surprised, and concerned. "Casualties will be very heavy."

To this point they had been remarkably light.

"One does not make an omelette without breaking eggs," Putnik remarked. "However, there is more than one way to skin a cat. We will mount a slow frontal assault here, while you, Petrovich, and you, Magrinovich, take your people through the mountains to arrive in the rear."

General Magrinovich pulled his nose. He commanded one of the finest divisisons in the Serbian army, but they were largely on foot. "That is very difficult country," he pointed out. "It will take time."

"You have four days," Putnik said. "Then I wish you to close on the rear of the Turkish position. I assume you will not need as long, Petrovich."

The brigadier-general studied the map. "My route is also difficult," he pointed out, "but I think we can do it in three."

Putnik nodded. "You will be in position in plenty of time for your attack at dawn on the fourth morning. Magrinovich, you will have to assault immediately you reach your position." He marked them on the map. "Good fortune, gentlemen."

Both wings of the enveloping movement left immediately. Now the weather had definitely turned wintry, and the cavalry plodded along while the rain bounced off their caps and soaked their greatcoats. They were being guided by Macedonians, who presumably knew the best mountain trails, but even so they often found it necessary to dismount and lead their horses.

"Makes you almost yearn for the old Sudan," Lockwood remarked. "At least we didn't have any rain."

Because of the weather, their progress was slower than Petrovich would have liked, and their stops were kept down to a few hours at a time, bivouacking as best they could. The sight of a mountain village was like manna from heaven, as at least it meant they could get out of the wet for a brief spell.

The villagers fed them hard bread and goat stew, and gathered round to stare at the soldiers, the children whispering among themselves. They were desperately poor, judging from their clothes, their houses and their food, but there could be no doubt that they hated the Turks and looked on the Serbs as their saviours. So much so that, having wrapped himself in his cloak and settled down to sleep as best he could for an hour, Berkeley awoke with a start to find a warm young body snuggling in with him. He sat up, looked down at the girl – she could hardly be much more than fifteen, he estimated – and looked across at the guide, who was only a few feet away.

The guide grinned. "She would deem it an honour, famous sir."

Well, Berkeley thought, Caterina was a long way away, Julia even further.

Next morning his men were in fine humour; it appeared that almost every man had been serviced by the mountain women, all of whom regarded it as a privilege. Now even the rain hardly seemed to matter. But that afternoon their advance guard was fired upon.

Berkeley's first thought was that it was, after all, angry and jealous villagers, but his men galloped back to tell him they had encountered a Turkish outpost. Berkeley immediately deployed his command and went forward himself, with Lockwood and Horovich, to oversee the situation.

"We returned fire, your excellency," said Sergeant Dragovich, who had maintained his position with half a dozen men, dismounted and crouching amid the rocks.

"You are sure they were Turks?" Berkeley asked.

"It sounded like Mausers, sir."

The Turks, Berkeley knew, were being supplied by the Germans; there was even a rumour that they were employing German officers.

"Well, we must move them, quickly."

He drew both sword and revolver, waited for Horovich to bring up his dismounted squadron and moved along the trail, the guide prudently keeping to the rear. Then he led his men forward at a rush. He was actually surprised that he had not yet been wounded in this campaign. Perhaps twice was enough for fate. More probably it was because Turkish marksmanship was extremely poor, and the Serbs had not yet encountered any real resistance.

Nor did they now. They discerned the Turkish position easily enough, from the detritus lying about, but there was no sign of any enemy.

"Well, that's that," Berkeley remarked to Horovich. "Now they surely know we're coming."

He sent a message to Brigadier-General Petrovich, who arrived an hour later.

"I reckon those fellows will be scuttling to Prilep just as fast as they can go," Berkeley said. "To warn the main body."

Petrovich nodded. "But that is all to our advantage, Colonel. Is there not a saying in chess that the threat is greater than the execution? So the Turks will know we are turning their position. They must either detach a sizeable force to stop us, which will weaken their position in the pass, or they must accept that they have been outmanoeuvered and withdraw."

The Turks abandoned the pass. Before they had reached their destination, Berkeley and his men looked down on the valley and a huge body of men moving to the south-west.

"Talk about bloodless victories, sir," Lockwood remarked. "It seems to me that this General Putnik is a sizeable soldier."

Berkeley wondered how he would do against troops who were better trained and equipped and better led than the Turks; and had higher morale. But there could be no faulting the old general's energy, as he drove his men in pursuit. Strategically, he had already gained a great victory. Having failed to hold the Serbs at the pass, the Turks were left with either retreating on their army attempting – quite successfully to this point – to hold the Greeks, or retreating to the south-west. The latter meant cutting themselves off from the rest of the Turkish Empire in the Balkans, and any real hope of succour. Macedonia was lost.

"However," Putnik told his officers, "they still have an estimated forty thousand men in the field, and they have a very strong fortress here." He prodded the map at the town of Monastir, on the south-west border with Albania. "He will take shelter there, and wait either to be evacuated by sea, or for a Turkish offensive in Thrace which may reverse the situation. We must have him, now, gentlemen."

The army sang as it marched along. Even if they had not yet won any great victory, they were confident of doing so when the occasion arose. And that the Turks were in headlong retreat could not be doubted, from the amount of discarded *matériel* they picked up as they went along. Petrovich's cavalry was sent ranging ahead of the infantry, and they did bring in some Turkish stragglers, terrified conscripts who were intent only on keeping their lives – and their manhoods: they had apparently been fed a rumour that the Serbs would castrate every prisoner they took.

Berkeley hoped it was only a rumour, as he sent them to the rear.

A few days later his scouts sighted the roofs of Monastir. He sent a galloper back to Petrovich, and commanded his men to halt to await the arrival of the main body. He himself, with Horovich and Lockwood, went forward to the next high ridge to gaze at the fortified town. It was November 4, and it was amazing to consider that this war had only started a fortnight previously. In that short space of time the Serbs had overrun all of Macedonia but for this last little pocket of resistance, close to the Albanian border; and there would be little refuge there for any Turk.

In that fortnight he had not bathed or changed his clothes, so rapid had been the advance. He had only had half a dozen hot meals, and hardly more than a couple of dozen hours of sleep. He knew that he and his men were on the edge of physical collapse, yet the morale of continuous victory, continuous advance, remained high. And surely this was the end.

"What then, sir?" Lockwood asked.

"Do you know, Harry, I have no idea," Berkeley said. His first priority would be to get in touch with Gorman.

They had their usual couple of hours sleep, kept half-awake by the tramp and rumble of the infantry and artillery arriving. It was a still night, although the clouds were low – there was even a flurry of snow at dawn – and the Turks could hear the arrival of their enemies too. There were distant bugle calls, and Berkeley could imagine the defenders standing anxiously to their guns.

Dawn revealed that the Turks had accepted they would have to fight, and were determined to make the best of it. Their army, or the main part of it, had marched out of the town and taken up a position in front of it, in a distinctly nineteenth-century fashion: horse, foot and guns all carefully arranged. Brought up in his staff college days on the encounter battles of the American Civil War or the Franco-Prussian War, and having since then studied similar battles of the Boer War and the Russo-Japanese conflict, he had to form the impression that the enemy were inviting defeat.

General Putnik thought so too. He arrived soon after daybreak, followed by the main part of his army, and studied the Turkish dispositions through his field glasses. "Well, gentlemen," he said, "they are lambs to the slaughter. General Petrovich, your cavalry will undertake a turning movement on the right. Proceed in full view of the enemy, but keep out of range. This will distract him. You will not, however, charge, until his centre is broken."

Petrovich saluted and summoned his officers.

Putnik frowned. "What is that madman doing?"

The infantry division on the extreme left of the Serb army, led by Major-General Magrinovich, had not formed up like their comrades, but continued advancing, marching down the slope towards the town and the Turkish forces, flags flying and drums beating.

"We must get him back," said one of the staff officers.

"I will have him court-martialled," Putnik growled. "Yes, call him back."

A junior officer wheeled his horse and galloped down the slope. But it was too late. The Turkish general had no doubt been as surprised as anyone to find himself being attacked by a single division. Now he reacted vigorously, and detached virtually his entire right wing to assault the impetuous Serbs. These halted their advance and attempted to deploy, but they were outnumbered and quickly surrounded.

Putnik cursed and swore as he saw his men being cut to pieces, while a ripple of alarm and apprehension ran through the entire army. To have come so far, so successfully, and then to have the cup of victory dashed from their lips by the overenthusiasm of one divisional commander . . .

Berkeley, already starting to lead his regiment away to the right, checked his horse and held up his hand. His men halted behind him, while he studied the Turkish ranks through his glasses.

"Hold the regiment here," he told Horovich, and galloped to where Petrovich was marshalling the rest of the cavalry. "Down there, General," he said.

Petrovich levelled his glasses and saw what Berkeley's keen eye had spotted. The Serb division was fighting desperately, but was clearly about to be overwhelmed. Now it was the Turkish turn to become overenthusiastic. Men were streaming away from the centre to take part in the coming massacre.

"By God," Petrovich said. "Have your men ready, Colonel." And he himself rode to Putnik.

The general had been watching the destruction of his left wing shoulders humped, cap pulled down over his eyes. Now he turned back sharply as Petrovich indicated the situation in the Turkish centre. He waved his cap in the air, and Petrovich galloped back to the waiting cavalry, the entire brigade now formed into line, lances at the ready.

"The brigade will advance!" Petrovich shouted.

"Hurrah!" Berkeley yelled, and drew his sword as the bugles sounded. The Serb cavalry trotted down the hill, pennons fluttering from their lance heads. Behind them the lead divisions of the infantry also advanced, at the double, and behind them the artillery sent several salvoes crashing into the Turkish ranks.

Too late the Turkish commander realised his mistake. Bugles rang out, staff officers were sent chasing after his disintegrating centre.

But the Serb left wing, realising that they might yet be rescued, were holding their ground and dying where they stood, while the Turks were caught in a maelstrom of conflicting orders and sudden fear.

"Cavalry will charge!" Petrovich roared, and the lances came down, while Berkeley levelled his sword. With Horovich at one shoulder and Lockwood at the other he led his men into the Turkish centre. Blue-uniformed infantry, wearing fezzes and dark moustaches, presented rifles and bayonets, and several fired, but they were too distracted by the wall of horsemen careering down on them to take aim. Then Berkeley was into their midst, sword arm held rigid and wrist turned, thumb lodged in its slot on the haft of his weapon. The man immediately in front of him attempted to step aside and jab with his bayonet, and was struck by the horse's shoulder and sent sprawling, to be ridden over by Lockwood. A second man appeared, and held up his rifle like a quarterstaff. Berkeley's sword point struck him in the face with a jar that travelled right up his arm and into his shoulder, but the man went down with blood splattered across his tunic and on his face.

Now there were only running men in front of him, streaming in every direction. And not only from the shattered centre. Those on the Turkish left were also pouring from the field, as were those on the right, abandoning their assault on the Serb division which had precipitated this extraordinary battle with its even more extraordinary result.

Now it was a business of controlling his own men, who were pursuing the fleeing Turks, and also heading towards the now exposed town behind. The gates were open, and the Serb horsemen were making for the pillage they knew awaited them.

"Bugler!" Berkeley shouted. "Sound the recall."

There was no response, and he swung round to look behind him. The bugler was gone.

Lockwood was there. "He stopped one, sir."

"Then we'll have to do it manually."

His horse was exhausted, and it took some time to bring his men back. But by then the battle was over. The Turks had fled, those who could. An enormous number were scattered on the ground, dead or dying. A far greater number had surrendered.

"I estimate we have cut their army in two," Petrovich said. His face was lined with powder marks, his uniform had been slashed; Berkeley supposed he hardly looked any better. But they had triumphed.

The war was effectively over, for on the same day as the Battle of Monastir, the Greeks overwhelmed the remaining Turkish forces in Macedonia at Venije. The survivors of Monastir fled to the fortress of Yannina, and were besieged there by Greek units. Other Greek units rushed on to Salonika, arriving there and taking possession only twenty-four hours before the Bulgarian army caught them up.

"Oh, let them squabble," General Putnik said. "We have Macedonia."

King Peter himself, very old and frail but wearing uniform and erect on his horse, came down to inspect his victorious troops and hand out medals. All the officers from regimental commanders up were so honoured, and the old monarch gave Berkeley a special handshake.

"I have heard much of your cavalry charges," he said. "You will have a brigade."

Now that the fighting appeared to be over, Berkeley was more interested in contacting London to find out what he was to do next; the war had ended far more quickly and decisively than anyone had anticipated, or, from his point of view, was really to be desired. Far from being at all weakened by the conflict, Serbia was now on a high, with an army which had gained what could be called a succession of great victories – even if against negligible opposition – and having just about doubled its territory by the acquisition of Macedonia. There were undoubtedly going to be a large number of hotheads, in the military and out of it, who would regard Austria as less of a threat and more of a target in these new circumstances.

His application for leave was immediately granted; he was one of the heroes of the hour, but, having given Lockwood a position in the regiment he could not at the moment be considered a valet, and had to be left behind.

Petrovich naturally supposed that Berkeley wished to return to Sabac, to see Caterina and the children. He did want to do that, but Athens was more urgent, and as he had to admit to himself, not entirely for political or military reasons. Besides, at the moment it was so very much closer, just over two hundred miles from Monastir, whereas Sabac was three.

With the railways disrupted and people still in a state of some agitation, it took him a week to reach the Greek capital. Not that he wasn't welcomed wherever he went; the Serbs were the heroes of the hour, as far as the Greeks went, and Berkeley, having bathed and shaved and changed into a new uniform, was the epitome of a dashing Serb cavalry officer, one of the men who had driven the Turks helter-skelter from Macedonia. And who would now assist the Greeks in their aim of obtaining some of Thrace from the Bulgarians? Certainly there were considerable anti-Bulgarian sentiments to be heard on every side, but were these people so limited in their vision that they would fight amongst themselves over the spoils with Turkey still a major power, and still in the field? Berkeley sincerely hoped he would not be required to take part in such a self-destructive process.

Once in Athens, he returned to the Excelsior, where he was made even more welcome than on his previous visit. He bathed and changed and generally spruced himself up, then, wearing civilian clothes, called at the British Embassy.

"Major Townsend?" Andrews was astounded. "We have been hearing the most amazing rumours."

"That I have been fighting for the Serbs?"

"Indeed. Did London know about this?"

"I think you had better ask London," Berkeley suggested. "My wife is Serbian, you know. I felt I should do my bit."

"Yes," Andrews said doubtfully. "Actually, our new military attaché is an acquaintance of yours. Colonel Smailes?"

Berkeley hastily suppressed a frown. "Toby Smailes is in Greece?"

"Or Thrace, or somewhere. He is with the Greek army. While he was here, however, he did ask if there was any means of getting in touch with you. He seemed quite anxious to do so. Well, I told him you would probably be in Sabac, and I believe he was meaning to go up there, when he was overtaken by the outbreak of war."

Berkeley was suddenly faced with a very difficult, and possibly dangerous, situation. Gorman had ordered him to join the Serb army. That had admittedly been several months ago, and while he had been with the cavalry, whether at Novi-Sad, Nish or in the field, it would not have been possible to contact him again. So, whatever had happened to change Gorman's mind, it had been something so important he had deemed it necessary to send his own right-hand man to find him.

But what could have happened?

"When do you expect Colonel Smailes back?" he asked.

"It's impossible to say. I imagine as soon as things settle down. Will you remain in Athens?"

"I cannot do that. I am on leave from the army and must rejoin my command."

"Then where may Colonel Smailes find you, when he does return?"

"I don't know that either, dammit. If he wishes to see me urgently enough, tell him to go to Sabac, where I am sure he will be welcomed by my wife, and wait there. I should be able to get home in a month or so."

Andrews looked more doubtful yet. But he said, "I will do so. It may be more useful, however, for him to stay with our new man in Belgrade. He is a friend of yours: Harvey Braddock."

Berkeley could not believe his ears. "Harvey Braddock is the consul in Belgrade?"

"That is correct. He took up his post a month ago. Did he not contact you?"

"No, he did not. He could not, as I was with my regiment in the north." Berkeley hesitated. But he was entitled to ask after an old friend. "Did Mrs Braddock accompany him?"

"Yes, she did. But he sent her back here when the crisis worsened."

"You mean she is in Athens?"

"Yes, indeed."

"I feel I should call."

"Of course. I will give you the address."

At least, he thought, his journey had not been entirely wasted. And it might still be possible to obtain more.

"I shall need the use of your code room again."

Andrews raised his eyes to heaven.

Berkeley sent: War over. Am promoted brigadier. Please advise on acceptance.

He reckoned it was best not to indicate he knew anything about Smailes' appointment, which would leave the ball squarely in Gorman's court.

"I'm staying at the Excelsior, as before," he told Andrews. "Will you let me have the reply to that the moment it comes in."

Andrews made a face. There was, Berkeley noted, no invitation to lunch this time.

But there was also no chance of a reply being received for several hours. He went to the address Andrews had given him.

The door of the apartment was opened by a maid.

"Mrs Braddock in?" he asked.

"Berkeley!?" Julia had been within earshot. "Oh, Berkeley." She hurried forward, then checked. "Thank you, Irene."

The maid gave a little curtsey and withdrew, casting Berkeley a curious glance; her mistress's pleasure at the visitor was unmistakeable.

Julia held his hands and drew him into the small withdrawing room. "I was so afraid . . . They told me you were fighting with the Serbs."

"I didn't have too much choice."

"But you survived."

"I usually do." He glanced at the doorway, but the maid had disappeared. He took Julia in his arms, kissed her again and again. "I've even been promoted, I'm a brigadier."

"Oh, Berkeley!" She held him close. "I got Harvey posted to Belgrade."

"So I heard."

"Then I sent a message to Sabac asking if I could visit, but there was no reply."

He nodded. "I was with the army."

"But your wife . . ."

"Oh, I think she received the message. As to what she made of it . . . No doubt I shall find out when I go home."

"And then Harvey sent me down here to be safe. He thought the Serbs would be smashed and the Turks would overrun the country."

"He never was much of a military man," Berkeley said.

"Now he wants me back."

"Ah," Berkeley said. "When?"

"I was going to leave tomorrow. He says there are trains running."

"There are. This couldn't have worked out better. We'll go together."

She gazed into his eyes. "And? You said the war might last for years."

He kissed her. "So I'm not much of a military man either, I suppose. The Turks didn't put up much of a show."

"But with the war over . . ."

"Yes," he said.

Everything was happening too quickly. He was virtually promised to two women, and what women! Julia was everything he could and did love, and want; and was married to another man. Caterina was everything any man could want, physically, but they no longer loved each other. And she was capable of bearing the most terrible hatreds. She could also kill.

But Julia could know nothing of that. Or of how dependent he was upon a satisfactory reply from London.

"What do you want me to do?" Julia asked.

"Get rid of the maid," he suggested.

They went out to eat. It was a bleak late November day with rain sweeping in from the Aegean Sea, but inside the restaurant it was snug, and the mood jolly; all of Greece was celebrating.

"You'd think the war was over," Julia remarked.

"Well, it is, from their point of view. Even more from the Serb point of view. They've got what they want."

"But the Bulgarians are still fighting, aren't they?"

"Well, they want everything that's left of Turkey in Europe."

"Will they get it?"

"It looks so at the moment."

"Won't that make them the strongest Balkan power?"

"They already are the strongest Balkan power. It will increase their strength, certainly. But it should also satisfy them. Let's talk about us."

"Just tell me what you want me to do."

"I think," he said, "that you should let me sort out my side of the equation first. I would really like an amicable parting from Caterina, and you must understand that I would like to have both access to and some say in the upbringing of my children."

"Will she agree to that?"

"Nothing ventured, nothing gained. I am her sole source of income. I think we should be able to sort something out."

She held his hand. "I am so very sorry."

"About what?"

She flushed. "So disrupting your life."

"I think it was going to happen anyway. You just happen to be the catalyst."

"And what do I do, in the meantime? To be so close, in Belgrade . . ."

"I will let you know what is happening, as soon as I know what is happening."

"Between you and Caterina?"

"There are other matters involved."

"Which you cannot discuss with me."

He smiled. "Back to square one, eh?"

She toyed with her glass. "Harvey told me that it is supposed in the Embassy that you are a spy."

"Did he, now?"

"Something else you cannot admit to me."

"Would you expect me to?"

She raised her head. "Perhaps. If you truly loved me. If we are going to destroy two marriages and cause a great scandal, just to be together."

"I must turn the coin over, Julia. I would expect you not to ask, to trust me, absolutely . . . if we are going to destroy two marriages and cause a great scandal, just to be together."

They gazed at each other.

"I should be getting back," she said.

"But you would rather I did not accompany you."

"I think we both need to do a lot of thinking," she said.

After so many years, he thought, we still need to think? But he didn't say it. "Will I see you on the train, tomorrow?"

"I shall look forward to it."

The Assignment

S o, where do we go from here? Berkeley wondered as he returned to the hotel, to find Andrews seated in the lobby.

"This came, almost by return," the secretary remarked, holding out the envelope.

"Thank you." Berkeley took it.

As usual, Andrews hesitated, face twisting. "I suppose it is nothing the ambassador should know?"

"If it is, I am sure London will inform him," Berkeley said.

"One day, Major Townsend . . . Oh, I forgot, you are a colonel now, in the *Serb* army."

"No, no, Mr Andrews, I am now a brigadier-general in the Serb army. Thank you."

Andrews left, and Berkeley went up to his room, locked the door, slit the envelope and got out his code book.

Gorman had written:

Imperative you contact Smailes at earliest possible moment. Understand he has left Embassy to join Greek army in hopes of finding you. Follow and find. Take your instructions from him, as if from me. This is a vitally important matter. G.

Berkeley considered the transcript for several seconds, then struck a match and burnt it. He leaned back in his chair and gazed at the ceiling for several more minutes. Gorman's orders had been clear and precise: follow and find, but once again the general was underestimating just how large and complicated the Balkan Peninsular was. Yet he had received a definite order, and there was no doubt that he could find Smailes, and very quickly, simply by going to Salonika.

And thus foregoing the pleasure of Julia's company on the journey up to Belgrade, with all the promise of what might come after.

The alternative was to cut his links with the British army, and thus with Britain. As a Serbian brigadier, he no longer needed his English pay. But he would never be able to bring himself to do that;

quite apart from his oath, it would mean he would never be able to go home.

Besides, it would mean tying himself irrevocably to Caterina for the rest of his life, and that he could not contemplate.

He considered sending a message to Julia, decided against it. Whether he told her he could not come with her, or just didn't turn up at the railway station, she would take it in the same way. That was something else the future would have to take care of. He hired two remounts, and left for Salonika.

This was a journey of some 200 miles, relatively simple, as the road followed the coast for the most part, past places famous in history or legend, such as the pass of Thermopylae, and the towering, snow-clad heights of Mount Olympus. But it still took Berkeley more than a week. Technically, he supposed he was absent without leave from the Serb army, but he didn't think anyone was going to take that too seriously in the case of a brigadier who was also a hero.

Salonika itself was nearly as old as Athens; it had been founded by Alexander the Great and named after one of his sisters. In the more than two thousand years since then it had undergone more vicissitudes than most Balkan cities, having been sacked on several occasions, the most terrible being the massacre of the inhabitants by Sultan Murad in 1430. Immediately preceding the outbreak of the recent war it had been the headquarters of the Young Turk movement which was now dominating Constantinople.

Salonika's importance lay in its position, at the head of the Gulf of Thermaikos. It had a harbour to equal Piraeus, and in fact was more sheltered. The town itself sprawled over a succession of foothills in a most attractive fashion; even if the evidence of the recent conflict was everywhere, with burned-out farms, trampled fields, and some wrecked houses in the city itself. But the Greek flag flew proudly from the famous White Tower. The inhabitants, who appeared to be a mixture of every nationality in the peninsular, seemed somewhat uncertain of themselves, as well they might be, Berkeley supposed, but they raised a cheer at the sight of a Serbian general, however oddly travelling without either staff or servant. There was not a Turk in sight.

He reported to the military headquarters in the town, where he was welcomed by General Athenaikos. "You come from General Putnik?" the Greek asked.

"No, sir, this is a private visit."

"Ah. But you will observe, eh?"

"Are the Turks still close?"

"The Turks." Athenaikos gave a short laugh. "No, no, they have fled all the way back to Adrianople." He indicated the town, only twenty-odd miles west of Constantinople itself, on the wall map. "But all of Thrace is occupied by Bulgarian troops."

"Why say but?" Berkeley asked. "Are they not our allies?"

"Oh, indeed. But they are ambitious allies. Do you know that we reached this position only one day before them? Our advance guards exchanged fire before they withdrew. Yet they remain, on those heights over there, watching and waiting. They want Salonika. It would be their window on the Aegean, and hence the Mediterranean. Right now, all their seaports are on the Black Sea, which means they cannot get in or out by sea, as long as the Turks control the Dardanelles."

"But they would never attack you, surely."

Athenaikos tapped his nose. "Who can tell, General Townsend? Who can tell? Now tell me the real reason for your visit."

"I'm trying to find an old friend of mine, Colonel Toby Smailes. He is a British observer."

"But of course. Colonel Smailes is here in Salonika. I will send out to find him for you."

"Thank God you've finally turned up." Smailes peered at Berkeley's insignia. "Should I be calling you, sir?"

"Only if it makes you happy. As for turning up, you're damned lucky I am here at all. In case it has escaped your notice, I have been fighting a war."

"And doing famously," Smailes said. "We need to talk. Somewhere very private."

"I gathered that from Gorman's telegram," Berkeley agreed.

The most private place Smailes could think of was the open air, where they could see anyone approaching them. He secured a bottle of wine, and the two officers rode out of town to dismount and seat themselves on a grassy slope looking down on the water. It was a surprisingly good November day, but the breeze was chill and there was the threat of colder weather in the dark clouds gathering in the mountains to the north.

"Let's make it brief," Berkeley said.

"If we can. First, give me your assessment of the situation here. You know the Turks are suing for peace? There's to be a conference in London."

"I heard a rumour."

"Will they get it?"

"From Greece and Serbia, certainly. They have obtained everything they want. Bulgaria now . . . she's still fighting isn't she?"

"She is, and she has to be stopped before her armies get to Constantinople. That would be quite unacceptable."

189

"What are the powers going to do about it? Send the fleet to the Dardanelles?"

"Back the peace conference."

"You are assuming that the Bulgarians will accept whatever terms are put forward."

"It will be necessary to bring some pressure to bear. The Russians are in a good position to do this. However, there are problems."

"Aren't there always? I assume you are talking about the Austrians? They're not actually friends of the Bulgarians."

"Oh, quite. However, they do regard the Balkans as their backyard. Our people in Vienna report that the Austrian government is rather upset about the way this war has gone. I am talking about the speed with which it has been concluded and the absolute victory gained by the allied states. The Austrians were looking for a long, drawn-out war which would end in a Turkish victory. They would probably have been quite happy with a Turkish occupation of Serbia. The Austrians have always felt they could get the better of the Turks, as they proved in Bosnia-Herzegovina."

"I take your point. But I don't see what I can do about it. I did my best to see off the Black Hand, but I'm afraid there are indications that it may be about to resurface. And right now the whole Serb nation is cock-a-hoop."

Smailes frowned. "You think they may attack Austria?"

"No. I think both King Peter and his chief army officers know that would be a mistake. But I don't think they will put up with any more Austrian aggression, in *their* backyard."

"Oh, quite. But we feel this is a remote possibility, at the moment. The Emperor is very old, very sad, very uncertain. His life has been one long tragedy, really: wife murdered, son a suicide, his appointed heir, Franz Ferdinand, now a morganatic husband. It is all very distressing for the poor old soul. He had to be bullied into occupying Bosnia-Herzegovina. No, no, I think we can safely say that as long as Franz Joseph is Emperor, Austria will undertake no more military adventures. Or, for that matter, political ones either. Unfortunately, as I say, he is eighty-three years old. It is a certainty that within the next couple of years Austria-Hungary will have a new Emperor. And it is going to be Franz Ferdinand."

Berkeley gazed at him. "I hope you are not saying what I think you are saying."

"I am merely stating one or two facts," Smailes said smoothly.

"General Gorman sent you all of this way to give me a political lecture?"

"The general would like you to take a very broad view of the situation, Berkeley. There can be no doubt whatsoever that unless there is a most dramatic change in the political climate, at some time in the next ten years we are going to be at war with Germany. This is accepted even by some government ministers; one only has to read some of Lloyd George's speeches to know that. Of course, this sort of thinking is anathema to the Liberal Party as a whole, but still, if a war were to be dumped in their lap, they would have to fight, or they could lose the next election to the Tories, especially with all these problems in Ulster. We would have as our allies Russia and France. Germany would have Austria-Hungary, and possibly Italy. We don't know about Italy; she is in alliance with Germany and Austria, but she hates the Austrians. On the other hand, Germany might also be able to call on Turkey. There are already a considerable number of German officers serving in the Turkish army, and they are certainly supplying them with arms. And after what has happened these last few months, the Turks will be looking for revenge. So . . ."

"You are talking of a general European war. Back to the days of Napoleon."

"It is certainly possible. And has to be considered. We have to consider life and death. Some in particular. Dynasties. Let's consider dynasties, Berkeley. Those which may hold the future of Europe in the palms of their hands. When Franz Joseph goes the way of all flesh, he will, as I have reminded you, be succeeded by Franz Ferdinand. This man considers himself a soldier. However, the estimates of our people in Vienna are that he is a sensible man who realises that to dabble militarily in the Balkans might not turn out well. The estimation is that he will have to be pushed. So let us consider who is likely to do the pushing."

"His German allies," Berkeley suggested.

"Absolutely. But the German soldiers and sailors are also sensible men, some of them. They know Russia is recovering from the catastrophe of the Japanese war. They know France is arming as quickly and ambitiously as she can, just as they know the French will never forgive them for the defeat in 1871 and the German annexation of Alsace and Lorraine. They know, because they can read, that Britain is becoming more and more antagonistic to them, even if we are not yet officially a party to any alliance directed against them; you can be quite sure they know that the British and French armies have been conducting secret talks. The Germans have always had this fear of being hemmed in. This is growing with every day. Thus they are faced with a dilemma: shall we push, or shall we wait until we are forced to jump? And who has the ultimate power of decision? The Kaiser. There is no statesman in Germany, no general and no admiral, capable of standing up to Wilhelm II. And the Kaiser, as we all know, is a megalomaniac who sees himself as the great warlord of the twentieth century."

"You think the Kaiser will push the Austrians into a war with Serbia? You'll have to explain to me how he will benefit from it."

"There can be no doubt that if, for whatever reason, Austria goes to war with Serbia, Russia will intervene. Now, the Germans are obliged under their treaty to go to war on Austria's side, certainly should the French come in on the Russian side, as *they* are obliged to do. Thus we will have a general European war, with Germany and Austria, and they would hope, Italy, against Russia, France, and Serbia which, let's be frank, would be crushed out of existence in a week. And we know the Germans have a plan to deal with France very quickly, as they did in 1870, and then turn their whole military might on Russia, supported of course by the Austrians. They have every expectation of emerging from such a conflict as the dominating nation in Europe. And thus the world."

"Would we stand by and see that happen?"

"There's the rub. We are not contractually required to fight with either France or Russia. Indeed, the Tsar and his regime are probably more loathed in Britain than anywhere else. And it must be remembered, and is certainly remembered by the Germans, that however far our *rapprochement* with France has gone, only fifteen years ago we were on the point of declaring war on her, over that Fashoda business. Would we really go to war on her side, now? In the German estimation, the answer is no. But as I have said, public opinion in Britain is gradually taking on a more and more anti-German stance, whipped up by the politicians, to be sure. So logically, if there is to be a European war, from the German point of view it is best fought now, rather than in ten years time, by which time Great Britain and France may well have concluded a formal alliance. And the lynchpin in all of this thinking is the Kaiser."

Berkeley stroked his chin.

"But we are talking about dynasties," Smailes went on. "Where they matter. With all the respect in the world, if King George were to drop dead tomorrow, it would mean absolutely nothing in the context of European politics, because we are a democracy. The same goes for France. Well, they don't have a dynasty at all, at the moment; if Monsieur Poincaré were to die they would simply find another Prime Minister. But in the three autocracies, well . . . If the Tsar were to die, he would be succeeded by a young boy who is reputed to be terminally ill. This would be greatly to the advantage of Germany and Austria. Unfortunately from the German point of view, Wilhelm and Nicholas are first cousins, and one will hardly wish the death of the other. When Franz Joseph dies, he will be succeeded by Franz

Ferdinand, a man who will need time to find his feet, but who is very capable of being pushed by the Kaiser. But when the Kaiser dies . . ."

"There is the Crown Prince," Berkeley pointed out.

"Oh, yes. We have had an eye on him for a long time. An utter weakling. He cannot even make up his mind what clothes to wear and has to be told by his valet. The thought of plunging Europe into a general war would give him a seizure. With the Crown Prince ruling Germany, European peace would be a certainty for at least ten years, by which time the entire situation may have changed dramatically."

"Wishful thinking," Berkeley suggested. "The Kaiser is fifty-four years old, is in the best of health, and comes from a family which has a habit of living a long time."

"Absolutely. If we are going to achieve the situation we need, he would have to be assisted."

Berkeley raised his head. "You seem to have forgotten that in addition to being a cousin of the Tsar, the Kaiser is also a cousin of King George."

"And as I have just reminded you, Berkeley, King George does not rule England. He represents us."

"And you are telling me that the government of Great Britain, a Liberal government, is willing to contemplate the assassination of the Kaiser?"

"Ah . . . no. Most of the members of the cabinet would be utterly shocked, not to say horrified, by such a suggestion. But then, does the government, the Liberal government, really know what it is about? It was elected on a certain platform of measures, several of which it has managed to carry out. But in the main, it was elected on an understanding by the people of England that such a government would keep us out of a European war. Now, as I have explained, we are inexorably drifting towards such a war, and the government, as a group, can do nothing about it save build more and more Dreadnought battleships at vast expense. Were the mainspring of this drift towards war to be removed, whoever accomplished such a deed would be doing both the government and the people of Great Britain an inestimable favour."

"A very Balkan, or Japanese, suggestion," Berkeley observed. "And an utterly distasteful one. Well, Toby, I wish you luck."

"It is your luck with which we are concerned, Berkeley."

Berkeley stared at him. "You must be mad. What do you take me for?"

"An English officer, who will carry out any command given him by a superior. I am here as the mouthpiece of General Gorman."

"Well, you can tell the general, nothing doing. If I am to be considered as disobeying the orders of my superior, then I will offer you my resignation, here and now."

"My dear fellow," Smailes said, "you can't resign. Nor can you refuse to obey your orders."

Berkeley looked him up and down. Smailes wore a revolver, but then so did he. And he suspected he was a better and quicker shot. He also wore a sword.

"Try me," he said.

Smailes smiled. "Oh, I have no physical jurisdiction over you. Should you persist in this madness, I shall, most regretfully, return to Athens and wire the facts of your refusal to the general."

"Then there is an end to the matter."

"Not quite. When I do that, the general will feel obliged to release to the Serbian government the facts of your employment over the past few years. We obviously have kept the transcripts of all your messages to us, and of our replies."

"What a nasty lot you are," Berkeley remarked. "So what are you going to prove? You can prove that I have been a British agent for the past four years. You cannot prove that I have in any way harmed, or tried to harm, the Serbian government or their armed forces. Or that I have ever given any information regarding either the political or the military situation in Serbia."

"Ah, but do the Serbs know that? If they are in possession of the certain fact that for the past three years, while serving in their army, you have been actually a British spy, will they not feel that the messages they will see are only a small part of the messages that were actually sent? Of course you know these people better than us, but our impression of them is that they are conditioned to suspicion, to a fear of betrayal, and that they are very inclined to shoot first and ask questions afterwards. Would you not agree that is an accurate estimation of the situation?"

"You unutterable bastards," Berkeley remarked.

"Quite. Then you do agree."

"You people live in never-never land," Berkeley said. "What you require me to do is travel to Berlin, demand an audience with His Majesty, walk up to him, shoot him, and presumably be immediately shot down by his guards, to the great relief of everyone."

"I suspect you are becoming something of a Serb yourself," Smailes said. "No, no, we will choose the time and place. We would prefer it if the deed was done and you escaped, just in case you were caught and required to confess. We do not think it would be a practical proposition in Germany itself, which is a very heavily regimented society. However, Hungary is a different matter."

194

"Does the Kaiser ever go to Hungary?"

"Yes, he does. Almost every year. He goes in the spring, for the shooting at Lake Balaton."

"Accompanied, no doubt, by a considerable entourage."

"Oh, indeed. But then, you have access to a considerable entourage, have you not?"

Berkeley frowned at him.

"I am speaking of the Black Hand."

"Which you required me virtually to disband."

"But which you yourself have told us is still there, waiting to be resurrected. A body of desperate men who look to you as their natural leader."

"The Black Hand was created to fight against Austria," Berkeley said. "Even if they could be reunited, which I doubt, they have no quarrel with Germany; certainly not when it may involve the loss of their lives."

"Not even if you convince them that the Kaiser is the mainspring of all Austrian acts of aggression? You have a network of agents and anarchists already in existence in Hungary, have you not?" Smailes asked. "All they need is to be activated. You have every prospect of getting to Lake Balaton, doing the job, and getting out again. As you and Anna Slovitza did back in 1908."

"Which cost Anna's life."

"All the more reason for you to survive."

Which didn't make much logical sense. But of course Smailes was stating facts. However much he might have denied it, Berkeley knew the Black Hand was still very much in existence and was recruiting all the time, principally from among people like the schoolboys at Gregory's establishment. He also knew that people like Szigeti in Kiskunhalas were still there, and would respond if called upon again to serve the cause. The proposition was a practicality, even if getting away again afterwards was not so probable. And what was the alternative? He knew just how ruthless Gorman was. If he refused he would very probably wind up against a wall, being shot by the very soldiers he had led to victory in the recent war.

"And afterwards?" he asked. "Just supposing I carry out your orders, and get away with it?"

"The world will be your oyster, my dear fellow. Certainly you will find that we will be everlastingly grateful."

"We, being you and Gorman."

"I'm sure you understand that even the general could not undertake such an action on his own. We, as I use it, may claim to represent a substantial group within the Establishment. We would never be able to acknowledge you, or what you have done, but

195

we would, as I say, be most generously grateful. And you would have the knowledge that you have saved Europe from a most devastating war. Shall I communicate to the general that you accept our commission?"

Berkeley sighed. "I don't seem to have much choice. I will need considerable documentary support."

"Such as?"

"New passports for Lockwood and myself."

Smailes nodded.

"You will leave the photograph spaces blank. We will see to that locally."

Another nod.

"I will also need considerable funding."

"Whatever you require will be paid into your account in Belgrade. How much time will you need to set it up?"

Berkeley considered. "I'm afraid, a few months."

"And it is now nearly December. Are you saying it is unlikely you will be ready before next spring?"

"I'm afraid there's no chance of that. Recreating the Black Hand is going to take time, as will reactivating our agents in Hungary."

"I see. This is a pity, but I understand the situation. Very well. Target date will be the spring after next, 1914. Now, how you organise the mission and carry it out must be entirely your business: we do not want to know. And, of course, you understand that if you are taken, whatever you might say to your captors, His Majesty's Government will deny any knowledge of you beyond the fact that you were retired as unfit four years ago and have since been serving with the Serbian forces."

Berkeley nodded. "There are people at the Embassy in Athens who know that I am still employed by the army."

"Leave the people in the Embassy in Athens to me," Smailes said. "So, we will keep you informed as to the Kaiser's movements, or projected movements, as soon as we know of them. Our messages will be very simple, a place and a date. Nothing more. The rest is up to you."

"Yes," Berkeley said thoughtfully.

Smailes held out his hand. "I will wish you good fortune, and every success."

"If you don't mind," Berkeley said, "I won't shake your hand, right this minute."

He returned to Serbian army headquarters, which had been established in the town of Skopje. This was close to the Albanian border. Yannina had fallen to the Greeks and the last Turkish army in the south-west of the peninsular was no more; but General Putnik was still keeping an eye on things while the London peace conference got under way.

"You have been gone a long while," he remarked mildly, when Berkeley reported to his office. "Is there trouble at home?"

"I'm afraid I did not go home, sir," Berkeley said; he was pretty sure the general had found that out, anyway. "I went to Athens and then Salonika, to see for myself what is happening in the east."

"That is very interesting. Very enterprising," Putnik said. "Did you discover anything of value?"

"That the Bulgarians are maintaining a very large army in Thrace."

"They have also a considerable force just across the Macedonian frontier," Putnik told him. "And are claiming that they have not received a fair share of the spoils."

"Will we give them some of Macedonia?"

"Certainly not. This is our country now."

"So we are maintaining our army in the field?"

"Until we see what comes out of London, certainly."

"Ah," Berkeley said. "I came here to resign my commission."

"Resign?" Putnik shouted. "When you have just been promoted, and are one of our best cavalry commanders?"

"I have a wife and family to see to."

"Don't we all? I cannot accept your resignation, General Townsend. Certainly not until this business is finished for good and all."

"Then, sir, I must ask for some more leave, to visit my family."

"For Christmas, eh?" Putnik chuckled. "If I give you leave, must I not give every married man in the army leave for Christmas? You will get your home leave, General, in due course. As to whether it will be for Christmas, I cannot say. Be patient. Your family will not go away."

Berkeley had not supposed that getting out of the Serb army and reconstructing the Black Hand was going to be either simple or quick, which was why he had told Smailes he could not possibly be ready by the spring of 1913. But even the year's extension he had been given was not all that long, in view of the immense amount of work that had to be done.

To what aim? The assassination of a ruling monarch: a man he had never seen, and had no personal reason to hate. The deed itself did not hang heavily on his conscience – he had killed sufficient men in his time – although he could certainly hope that during the next fifteen months something would happen, such as a natural death, to prevent him having to carry out his horrendous orders. But as he had reminded Smailes, the Kaiser was relatively young and in perfect health, so far as was known. Nor did he discount his chances

197

of committing the crime and escaping, if he could get sufficient support.

But the whole idea went against those, no doubt absurd, notions of honour that had dominated his youth. The stakes were very high: if Smailes, or Gorman, were to be believed, the entire future of Europe might be at stake. That meant the future of Caterina, and more important, his children.

And Julia? Probably hers too.

Then what of that future. The trouble with being encamped, with nothing to do but drill his brigade and drink in the officers' mess, was that it gave him too much time to think. And plan? He was strangely reluctant to do that. Because however much he knew he had fallen in love with Julia, she still wanted to dictate her own terms for their lives. And however much he knew he had fallen out of love with Caterina, he knew that was because he had not been able, and had not wanted to be able, to equal her hatred, her burning desire for revenge. But if he did reconstitute the Black Hand, even if only for this one supreme occasion, Caterina would be as loving as ever in the past. Would he then fall in love with her all over again? Could he?

Lockwood, who obtained Christmas leave and returned to Sabac to see his own wife and child, could tell that his master had a great deal on his mind. He was also somewhat confused, as like everyone else, he had supposed Berkeley had returned home the previous month. "Mrs Townsend was hoping to see you, sir," he remarked.

"I had things to do, Harry."

"Of course, sir." Lockwood waited, but Berkeley did not feel he was in a position immediately to enlighten his faithful old friend as to what was going on. In fact, he was not sure he could call on Lockwood at all for what might well turn out to be a suicide mission, however much he might feel the need of his support.

It was a bleak winter in and around the mountains of Macedonia, while the talking continued in London and the recent antagonists waited. Berkeley exchanged letters with Caterina, warmly enough, but despite what Lockwood had said, Berkeley did not feel his wife was particularly anxious to have him back; that he was serving with the Serbian army was sufficient. But at last, at the beginning of March 1913, his turn for another furlough came up, and he could ride for Belgrade.

He went first, as he always did, to see Colonel Savos. The colonel was older and slightly more grizzled, but was as hard-faced as ever, and yet, as usual in recent years, genuinely pleased to see his old friend.

"You have had a great war, I believe, General," he remarked.

"A successful one, at any rate," Berkeley agreed.

"Fate plays funny tricks," Savos remarked. "When I first saw you sitting in that chair, I honestly thought I would not see you again. How long ago was that?"

"Four and a half years," Berkeley said.

"Only that? It seems much longer. Now you are one of our most famous soldiers, as well as a husband and a father and a prominent citizen."

"Correction," Berkeley said. "I am not a Serb citizen."

"With your war record, you could be, any time you wish."

"I have the matter under consideration. Now tell me, Colonel, have you any news of any of our friends?"

Savos' eyes had a disconcerting habit of suddenly appearing to have closed, while remaining open. "They are keeping out of sight, until the war is over."

"The war *is* over."

"Not everyone is convinced of that."

"And if, or perhaps I should say when they reappear, will you do something about them?"

"If they commit no crimes inside Serbia," Savos said smoothly. "I should have no reason to do anything about them."

Berkeley went to see Gregory.

"Berkeley, my old friend!" The schoolmaster embraced him. "But it is good to see you again, looking so well, and so famous, as well."

"You mean I look famous?" Berkeley asked.

Gregory poured wine. "And you are on your way home, to see your wife?"

"I am."

"Then it is good of you to take the time to call on me."

"We may have some business."

Gregory gazed at him for some seconds, then was distracted by a knock on the door. "Come," he said.

The schoolboy who entered was thin with pinched features. He stopped in embarrassment when he saw Berkeley. "I apologise, sir. I did not know you had a visitor."

"A famous man, Gavrilo," Gregory said. "Brigadier-General Townsend."

Berkeley stood up and shook hands.

"Princip is one of my best pupils," Gregory said. "One of my most faithful pupils."

Gavrilo Princip's eyes flickered over Berkeley's uniform.

"Was it important, Gavrilo?" Gregory asked.

"I will return later, sir," the boy said and withdrew, closing the door.

"Have you many who are that faithful?" Berkeley asked.

"Not quite enough at the moment, but their numbers are growing."

Berkeley sat down again. "Suppose I told you that I am interested in reactivating the Black Hand."

Gregory's eyes narrowed. "I think I would like to be told why."

"It is a simple matter. By our success in this war, Serbia has, virtually overnight, doubled her territory. This is disturbing to Vienna."

"If we have doubled our country, then we have also doubled our strength," Gregory pointed out. "The Austrians would not attack us before, why should they risk it now?"

"I believe they may well be planning to do so," Berkeley said. "I do not agree that the mere fact of doubling your country has meant a doubling in your strength. What it really means is that your army, which has not grown in size, now has double the territory to defend."

"I do not believe," Gregory said, "that old man in Vienna has any longer the will to go to war with anybody."

"But that old man, Gregory, simply because he *is* an old man, is not going to be around very much longer."

Gregory got up and poured them each a glass of wine. "I agree that that is a point. Then we would have to deal with Franz Ferdinand. So, you would reactivate the Hand to that end?"

"I would reactivate the Hand to oppose Austrian ambitions," Berkeley said carefully. "I do not think Franz Ferdinand is a threat, in himself."

"That may be. But he will be less of a threat if he is dead."

"If he is dead," Berkeley said, equably, although he was not pleased with the way the conversation was going, "he will merely be succeeded by his brother, or his nephew, or whatever, when the old man dies."

"He is our threat," Gregory said stubbornly.

"You will have to permit me to be the judge of that," Berkeley told him.

"You?"

"You once invited me to lead you. Now I am prepared to do so."

"What has changed your mind?"

"I am now dedicated to your cause," Berkeley said. If he had often in his life regretted the number of lies he had had to tell people, beginning with his own parents, he had at least had ample practice.

Once again Gregory studied him for some seconds. "Have you told your wife of this?"

"I have not told her yet. I will do this when I get home. She will be very pleased to know that the Black Hand is being revived."

"No doubt. And you have a specific manoeuvre in mind?"

"Yes."

"I think I am entitled to know what it is."

"You shall, in due course. For the time being, let us find out who is still willing to work with us."

"How many men will you need?"

"Three. Three good men. Karlovy, for a start. If he will serve under me."

"Oh, yes, I think he will serve under you."

"Do you know where he can be found?"

Gregory nodded. "I will send him to you, and you will tell him whatever you wish."

Berkeley had one last call to make before returning to Sabac. He did not suppose he was ever going to see Julia again, either because he was not going to return from this mission, or because Harvey Braddock would be one of those shifted out of the Balkans for knowing too much about Berkeley Townsend's activities.

He continued to feel oddly ambivalent about the whole situation. He had known from the beginning that the army would not have placed him in the Balkans, for what might have been a considerable time, paying him a good salary, merely for the few small items of interest he had been able to send them. And while he supposed they gave him credit for supressing the activities of the Black Hand, once that was done they had had no reason to leave him *in situ*. No, they had all along had bigger things in mind: firstly, that he should rise in rank and esteem amongst his Serb associates, and thereby perhaps be in a position to influence her foreign policy – a very long shot – and secondly, and far more sinisterly, that when they were ready to use it, he would be able to reconstitute the Black Hand, only this time it would be carrying out London's secret plans, not those of Belgrade.

This he had now been ordered to do. To commit the crime of the century. Which might, if London were right, save Europe from a vast and destructive war. But which, if London were wrong, could easily bring about that war. His not to reason why, his but to do and die. Or not, if he could manage it.

But that still left his emotional life in a mess. Of course, if he died, that would be the end of the matter, at least from his point of view. But if he succeeded, and got away with it, Caterina would certainly return to him, body and soul; he could not doubt that. But Julia . . . no matter how secret these matters, they always came out in the end . . . Julia would be shocked and horrified at what he had done. She had never really cared for the army way of doing things.

He knocked on the door of the consul's residence, and was admitted by a maid. "Mr Braddock is at the consulate, sir."

"Ah. Then I shall go along there shortly. Would Mrs Braddock be at home?"

"Indeed, sir. Who shall I say is calling?" She was eyeing his uniform appreciatively as he gave her his cap and gloves.

"I know the gentleman, Sophie," Julia said from the drawing room doorway.

She stood back to allow him to pass, and closed the door. "You continually surprise me."

Her tone was understandably cold.

"I am sorry. I was required elsewhere."

"Could you not have sent a message?"

"I considered it best not to."

"Well." She sat down. "You were to instruct me. Or have you changed your mind about that also?"

He sat beside her. "Believe me, I would prefer not to. But . . ."

"You are required elsewhere."

"Yes."

"I see. For how long?"

"I have no idea. But it will not be for a few months, yet. We could perhaps meet . . ."

"To what purpose?"

"I had supposed you enjoyed my company."

She got up, restlessly, moved about the room. "You wish me to become the ultimate mistress."

"Once you said you would be happy with that."

"Once you offered me more," she countered.

He sighed. "I can offer you nothing until this mission is completed. Believe me, this is for your sake as much as mine."

"A mission which you say may take a year or longer."

"I'm afraid so."

"And where do you go now? To Sabac?"

"Why, yes."

"To be with your wife."

"And my children. You said you might visit us."

"So that you could steal into my bedroom in the dead of night, like a thief?"

Berkeley stood up. "I am sorry. We seem to alternate between passionate love and passionate quarrelling. You know the situation, Julia. I am a soldier, and I must obey orders. I have been given certain orders, which will take approximately a year to carry out. Until then,

202

I am not a free agent, either as regards time or movement. I thought you understood."

"When you thought that, we were not thinking in terms of years," she said bitterly.

"One year. Then I will be able to come to you."

He had not meant to make such a rash promise. It had just slipped out.

"One year," she said. "Here?"

"If you are still here," he said cautiously. "But wherever you are."

"Well, then," she said, "I will wish you every success in your mission."

They gazed at each other, but she was offering nothing more at the moment, nor was he in the mood to seek it. He kissed her hand, and left.

Berkeley always felt an intruder when he came to Sabac. It was his home, but he did not belong here: he was not, and could never be, one of these people. But he was at least sure of a welcome nowadays, especially as the people caught sight of his uniform, and clustered round, all wishing to shake his hand and pat him on the back, ask him questions about the war, congratulate him on the army's success.

There could be no doubt that Caterina knew he was coming long before he reached the tall, dark house. Today the doors were open and she stood there, Baby Alicia in her arms, the two toddlers clinging to her skirts. She was so beautiful, and today so adoring, as he hugged and kissed her and the children, and smiled at Marie Lockwood, waiting behind her.

"It is so good to have you back," Caterina said. "So good. And so triumphant."

They sat together in the drawing room after the children had been put to bed.

"How long can you stay?" she asked.

"A week."

"And then?"

"I must return to the army."

She pouted. "But the war is over."

"No one seems to be quite sure about that," he told her.

But for the week, at any rate, they recaptured the relaxed and loving gaiety of their first two weeks together, taking long rides in the countryside, walking the streets of Sabac hand in hand, enjoying the company of their children when at home.

Yet there remained tensions.

"Do you remember a woman named Julia Gracey?" Caterina asked one day.

"Indeed I do. I was returning from a visit to her home when I was shot."

"Absolutely. Did you know that she is now married, to someone in the British Foreign Office named Braddock?"

"Is that a fact? I recall there was some talk of it when last I was in England."

"She is now living in Belgrade."

Berkeley raised his eyebrows. "What is she doing there?"

"Her husband is consul."

"Good Lord! How did you find this out?"

"She wrote to me, oh, some time ago. During the campaign. Asking if she could come to visit."

"And did she?"

"No, because I never replied to the letter."

"Don't you think that was rather rude?"

"Perhaps. I did not wish to see her. Did you ever have a relationship with her?"

"Well," Berkeley said, "as our families were near neighbours, we saw a lot of each other as children, and I suspect there was some sort of understanding between our parents, but it was never a possibility. She isn't my type, and I think she always preferred Braddock."

"I am glad of that," Caterina said.

The next day Karlovy arrived.

He entered the house somewhat suspiciously, as well he might, Berkeley supposed. He received him in the reception room, and closed the door.

"Gregory said you had business," the anarchist said.

He looked somewhat down at heel, having lacked regular employment for the past couple of years.

Berkeley poured them each a glass of wine and gestured Karlovy to a chair.

"Did he tell you what this business might be?"

Karlovy's eyes were opaque. "No, he did not."

"It is my intention to reactivate the Black Hand."

"You, General? What brought on this change of heart?"

"My knowledge of what is happening in and around Serbia."

Karlovy stroked his chin.

"Specifically," Berkeley said, "I wish to restore our contacts in Hungary, with a view to getting in and out of the country as we require. I am thinking of people like Paul Szigeti, and any other of Anna's people who might still be willing to help us."

"It will take time."

Berkeley nodded. "You have the time. I wish everything in place by the end of this year."

"It will also take money."

"You shall have it."

"You also understand that, now the Austrians control Bosnia-Herzegovina which includes Slovenia, getting in and out of Hungary can no longer be a simple matter."

"Was it ever?" Berkeley asked.

Karlovy gave a quick smile. "You also realise that crossing the border, legitimately, with anything like a machine gun, is no longer as easy as it was."

"We will be a hunting party, and will carry only hunting weapons."

"Next year."

"I will tell you when. I have said I wish our agents activated by the end of this year."

Karlovy nodded. "I will attend to it. Are we going after another payroll?"

"I will tell you what we are going after when the time is right."

"Very good." He stood up, and the door opened to admit Caterina. She gazed from one to the other in surprise.

"It's all right," Berkeley said. "We are not about to kill each other."

"What are you doing here?" Caterina asked.

"Your husband will tell you, madame," Karlovy said, and left.

Caterina looked at Berkeley.

"Briefly," he said, "I have decided to resume our campaign against Austria."

She gaped. "With Karlovy?"

"With the Black Hand, yes. Karlovy is going to reactivate all of our agents."

"Oh, Berkeley," she said, and went to him, hugging him tightly. "Does Gregory know?"

"He does. He found Karlovy for me."

"Oh, Berkeley," she said again, "I am so proud of you. And I shall ride at your side, just like Mother."

"Ah . . . we'll have to talk about that, when the time comes. You understand that it cannot be for a while. Karlovy has to put things back in motion, and I have to get out of the army. That cannot be done until peace has definitely been concluded."

"But it will happen." She hugged him again. "You have made me the happiest woman in the world."

When Caterina was the happiest woman in the world, she was also the most loving, and the most loveable woman in the world.

When he lay in her arms, to leave her for another woman, even a woman like Julia, became unthinkable. And Julia was surely now gone forever.

Now the lead weight of what he had been ordered to do became heavy indeed. And yet, without it, the total reconciliation with Caterina could not have happened.

He returned to the army to be summoned immediately before General Putnik.

"I am glad you are back, General," Putnik said. "Have you heard the news?"

"I'm afraid not, sir."

"King George of Greece has been assassinated. Shot through the heart as he took his morning walk."

"Good God!" Berkeley's mind immediately turned to Gregory. But what possible reason could any Serb have for murdering the King of Greece, their ally? "Do they know who did it?"

"Oh, they have the assassin. He is a peasant, named Alexander Schinas."

"But why?"

"He refuses to talk, either about his employers or about such mundane matters as where he got the gun, and the expertise to kill with a single shot."

"So, presumably . . ."

"Oh, the Greeks will beat it out of him if they can. But whether they do or not, *we* can have no doubt as to who was responsible. So, we must prepare ourselves for another campaign."

"You think this was inspired by the Turks?"

"The Turks no longer matter, General. The people we are now going to fight are the Bulgarians."

The Hand of Fate

It appeared that Serbia and Greece had signed a secret treaty, not only jointly to oppose any further Bulgarian claims, but also to regain some of the territory Bulgaria had already claimed, and of which she was in possession. Berkeley was less astonished than Putnik had supposed might be the case, but now the assassination of King George gave them a *casus belli*, supposing it could be proved that Bulgaria was behind it. He had no doubt that London already knew of the murder, and had formed its own opinion as to who was responsible, but as to whether the War Office knew of the secret treaty was another matter. He gave Lockwood leave of absence from the brigade and sent him off to Salonika to find Smailes, hoping he was still there. The colonel had in fact returned to Athens, but Lockwood caught up with him. He returned three weeks later to tell Berkeley that Smailes was already aware of the situation, but that the great powers, who had been monitoring the settlements in London, had forbidden the Serbs or the Greeks to take any aggressive action. This was reassuring, but only the following week it was Bulgaria which declared war and crossed the frontiers in great strength.

This war lasted little more than a month. The Bulgarian calculations had been based on three facts. Firstly, that it was necessary to sort the situation out by force before a final settlement was imposed by the powers. Secondly, that they possessed the largest army in the Balkans, and thirdly, that it was battle-hardened from the recent war. But it still remained a wild throw, inspired entirely by the Bulgarian commander-in-chief, General Michael Savov, without consulting his government. This hastily disavowed his action, but by then it was too late. The Greeks and the Serbs were already mobilised, and now they had the excuse to take unilateral action. Their combined numbers were not so inferior to the Bulgarians, and their men were just as battle-hardened. Putnik and his men advanced, the cavalry brigades to the fore, and gained a series of smashing victories. The Greeks in the south were no less successful, while the Turks in Constantinople immediately resumed activities. Bulgaria had been utterly defeated before the powers could react.

Unfortunately, the war again exceeded parameters acceptable to the men who supposed they ruled Europe. The Albanians had taken advantage of Serb preoccupations in the east to cross the frontier into Macedonia and see what they could pick up for themselves. Berkeley was ordered to clear them out and occupy their country. This he did very rapidly, supported by an infantry brigade. Whereupon the powers, or at least Austria, did sit up and take notice. A Serbian-held Albania not only gave the Serbs access to the sea, but it reversed the situation in Bosnia-Herzegovina, in that the provinces were now surrounded on two sides by the Serbs.

General Putnik himself arrived to inspect the troops. He was greeted with acclamation by his men, but when he entertained his senior officers he was very serious.

"We have been ordered to evacuate Albania," he told them.

"May we ask who by?" Berkeley enquired.

"Austria. She has given us an ultimatum, to be out in eight days." They stared at him in consternation.

"Then it is war at last," General Palich said, "with the old enemy."

Putnik sighed. "There will be no war."

Once again they stared at him.

"The Austrians have two army corps mobilised in Bosnia-Herzegovina," he said, "just across the border. That is superior to any forces we have. We cannot fight them without being massacred."

"But, Russia . . ." someone ventured.

"Is proving, as usual, all bluster and no substance. They tell us the recent famine in the Ukraine, and the political uncertainty since the assassination of Prime Minister Stolypin, has made it impossible for them to act on our behalf."

"So, we are going to crawl away with our tails between our legs," someone said, bitterly.

"I'm afraid that is what we are going to have to do. This time. One day, perhaps . . . I thank you, gentlemen. I thank you all. General Townsend, a word."

Berkeley waited while the other officers filed from the room.

"You tendered your resignation a few months ago, and I could not accept it. You are welcome to tender it again, now."

"Will you tell me why, sir?"

Putnik shrugged. "It would appear that our fighting days are done, without Austrian permission. That is an intolerable situation, but it is one we have to face. I do not think you, as an Englishman, should be required to endure it. My advice to you would be to leave Serbia. Take your wife and children back to England and resume your life there."

"But you still expect to fight Austria, one day."

"It is my hope, certainly," Putnik said. "One day. If I live long enough."

"Then, sir, while I will accept your permission to retire from the army and attend to my own affairs, I will remain in Serbia, so that you may call upon me when that day arrives."

Putnik clasped his hand. "I wish there were more like you, General Townsend."

How Berkeley wished it could be possible to tell this gallant old gentleman the truth of what was happening, or about to happen!

"Strange, but I really feel as if we are going home," Lockwood remarked, as they walked their horses north.

Sabac was in fact the only home he had ever truly had, and his wife and family were there. Unlike Berkeley's his had been an entirely happy marriage.

They had changed from uniform into civilian clothes so as not to attract attention.

"At least temporarily," Berkeley agreed.

Lockwood glanced at him. "Is there something on, sir?"

"I'm afraid there is," Berkeley said, and repeated the gist of his conversation with Smailes.

Lockwood gave a low whistle. "Some do."

"A highly dangerous do. I am not insisting that you get involved, Harry."

"But you wouldn't have told me if you didn't wish me to be involved, sir."

"I have told you because you are the only person in this entire world I can trust. And I do need to trust someone. But it might be equally important for you to remain in Sabac to take care of things there, supposing I don't come back."

"But you do expect to come back?"

"Haven't I always?"

"Indeed, sir. I would like to accompany you, sir."

"And Marie, and the children?"

"Well, sir, if you intend to come back, then I do also. If I do *not* come back, well, Marie knew she was marrying a soldier. And also, if I may say so, someone with already established loyalties which she has always known I would honour even above marriage."

Berkeley clasped his hand.

"So, you are giving up soldiering, again," Colonel Savos remarked, when Berkeley paid him his customary visit. But now the situation was entirely reversed; Berkeley no longer needed to obtain information from the policeman, but he did wish to know just how much Savos knew about what was going on.

"There comes a time," Berkeley agreed.

"Absolutely. So, are you now going to retire, General?"

"I think so."

"Ah. Tell me, do you still see anything of Gregory Masanovich?"

"I paid him a call the last time I was in Belgrade," Berkeley said, having no doubt at all that Savos already knew that.

"But he too is retired, eh?"

"As far as I know."

"Would it be possible for you to find out?"

"I am not a police agent, Colonel."

"Of course not. But you are an old acquaintance of the good doctor, and I believe you have the well-being of Serbia at heart. After all, you have spent the last couple of years fighting for us, have you not?"

"Does that have anything to do with Gregory Masanovich?"

"It may. You are of course aware that there is considerable tension between Serbia and Austria. *Déjà vu*, eh? That ultimatum . . . the Austrians are just dying to get at our throats."

"We accepted the ultimatum, Colonel. Which is why I am here."

"Absolutely. However, we are again in a position where any overt act of aggression towards Austria could have the most serious consequences."

"And you think Gregory is planning some such action? My dear Colonel, the Hand has been disbanded."

The two men gazed at each other. He does know something, Berkeley realised.

"As I said to you once before, General, I do not believe societies like the Black Hand ever disband, entirely. Certainly not as long as there are one or two principals left. Did you know that shooting has been heard coming from that school of his?"

Berkeley frowned. "Shooting?"

"We think it was target practice. These are schoolboys, you understand. Do you consider target practice should be a part of the normal school curriculum?"

Berkeley stroked his chin. "You are not suggesting that Gregory would use schoolboys to raid into Austria?"

"I believe he is training them for use somewhere. I think it might be a good idea for you to have a word with him."

"You mean, warn him off."

"That is what I mean, yes. It would be best coming from you rather than, officially, from me."

"I'll see what can be done," Berkeley agreed.

He knows nothing of Karlovy, he thought, with some satisfaction.

As it was now August, the school was shut for the holidays and Gregory was not to be found. "The doctor goes into the country, for the air, during the holidays," the concierge explained.

"And all the pupils go home," Berkeley suggested.

"Indeed, sir."

"Some, I believe actually live abroad. In places like Bosnia."

"Well, they did. But most of their families have moved out, since Austria took over the provinces."

Berkeley nodded, thoughtfully, and made his way to Sabac.

He was more disturbed than he had allowed himself to reveal by what Savos had told him. He couldn't criticise Gregory for attempting to recreate the Hand, using entirely fresh, and very young, blood. Schoolboys, and schoolgirls for that matter, are always more eager to sacrifice themselves for a cause than their elders, however unpleasant the thought might be of using such essentially immature and innocent material to carry out crimes which could take them to the gallows.

What he did not want, and could not allow, was for Gregory to embark upon some scheme which might cause a crisis which could result in the borders being closed and travel in Hungary restricted, at any time before next summer. Berkeley and Lockwood rode into Sabac, thus arriving before the train. In any event, no one at the Slovitza House was expecting them so soon. Marie seemed over-whelmed to see them, hugging Lockwood with desperate pleasure while the valet looked extremely embarrassed.

"I hope you're glad to see me as well," Berkeley remarked.

"Oh, General, sir, but . . ." She took in the civilian clothes for the first time. "You have left the army?"

"That we have. Is Mrs Townsend up?"

"I think she will be in the nursery, with the children. Or perhaps . . ." she changed her mind about what she would have said.

"Yes?" Berkeley asked.

"She will be in the nursery," Marie said, with great determination. "Shall I tell her you are here?"

Townsend wished, just once, that he was not be surrounded by deceit, or half-truths. On the other hand, was he not deceiving all of these people, all of the time?

"I will tell her myself," he said, and went to the stairs. Then paused, and looked over his shoulder. "Has Mr Karlovy called?"

"No, sir. I have not seen Mr Karlovy. Dr Masanovich was here . . ."

Foot on the bottom step, Berkeley frowned. "Dr Masanovich? When?"

"A week ago, General. He came with a friend."

"What friend?"

"A very young man, sir. Only a boy. I think he was a pupil from the school."

"They saw madame?"

"Oh, indeed, sir. They spent some time together."

"Thank you." Berkeley went up the stairs and paused at the first-floor landing, as he listened to the unmistakeable sound of revolver shots coming from the backyard. He crossed the reception room and looked down. Caterina was alone, her hair bound up in a scarf, shooting at a target at the far end of the yard.

Berkeley stroked his chin, then went on up to the nurseries.

"General!" As with everyone else, Alexandrina the nurse was astonished to see him.

"Papa!" Anna was in his arms. "We did not know you were coming."

"So it seems." He hugged John and Alicia, still very much the baby of the family, in turn.

"Tell us about the war, Papa," Anna begged. "Did you kill a lot of the enemy?"

"Lots and lots," he assured her, and listened to the soft footfall outside the door.

"Mama!" Anna shouted. "Papa's back!"

Caterina opened the door. "We did not expect you," she said.

"So everybody tells me." He stood up to take her in his arms, but it was a few seconds before she relaxed.

"What has happened in the war? We have not been defeated?"

"Yes, and no."

"What do you mean?" Her hands were tight on his.

"We beat the Bulgars, easily enough. But then had to take orders from the Austrians."

"So that's what—" she bit her lip.

"Gregory meant?" he prompted.

She freed herself.

"I know he was here. Perhaps you'd tell me what he had to say. And who was his companion?"

"One of his pupils." She led him out of the nursery and into their bedroom.

"He brought one of his pupils to see you?"

"The boy was accompanying him on holiday."

"I find that rather odd. What did he have to say to you?"

"He said there was great tension between Austria and our people."

"And suggested you practice shooting?"

"Well," she said, "everyone needs to know how to shoot. Especially where we are, only a few miles from the Bosnian border."

"I've been thinking about that," Berkeley said, watching her. "You really are very exposed here. And the children. Perhaps it would be a good idea to sell up, and move to Belgrade."

"No," she snapped, and flushed as she glanced at him. "This is my home. I will not abandon it because of any threat from the Austrians."

Berkeley nodded. "I didn't suppose you would. What else did Gregory have to say?"

She sat on the bed, her hands in her lap. "That you and he are working together to revive the Hand."

"I suppose that's true. And . . ."

"That you are planning something very big. With Karlovy."

"Who seems to have disappeared. Did he tell you what this big thing was?"

"He would not."

"Because he does not know. Nobody knows, except me."

She sniffed. "You will not even tell your wife."

"I think it is best this way. And Gregory told you nothing else? Apart from that you should practice shooting?"

"No," she said.

She was lying to him. Gregory was indeed planning something on his own. Something which could involve Caterina? Berkeley was well aware that for all her indications of domesticity, her hatred of the Austrians and her determination one day to avenge her mother and father was as strong as ever.

He would have to be patient. In the meantime . . .

"It is important that I see Gregory. Do you know where he has gone?"

"No."

"Will he be coming back here before term starts?"

"I do not know."

"Ah. Right." He had come home wishing only to take her in his arms and hold her there for a long time. Now he no longer wanted to do that. "Well, I must have a bath and a change of clothing." He rubbed his chin. "And a shave. By the way, what was the name of this schoolboy he had with him?"

"I think it was Princip."

"Gavrilo Princip?"

"Yes, I think that was it. There is mail for you."

She indicated the envelopes lying on the table. Two were from his parents, and he put them into his pocket to be read at leisure. The third was also from England, a large and thick manila envelope. It was heavily sealed, and the seal had not been broken. He opened it. As indicated by Smailes, one of the sheets was simply a list of dates

213

and place names. As these included such things as the sites of various army manoeuvres, as well as royal cities such as Potsdam and Berlin, Berkeley presumed any intelligent person would be able to work out they were the itinerary, if not of the Kaiser, certainly of someone in his entourage. But the important one remained, Lake Balaton, June 3 to 21, following which the subject was departing for a Baltic cruise on the royal yacht.

Lucky for some, Berkeley thought. But that was one holiday he would never take.

Also in the envelope were two passports and various other documents pertaining to a Mr Peter Carruthers, businessman of Athens, and his servant, Charles Brent. As promised, in each passport the space for the photograph and signature had been left blank.

"I hope it is not bad news," Caterina said.

"Not at all," Berkeley said, as he burned the itinerary.

Much to Berkeley's relief, Karlovy appeared at the beginning of November. It had been a tense period, not only because Berkeley could make no concrete plan until he knew he had a way in and a way out, but also because of the tension that existed between Caterina and himself: each had a secret they would not, dared not, divulge to the other. There was no sign of Gregory during the holidays, and no word from him either, and Berkeley was just determining that he would have to go to Belgrade, when Karlovy was announced.

Berkeley received him in the reception room. The anarchist looked tired and travelworn, but he seemed ebullient enough.

"I have made all the contacts you require, General," he said. "They have been paid, and are standing by. All they wish is the word from you." He paused, hopefully.

"I congratulate you. Now, how many men have you got to go with us?"

"These still have to be recruited. It would be a great help if I can tell them what we are going to do."

"Did Anna ever tell you her plans, before she was ready to carry them out?"

"No," Karlovy acknowledged.

"Then you must be patient. As I told you, we need three good men. You can tell them we are going to strike at the very heart of Austria. Exactly how will be revealed when the time comes."

"And that will be?"

Berkeley grinned at him. "That too must wait. But it will not be until next year. Go and spend Christmas with your family. You do have a family?"

It had suddenly occurred to him that he knew absolutely nothing about this man, save that he was a violent rogue.

"I have no family," Karlovy said.

"But you have a woman?"

"I have many women," Karlovy said. "When do you wish me to return?"

"As I have told you, I wish you to do nothing, save recruit your men, until next May. At the beginning of May, I wish you to go into Hungary, visit Szigeti, and tell him that we shall be coming to him the first week in June. We will need to hire horses. He must arrange this. There is no need to tell him more than that."

Karlovy grinned. "I cannot tell him what I do not know myself."

"Absolutely. But you may tell him that it is possible we will need to use his house on the way back as well."

"Which will be when?"

"I will tell you that when we are on our way. After you have seen Szigeti, you will return to Belgrade, and come to Sabac on the first of June."

"These men I am to recruit. Must they be armed?"

"Yes, I wish them each to be armed with a hunting rifle."

"Because we are going hunting," Karlovy said thoughtfully. "In Hungary."

"You are thinking too much, Karlovy. Your people may also bring their personal sidearms."

"I will need money until then. And for the men."

Berkeley paid him.

"The first of June," Karlovy said, and left.

"Why do you deal with Karlovy, and not Gregory?" Caterina asked.

"Simply because I am in field command of our people, and Karlovy is my second-in-command. Gregory prefers to keep out of the firing line, as you well know. Why, did he tell you something different when he was here?"

"He told me nothing when he was here, save that you and he are again working together."

Another lie.

"I am going into Belgrade next week," Berkeley said. "Would you care to come with me?"

"I would rather stay here."

"As you wish. I shall probably be calling on Gregory."

"Give him my regards," Caterina said.

The temptation to grab her and shake the truth out of her was enormous. But he knew such tactics would never work with Caterina, and now was no time to have an open split. He had to believe that he would survive the Kaiser's assassination, that he would return to Sabac, and that he would be able to pick up the threads of his life again – with his wife.

All that was necessary was to warn Gregory off.

He called at the school and was, as usual, shown into the head-master's study.

"I missed you, in the summer," Berkeley said. "Both here and at Sabac."

"So I understand," Gregory said smoothly. "But then, no one expected you home so suddenly."

"Obviously," Berkeley agreed. "Caterina is being rather mysterious about your visit."

Gregory bristled. "I hope you are not suggesting there has been any impropriety between me and your wife."

"Of course I am not," Berkeley said, "because I am sure you are well aware that if I suspected that I would kill you."

Gregory gulped.

"Besides, you had company, did you not?" Berkeley said. "The boy Princip. One of your favourite pupils, you told me."

Once again Gregory attempted to bristle. "Are you saying—"

"I am saying nothing, Gregory. What you do in private, even with your own pupils, is up to you. Although I suspect that the boy's parents, and equally Colonel Savos, might be interested."

Another gulp.

"However," Berkeley went on, "I will also take a somewhat sombre view of anyone who attempts to involve Caterina in any plots."

"Caterina wishes to emulate her mother. You cannot blame her for that."

"She is my wife and the mother of my children. That is all that matters to me. Now tell me what you went to see her about."

Gregory licked his lips.

"The matter is interesting Colonel Savos," Berkeley said. "He knows that you have been training some of your schoolboys in anarchy, and he is not happy about it. That he has not yet arrested you is simply because I have asked him not to. But I have to be certain that you are not planning any move against Austria."

"While you do."

"What I do is my business. Tell me why you went to Sabac."

Another quick flick of the tongue round his lips.

"I went to ask Caterina to give shelter to any of my people who might need it. Sabac is close to the Bosnian frontier. It is the obvious place for them to go to ground, and the Slovitza house is the obvious place for them to seek concealment until they can be returned here."

"And Princip is a Bosnian, you told me."

"He was."

"Well, you can forget all about that idea, for two reasons. First of all, Sabac is sufficiently close to the border to come within the range of an Austrian punitive raid, which they might well risk if they felt they might catch a wanted criminal. That would certainly put Caterina and my children in the firing line if they were found giving shelter to the criminal in question, and that I will not permit. Understand this very clearly. The second reason is that there is to be no action in either Austria, Hungary or Bosnia until I say so, and I have not said so yet."

"You think you can give me orders?"

"I am giving you orders, Gregory. I have taken command."

"And you are planning something. But you will not tell me what it is."

"No, I will not. It is best this way."

"And Karlovy?"

"Karlovy knows nothing, save that he will accompany me."

"Suppose I told you that I do know what you are planning, and that I am working to help you."

Berkeley considered him. "There is absolutely no possibility of you knowing what I am planning, Gregory. All you have to do is sit tight and wait to hear from me." He got up. "And keep your schoolboys at home."

Gregory leaned back in his chair. "Do you wish to know the real reason I went to see Caterina?"

"I would, yes."

"I went to ask her if we could use her house for shelter, certainly. But I also had a piece of information that I felt would interest her."

"Yes?"

"I have learned that the man who signed the death warrant for her father, and who was therefore indirectly responsible for her own rape and torture, was the Archduke Franz Ferdinand."

"That was a very long time ago," Berkeley said.

"Not to Caterina," Gergory pointed out.

Damn, he thought as he went out on the street to walk back to where he had stabled his horse. Damn, damn, damn. Once he had reminded Caterina that she did not even know the men who had hanged her father and ill-treated her, and he thought she accepted that reasoning. But if she knew the name of the man who had signed the death warrant . . . He could only thank God that the Archduke was many hundreds of miles away, in Vienna.

And he did not suppose that Caterina was in a minority of one when it came to Serbs, or Bosnians for that matter, who hated all Austrian archdukes.

"General Townsend."

He turned, sharply, recognising the voice. As usual, Julia Braddock was dressed in the height of fashion, wearing a fox-fur winter coat and a fur hat, and carrying an umbrella.

"Mrs Braddock." He bent over her hand.

"It seems a long time since we met."

"I'm afraid so."

"And you have been fighting more wars."

"I'm retired now."

"Ah," she said, and waited. But when he did not speak, she said, "Harvey has been transferred."

As Smailes had promised. But he said, "Isn't that rather sudden? He has only been here a year or so."

"Yes," she said. "It came as a surprise to both of us. I don't suppose . . ." Cheeks pink, she glanced right and left, although as she was speaking English there was little chance of any of the passersby eavesdropping.

"Certainly not here in Belgrade," Berkeley said.

"I was thinking of Athens."

"If anyone in Athens got to know of it, I am very sorry," he said. "Does Harvey know?"

She shook her head. "Not so far as I am aware. So, I suppose it's goodbye."

"I'm afraid it is."

She licked her lips. "If you were to . . ."

"Dearest Julia, we have been through this so many times. I am still a serving officer, in the British army at any rate. I have been given a job of work to do, and I am not a free agent until that job is completed. For you to do anything as dramatic as leaving Harvey right this minute would be incredibly foolish."

"But when this job is over . . ."

"Yes. If it is possible. Have you any idea where you are being sent?"

"Yes. Sarajevo."

"Good Lord. I didn't know we had a consulate in Sarajevo."

"It was opened several years ago, when the Austrian occupation became an established fact. We're told it's one of those old provincial towns where nothing ever happens."

"Let's hope you're right. When do you go?"

"As soon as Harvey's replacement arrives, which will be within the month. As to how long we will stay in Sarajevo, I don't know."

He nodded. "I will try to be in touch, later in the summer."

"But if we're not there . . ."

"I'll find you."

He hurried away. Emotions, feelings, whether his own or other people's, now had to be put on hold. Only Lake Balaton mattered.

Berkeley did not mention the matter of Franz Ferdinand when he returned to Sabac. Far better, he decided, to let that one lie.

It was a peaceful period. If he spent much of his spare time studying maps and roads and correlating them with the positions of the various agents Karlovy had reactivated – Berkeley had even had him look up old Dittmann at Seinheit, in case they found it necessary to escape to the north into Russian Poland – he was also able to devote a good deal of time to his family and affairs.

He supposed that knowing one is virtually under a sentence of death greatly sharpens one's perspectives, one's understanding of the truly important things in life. His children were a delight. Anna was now five, and already a capable horsewoman. At four, John was becoming interested in weapons, encouraged by his mother. And Alicia watched her elder brother and sister with envious eyes. For the present they were merely happy children. Berkeley could not doubt that with him dead and gone Caterina would instil in them her own hatred, and that they might well have short and unhappy lives.

And there was nothing he could do about that, save love them while he had the chance.

And Caterina? She too seemed to have recaptured some of the *joie de vivre* of a few years back. She loved him with almost as much desperation as he loved her, at least physically, so much so that he had to wonder if she had an inkling of the immediate future. Perhaps he talked in his sleep! Or perhaps, now that she was able to concentrate her hatred upon a single man, she too was able to love again, with at least part of her mind.

Christmas was a happy time, but once it was over, it became necessary to prepare himself for what lay ahead. Certainly as he observed what was going on around him, Berkeley could believe that Smailes and Gorman and their secret masters had a point, no matter how drastic their proposed remedy. That all the powers were preparing for an eventual war was certain; the exception was Britain herself – but she seemed to be preparing for a civil war, in Northern Ireland.

Meanwhile, in March, Tsar Nicholas II announced that he was increasing the size of the Russian army from 460,000 men to 1,700,000. This made the Serbs very happy. Austria responded by making provision for increasing the size of *their* army the top of their budget priorities, while Germany held vast manoeuvres at which the Kaiser was prominent. To further increase the tension, Albania remained in a state of incipient civil war, and disturbing reports began to circulate of atrocities committed by Serb troops on Albanian Moslems along the Macedonian border. Granted the deep-seated hatreds and frustrations on both sides of the border, the possibility of such things happening could not be discounted, but Berkeley became more than ever determined to get out of the Balkans, once his task was completed – even if it meant kidnapping Caterina all over again. He could never be one of these people, even if he sympathised with many of their problems and had fought for them.

In the new year he set his plans in motion.

"I am thinking of growing a beard," he told Caterina. "Would you like that?"

She appeared to size him up, as if she did not know what he truly looked like. "That might be amusing," she agreed.

"Lockwood is going to grow one too," he said.

The beards grew rapidly, and by the middle of May were sufficiently full and bushy for them to be able to go into Belgrade and have the photographs taken, to be placed on their passports.

"I feel I am making love with a stranger," Caterina giggled. "How long do you mean to grow it?"

"I shall probably shave it off in the summer," he said.

Which was now only a few weeks away. On June 1 Karlovy arrived.

"I am going on a journey," Berkeley told Caterina.

"With Karlovy?"

"That is correct."

"You are going on a raid."

"I am going on a journey with Karlovy. I will be gone about a fortnight."

He paused, waiting for her to insist upon accompanying him, as she had done so often in the past. But to his surprise, she merely said. "I will wish you good fortune."

Karlovy's three men were waiting outside the town, and the party of six took the train up to the Hungarian border.

"Perhaps you would be good enough now to inform us what we do?" Karlovy asked.

Berkeley had given a good deal of thought as to how to handle the business. "We are going to rob the Anhalt Bank in Buda," he told them; the group were alone in the compartment.

One of the men whistled. "That will be very dangerous."

"Not as I have planned it," Berkeley told them. "I have spent the last year obtaining plans and learning about the alarm systems. We will be in and out before anyone even knows we are there. This is necessary if we are to relaunch the Hand. We need money."

"What are these plans of yours?" Karlovy asked.

"I will tell you when we are across the border. For the moment we are going to Lake Balaton to hunt."

Karlovy grinned.

With his beard Berkeley did not think there was any chance of his being recognised, and he had his new false papers.

"Mr Carruthers," said the border guard. "Mr Brent." He glanced at Lockwood, and then checked out the Serbs, who were also travelling under assumed names and had false papers. "Going to Balaton, to hunt. Let me see your weapons, gentlemen."

They showed him their Mauser hunting rifles, equipped with telescopic sights, and Lockwood also had his trusty shotgun. Their pistols they kept concealed, and their baggage was not searched.

"It is quite busy, at Balaton, at this time of year," the guard said. "Please be careful to shoot only birds and deer."

Szigeti met them at Kiskunhalas.

"It is good to see you again, Mr Jones," he said.

Berkeley wasn't so sure of that; the little man's eyes were shifty.

"The name is Carruthers this time," he told him.

"Carruthers," Szigeti said, as if committing it to memory. "That is very English."

In the six years since Berkeley had last been here, both the Szigeti daughters had got married and moved away from home, so that only their mother was left. She made the travellers welcome, but said little and was clearly uneasy.

"You are on your way to Buda?" Szigeti asked.

"No, Lake Balaton."

"Ah. Always Lake Balaton."

"You have the horses?"

"Their hire has been arranged from the livery stable. You will return them here?"

"Of course," Berkeley said smoothly. "We will also leave some spare clothing with you, to be picked up on our homeward journey."

He suspected they were going to need it.

They obtained the horses the next morning, and set out for Lake Balaton. They also hired tents and camping equipment, and two pack animals.

"When do we turn north?" Karlovy asked.

"We are going to Lake Balaton," Berkeley told him. "We will hunt and shoot and fish, for a week or so. We are not due in Buda until the middle of the month."

This time they followed the road, actually passing through Mohacs, but there were no manoeuvres on at the moment. Then they swung north through Tolna.

"This is dangerous," Karlovy grumbled.

"No one is going to recognise us, after six years," Berkeley told him. And it seemed no one did. The following day they were overlooking the lake from a slight rise. They pitched camp and for the next week acted the part of leisured gentlemen enjoying the fishing and the shooting; the area abounded in game as well as birds, and the lake teemed with fish. As Szigeti had indicated, it was a popular area in June, but there was as yet no sign of any Germans. None were expected until the 18th of the month so Berkeley was not worried, and when buying supplies in the village, he gathered that they would certainly arrive, and was able to inspect the ground where the imperial entourage would pitch their tents.

It was on the night of the 17th that he told his men what they were going to do.

"That is suicide," Karlovy declared.

"Not for you," Berkeley said. "Your business is to create a diversion." He spread his map on the ground. "The Germans will be going here, you see, and it is reasonable to suppose that the Kaiser's tent will be here. You will attack the camp here."

"Attack?"

"Make it look good. Fire as many rounds as you can. Once you have have drawn the guards towards you, you may leave. Ride like the Devil!"

"Where?"

"Back to Szigeti, if you wish. Or straight for the border. The important thing is for you not to be identified as Serbs."

"While you do what?"

"Mr Lockwood and I will take advantage of your diversion, ride into the camp, execute the Kaiser, and hopefully ride out again before anyone realises what is happening."

Karlovy pulled his beard. "I do not think you will survive."

"That is our business. All you have to do is play your part."

"And you say this will help Serbia?"

"It will throw Germany into confusion for the foreseeable future. Without German support, Austria can do nothing. And all the while Russia grows stronger. Yes, it will help Serbia."

Some more beard pulling. "Gregory knows of this?"

"Of course he does," Berkeley said. "We planned it between us."

"Then we will do it."

"Give me your hand."

The two men clasped hands.

The next morning, Berkeley rode into the village. He went to the post office, which doubled as a general store. "I suppose my people will have to move," he remarked.

The Hungarian raised his eyebrows. "So soon?" Over the past week Berkeley had been an excellent customer.

"Oh, I would rather stay," Berkeley assured him. "But is it not true that when the German royal entourage arrives, they take over the entire east side of the lake?"

"Oh, yes," the postmaster agreed. "That is true. But you do not have to worry, Herr Carruthers. They are not coming this year."

"What did you say?"

"The hunting party has been cancelled."

"When?"

"Quite recently. I only found out today. The Kaiser is instead going to Bremen to launch this new liner, the *Bismarck*. They say it is the largest ship in the world. There it is in the newspaper."

Berkeley grabbed the broadsheet, stared at it. There could be no doubt about it. The Kaiser was going to Bremen. He felt like a man actually standing on the gallows who has been handed a reprieve and who doesn't know whether to laugh or cry. When he thought of the year of preparation, the plans, the money, the elaborate secrecy . . . all reduced to nothing at the whim of a lunatic warlord!

Then his eye, almost unconsciously, flickered down the page.

ARCHDUKE TO VISIT SARAJEVO. The Archduke Franz Ferdinand and his wife will visit Sarajevo next week on the occasion of their fourteenth wedding anniversary. Until now the visit has been kept secret for fear of demonstrations against Austrian rule, but considerable precautions are being taken to prevent any trouble.

Another secret. But one that Gregory, with his huge network of spies, had discovered. And laid his plans accordingly. He had even supposed that Berkeley had been planning along the same lines. A week! It had to be stopped: the consequences of an attack upon the Archduke were incalculable.

Sarajevo! Julia was in Sarajevo. Of course, the British Consul and his wife would have nothing to do with a terrorist outrage . . . but they might get too close to one. And his mission here was in any event aborted. In every possible way his duty pointed towards Bosnia, just as quickly as he could get there.

"Then perhaps we'll be able to stay," he said to the postmaster, and went to his horse.

Outside the village he whipped the animal into a gallop. Time. There was time. He could be back in Belgrade in three or four days. All would depend on how soon Gregory despatched his assassins.

His schoolboys!

He drew rein to give his horse a breather. It was still fairly early in the morning, and there did not seem to be anyone about. The camp was only a mile or so further on, and from the slight rise on which he sat his horse he could see the glistening waters of the lake. A flutter of birds rose from a copse some distance to his right. Berkeley frowned, and slipped from the saddle. He was unarmed, save for his pistol, but he did have a pair of binoculars. These he levelled and focussed. The copse was about half a mile away, but he was sure he could make out the gleam of metal amid the trees.

The camp was about to be attacked!

Another betrayal! But he could not abandon his people. They had to be warned to resist the attack from . . . it could only be Hungarian police. He looked left and right. The last couple of days had been dry, and this morning there was a good breeze, blowing from the south, towards the copse. He hunted around desperately, gathered brushwood and stacked it, struck a match and carefully fanned the flames, then scattered the burning brush across the grass. It caught almost immediately, and put up a wall of dense smoke, moving towards the copse and spreading to right and left.

He heard shouts in the distance, but could not see through the smoke. He regained his mount and kicked him again into a gallop, riding down the lee side of the smoke wall. Now there were more shouts and even some shots, but the Hungarians could no more see him than he them.

Disturbingly, there was no reaction from the camp which he could see clearly. But now Lockwood appeared, at the head of the low rise which led down to the beach. He had his fishing rod in his hands and looked utterly bewildered.

"Mount up!" Berkeley shouted. "Ride!"

Where the Devil was Karlovy and his men? He suddenly knew – there was only one horse left on the stake line.

Lockwood reacted as quickly as ever, having the coolness to run first to his tent and secure his haversack and shotgun, before freeing his horse and leaping into the saddle. As he did so, several mounted policemen came round the edge of the smokescreen waving and shouting, and firing their carbines. From the backs of their horses they could not find a target. But Berkeley had brought his mount to a halt, and now he drew his pistol, and sighted very carefully, using both hands, before squeezing the trigger.

The policemen were close together, and he certainly hit one of them, as there were more shouts. They wheeled their horses and rode back, one man hanging from the saddle.

"What's going on, sir?" Lockwood panted.

"Nothing very nice," Berkeley said, and wheeled his horse. "Let's get the hell out of here."

They rode south, away from the blaze. They had a considerable start, as Berkeley guessed that the police would be anxious to beat out the fire before it did too much damage in preference to mounting an immediate pursuit. After a couple of hours they reached another small wood, and found a stream.

"Now," Berkeley said, "let's get rid of the fungus."

They used their knives to shave, somewhat roughly. Then they tore their false passports into tiny pieces and dropped them into the rushing water. Berkeley would have preferred to burn them, but he dared not risk another fire, as the police had to be close.

"Do you think Karlovy got away?" Lockwood asked.

"Karlovy set this up," Berkeley said.

"Sir?"

"When did he and his people leave?"

"Almost as soon as you did, this morning. They said they were going shooting."

"They were going to the Hungarian police. I think killing the Kaiser was too rich for their blood."

"But how are we going to do it now, sir, on our own? And with the police looking for us."

"We aren't, Harry. There's been a foul-up." He repeated what he had learned in the village.

"God Almighty!" Lockwood exclaimed. "You mean we've been absolutely done."

"*We* haven't, Harry. London can hardly blame me for a last-minute change of plan on the part of the Kaiser. But we have to stop that crazy schoolmaster from starting a war."

To All Eternity

It took them longer than Berkeley had estimated to regain Kiskunhalas. This was because it was necessary to avoid not only the police, who were scouring the countryside, but also places like Tolna, where without their beards, they could conceivably be recognised. It was June 23, a Tuesday, before they reached Szigeti's house, hungry and dirty. But there were still five days in hand.

Szigeti was in his garden, and appeared amazed to see them.

"Mr Jones?" he asked, uncertainly, as that was how he remembered Berkeley without the beard. Although the two Englishmen had again not shaved for several days.

"The very man," Berkeley said, dismounting and handing his reins to Lockwood.

"But, Karlovy . . ."

"Let's go inside," Berkeley suggested, "and you can tell me all about Karlovy."

Szigeti licked his lips and led the way into the house, where his wife was entertaining one of her daughters, who had a small child on her lap. Both sprang up at the sight of Berkeley.

"But, you are dead!" Madame Szigeti exclaimed.

"Ah. Is that what Karlovy told you? When?"

"He was here yesterday. He said you and Mr . . ." She glanced at Lockwood, who having stabled the horses, was just coming in.

"And how were we supposed to have been killed?"

"He said a police raid, there was shooting . . ."

"From which he and his men escaped," Berkeley said grimly. "Where is he now?"

"As I told you," Szigeti said, "he came here with his people, told us you had been killed, and then they took the train. I returned their horses to the stable. You understand, sir, that it is not my business to do more than act as a go-between."

"Oh, quite," Berkeley said. "Now, we also wish to take the train."

"There is no train now, until tomorrow."

"Then we will have to spend the night here," Berkeley said equably. "I am sorry to inflict this upon you, madame, but it is necessary."

Madame Szigeti swallowed, and looked at her daughter.

"Your name is?" Berkeley asked.

"Anna," she gasped.

"Well, now there's a step in the right direction. You have a husband, I believe," Berkeley said.

She nodded. She was actually quite a pretty thing, but so terrified at the moment that she seemed almost ugly.

"What does he do?"

She licked her lips. "He is a soldier."

"Ah. Stationed here?"

"No, sir. He is in Budapest."

"Then you are all alone at home? Or do you have other children?"

"No, sir." She hugged the little boy to her breast.

"Then no one will be disturbed if you spend the night here with your parents."

She gave her mother a quick glance. Madame Szigeti nodded.

"Good," Berkeley said. "Now, we need to eat and bathe and sleep. Szigeti, you may return our horses to the stables"

Szigeti opened his mouth and then closed it again. He also glanced at his wife.

"And you should bear in mind," Berkeley said, "that at the slightest suggestion of treachery, we shall kill you, your wife and your daughter."

The Szigetis trembled.

"But if you do as you are told, and help us to get out of the country, we will pay you a hundred English pounds sterling."

Szigeti hurried off and the women prepared baths and food. Having eaten and changed, Berkeley and Lockwood felt a whole lot better. By then Szigeti had returned. He had nothing to report, as the news of the fracas at Balaton had not yet reached Kiskunhalas, nor had the police tracked the fugitives as yet.

"But they'll have the border closed by now, sir," Lockwood suggested.

"They aren't looking for us," Berkeley pointed out. "They're looking for two bearded gentlemen named Carruthers and Brent."

"But if Karlovy did betray us . . ."

"Karlovy is assuming we are dead by now, as he told Szigeti."

Lockwood pulled his nose. His master's confidence was sometimes frightening.

"What about these people?" he asked. "Do you think they can be trusted? Even with the promise of a hundred pounds?"

"Probably not," Berkeley agreed. "We'll just have to make sure of it."

They had been speaking English, while the Szigetis watched them anxiously.

"Now," Berkeley said, reverting to German. "Mr Lockwood and I are both desperately in need of a good night's sleep. We will use your spare bedroom, if we may, and you, Miss Anna, will sleep with us."

"Me?" Anna cried. "I am a respectable married woman."

"I have no doubt of it. And we are not going to interfere with you or embarrass you in any way. We just require your company to make such that no one attempts to interfere with *us*. I suggest we none of us undress, just lie down and have a good sleep. I am sure you can take care of your grandchild for the night, madame."

An intensely embarrassed Anna was placed in the big double bed between them, having removed her boots, as did Berkeley and Lockwood. In fact they all slept heavily, and were up at dawn, totally refreshed. Berkeley inspected the yard and street from the bedroom window but they looked deserted, and the Szigetis seemed normal when they went down to breakfast.

"You'll be glad to see the back of us, I'd say," Berkeley remarked.

"Well, sir," Szigeti said, "if the police are after you, and they come here . . ."

"Is there any reason for them to do that?"

"Well, no, sir. But—"

"What time is the train?"

"It leaves in one hour."

"Then we had better make haste. You go and pack a bag."

"Me, sir?"

"You are coming with us," Berkeley explained.

"Me?" Szigeti asked again, his voice higher.

"Just as far as the border. Or across it. Then you are welcome to return."

"You do not trust me," Szigeti complained.

"Right this minute, I am not in a position to trust anybody," Berkeley said.

"And the money?"

"Will be paid to you once we are on Serbian soil."

Szigeti bade his wife and daughter an almost tearful goodbye, clearly under the impression he might never see them again, and they went into town and boarded the train. There did not appear to be more than the usual number of policemen at the station, which indicated that the search for the fugitives had not yet reached Kiskunhalas. Berkeley did not suppose it was a very serious search anyway. He had no idea what Karlovy might have told the Hungarian police, but even if he had revealed that Berkeley was after the Kaiser, the fact was that had not come off. True, he had started a fire and shot and wounded a policeman, but as he was quite sure Karlovy would not have dared reveal they were all members of the Black Hand – he would have been arrested on the spot, no matter what information he had to give – the police had no reason to come this way.

But no matter how confident he felt about the safety of himself and Lockwood, Berkeley was acutely aware that time was passing. This was Wednesday June 24. In four days time the Archduke would be in Sarajevo. If Gregory was planning anything, the plan would already have been set in motion. But Berkeley would be in Belgrade tonight.

There were additional police at the border, and severe checking of documents, but the famous Serbian general and his servant returning from a visit to Budapest, were let through without trouble, as was Szigeti. Szigeti had some trouble on the Serbian side, but Berkeley explained that they were merely carrying out a business transaction, whereupon he shook hands with the agent, and told him to wait for the next train north. He also gave Szigeti the promised one hundred English sovereigns, which cheered him up considerably.

"Will I be hearing from you again, General?" he asked.

"Perhaps," Berkeley said. He needed to keep the little man at least interested.

Then the train continued south.

That afternoon they were in Belgrade. They went directly to the school. Everything seemed normal, boys and masters hurrying from one classroom to another, and as usual they were shown straight to the headmaster's study.

"Berkeley?" Gregory was even more surprised than Szigeti to see them – and a good deal more frightened. "I was told you had gone away."

"Who told you that?" Berkeley asked.

"Well . . . it must have been Caterina."

"You have been to see my wife, again?"

"No, no. She came to see me."

"She came here?"

"Yes. She happened to be in Belgrade, and she did me the honour of calling."

"Gregory," Berkeley said, "you are lying. My wife would never come to Belgrade on her own. In fact, she would never come to Belgrade at all."

Gregory goggled at him.

"So who told you I had gone away?" Berkeley asked.

"Well . . ." Gregory licked his lips.

"Karlovy, I expect. Where is he?"

"How should I know. If he went with you—"

"How do you know he went with me?"

Gregory began to pant.

"Because you have seen him, yesterday, or perhaps even today. And he told you I was dead, killed by the Hungarian police."

Gregory was clearly trying to think. "He came here and told me this, yes," he said. "He said you had been ambushed. But he managed to shoot his way out."

"With all three of his people," Berkeley remarked. "Isn't he a fortunate fellow. Now tell me where he is."

"I do not know."

Berkeley knew he was lying. But Karlovy could wait. "Very well. Tell me what you are planning in Sarajevo."

"Sarajevo? Me? Planning?"

"Gregory, I am losing patience. You are planning an attack on the Archduke Franz Ferdinand, when he goes to Sarajevo at the end of this week. You have got to stop it."

"Me? How can I do this?"

"Because you set it in motion. You know who is involved: the boy Princip, for a start. They will carry out the attack, and then escape across the border and take shelter in my house. Is that not correct? Because you have suborned my wife into giving them refuge. Is that not correct?"

"I know nothing of this. I . . ."

Berkeley drew his pistol and presented it to Gregory's head. "You had better know something about it, and how to stop it, or I am going to blow you apart."

"My God!" Gregory cried. "Murder! He means murder!"

The door burst open with such force that Lockwood was pushed to one side. Berkeley turned away from Gregory, and faced Karlovy who was accompanied by two of his men. All carried pistols, but Berkeley fired first; his bullet struck Karlovy squarely in the centre of the forehead, and he fell backwards with a thump. His men fired, but were distracted by the death of their leader, and also by Lockwood who had regained his balance and now swung his shotgun with tremendous force catching the nearest man on the shoulder and tumbling him against the wall.

The other man dropped his gun and raised his arms, looking death in the face. Berkeley levelled his own weapon but did not fire; the man had only been acting under orders. Berkeley was now distracted by a groan from behind him.

"Keep them covered, Harry," he said, and turned back to Gregory, who was slumped in his chair, blood oozing from his jacket, clearly dying. He bent over the stricken man. "Listen," he said. "This madness must be stopped. Tell me the arrangements."

"It cannot be stopped," Gregory muttered. "It will happen." His lips parted in a ghastly smile. "So you killed Karlovy. All of this could have been avoided, if he had killed you in England."

So it had been Karlovy, all along. And no doubt he had been set up again, Berkeley thought, just to get him out of the way while Gregory carried out his master plan.

"It will be stopped," he said. "Tell me who leads the group."

Gregory uttered a little sigh. "Hamid the Cobbler . . ."

"Who is Hamid the Cobbler? Where is he?"

Gregory made a noise which could have been a chuckle. "Too late," he whispered. "Caterina . . ." His head slumped on to his chest.

Berkeley stared at him in consternation for several seconds. What had he been going to say about Caterina?

He stood up, looked at the two terrified anarchists guarded by Lockwood's shotgun. There was a considerable amount of noise from below the stairs, the gunshots having been heard. But no one was prepared to risk investigating.

"What do you know of this?" he asked.

"Nothing," the first man said. "We did what Karlovy told us."

Berkeley reckoned that was probably true. He picked up their guns. "Let's go," he told Lockwood.

"Shouldn't we report this, sir?"

"We haven't the time to waste in a police cell, Harry." He ran down the stairs, Lockwood behind him. At the sight of the two heavily armed men the crowd of boys and masters hastily retreated. "There are two dead men up there," Berkeley told them. "Someone had better tell the police." Then they were in the saddle and galloping out of the city.

They had to hire fresh horses and it took them three hours to reach Sabac; it was dark and their mounts were all but dead when they dismounted before the Slovitza house.

They had been the longest three hours of Berkeley's life. Now he ran up the steps. The door was opened for him by Marie. "Oh, General, I am so glad you are back."

"I'm glad to be back. Where is madame? Upstairs?"

"No, sir. Madame is not here."

Huge lumps of lead seemed to be gathering in Berkeley's stomach. "Not here? Where is she?"

"I do not know, sir. Only that she has gone away."

"With the children?"

"Oh, no, sir. The children are upstairs with Alexandrina. Madame just said she was going away for a few days."

"By herself?"

"No, sir. She had some people with her." She looked embarrassed. "Young men."

Berkeley stared at her for several seconds. This was far worse than he had feared. He had realised that Caterina was involved, but not that she would actively take part in it. She was again dreaming of emulating her mother. And Gregory had recruited her with that ruthless intensity that had led him to employ his own schoolchildren. They could only have gone to Sarajevo – to the house, or shop of this Hamid the Cobbler? That was all he had to go on.

He went upstairs to see his children, who were just being put to bed. They were, as always, boisterously happy to welcome him, perfectly certain their mother would soon be back. Even Alexandrina did not seem the least perturbed by Caterina's sudden departure. "She said something about going to a function at Dr Masanovich's school in Belgrade," she explained.

"Listen to me very carefully. I wish you to pack some clothes for the children, and some of their toys. And of course, clothes for yourself."

"We are leaving Sabac?" She was astounded.

"Tomorrow morning. You will go to Belgrade, and put up at a hotel there. Hopefully, Mrs Townsend and I will join you very shortly."

"But . . ." The poor woman was obviously completely confused. "If Mrs Townsend is there now . . ."

"Just do as I ask. Mr Lockwood will take care of everything." He went outside, where Lockwood waited.

"Here's a pretty kettle—"

"I'm putting you in charge, Harry." Berkeley sat at his desk and wrote a cheque. "They will cash that at the bank in Belgrade, and here is some cash to get you there. Take Marie and your children, and Alexandrina and my children, and go to a hotel, and wait there until you hear from me or of me. Shut this house up. Take the horses and stable them in Belgrade."

"You're going after Mrs Townsend? Shouldn't I come with you?"

"I don't think two of us is going to be any better than one, this time, Harry. Now listen. If by any chance you learn of my death, it will mean that Mrs Townsend is also dead. You will then take my children, and yourself and your children, back to England. You will place my children in the care of my parents, and . . . well, old friend, you will have to fend for yourself."

"I shall do as you wish, sir," Lockwood said. "But I'd take it very kindly if you were to come back."

"It's my intention to do so," Berkeley assured him. "By the way, if Colonel Savos wishes to have a word with you, as I think he probably will, tell him exactly what happened; you didn't shoot anybody, so there is no reason for him to hold you, except as a witness. I assume they will perform a post-mortem on the two dead men, in which case they will find that the bullet which killed Gregory came from a Mauser pistol, as used by Karlovy, while the bullet that killed Karlovy came from my Browning. I was shooting in an attempt to save not only my own life but Gregory's. Right?"

"Absolutely, sir."

"Well, then . . ." They clasped hands. "It was always likely to end this way," he said.

Berkeley snatched a few hours sleep, as there was no point in arriving in Sarajevo exhausted. At dawn he took two horses so that he would have a remount, and rode for the border. He did not know what was happening in Belgrade, but as no policemen had come down to Sabac after him, he had to assume that Savos was following his own agenda – as he always had done. Equally, as he had no idea what plans the Black Hand had laid, there was only one way he could handle this, while hoping that he could still extricate Caterina from catastrophe. He felt he had some time, as it was still only Thursday, and Sarajevo being only just over a hundred miles from Belgrade, although the country was fairly rough, he reached the Bosnian capital on Friday afternoon, changing his mounts regularly. He had no trouble at the border; he was travelling as Major Berkeley Townsend, British army, retired, and also as Brigadier-General Berkeley Townsend, Serbian army, retired. While he had no doubt his entry into Bosnia was recorded and would be forwarded to Sarajevo, no one had any reason to stop him for the time being.

The first thing one noticed about Sarajevo was the pronounced Moslem flavour, not only in the many mosques and minarets, but also in the general architecture, all of which contrasted oddly with the motor cars on the streets. Berkeley, who had not been here before, assumed a large proportion of the population remained Moslem.

Equally he observed that while there were already some red and white flags draped from various buildings and wrapped around lamp-posts, there was no evidence of any increased security.

He went straight to the British Consulate, gave his name, and after a short wait was shown into the consul's office.

"General Townsend? Berkeley?" Harvey Braddock clearly didn't know whether to be pleased or dismayed. "What brings you to Sarajevo?"

"A matter of the most vital importance," Berkeley told him.

Braddock showed him to a chair.

"Have you ever heard of the Black Hand?" Berkeley asked.

"Ah . . . rumours. It is some kind of secret society, is it not."

"That is correct. Now, Harvey, I do not propose to answer any questions as to how I come by my knowledge, but I can tell you that this Black Hand is planning an attempt on the life of the Archduke Franz Ferdinand, when he comes here at the end of the week."

Braddock gaped at him. "They must be stopped."

"Exactly."

"But how? Do you know these people? Can you identify them?"

"I can identify them if I see them," Berkeley said. "I know they are somewhere in the city, but I do not know where they are currently hiding." He had no intention of telling anyone about Hamid the Cobbler until he had found Caterina.

"Then what can we do?"

"We, you, can go to the authorities and get them to postpone the Archduke's visit. A week will do. Meanwhile, I will find these people. I am sure I can."

"You'll need police assistance."

"I can manage on my own."

"I have to ask this, sir: for whom are you working?"

"I am working for the Serbian government. These are my credentials. I am a brigadier-general in the Serbian army, at this moment on the retired list. I am also a British military attaché. I know it's complicated, but there it is. My business is to prevent hostilities between Serbia and Austria-Hungary."

"Am I allowed to tell the Sarajevo police this?"

"It would be better if you didn't. Just get them to postpone the visit, and leave the rest to me."

Braddock swallowed. "I will certainly try. You understand I have only been here a short while. I will have to make an appointment, and at this hour . . ."

"Then would you do so? I'm sure you appreciate that this is a most urgent matter. Now, one more thing: I need somewhere to live until I find these people."

"Ah, yes. I can recommend a good hotel."

"I cannot go to a hotel, Harvey. As you will know, it is the police custom to visit each hotel every morning and check through their registers. If my name is found, I will be questioned, and certainly I shall be under surveillance all the time I am in Sarajevo."

"Oh, quite. Yes. Well . . ."

"I would like to stay at your residence. It is only a matter of a couple of days."

"I suppose you will have to. I had better come with you."

"Just agree, and I will go on my own, if you will direct me. You must get on to the police right away."

"Yes, of course," Braddock said, more doubtfully yet.

He was clearly not a man of great decision.

"Berkeley?" Julia was even more astounded than her husband, as she gazed at her travel-stained, unshaven lover.

"I am to stay with you for the next few days."

"Stay? Here?" She waved her hand, and the servant who had admitted him left the room. "I'm not sure Harvey will agree."

"Harvey has already done so. This is a most vital matter, Julia."

"To do with us?" There were pink spots in her cheeks.

"No. It is an international business. I may as well tell you, Caterina is in Saravejo with some of her friends."

"You mean she has left you again?"

"No. She is working for a secret organisation, which means to assassinate the Archduke when he comes here on Sunday."

"Caterina? Murder? That sweet little girl?"

"Believe me, she comes from a long line of assassins."

"Good Lord!" She got up, poured them each a glass of sherry. "When did you find out?"

"I knew it before I married her. It is a very long story, and I really do not wish to go into it now. The important thing is that she, and her friends, are stopped. I have sent Harvey to warn the local police. My job is to find her."

"Do you know where she is?"

"Not precisely, but I think I can find out. All I need is somewhere to stay, out of the eye of the police, until I do that."

"And then?"

"I shall carry her across the border to Serbia, and make sure she doesn't do anything like this again."

She sipped her drink. "And us? When do you complete your mission? Or is this a part of it?"

"My mission is completed."

"Well, then . . ."

"But I must sort out this mess before I can consider anything else."

"I see," she said coldly.

"Look, Julia, please be adult about this," Berkeley said. "I cannot stand by and allow my wife either to commit murder or be hanged."

"Of course. I understand where your duty must lie, Berkeley. And I must stand back and act the good wife to Harvey and wait, patiently. I will show you to your room."

"I am grateful for your understanding," Berkeley said. "And for the use of your house. But the sooner I start on finding Caterina the better for all of us. I will see you at dinner."

He kissed her hand.

Berkeley headed towards the old part of the city and asked a policeman for the whereabouts of Hamid the Cobbler. The directions were simple enough, the distance not far. There were crowds of people on the streets, but few took much interest in the tall, well-dressed and obviously foreign gentleman who walked with a slight limp, swinging his cane, even if he was also untidy and unshaven.

He entered the shop, where a big, heavy man was bent over a workbench.

"Hamid?" Berkeley asked.

The cobbler looked up. "I am Hamid." He spoke Serbo-Croat.

"I am looking for my wife."

Hamid gazed at him.

"Her name is Caterina Townsend," Berkeley said.

Hamid's eyes flickered. "I know no one of that name."

Berkeley glanced at the street and the people, then at a door leading to the interior of the shop. "I think we need to speak in private."

"I have no desire to speak with you in private," Hamid said.

Berkeley unbuttoned his jacket to reveal the Browning in his belt. "I think you do."

Hamid gazed at the gun, swallowed, and laid down his hammer. "Why do you wish to find this woman, Caterina Townsend?"

"Because she is my wife."

"I know a woman called Caterina Slovitza," Hamid said.

"She'll do. Where is she?"

"I do not know. But she is coming here, tomorrow."

Berkeley considered him: the man was clearly lying, but about what? The Englishman had very little choice – to start a fracas now, even if it meant taking this man inside and shooting him, would not bring him any nearer to finding Caterina. It might, in fact, make it impossible.

"Very well," he said. "I will return tomorrow. At what time?"

"She will be here at ten o'clock in the morning."

"Thank you. And Hamid, if she is not here, I am going to place you under arrest and hand you over to the police to be hanged for conspiracy. Please bear this in mind."

Hamid glowered at him and picked up his hammer.

Berkeley returned to the consul's house, slowly. He had no desire to be alone with Julia right now. His relations with her, and with Caterina, were simply too ambivalent to be considered. He could

236

only concentrate on the immediate business of saving Caterina's life . . . and preventing a war!

Braddock was already at home when he returned. The consul was in a very excited state. "They won't hear of it," he said.

"You told them of the plot?"

"They were totally contemptuous. There are always plots, they said. If we were to cancel or postpone every visit by royalty because of a supposed plot, no one would ever leave Vienna. And even in Vienna there are plots. Have you found your wife?"

"Not yet."

"Then what are we to do?"

"I think I am going to be able to find her, tomorrow."

"And her accomplices?"

"I'm working on it. Look, you have done all you can. You heard of this plot, and you did your duty and warned the police. If they choose to ignore your warning, that is their business. No blame can be attached to you."

"But if they find out that I have you staying in my house . . ."

"I shall be gone before they can make anything of that." Berkeley smiled at them both. "I'm for an early night. Tomorrow may be a busy day."

"You realise that Julia and I are on the official guest list, to meet the Archduke at the town hall?"

"Then I suggest you get a good night's sleep as well," Berkeley recommended.

He was less sanguine than he made himself appear. He was still working very much in the dark. He did not know how many of Gregory's pupils were involved, and he did not know the extent of Caterina's own involvement. Nor did he yet know the exact assassination plot. These were things he would have to find out tomorrow. And then? He could not hand the conspirators over to the police without involving Caterina. And merely to remove Caterina would not prevent the plot. He simply had to overawe them, use his position as field commander of the Hand to make them abandon the conspiracy.

Schoolboys!

"What are you going to do when you find her?" Braddock asked at breakfast.

Berkeley had, somewhat to his surprise, slept well; even Julia had had the sense not to attempt to come to him with her husband in the house.

"I may bring her back here, in the first instance," he said. "Will that be all right?"

Braddock glanced at his wife nervously. "I suppose so. But it does involve us rather heavily."

"My wife is a British citizen," Berkeley reminded him. "And therefore is entitled to the protection of the British consul until I can get her out of the country."

"Yes, I suppose that is true. But if she is involved in anarchy . . ."

"She will, at worst, have to be deported. But I would still hope to get her out of the country before it comes to that."

"I see. And her friends?"

"They may have to take their chances. But they are all very young. We may be able to work something out there. Now I must be off."

"And good luck," Braddock said.

"I'll put out fresh towels," Julia volunteered. "For Caterina, when she comes."

"Thank you," Berkeley said.

He hurried to the cobbler's shop. As it was a Saturday, the streets were even more crowded than the previous day, and now, as he had changed his clothes and shaved and wore a top hat, he was even more conspicuous.

He looked for an increased police presence but there was hardly a uniform to be seen. Either the authorities were indeed determined to ignore Braddock's warning, or they were using plain-clothes men to infiltrate the crowds. He had to hope it was the latter.

Hamid the Cobbler was working as before; the shop was otherwise empty. But he seemed in a better humour today. "Ah, General Townsend," he said. "I will put up a plaque, that on the twenty-seventh of June 1914 my shop was visited, a second time, by so famous a man."

"Where is my wife?" Berkeley demanded.

"Inside."

Berkeley was surprised. This was too easy. "Is she alone?"

"Of course."

As before, Berkeley had no doubt he was lying. "If she is not," he said. "I will come back and talk to you about it." He unbuttoned his jacket, went to the door, tried the handle. The door was not locked, and he pushed it in while remaining in the shop.

There was a lantern glowing to illuminate the otherwise dark interior, revealing a poorly furnished Moslem dwelling. Caterina stood on the far side of the room, facing him. Her face was composed, but defiant.

Berkeley stepped inside, keeping his back to the wall, while he took in the rest of the room. It certainly appeared to be empty. "You are an incredibly silly little girl," he remarked, in English.

"You have always carried out your duty, obeyed orders, and been proud of it," she said. "Women can have orders, duty, too."

"Killing, and being killed, is man's work."

"That is a matter of opinion."

"And who gave you these orders that have to be carried out?"

"Gregory."

"Gregory is dead."

Her mouth dropped open. "You killed him? You killed Gregory?"

"No, I did not, Karlovy did that. Actually, he was shooting at me. Still, the fact is they are both dead. Therefore I am now in command. And I am aborting this conspiracy, now. You will return with me to Sabac."

"You were never in command," she snapped. "If Gregory is dead, then *I* am in command. And I will avenge my parents."

"Caterina . . ." He stepped towards her, and the door behind him opened. He had been careless – too many years of relying on Lockwood always to guard his back. But Lockwood was in Belgrade by now.

His hand dropped to the Browning, but Caterina had already drawn her weapon. "Please do not make me do it," she said.

Berkeley hesitated. He could kill her, but equally she could at least hit him. And if he died now, it would not stop what was going to happen.

Even supposing he *could* kill Caterina.

A gun muzzle was thrust into his back, and a hand came round to secure the Browning.

"Do not harm him," Caterina said. "I am sorry, Berkeley, but you must remain here for the next twenty-four hours. Then you will be free to go. I give you my word."

"You foolish girl," he said. "You are going to get yourself killed."

"I will have done my duty."

There were several men in the room now, and one came round in front. Berkeley recognised Princip.

"Why has he come here?" the boy asked.

"To tell us that Gregory is dead," Caterina said.

"Gregory? You killed him!" Princip accused.

"No, Karlovy killed him," Caterina said, "apparently by accident. Nothing has changed, except that we owe it to Gregory to succeed in our mission."

"And him?"

"My husband will stay here until our task has been completed."

How like her mother she had become.

"Take him into the inner room," she said, and opened the door behind her.

This led into a bedroom, with a single four-poster bed, a table, a straight chair, and another table with a washbasin and ewer. Through another open door there was a toilet.

"I'm afraid we must tie you to the bed, Berkeley," she said. "There will be someone with you at all times, to release you to use the toilet or to eat. This man will be armed, and he will not hesitate to shoot you if you attempt to attack him or escape. Please be sensible. And perhaps it may be possible . . . Well, all things are possible."

"You are committing suicide," Berkeley said again.

"I am doing what must be done," she said. "Please lie on the bed."

There were now seven people in the room with him. All were very young and therefore inexperienced. But he did not suppose he could take them all on together. On the other hand, if they intended to leave him with but a single gaoler . . . Even Caterina, who had seen him in action, did not really know with what she was contending.

He lay on the bed, and his arms and legs were extended and secured to the four uprights. Caterina gazed at him for several seconds, but with no suggestion of love in her eyes, then went to the door, followed by her henchmen. One of the boys remained. He sat on the chair behind the table, facing the bed, ostentatiously placing a revolver on the table in front of him.

Berkeley did some calculations. It was now getting on for midday on Saturday. There were still twenty-four hours to go. The first priority was what Braddock and Julia might do if he did not return to lunch. Go back to the police? That was a possibility. But as they had no idea where he had gone, he doubted they would do that.

More likely they would just sit tight and hope he would turn up. That was certainly Braddock's line of behaviour, whether or not he suspected a liaison with his wife. So, forget them.

He had twenty-four hours to get out of here. The only way he was going to stop an attack on the Archduke was by arresting all the Hand members in Sarajevo. Which might mean having to kill them. Including Caterina? And he did not know how many of them there were.

"So tell me," he said pleasantly to the boy, "what is going to happen tomorrow?"

"You know what is going to happen, General," the boy said. "We are going to execute the Archduke."

"And his wife?"

"If she gets in the way."

"I see. How are you going to do it?"

"A bomb will be thrown into their car while they are going to the town hall for the official reception."

"You are likely to kill more than just the Archduke. And his wife."

"That is the fortune of war," the boy said.

Berkeley forced himself to be patient, to give the other conspirators time to leave the shop, but as it happened, before he was ready to make any move, Hamid came in with his lunch. The food was for all three of them, and the two men sat at the table, both with loaded revolvers in front of them, while Berkeley sat on the bed and ate the mutton stew, washed down by some rough red wine. He was then allowed to use the toilet, again watched by both men.

Caterina was not as innocent as he had supposed.

This went on for the rest of the day. One of the men was always with him, while presumably the other slept, but whenever he needed to be released the second gaoler was always called.

Here was a problem. They always kept their distance, and he was required to eat with his fingers. There seemed no way he could get at them. Unless . . .

That evening, when being allowed to use the toilet, he suddenly gasped and collapsed on the floor. Neither man approached him.

"What has happened to him?" the boy asked.

"It is some kind of attack," Hamid said.

"What should we do? Suppose he dies?"

"Then he dies," Hamid said. "It could also be some kind of a trick. Let him lie there."

They waited, and after a while Berkeley gave up: lying on the cold stone floor was distinctly uncomfortable.

"That was a nasty turn," he said, raising his arms as they pointed their guns at him.

They tied him to the bed.

Now he was becoming quite desperate. The hours were ticking away. This evening the Archduke and his wife and entourage would be arriving in the city. The boy had said a bomb would be thrown the next day outside the town hall, but there might also be an earlier attack.

And he could do nothing about it.

He fell asleep from sheer mental exhaustion, trying desperately to think of some way of getting out of his prison without being instantly shot. But there was none. He awoke with a start and in a cold sweat. Sunday morning; it was going to happen within a couple of hours.

He turned his head and saw to his amazement that there was no one sitting at the table. He frowned, looked left and right. The lantern had been turned down and the room was very gloomy, the only daylight seeping in from under the door. But he was definitely alone.

Now was no time for finesse. He began to strain on his bonds, working both arms and legs with desperate urgency. The bed creaked noisily but no one came in. When he listened, he deduced there was no one in the shop either.

Equally, there was no great noise on the street. Nothing had happened yet.

He resumed work, panting and gasping. He knew there was no rope which would not slacken over a period of time. But how much time? He had no means of telling, save that even in the closed room it gradually grew brighter as the sun got higher; and hotter too, although that was at least partly his own body heat caused by his exertions.

He was almost despairing when there was a crack, and one of the posts fell in. The others followed immediately, and he could only be grateful that there was no canopy, or he might have been smothered.

But the collapse of the bed had slackened the ropes, and within ten minutes he was free. He seized the ewer, took a drink, and then poured some over his face. Then he contemplated the door; but that was not going to stop him now. He hurled himself against it, and it cracked. It took him several charges, and a badly bruised shoulder, before one of the panels splintered sufficiently for him to tear it out and get his hand through to slip the bolt.

The next room was empty, as it had to be or someone would have heard what he was doing. The street door was also closed, but as he went towards it, it swung in, to reveal Hamid.

"You were careless," Berkeley said.

"The boy would go to see the fun," Hamid said, and swung the hammer he was carrying.

Berkeley caught the wrist in his left hand and hit the cobbler with his right, putting all of his pent-up fury, frustration and fear into the blow, which struck Hamid in the stomach, and had him on his knees, gasping for breath. Berkeley wrenched the hammer from his hand, and as Hamid made another grab for his knees, used it to strike down. Hamid struck the floor on his face without a sound. Blood trickled from his scalp. Berkeley did not know whether he was dead or not, and he did not have the time to find out.

The street door had swung shut behind Hamid when he had come in. Berkeley took a deep breath, opened it and stepped outside, uncertain what he would immediately have to face. He blinked in the fierce sunlight. The street was empty, save for a couple of stray dogs. Everyone had gone to see the Archduke, and from not so very far away he could hear the sound of cheering.

He ran in the direction of the sound, panting and staggering; his legs were still not working at their best. Now he caught up with people, who glanced at the big unkempt figure with the two-day growth of beard. But no one attempted to stop him.

He rounded a corner, and came in sight of a large crowd, not in the least held back by only one or two policemen. Those apart, there was not a soldier to be seen. The Bosnian authorities definitely did not believe there was going to be any trouble, no matter how many warnings they might have received. Or they did not care.

He pushed his way into the throng until he was on the street itself. To his right a line of cars was approaching, travelling very slowly because of the people who kept darting to and fro across the street, shouting and cheering. All the cars were open, but here at last there was some protection: mounted policemen rode in front, and the lead car contained only men, obviously plain-clothes policemen. The Archduke and the Archduchess were seated in the back of the second car, the Archduke in full uniform, nodding to the crowd and occasionally raising his hand, while the Duchess, who carried an enormous bouquet of flowers, smiled from beneath her broad-brimmed hat. There were several cars behind, each filled with both women and men.

Berkeley looked away from them. In sight to his left was the town hall, its steps and doorways crowded with dignitaries, amongst them no doubt an anxious Harvey and Julia Braddock. Then he looked over at the faces of the crowd itself, and found himself gazing, on the other side of the street, at Caterina.

She had not seen him and was staring at the approaching cars. She carried a large bag, and was flanked by two of the boys who were members of her party. Both were smoking cigars. But then, so were several other men in the crowd.

The cars were very close. Berkeley took a deep breath and stepped forward, and was immediately pushed back again by a policeman.

"Keep back," this worthy shouted. "Out of the way."

The horses came abreast and passed them, and the first car. Berkeley recovered his balance. "Caterina!" he shouted, as loudly as he could.

He doubted it she had heard him, above the noise of the crowd. He could only watch, in horror, as she delved into her bag and pulled out the grenade. One of her companions touched the very short cord with the end of his cigar. It glowed immediately, and she tossed it straight into the archducal car, as it drew abreast of her.

For the moment it seemed that only the Archduke realised what had happened; he reacted very promptly, leaning down, seizing the bomb, and throwing it over his shoulder out of the car.

The crowd gasped, at last realising something was happening.

The bomb landed in the car behind and immediately exploded. There was a moment's silence, broken by someone shouting, "Drive! Drive!"

The horses were neighing and stamping but were pulled out of the way, as the first two cars put on speed to reach the town hall steps, scattering people before them. The third car was a total wreck, with several bodies lying in it or on the street. Of Caterina and her accomplices there was no sign, but police whistles were blowing, men were shouting, and there were several gunshots; while above them all rose a huge wail from the watching crowd.

Berkeley had no idea what to do. Going after Caterina seemed a waste of time, partly because the police were already doing that, and had a head start, and partly because he had to assume that the conspirators had a hideaway and an escape route already prepared. And he was unarmed.

While the Archduke . . . At least total catastrophe had been avoided. The car was at the town hall steps, and officials and policemen were clustering round. Berkeley allowed himself to be carried forward with the crowd, as the car door was opened and the Archduke slowly stepped down. Berkeley wondered if he realised what had happened to the car behind him; certainly he gave no sign of it, merely looking extremely angry. The mayor was attempting to welcome him, and he said loudly, "I come to your city as a friend, Herr Burgermeister, and someone throws a bomb at me."

People continued to fuss. Berkeley saw the Braddocks with the other guests at the top of the stairs, but it appeared that the Archduke was not staying; the reception was apparently being at least postponed. After a very brief greeting he got back into the car and the motorcade prepared to move off.

Berkeley couldn't blame him for wanting to get away from the scene of the tragedy; shouts and screams were still rising from amongst the injured people as the police tried to clear the street. Now he had to think about Caterina, and indeed himself. The attempt had failed, as so many of Anna's attempts at murder and mayhem had failed. Now he had to concentrate all his efforts on saving Caterina, supposing he could find her. And afterwards?

He found himself still in the midst of the crowd, following the Archduke's car, as the motorcade continued on its way, still very slowly. Neither the Archduke nor his wife were smiling now, but looking grim-faced from left to right. The cars reached the corner and slowed almost to a stop, for some incomprehensible reason apparently uncertain which way to turn. In that moment of hesitation, Berkeley saw Gavrile Princip. The boy stepped out of the crowd and levelled what, even at a distance, Berkeley recognised as his own Browning pistol.

He did not hear the shot, but he saw the Archduke half turn, blood spurting from his neck. Instantly, the Archduchess threw herself forward across her husband. There was another shot, and she slumped over his knees.

Once again, pandemonium. Princip had not acted as promptly as Caterina, and had hesitated for a second after firing the second shot; Berkeley would have liked to feel that he was appalled at having hit the woman. In any event, he was already being seized by passers-by and appeared in some danger of being lynched – which would be no more than he deserved, Berkeley supposed. There were people running from every direction. Some jostled him as he stood still, trying to understand the total calamity that had overtaken both himself and history.

At every level, he had failed. Idle to say the fault was not his. He doubted Gorman would see it that way. Now only Caterina remained.

He hurried back to the consul's residence. Only the servants were there, and they were in a state of high agitation as rumour spread across the city. Berkeley ordered a bath and poured himself a glass of brandy. He had just finished dressing in clean clothes when the Braddocks returned.

"My God!" Harvey shouted. "Where have you *been*? Don't you realise what has happened?"

"I was there," Berkeley said. "As to where I've been, it's too long a story. How is the Archduke?"

"The Archduke is dead." Julia virtually spat the words at him.

"Shit! Listen, Harvey, you must find out if they have taken Caterina."

"Me?"

"You are the British consul, and she has British citizenship. If they have taken her, she is your responsibility."

"My dear fellow, I cannot involve His Majesty's Government in a sorry business like this."

"You are going to do it, Harvey," Berkeley said.

Braddock opened his mouth, looked at his wife whose face was expressionless, and then closed it again.

"You do not think she may have got away?" he asked.

"I hope she did. But I have to find out. Do you know what they will do to her? She was in their hands once before, when she was thirteen. She was raped and beaten and then forced to watch her father hanged. That event has coloured her entire life. Were it to happen again it would drive her out of her mind."

"If they have taken her, will it not already have happened?" Julia asked, quietly.

Berkeley shot her a glance, then turned back to Braddock. "I am not asking you to risk anything, Harvey. Surely you can make discreet inquiries?"

"Well, I suppose I can." He went to the sideboard and poured himself a brandy.

"Every moment counts," Berkeley said.

Harvey gulped his drink and went to the door. "I'll be back for lunch," he said.

"It'll be late," Julia said with a sigh.

How these people wished to resume the normality of their lives, Berkeley thought.

"Would you like a drink?"

"I've already had one, thank you."

"Suppose the police do have her; what will you do? What can you do, save involve yourself?"

"I told you: I will get her out, and back to Serbia."

"You, alone? Surely you cannot expect Harvey to help you? It would cause an international incident."

"Don't you think we already have an international incident? Perhaps Great Britain is not yet involved, but she soon will be. No, Julia, I do not expect Harvey to give me any practical help."

"You said something about bringing her here, if you can get her out of the hands of the police. That would be very risky."

"Of course it would. I shall not do it, if it disturbs you that much."

They gazed at each other.

"And if you do not succeed in freeing her?"

Berkeley shrugged. "I have other duties. To my three children."

"Do you not suppose they are your prime duty? If both you and Caterina were to be killed . . ."

"They'd be taken care of. But I'd rather do it myself."

"With no room for anyone else."

"At this moment, no. You'll forgive me, Julia, but I have rather a lot on my mind."

"I'm sure you do. I must go and see what cook has for lunch."

Braddock was back in an hour. "They have her," he panted.

"Where?"

"At one of their police stations."

"Show me."

Braddock spread a town plan and indicated the position.

"Do you know if she's hurt?"

"I cannot say."

"What about Princip, and the others?"

"They have Princip, certainly. And I think one or two others."

"So what happens now?"

"They will be interrogated." He flushed. "You understand . . ."

"I know what that means," Berkeley said.

"Well, then they will stand trial. Quite apart from being caught red-handed, they will by then have confessed. They will certainly be condemned."

"To death?"

"Well . . ." Another flush. "By Austrian law, Princip is a minor. He cannot be executed, but he will be imprisoned for life."

"And Caterina?"

"Caterina, unfortunately, is an adult."

"I see. Thank you, Harvey. You've been a great help. Now, I don't suppose you have a weapon? Those children took away my gun."

"A weapon? My dear Berkeley, I must advise you most strongly against attempting to use force. You will get yourself killed to no advantage. And you will be involving His Majesty's Government. Listen to me. We will employ the very best lawyers."

"To what purpose? You have just agreed that by the time the case comes to court Caterina will have confessed."

"Well, people do have a habit of confessing under extreme . . ."

"Torture."

Braddock sighed. "We will demand that your wife is examined by our doctor. And if there is any sign of physical harm, we shall claim that any confession was extracted by torture. Torture is illegal in Austria-Hungary."

"Harvey, you are living in never-never land, where all the men are gentlemen and all the women are ladies." Come to think of it, he realised, that was the land in which the average Foreign Office official, having been to Eton and Oxford, was brought up. "There is not going to be a trial for several months, by which time any physical damage Caterina may have suffered will have disppeared. And even if it hasn't, do you think the Austrians will give a damn, no matter what protests you make? This is the heir to their throne that has been killed."

Braddock gulped.

"But again, thanks for your help," Berkeley said, and went to the door. "I will not involve you, or His Majesty's Government, I promise."

"I have the power to place you under arrest," Braddock said.

Berkeley turned back to face him, and look past him at Julia, standing tensely by the sideboard. "Do that and I will kill you," he said, and left the room.

Oh, to have Lockwood, he thought as he made his way towards

the police station. Or Karlovy, who might have been a thug but was a good man in a fight and utterly faithful to the Slovitzas. Or both.

But he had neither.

He reached the police station, having to make his way through a considerable crowd that had gathered outside, chattering and occasionally shouting. At the door he was checked by a policeman.

"What do you want?"

"I am a representative from the British Consulate," Berkeley said. "You are holding a British citizen."

"I have no knowledge of that."

"Let me speak with an inspector."

The constable hesitated, but Berkeley had such a confident air of authority that after a moment he stepped back and allowed him through, at the same time calling for his sergeant. That official bustled out of an inner office.

"Gentleman from the British Consulate, says we are holding one of his nationals, Sergeant."

The sergeant looked Berkeley up and down.

"She is probably going under the name of Slovitza," Berkeley said.

"You are saying that Caterina Slovitza is a British citizen? How can that be?"

"Simply that she married an Englishman," Berkeley said.

"And where is this Englishman now?"

"I have no idea," Berkeley said. "His whereabouts do not affect my business, which is to see his wife and make sure she is being properly treated."

"You realise that this young woman threw a bomb at the Arch-duke, and was clearly a member of the gang that shot him a few minutes later."

"That does not affect her status as a British citizen," Berkeley said, patiently, "nor my duty to interview her."

"Well, it is not possible," the sergeant said.

"If she has been unnecessarily harmed," Berkeley warned, "I will bring charges."

"Unnecessarily harmed," the sergeant said. "Ha! The lady is dead."

Berkeley stared at the man in total consternation.

"You mean you murdered her."

"No, sir, we did not murder her," the sergeant said, also patiently. "She was brought here, and received a preliminary questioning. That was before we knew the Archduke had been shot, and was dying. When that news was received, she was locked in a cell while we awaited the arrival of the other prisoners. She was alone. I admit this was careless of us, but there was so much going on. Anyway, in a matter of seconds she had taken off her stockings, looped one end through the bars of the cell window and hanged herself."

God, God, God, Berkeley thought. When he had first gone to Sabac he had wondered if, far from entering the vampire's den as a possible victim, he was not to be the agent to destroy them utterly. But hadn't Caterina been bound for an end like this, almost from the day she had been born? She was Anna Slovitza's daughter.

"Let me see her body," he said.

The Austrians allowed Berkeley to have a coffin made, and released Caterina's body to him. They were embarrassed at having her die on their hands, especially if she actually was a British citizen. He did not return to the Braddocks' house but stayed at the police station until he could leave, having hired a horse and cart. He neither slept nor shaved nor ate for some forty-eight hours while he drove slowly back to the border. He was carrying Caterina back to be buried alongside her mother.

What a waste, he thought. Two of the most exciting, desirable women there can ever have been, devoting their lives to death and destruction, including their own.

He buried Caterina, with only the servants attending; bathed and changed and ate; stood in that never-to-be-forgotten drawing room for a last time, looking at the silver-framed photographs, including some of himself, and Caterina, and the children.

Then he went into Belgrade, to Colonel Savos.

"Have you a warrant for my arrest?" he asked.

"For Karlovy? As I understand it, you shot him in self-defence. But this business in Sarajevo . . . Had you anything to do with that?"

"I tried to stop it."

Savos nodded. "Well, it is done now. The Austrians have issued an ultimatum. They know it was the Black Hand. They are certain the organisation has been supported by our government. They are demanding the right to send their own people into Serbia to carry out investigations and arrests."

"Will you allow this?"

"No," Savos said. "We will fight."

"Serbia will fight Austria?"

Savos nodded. "This time we are ready. We will have Russian support. It has been promised."

"And France will support Russia, and Germany will support Austria. You are talking of a general European war."

Everything that Gorman and Smailes had been working so feverishly and illegally to prevent.

"Yes," Savos said. "It will be the ultimate settlement. Will you come back to the colours?"

"No," Berkeley said. "I am going to collect my children, and my valet and his wife and children, and go back to England."

Savos raised his eyebrows. "You have lost your stomach for fighting? *You*? What will Caterina say?"

"Caterina is dead," Berkeley told him. "The Slovitzas are no more."

Except in my three children, he remembered.

"Ah, Berkeley," General Gorman said. "Welcome home. Who have you brought with you this time?"

"My three children," Berkeley said. It had taken Lockwood and himself five weeks to get from Belgrade to Athens and thence to London. "Are the rumours I have been hearing correct?"

"That we are at war? Yes, they are correct. We declared war on Germany yesterday morning. I never knew you had three children. Is your wife well?"

"My wife is dead, sir."

"Oh, what a shame. Still, these things happen. I would say you're due for a spot of leave."

"May I ask, sir, why we are at war?"

"Well, Belgium, I suppose. The Germans really shouldn't have invaded Belgium. Still, don't you know, we were going to have to fight them some time, some place. Now is as good a time as any. I'm not blaming you, Berkeley. If you'd managed to nab the Kaiser, well, things might have been different. But, man proposes and God disposes, eh? As for reactivating the Black Hand, I think we need to keep that a secret, between you, me and Toby Smailes. Oh, by the way, the Braddocks were here a couple of days ago. Well, Mrs Braddock was. Her husband is still in Sarajevo. But he'll have to be pulled out now, I suppose. Anyway, she wishes to be in touch."

"Yes, sir. Am I going to be employed, now that we're at war?"

"Well, now," Gorman said. "Yes, I think we will be able to find something for a man of your peculiar talents to do. Death and destruction is your natural state, is it not? I'll be in touch."

"Thank you, sir."

"And don't forget to chase up Mrs Braddock, eh? Weren't you engaged to her once?"

"No, sir," Berkeley said. "We were never engaged."

I don't think we ever really liked each other, he thought, as he went down the stairs.